PENGUIN BOOKS

DEMO

'Miller is full of hard-hitting observations about class, money and gender, and the agony/ecstasy of being young' *The Times*

'The real strength of this witty, warm, spirited novel lies with its vibrant characters. They may endlessly discuss the impact of international events on their lives but, as Miller deftly dramatises, the real emotional, life-changing conflicts are with each other' *Guardian*

'*Demo* is a stylish debut that explores sexual and social politics, anti-globalisation and gender through the lives of two very different women and is cut through with flashes of brilliant dialogue' Louise Welsh

'A very subtle, beautifully crafted story . . . Miller is a new writing talent to be reckoned with' *Press and Journal*

'Miller's tales of four protesters define the *zeitgeist* . . . the sub-text of the book touches on a spectrum of political issues: the clash of Clare's father's Clydeside socialism with the new single issue protests; the presence of radical Islam in multi-cultural Scotland; the fact that the Iraq war went ahead, despite the vigorous protests against it' *Scotsman*

'From the first paragraph you are hooked' *Glasgow Evening Times*

'A crackling debut . . . The novel's intimate characterisation and dissident politics should guarantee it an audience' *Big Issue*

'The politics of resistance provide a framework of impassioned idealism to the individual struggles of two women . . . the ways the personal and political affect [these] two different, and very contemporary women comes across as urgent and exciting' *Metro*

'Full of pace . . . Miller's keen ear for language and dialogue remains an engaging and delightful aspect of her writing throughout. When she writes about the anti-war movement, whether the mass demonstrations with all their colour and sounds and costumes and home-made banners, or the crushing feeling when the bombs fell on Baghdad and Bush got re-elected, or the almost unbearable excitement of going to demonstrate abroad, Miller captures the atmosphere perfectly' *Socialist Review*

'Clare is a feisty heroine ... Miller's writing is effective, particularly when she allows Clare her own voice' *New Statesman*

'An utterly convincing central character, a genuine poignancy and a sparkling sense of humour' *Herald*

'Trust-fund revolutionaries, drunken toffs, white men with dreadlocks and the honest working class, they're all here. And it's wonderful' *Laura Hird Website*

ABOUT THE AUTHOR

Alison Miller grew up in Orkney and now lives in Glasgow. She worked for the WEA (Workers' Educational Association) in an adult education project in Castlemilk, Glasgow, and more recently co-ordinated the counselling and group work service in the Centre for Women's Health. In 2003 she graduated with Distinction from the M.Phil in Creative Writing run by Glasgow and Strathclyde Universities. Now, as well as writing, she works freelance as an adult educator and counselling supervisor.

Demo

ALISON MILLER

PENGUIN BOOKS

PENGUIN BOOKS

Published by the Penguin Group
Penguin Books Ltd, 80 Strand, London WC2R ORL, England
Penguin Group (USA) Inc., 375 Hudson Street, New York, New York 10014, USA
Penguin Group (Canada), 90 Eglinton Avenue East, Suite 700, Toronto, Ontario, Canada M4P 2Y3
(a division of Pearson Penguin Canada Inc.)
Penguin Ireland, 25 St Stephen's Green, Dublin 2, Ireland
(a division of Penguin Books Ltd)
Penguin Group (Australia), 250 Camberwell Road, Camberwell, Victoria 3124, Australia
(a division of Pearson Australia Group Pty Ltd)
Penguin Books India Pvt Ltd, 11 Community Centre, Panchsheel Park, New Delhi – 110 017, India
Penguin Group (NZ), cnr Airborne and Rosedale Roads, Albany, Auckland 1310, New Zealand
(a division of Pearson New Zealand Ltd)
Penguin Books (South Africa) (Pty) Ltd, 24 Sturdee Avenue, Rosebank, Johannesburg 2196, South Africa

Penguin Books Ltd, Registered Offices: 80 Strand, London WC2R ORL, England

www.penguin.com

First published by Hamish Hamilton 2005
Published in Penguin Books 2006
1

Typeset by Rowland Phototypesetting Ltd, Bury St Edmunds, Suffolk
Printed in England by Clays Ltd, St Ives plc

ISBN-13: 978–0–141–02537–7
ISBN-10: 0–141–02537–9

For Irene Eliza Miller

Rise like lions after slumber
In unvanquishable number –
Shake your chains to earth like dew
Which in sleep had fallen on you –
Ye are many – they are few.

'The Mask of Anarchy', Percy Bysshe Shelley

PART ONE

Glasgow – Florence

November 2002

It was deadead good they let me go. I've never went abroad before except Majorca or Tenerife. And only in the summer to lie about on the beach and that. This was November and I'm like, will I take my big coat or will it still be warmer than Glasgow? My ma didny know. My da says, Oh aye, Italy can be cauld this time a year. Willy Bauld. And he showed me the world temperatures in the *Herald*: Venice 6 degrees Celsius, Rome 9 degrees, Florence 8, Glasgow 10. Like it was football scores. Aye, hen, take your coat, he says.

I goes, Puck, puck, puck, puckeck and flap my elbows, cause I don't like it when he calls me hen, and I dodge behind the sofa before he can swipe me with the paper. A right comedienne, he says.

My daddy's alright really. He wasny that keen at first when I says I wanted to go on the demo. Och, Da, it's no like it's for a daft holiday; it's a good cause. Anti-war, anti-globalization! I bet you'd have went if you were my age. It's everything you're always goin on about.

You're too young, he says, sixteen's too young to be gallivantin about Europe. Like I'm still a wean!

But I says, Danny'll be there, he'll look efter me. He's organizin the bus and runnin the Glasgow end a the trip.

Oh aye, my da says, that's reassurin; couldny run a menodge, that brother a yours.

That's no fair, my ma says; you're too hard on the boy. And that pure sets my da off on wan.

Hard? Listen, when I was twenty-four I was bringin in a

wage tay keep my wife and family . . . blah blah blah . . . and the vein's standin out on his forehead and he's went pure puce. And my ma's at the sink with her back to him, but you can see she's mad cause she's rattlin the dishes and clashin them ontay the drainin board an shakin her head. My da keeps goin on about Danny no havin a job. Like it's his fault he got his books fae the Call Centre. They're always arguin. My da givin it, When ye gonny grow up and shoulder your responsibilities? At least the Call Centre was a *job*.

Danny used to say nothin, but since he joined his group he's more able for my da and he gives it, So where's your politics now? The big socialist, eh? The Big Red Clydesider. That kinda work's crap and you know it. You're no even allowed out for a pish. Some a they boys in there have never even *heard* of a union.

Aye, well, my da says, if they didny turn the colour a biled shite at the mention of the word *work*, mibby they could get off their arses an *form* wan. And Danny's went the same red as my da by this time and just swears under his breath and goes through to his room and turns up his stereo dead loud.

Anyway, to cut a short story long, as my da would say, he eventually says I could go. I think he felt like . . . guilty about Danny. Or maybe my ma's went on at him. I don't know. But when Danny and me are just leavin to catch the bus, my da's went, Here, son, there a wee contribution. For the vino. Mind an look efter my lassie. And he hands a few notes to Danny. See he *is* alright my da, when it comes down to it.

But for a minute I think Danny's no gonny take the money; he just stands there lookin my da in the eye. And my da's like, Suit yersel, son. And I'm just away to say, I'll take it, Da, when Danny puts it in his jeans pocket and says, Thanks, dead low and goes out the room.

4

I looks at my da and his face is like deadead hurt and I goes, Thanks, Da, and I hug him hard.

He pats me on the shoulder and says, You look efter yoursel now, hen, and keep outay trouble. And I'm like nearly greetin and I think my da is too.

Danny comes back in then with his rucksack over one shoulder and says, Right, we ready to rock an roll, Wee Yin? And I'm glad he's makin an effort so I goes, Who you callin Wee Yin, Big Yin? And my da laughs and says, Away yous go, the paira ye. Have a good time. Say hello to the comrades for me. And come back in wan piece, will ye.

I hug him again and I burst my coldsore on his stubbly cheek and I'm like, See what you've went an did now! So he takes his hanky out an dabs my mouth dead gentle. And Danny says, She'll live – come on, Clare, or we'll miss the bus. Say cheerio to Ma for us. Tell her we'll text her when we get to Florence.

You and your mobile phones! Da says.

When we gets to the square there's buses standin and a lot of folk millin about smokin. There's this guy with amazin dreadlocks tied back and one a they black and white Arab scarfs round his neck with the tasselly points hangin down his combat jacket. Danny flings his rucksack on top of a heap of other bags at the back of one a the buses and shouts over, Hey, Julian. And the guy with the dreads looks at us, takes a draw on his roll-up, makes his eyes into slits, says somethin to the guy next to him and comes over dead slow. He doesny even smile nor nothin. I'm thinkin, Who is this guy?

Alright? Danny says.

And the guy Julian says, I'm good. Who's this then? And he's got like this posh voice, definitely no Glasgow. It sounds dead funny with the dreads. He's lookin at me with these huge

5

blue eyes. Lookin right at me. And I feel my face gettin hot and my coldsore's pure lowpin. I look down and his fag's burnin away in his hand. The ash is blowin off in wee grey flakes.

This is my wee sister, Clare, Danny says, and I could've kicked him.

Delighted to make your acquaintance, the guy says. And he flings his fag onto the red tar stuff they've went an covered George Square wae. Red Square, my da calls it. And he slaps the heels of his boots thegether and sort of like . . . bows and holds out his hand, keepin his big blue eyes on me the whole time.

Clare, meet Julian, Danny says.

I try to think of somethin clever to say but I can't so I just goes, Hi, and keep my hands in my pockets and look across the square. Folk are startin to move towards the buses now and I'm dyin to get on and get movin.

So how's things? Danny says to Julian.

Bit fragile this morning, he says. Mouth like the inside of a vacuum cleaner.

Vacuum cleaner! A vacuum cleaner.

Bit of a dodgy old tum, he says. And he rubs his belly under his green jacket.

Well, just as long as you don't spew your ring aw ower me on the bus, Danny says and laughs.

No way! Was this guy goin to be sittin next tay us? Great! I flings Danny a look and hope the guy Julian doesny catch it. But Danny's all over him and he ignores me.

Did you see the report in the *Guardian*, Julian says, about Firenze's preparations for the Social Forum?

No, Danny says, I've already telt you I don't read that bourgeois rag. Oh God, is Danny gonny go off on wan?

Well, terribly sorry, your Supreme Proliness. I forgot, the guy Julian says. God, sir, you jocks don't half have the old chip on the shoulder. The old deep-fried Mars Bar and chips. Mahz Bah, he says it like.

I'll give you a Mars bar. Anywhere you like, Danny says, I've taen my chib. Come on, Jules, drop the English Upper-class Twit act, why don't you, or you'll put my wee sister right off her Irn Bru.

Wot? Julian cups his hand round his ear and leans forward. Some of his dreads swing round over his shoulder. They smell of smoke and somethin else. They look that matted way my hair used to go at the back when I was wee. I would like to touch them, see what they feel like. A bit clatty but. Could be introduced to a bar of soap, my ma would say. Wot's that you say? Class act you say? Well, of course. And he staggers towards the bus with a kid-on walkin stick and his hand shakin like he's an old old man. When he gets to the door he straightens up and turns his lamps on me. Ladies first, he says.

Come on, the driver says, what's the hold-up? He's in a right bad mood! I take my rucksack off, hold it in front of me and climb on. The driver's a wee fat man with greasy black hair. He draws me a dirty look.

It's already half full, the bus, and I don't see anybody I know. It's a shame my pal Farkhanda couldny come with us; her da wouldny let her. I was dead disappointed when she telt me. We would a had a good laugh. Everybody's older than me and they're all dressed kinda . . . weird. Like students and sort of like . . . hippies. Well, no really hippies, cause my da says they were a sixties phenomenon, a product of post-war affluence in the West. He uses a lot of big words, my da. His mates at work say, You swally a dictionary, PK? They never call him Peter. Just because I don't read the *Record* or the *Sun*, my da says. Rot your brain, they rags.

So I'm lookin for two seats thegether for me and Danny,

and suddenly he's right at my back and says, This'll dae for the three of us. And he swings his polybag fulla books and leaflets up on the rack and goes to take my rucksack off us and stick it up too. But I'm like, I want to keep it on my knee the now. And I squeeze into the window seat.

Suit yersel, Danny says, like he knows I'm pissed off, but isny gonny ask me what it's about. There's a seat for you, Jules, he says, and he points at the one across the passage. Then he paps hissel down on the seat next to me.

Great, Julian says, and sits in the seat next to a lassie with dyed purple hair. I'm tryin no to watch him but it's dead hard no to. He keeps movin his head up and down against the back a the seat, like he canny get comfortable for his dreads. So he sits up, pulls the black scrunchy off at the back, holds it in his mouth, and pulls all his hair up on top of his head, twists the scrunchy on and lies back against the seat. Ah, that's better, he says. I'm tryin no to laugh. All the ends ay his dreads are movin about like fingers growin out his head. The guy's a pure weirdo.

Danny does laugh. You look like a – thingmy, whatdyecallit – sea anemone.

Yes, creature of the deep, that's me. Hidden depths . . . still waters and so on.

I get my CD player out my rucksack and feel about for a CD. The bus is full now and the driver's arguin with a couple a guys that are tryin to get on.

I don't care if you're wae the official party of the fuckin Queen of Sheba, yous are no fuckin gettin on my bus.

The door hisses shut and he starts the engine. And the two guys are like bangin on the window and shoutin and givin him the finger.

Danny laughs. Dickheads, he says. Should've got here on time. And he leans over me, chaps the window and points to

8

the bus behind. There's still spaces on that wan, he says, talkin quiet but makin his mouth big so they can read his lips.

And next thing we're off, up the big hill at Rottenrow, headin for the motorway.

Time to knit up the old ravelled sleeve of care, Julian says. And he yawns and closes his eyes. The tentacles on top of his head waggle about a minute and then go still. His face is awful white but, kinda like . . . seethrough. Well, no really, but you know what I mean. He's got purply bits under his eyes that I've no noticed when his eyes are open. And he's got a wee kinda beard – no exactly a goatee – more straggly. More blondy than his hair too.

I take my Coke and my book and my crisps and my M&Ms out my rucksack and stuff them in the stretchy net pocket on the back of the seat in front and I stick my rucksack down at my feet.

Here, gie me that, Danny says, and he lifts it up on the rack for us, gets his own book out his polybag and plonks hissel back down. I plug my earphones in and switch on the White Stripes.

I wake up when somebody at the back a the bus shouts, Florence . . . at fuckin last! It's gettin dark and I'm achin all over. I look out the window, but I can't see much; just lights streakin past and a faint reflection of the seats at the other side. And my own face starin back at me with really big eyes. Like a slow loris. I'm burstin for a pee too; the toilet at the back of the bus has been disgustin since Newcastle.

Danny, I says. Danny. I poke my elbow in his side. Danny, we're here I think. Somebody up the back said it. Just now.

Danny sits up and blinks. What? Where are we?

We're here. Florence, I says.

Oh, yeah. So we are. He peers out the window.

Hey, Clare, there the Duomo, he says. And he's pointin to this huge church we're passin that looks like it's all white marble with coloured patterns and a big round red tower. Magic, I think, can we just get to a toilet afore I pee myself? I've been bitin my lip tryin to hold it in, so my coldsore's burst again. I can taste the blood.

When we eventually get off the bus and start walkin, my rucksack feels like twice as heavy as it did before we left Glasgow; the straps are pure cuttin into my shoulders. We leave Julian talkin to a bunch a guys outside the bus station, but Danny says he's stayin at the same B&B as us. Great! Just what I need.

The *pensione* Danny calls the place, but it says B&B on the door. The first thing I do when we get there is run to the toilet. It's all white tiles with a shower and a – whatdyoucall they things? A bidet. And it's pure Baltic too. My da wasny kiddin. The water's cold when I wash my hands and my teeth are chitterin. I look in the mirror above the basin. My face looks as if it's shrank. And my coldsore has went fae the corner of my mouth halfway across my top lip. There's this big red scab on it too. At least I'm no goin out clubbin this Saturday.

By the time I've came out, Danny's tryin out his Italian on the couple that owns the B&B. I've no got a scooby what they're sayin but they're smilin and they seem quite friendly. The woman looks at me and says, *Fa freddo*. And she rubs her hands thegether and shivers, so she must be feelin the cold too. I put my hands in under my oxters and nod at her and smile. She must've thought I've understood what she says, cause she comes out with a pure torrent of Italian. I looks at Danny but he's no got a clue either. I wish I'd've took Italian instead of Spanish at school. The man says somethin to the woman and she shrugs. She looks totally Italian – like they old women in the Olivio adverts. The guy turns to Danny. He's black and thin with a wee face, and he seems to be always smilin. He starts to speak dead slow in English.

We hope you OK here. Breakfast eight o'clock. Dining room downstairs. On ground floor. Beside reception. And they both smile and go out the room.

I'm like, Phew, and I fling myself on one a the beds. It's totally hard and doesny bounce and it's got a white duvet on top. In fact the whole place is white and more or less bare except for a picture of Our Lady on wan wall. Nay TV. Cheaper end a the market, Danny had said, but we're no goin for a luxury weekend; we're there to demonstrate, show Bush and Blair the error of their ways. Oh aye, I think, like they're really gonny be waitin with baited breath tay hear what Danny Kilkenny has to say! But I keep quiet. Danny can seem so old sometimes. When he's givin it, The Means of Production and Globalization and The Changing Economy, he sounds just like my da.

Well, whatdye think? Danny says. He's grinnin all ower his face and he looks dead chuffed with hissel.

I goes, It's brilliant. Great. I sit up on the bed and plant my feet on the floor. A kinda marble it looks like. Or no really marble but just as hard and cold. Kinda black and grey with a few orangey flecks. And there's a black border round the edge. It's like . . . pure Italian, I says.

Yeah, he says. Great, intit? Right, I'm just gonny text Ma and let her know we're here. Then it's out to see the sights of *la bella città*.

Good, I says, cause I'm starvin; wearin away tay a shadow. I'm holdin out the band of my jeans when the door goes and Julian walks in. Afore anybody even answers. He's taen his scrunchy off and his dreads are movin around all over his head.

Mmm, he says, a navel piercing. Well, you are full of

surprises, young Clare. I try to pull down my top but it's too short. I look over at Danny but he's in the middle of texting my ma. Tell me, he says, and his eyes are lookin right through me, Is any other part of your body pierced? And he flicks my belly button stud. I've got like a pure riddy by this time. I can smell his hair too, the cigarette smoke and the other sweet kinda smell. Waccy baccy I bet it is, and patchouli.

Hey, Jules – Danny's lookin over now – leave her alane, she's just a wean.

No I'm no, I says.

No, I bet you're not, Julian says. I feel as if his eyes can see right inside me.

She's strictly off limits, Jules; I promised my da I'd look efter her.

Stop talking about me like . . . like I'm no here, I says to Danny. And Julian gives a wee laugh. I can feel my face burnin; I must have even more of a riddy.

Well, if Comrade Kilkenny's decreed that his peach of a daughter's not to be tampered with, who am I to stage a coup? Wouldn't want to end up in a gulag now, would I? He's smiling at me when he says this, so I smile too, a wee smile so I don't split my coldsore again. Danny isny smilin but. He looks pissed off.

He's no a Stalinist, my da, so keep your fuckin insinuations to yoursel.

Hey, man, only joking, Julian says, and he holds his hands up and jiggles his dreads. Come on, let's go eat. Some of the other guys are meeting up in the trattoria round the corner . . . ah – Giovanni's, I think it's called.

Danny's like, Aye, right. Still in a bad mood. Julian's lookin at Danny, then he winks at me and taps the side a his nose with his finger. I put my big coat on and kid on I don't see him.

★

There's loads a people in the restaurant. I know some of the faces from the bus but there's a lot I don't know. Danny and Julian seem to know like . . . everybody and Danny's in a good mood again, huggin the lassies and clappin the guys on the back. It's funny, he's no the way he is at hame, Danny. There's candles in red glass holders on the red and white checked tablecloths and all the faces are glowin.

. . . This is Clare, Danny's *wee* sister, Julian's sayin to a lassie. Clare, meet my very good friend and *compañera*, Laetitia. Titty to those lucky enough to be admitted into a degree of intimacy with her.

I'm thinking, Titty! What a name!

Hi, she says, and she switches her roll-up into her left hand and holds out this wee white hand to me. She's got short black hair and big dark brown eyes and she's like . . . dead cool. No *cool* cool. But just . . . cool. Do come and join us, she says. She must come fae near Julian, cause she speaks the exact same way. She kinda like does ballet dancer hands at the empty chairs and Julian sits down beside her. I look around for Danny. He's sittin at a crowded table across the other side talkin to the guy next to him, givin it, Kyoto Agreement, fuckin American Isolationism, arms wavin, hand choppin down on the table – the full works.

The waiter's goin round takin orders. I sit down next to Julian, take my arms out my coat and let it fall over the back of the seat. Julian goes, Here, let the waiter hang that up for you. And he starts to pull it out from under me.

No you're alright, I says, I'll keep it in case I get cold. And I pull it round me a bit so it hides my belly. The fur round the hood tickles my back on the bare bit between my top and my jeans.

OK, Eskimo Nell, he says and he's got this kind of look in his eyes like he's laughin at me. I wish Danny was sittin next to us.

The waiter's reached us now and he's standin with his notebook and pencil and he says something to us in Italian. Le— Le— Titty or whatever her name is says, I'll have the *fettuccine al pesto Genovese, per favore*. The waiter writes on his wee pad and says, *Sì, signora*.

Julian turns to me: What about you, Clare?

I'm like dead flustered. I've no even saw the menu yet. I – I . . . I'm just gonny say I'll have a pizza when Julian says, We'll have the *spaghetti vongole*. That alright for you, Clare? And a carafe of house red, *un litro di vino rosso della casa, per favore. Sì, signore*, the waiter says. I just smile up at him and say, Thanks.

Grazie. Grazie, my dear, Julian says. It sounds like graah-tsee-ay. He does a conjuror's move with his hand. Twice. I canny be bothered to tell him I know the Italian for thank you; it's dead like the Spanish. When in Rome, he says . . .

Julian, don't patronize the girl, Titty says. She takes a draw on her fag and blows the smoke up over the heads of the two guys at the other side of the table. Her neck's dead white and smooth. She looks like she should be smokin thin black cigarettes out a cigarette holder instead of roll-ups, and wearin a long string a pearls with a knot in to swing in her other hand. And a shimmery silver dress with fringes. Like somebody out an old, old film. But she's wearin a black jumper with like holes in it and there's a green camouflage jacket and a brown scarf over the back a her chair.

I look round the room. Some folk at the side nearest the counter are finished eatin already. They look a lot older – my da's age mibby, some even older. They're all talkin fast and wavin their hands about. One woman's dead loud. She says, *Mais il n'est pas VRAI!* And I'm like, I know what that means! Cause I did French for two years at school. It's not true, she's sayin. Then a wee old guy gets up and taps the side a his wine glass and starts to speak. I canny make out much of what he's sayin, but the folk at his table are all listenin and clappin every now and again. He looks a dead nice wee old man. Then he starts to sing:

> Debout les damnés de la terre,
> Debout les forçats de la faim.
> La raison tonne en son cratère,
> C'est l'éruption de la fin . . .

And I'm nearly joinin in cause my da learnt me that song when I was ten: . . . Du passé faisons table rase, Foules esclaves, debout, debout. Le monde va changer de base . . .

Julian turns to Whatserface and says, Fucking French fucking communists! And I'm like dead shocked! My da's a communist. Then he stands up and shouts out, What did your lot do to us in the Spanish Civil War, eh? Shot us, didn't you, eh? Didn't you? Fucking wankers!

Julian, sit down and shut the fuck up, Whatsername says, dead low, and she pulls at his sleeve. He sits down. His face is white. Terribly sorry, old girl, he says, don't know what got into me.

My da's a communist, I says. He wouldny hurt naybody.

The folk at the French table haveny noticed anythin and the wee guy's still singin in a quavery voice. I look over at Danny, but he's stuffin forkfuls of pasta in his mouth and talkin to the guy beside him.

Sorry, Clare, Julian says, I wasn't talking about your father, of course. It's just the old enmities. Trots and Tankies. He turns right round and looks at me and smiles.

I look right back. I don't smile. I keep lookin right in his eyes.

Well, I thought we were all supposed to be marchin

thegether themorrow for like *World Peace*, I says. And anyhow, they're having mair fun at that table, if you ask me. I keep starin at him. He looks surprised.

The waiter comes up then with a tray of plates and a funny-shaped bottle fulla red wine. *Fettuccine pesto, signora?* he says to Titsy. *Grazie*, she says. And he sets hers down in front of her. She's got nay tits anyhow, as far as I can see. *Due spaghetti vongole?*

Here and here, Julian says, and he points to me and hissel. *Grazie*. I'm lookin at my plate. There's spaghetti and a sorta pinkish sauce over it, some onions and . . . like these wee kinda grey seashells. The waiter flicks his cloth over his arm and goes back to the kitchen.

So she has opinions, the young Clare, Julian says. I like a woman who knows her own mind.

Leave her alone, Boobsy says. Clare, pay him no heed. Eat up. And she like leans across Julian, pours some wine into my glass and flashes me a really nice smile. That's a nasty coldsore you've got there; I've just the thing for it in my bag. I'll find it for you when you've finished eating. *Buon appetito*.

I look at my plate again and my stomach turns over. I'm starvin but, so I'll have to eat some of it. I poke about in the spaghetti and try and wind it round my fork without touchin any of the shell things. I put a wee bit in my mouth. It's no as bad as I thought. A bit fishy but no too bad. I eat some more. I'm managin to keep away fae the shells pretty good considerin, and then suddenly there's this like . . . thing in my mouth. It's rubbery and kinda squashy and it's pure bowfin. I think I'm gonny be sick. I hold my napkin up to my face and put the thing out with my tongue. Julian's watchin me and he's got that wee smile on his face again.

Vongole not to your taste? he says. You don't know what you're missing. I sling him a deafie. I reach for a piece of bread out the basket in the middle of the table and spread it with butter. It tastes that good I want to cry.

Me, I love every kind of shellfish, he says. So does Laetitia, don't you?

Laetitia, Laetitia, that was it! I'm no gonny forget it this time.

Tell Clare what you compared oysters to.

Shut up, Julian, Laetitia says. She's only ate half her pasta and she's rollin a fag again. I'm looking at her plate. I think she must have saw me lookin, cause she says, Would you like some of mine? I can't finish it. And I'm like, Yes please.

Oysters, Titty, what did you say they're like when they slip down your lovely throat? Julian says.

Shut *up*!

A tongue in one's cunt. That's what she said. A tongue in one's cunt. What d'you think of that, young Clare?

You are an arsehole, Julian, Laetitia says.

I don't believe Laetitia had really says that. I mean like . . . use the c-word like that.

Why are you behaving like *such* an arsehole? She says it like *aahs*-hole.

Steady on, old girl, Julian says. Clare will begin to suspect you really like me.

Laetitia gets up. Clare, would you like to come to the loo with me and I'll dig out that coldsore lotion?

She leaves her fag burning in the ashtray, picks up this bag with sequins and ribbon and bits of lace all different colours and with like badges pinned on it and she starts to squeeze out past Julian. He grabs her arm as she passes and looks up at her. His eyes are kinda shiny and he's lickin his top lip, then bitin his bottom wan. Laetitia stops and turns to him and her eyes are black in the dim light. She takes his hand off her arm.

You're pissed, she says. And right enough, he's drank most of the bottle a wine hissel.

17

I get up, grab my bag and follow Laetitia. At the corner afore the lavvies I turn round. Julian's sittin with his head down and his dreads all spillin forward onto his plate.

Hey, Clare, Danny shouts across. Alright? He's dead happy-lookin and he holds up his glass of wine to me.

I'm fine, I says, and wave at him.

When I get in the toilet, Laetitia's already in one a the cubicles.

That you, Clare? she shouts.

Aye, I says. I go in the other one. I wait till Laetitia flushes afore I start to pee.

By the time I come out she's leanin ower the basin lookin into the mirror, puttin lipstick on, a sorta dark browny pink colour. She rubs her lips thegether. Then she clocks me watchin her in the mirror and smiles.

Lipstick revolutionary, that's me I'm afraid, Clare. Here, look. She rummages in her bag, takes out a wee tube of ointment and holds it out to me. Great for coldsores this stuff; I swear by it.

Thanks, I says. I take the tube, set it next the basin and wash my hands. I don't see any towel so I just shake them a bit in the sink. Then I unscrew the top of the tube. A wee white worm starts to ooze out the nozzle. I rub it on my finger and look in the mirror. My coldsore's even worse in the fluorescent light – dead scabby. I smear the cream quick onto my lip, screw the top on again and hold out the tube. Thanks, I says.

No, no, she says. You keep it.

Thanks a lot, I says.

She smiles, No need to keep thanking me. She's dead pretty. Like really beautiful.

What d'you think of Julian? she says, out the blue.

I'm like, I don't know. He's a bit . . . kinda weird . . . is he no? Laetitia's leanin back on the basin with her mad bag in front and her arms crossed over it. And she's lookin . . . sorta into the distance, except she's really starin at the toilet door. That stuff he says about you and like . . . oysters . . . I mean, that was pure . . . *mental*.

She turns to me then and smiles. Yeah, she says, pure mental. Only she says *pyaw*. Come on, honey child, better get back out there in case they start the revolution without us. And she pushes open the door into the restaurant.

It's dark and like dead noisy and hot and folk are singin. We walk over to our table. Everybody's standin up singin. I know this one too. *'Bandiera Rossa'*. I looks over at Danny; he's givin it laldy, punchin the air. The waiters are standin with their arms folded, watchin. Julian's no at our table but. He's over with the wee French guy, arm in arm and they're like conductin the whole thing with their other arms. Baith of them thegether. Julian's dreads are hittin the baldy head a the French guy so the wee guy stops conductin and grabs a bunch of them and holds them on top a his head like a mad wig. I looks at Laetitia and she looks at me and we both start laughin. And then we sing too.

> . . . *Avanti o populo, alla riscossa,*
> *Bandiera rossa trionferà.*
>
> *'Bandiera rossa la trionferà,*
> *Bandiera rossa la trionferà,*
> *Bandiera rossa la trionferà,*
> *Evviva il socialismo la bella libertà . . .*

Julian and Danny are still singin on the way back to the B&B. Different songs I don't know. They're walkin in the middle a the street but it's dead quiet; there's no traffic. I'm walkin behind with Laetitia. She's got her arm through mine and I've got my hands in my pockets tryin to keep warm.

Julian starts up a new song, '50 Ways to Leave Your Lover'. Danny joins in.

Oh Christ, here we go, Laetitia says. I look at her but she says nothing.

Julian's dancin about the road, wavin his arms.

> . . . slip out the back, Jack
> Make a new plan, Stan

What's the next bit?

. . . Don't give a fuck, Chuck . . .

Naw, that's no in it, ya bam!

Get yourself free . . .

There's a squeaky metal noise and then a bang. A guy up above has just threw open a shutter and he's shoutin something at us. Julian stops in the middle of the street and holds his arms up to the guy. *Buona sera, signor. Che bella città!* The guy looks like he's in his vest; he shouts again then goes away back into the room. Julian's shoutin, *Signor, signor . . .* and Danny's tryin to pull him away. Suddenly the guy's came back and he like . . . flings this water out the window. I see it kinda in slow motion, shining against the streetlights like melted gold. It just misses me and Laetitia. It splashes onto the cobbles and spatters onto our shoes and the bottoms of our jeans.

Fucking bastard! Julian shouts. But we all start walking again. Faster this time. And Julian and Danny have stopped singin.

The big heavy outside door of the B&B is still open, but there's only one wee light on in the reception bit, so we talk quieter. I didny know Laetitia was stayin here as well.

Where's your room? she asks.

Third floor, Danny says.

I'm on the second.

Come on up to ours, Danny says. There's nay weed, but at least we can finish the wine.

What wine? Laetitia and me says at the exact same time.

This wine! And he pulls a full carafe out fae under his jacket like he's doin a magic trick. It's got a couple a red napkins stuffed in the neck so's it willny spill.

You clever old thing, Laetitia says.

A man of many talents, Julian says.

Swiped it off the French table, Danny says. It would just a went to waste otherwise. So what d'you say . . . your place or mine?

Well, you've got the double room . . . lead the way.

Yes, lead on Macduff.

It's 'lay on', Julian, Danny says.

Well, rap my knuckles! Never could get to grips with the Scottish play. Not one of the Bard's best, if you ask me.

The stair's getting darker and narrower. Laetitia's in front. She presses a sorta round button on the wall and a light comes on.

You've got an answer for everything, ya know-all cunt.

Boys, boys! Laetitia says. Let peace break out, for goodness' sake. Make love, not war.

Is that an offer? Danny says. He's got the key in the door now but he's stopped and he's turned to Laetitia. It's funny but, when I'm lookin at him lookin at Laetitia, it's like he's no my brother. He's quite handsome. My pals at school say that: Your brother's gorgeous. And I laugh, cause . . . well, he's my brother. Now he's lookin at Laetitia as if there's naybody else there. He's got my ma's green eyes with like dead long dark lashes. My ma used to say, It's no fair, they lashes are wasted on a boy. But she was always smilin when she said it.

The stairlight clicks off. Come on, let us in for Christsake! I'm dying for a smoke, Laetitia says. You can just see her face kinda whitish in the dark.

Danny opens the door. Welcome to the humble Kilkenny abode, he says, and we all pile in. The room looks dead neat and white except for my bed. The duvet's crumpled and my book and my big red T-shirt for sleepin in are lyin on it.

OK, let's see what we've got for drinkin outay, Danny says, and he goes into the bathroom. Two here. He comes out with the toothbrush glasses from the metal circles above the sink. What else?

There's this, I says, and I pick up my empty Diet Coke can.

Great, and one ay us can drink out the bottle. What d'you say, Clare, shall we give the best crystal to our guests? He sounds just like Julian. I look round at Julian but he's went dead quiet. He's sitting on Danny's bed wae a face like fizz. His dreads are spread out over his shoulders and he's no even took off his jacket yet.

Danny pours some wine into one of the toothbrush glasses and hands it to Laetitia. She's sittin on my bed on top a her jacket with her bag on her knee, rollin a fag. She takes the wine off Danny and sets it on the wee table beside the bed.

Roll one for me, will you? Julian says.

Roll your own, Laetitia says, and clicks her lighter. A yellow flame comes up from the end a the wee thin roll-up, then settles down. She leans back on her elbows on the bed with her fag in her mouth.

Here, Danny says, and he pours wine into the other toothbrush glass and hands it to Julian. Get that down you. Then he takes the Coke can off us and sits down on the bed beside Laetitia. I don't know how he does it, but he manages to pour a thin stream of wine from the wide neck of the carafe into the hole on top a the can without spillin any.

Bravo! Laetitia says. Only it sounds more like Vravo! with her fag still in. She sits up and claps her hands and takes the roll-up out her mouth.

Here, Clare, Danny says, and hands me the Coke can. I wish it was Coke in it instead a wine – I'm thirsty. And the wine's no sweet like the kind I've drank afore at parties in Glasgow. But I take it anyway. There's nowhere for me to sit except on Danny's bed. Beside Julian.

He must've saw me standin wonderin what to do, but he doesny budge; he's still takin up most of the bed, leanin back on his hands, his legs spread wide, his eyes starin straight ahead. Danny and Laetitia are sitting close thegether on my bed. He's pourin more wine into her glass. I looks at Julian again and I sit down on the end a the bed. Danny and Laetitia are lookin into each other's eyes singin: 'Little Old Wine Drinker Me'.

I get a fright when I open my eyes cause it's pitch-black and I don't know where I am. I'm lyin there tryin to figure it out when I hear the snufflin noise in the room like somebody wae a bad cold.

Danny, I says, is that you? No answer. I remember there's a light above my bed, so I feel about for the cord and pull it. The room comes on like a headache and Our Lady's lookin down fae the white wall. Danny, I says again. But when I look over it's Julian's dreads I see on the pillow. It's Julian makin the funny noises. He's cryin.

I get out my bed. I don't even remember taking my clothes off last night. I just remember gettin dead tired and closin my eyes when Danny an them were drinkin an talkin. I don't remember putting on my big T-shirt either. I pull it down over my knickers and go over to the other bed.

Julian, I says, you OK? Julian? All I can see are his dreads like a big tangled nest. I touch his shoulder. Julian? He turns

over with his dreads all over his face and he shades his eyes
and looks up at me.

Clare, I'm . . . I'm . . . I just . . . And then he bursts out
greetin really loud and he's sobbin and snotters is comin out
his nose. He's a pure mess.

Julian, what's wrong? I says. But he can't stop cryin. I go
over and get my rucksack at the end of my bed and pull out a
big wad of paper hankies.

Here look, I says. And he takes some and rubs his nose but
he just spreads the snotters all over his face. And there's a line
like a snail trail across his dreads. Julian, wait a minute. I sit
down on the bed beside him and wipe the mess off his face
and dab at his dreads.

What's the matter?

Oh Clare, Clare . . . He reaches up and grabs my wrists. I
drop the hankies on the floor. Clare, oh Clare, oh Clare . . .
he says. And he puts my hand up to his mouth and kisses the
palm. His moustache tickles me. Clare, you won't tell Danny
or Laetitia about this, will you? Please. He's still heavin in
between words.

No, I says, I won't tell them. And he pulls me down on top
of him and he buries his face in my hair.

Oh, Clare, you're an angel, he says, and his voice is dead
thick. He's still got his combat jacket on and all his clothes.

It's OK, Julian, I says. You're alright. It's OK. And I try to
get up.

Don't leave me. Please don't leave me.

No, I won't, I won't. But look, you would feel better wae
your jacket off. And your boots.

Don't leave me, don't leave me.

I struggle out his grip, get off the bed and go to his feet.
See, I'll just get your boots off. I undo the laces and pull the
big scuffed brown Docs off his feet.

24

Pooh, I say, smelly socks! But they areny really. It's just what I used to say to my da when I was wee every time I took his boots off when he came in from work. I thought it might make Julian laugh, but he's still lyin there moanin. I set the Docs on the floor quietly.

There, is that no better? Sit up now and we'll get your jacket off. And he does sit up. I'm amazed. I unzip it and start to ease it over his shoulders. Come on now, you've got to help me, I says. And he starts shufflin his shoulders, shruggin it off.

Clare, will you stay with me tonight? he says.

I take his jacket and lay it on top of his boots. Well, I'm no goin anywhere, am I?

No, but will you *stay* with me? Here? And he lays the flat of his hand on the bed.

I look at his face. His eyes are even bluer in all that red puffiness and the dark bits underneath are like bruises. I sit down beside him.

Aye, I'll stay.

He gives a wee kinda gulp like you do when you've been cryin a long time and says, Clare. You're an angel! A beautiful red-haired angel. He pulls me down onto the bed beside him. His face is right close to mine now. The most beautiful red-haired angel in a red T-shirt in all of Florence. And he puts his hand up inside it and touches my navel stud.

Aahh, he says. His breath smells sorta sweet and sorta sour and I've got a funny feeling in my belly. He slides his finger down and hooks it in the top of my knickers.

Wait, Julian, I says. I've never did this before.

Oh, my sweet, sweet Clare. He starts kissin me all over my face, on my eyes and my nose and my mouth. His dreads fall onto me and it's like lookin through the branches of a tree. And then he lets go the band of my knickers and puts his

25

tongue in my ear. And he moves his hand up and plays with my stud. Then further up and touches my nipple. Then he takes my breast in his hand and like, just holds it. And strokes it. Oh, Clare, let me see you, he says. And he starts to pull my T-shirt up. He leans on one elbow and his dreads are fallin down so I can't see his face. He folds my T-shirt up over my belly and over my boobs.

Ohhh, he says, you're so lovely. And he holds me again, first one, then the other. And then he starts to kiss me and lick me. No on my face this time, but like on my breasts and my nipples and my belly and I don't know where else. All over. I don't remember where.

Then . . .

I feel his tongue inside me, right inside me, and I'm all wet and swollen and I want him further in. I can hear moanin and it must be me, it must be me. And then I don't know what happens. He's took his tongue out and he's lickin me down there and lickin and lickin. I stuff the sheet in my mouth and then it happens, oh God it happens and it's . . .

When it's died down I'm cryin and shakin and Julian's came back up beside me and he's saying, Shh, Clare, it's alright, it's alright, in between kissing my tears.

That was . . .

Shhh . . .

That was so . . . Oh my God . . . I've never . . .

And I put my arms round him and hug him tight.

You've got such a sweet cunt, Clare. Do you know that? A sweet, sweet cunt. He untangles my right hand from his dreads and puts it on the front of his trousers. It's hard. He moves my hand up and down. I know what to do now. I unzip him and put my hand inside his pants and hold him. I've never had one in my hand. Only felt it pressin against me when I was snoggin some boy at the club. It feels dead big. And hard. A bit scary. But I keep holdin it and Julian takes my hand and moves it up and down. I get a fright cause I feel like the skin might come off, slide off like the doobies you see lyin in the lane at the back of the scheme. But Julian keeps my hand there, movin up and down. He's startin to groan and then suddenly he holds my hand tight and stops it.

Clare, can I come inside you? he says. Please?

And I'm like, Yes. I want him to do that to me again.

He slides his jeans and pants down past his knees and pushes them and his socks off the rest of the way with his feet. I look down at him. His thing is standin up dead straight in front of his belly. It looks funny. The top is red and shiny with like this wee hole. His balls are red too and kinda sore-lookin under the hair. I can't believe I'm doing this. I reach down and put my hand round it again and I open my legs.

We both hear the voices outside on the landing at the same time and Julian dives on top of me and pulls the sheet up over us.

Shh, he says.

I don't breathe.

The voices get louder. A man and a woman. I can't hear what they're sayin, but I don't think it's English.

It doesny sound like Danny, I says, whisperin. He'll be sleepin in Laetitia's room.

Oh Christ, Julian says. Oh Christ, oh Christ, oh Jesus fucking Christ! He sits up. The voices go past the door.

What's the matter? I say.

Nothing. Nothing . . . Everything.

I sit up too. Julian's shakin his head. Everything, everything . . . His dreads swing round and hit me on the face, like skippin ropes hittin your bare legs in the playground. I hold his head and stop it movin.

Julian, what is it? He looks at me a long time. His eyes are still red.

Oh fuck! He takes my hands off him and jumps off the bed. He's only got a shirt on and a T-shirt. I look down at him, at his thing. It's wee now and pink and sort of crumpled. Peepin out at the edge of his white T-shirt. I think I'm goin to cry again. He grabs his clothes from the end of the bed and pulls on his pants. And then his jeans. Then he sits on the bed, unrolls his socks and plunges his feet in. He reaches round for his boots, sets them in front of him and swivels them on like he's stubbin out a cigarette. He stands up. He's no even did up the laces and he's pickin up his jacket and walkin to the door. He opens it. Then he turns.

It's not you, Clare. It's just . . . I can't . . . He stops and looks at me. You're a lovely girl, Clare. It's not you, believe me . . . and if . . . I'm sorry, Clare . . . I've got to go.

And he's went.

I sit looking at the closed door for ages.

When I wake up, I'm scared. There's a key really loud in the lock. The door opens and the light goes on. But it's only Danny.

OK, kid. Breakfast, he says, and he claps his hands and rubs them thegether. I keep my eyes half closed. He looks dead happy. You never see him this happy at home.

What time is it?

It's twenty to nine. Time to rise and shine. Here, I'm a poet! He walks over to the window and bends the shutters back. Sun comes pourin in. It's a crackin day! Chilly, but. Good demo weather. The gods are smilin on us.

You been out already?

You're rootin tootin I have. Come on. Cappuccino and brioches await you.

What's bree-osh?

They learn you nothin in that school these days? It's like

croissants. Some with jam in, some with chocolate. All mouth-wateringly delicious! He's talkin like Julian again.

Where's . . . everybody else?

Laetitia's in the dinin room on her fourth espresso. Julian's no appeared yet. Come on, come on. You'll miss the best of the day.

You sound just like my da. I fling the duvet off and head for the bathroom.

I'm goin to have a shower.

You and your showers, Clare. Too much washin can be bad for you.

You sound *exactly* like my da. I close the door behind me.

Danny shouts through it, See you down the stairs. Don't be long; breakfast is only on till nine thirty.

I've never saw Danny like this.

I look in the mirror over the sink. My coldsore's a lot better. It's shrank quite a bit. My hair's a mess, but. I pull some of the red tangles out with my fingers and smooth it down. I'm glad it's grew again; maybe I'll let it get really long this time. One of the toothbrush glasses is back in the metal bracket with a circle of dried red wine in the bottom and browny-pink lipstick marks on the side.

Or maybe I'll get it cut like Laetitia's. She just runs her fingers through hers and gives her head a wee shake and it falls back into place. As if she's just walked out the hairdresser's. It's worth payin extra for a good cut, my ma says. Saves you in the long run.

I pull my T-shirt up over my boobs and tuck it under my chin. I hold one boob in one hand and one in the other and look at them in the mirror. Even though they're no that big, they feel heavy. I think about Julian. My face gets hot and I turn away. I pull my T-shirt off over my head and step in the shower cubicle.

The white tiles are cold. I lean my cheek against them and close my eyes. The things we done last night come back dead strong and I get a warm melty feeling low down in my belly. I turn the shower on quick and the water's pure freezin. I gasp but I stay under it till it gets warm. Then I let it run and run over my head and face for ages. I've forgot to take my shampoo in with me, but there's a wee bar of soap on a dish inset in the tiles and I take the waxy pink paper off. It smells like roses. I run it under the water and rub it between my hands till it gets lathery. Then I rub the suds all over my hair and my body and I think about Julian. The feelin in my belly turns into a kind of an ache like period pains and I want him to touch me down there again. I put my hand on my pubes and I curl my finger round. I don't like the feel of it but. All the wee bits. Heather McLaren at school says she's saw hers. Looked at it in a mirror between her legs. Farkhanda and me didny believe her at first, but she says, Honest, it's true; her mother told her how to do it. They are a bit weird, right enough. Live in a bought house and it's pure manky. And her ma has straggly grey hair and wears like long purple skirts with bells and embroidery on. Find your clitoris, she says to Heather, and you'll never need a man for sexual gratification. Good job she doesny see the way Heather chases Scott Wilson.

My hair's still wet when I walk into the dinin room. The B&B guy with the smiley face is standing at a big silver coffee machine with a cup in his hand. Steam's hissin out and there's a strong coffee smell. He looks round and smiles at me.

Ah, buon giorno, signorina, he says.

Bon jurno, I say back.

You like cappuccino? And he points to the coffee machine. Is our new espresso maker, he says, and he pats the top of it like it's a wean and looks at me dead proud.

Yes . . . *grazie*.

Please. Sit. I bring to you.

I look round the tables. Most of them are empty. Danny and Laetitia are sittin at one in front of a big window. They're holdin hands on top of it, leanin towards one another, talkin low. The sun's shinin in on them and Laetitia's hands are whiter than ever on the green cloth.

Hi, I says.

They look surprised to see me, then Laetitia smiles and takes her hand out of Danny's.

Hi, Clare. Do come and join us.

Yes, do, Danny says. And Laetitia laughs and gives his hand a swipe. What kept you? Danny says. Sit down, I'll get you a coffee.

I've already ordered one off the guy. I sit down facin the window. It's right on the street and folk are walkin past, talkin loud.

The B&B guy comes over with my coffee and a wee basket with three pastry things in. *Cappuccino e brioches*, he says, and sets them on the table. *Buon appetito*. He smiles at me again and goes back to his shiny machine.

Oh good, Danny says, wan each.

Greedy boy, you've had yours, Laetitia says. These are for Clare. Her dark eyes are turned to me and she smiles. Did you have a good night?

I wish I could stop it but I can't. I feel the riddy comin up my neck and right over my face. Yeah, OK.

Your coldsore looks much better, anyway.

Aye, that stuff you gave us was great. Thanks.

Don't mention it. Better drink your coffee before it gets cold. Right, I'm off to my room to put on my slap; can't let the side down with this. She makes a face and points to it, then she twinkles her wee white fingers at us. *Ciao*. See you later.

Danny's smilin up at her. Aye, *ciao*, he says. His eyes follow her across the room. She stops and has a word with the B&B guy and points at his coffee machine. He nods and smiles and says somethin to her. *Ciao*, she says then and walks out through the door. Even with her holey black jumper she's beautiful.

Danny's still watchin the door. I spoon some chocolatey foam off my coffee into my mouth. I'm starvin. Some kind of orange jam oozes out the first brioche when I bite into it. It's warm and sweet and dead light. I eat the rest of it fast and wipe my greasy fingers on my napkin.

You and Laetitia in love? I mean, are you goin thegether?

What? He looks at me as if he can't remember who I am. His eyes are brilliant green in the light. The colour of leaves with the sun through them. In love? Don't know about *lurve*, but she's gorgeous, in't she? He pulls a face and talks out the side of his mouth. Put it this way, I wouldny fling her outa bed. When he sits back in his chair, his face looks dead soppy, but.

Better no let my ma hear you talkin like that. I take another brioche out the basket.

You better no fuckin tell her, he says, and looks back to the door. Julian, my man!

I nearly jump out my skin. I turn round and he's walkin towards the table. His dreads are tied back and he looks dead white. Strained. As if he's no slept. He's wearin the exact same claes as last night. He sits down in Laetitia's seat without saying a word.

You've missed breakfast, pal. But maybe my wee sister'll give you a bite of her brioche.

Julian looks at me then. Hi Clare, he says, dead low, then looks away.

Here, have the last one, I says. They're great. I hold the basket up to him.

He lifts his hand and shakes his head. A couple of his dreads snake out of the band at the back of his neck and hang down beside his sharp cheekbones. No. Thanks . . . coffee's all I need. D'you think they might bend the rules for that?

Well, why don't you try your ineffable charm on Mr Abensur? Danny says.

Who's Mr Abensur?

Guy that owns the *pensione*, ya tadger.

Julian's looked up then and his face is even whiter and his eyes are blazin. Who're you calling tadger, you Glaswegian prick. Even his voice sounds strained. Danny squares his shoulders and sits forward.

Danny, you're out of order, I says in a low voice, just like my ma does when him and my da are into wan. Stop it.

They look at each other for a bit longer. Danny leans back in his chair. Then Julian.

I look round and see the B&B guy still there. I don't think he's noticed anything. I didny know his name was Abensur either. What kind of coffee d'you want? I says to Julian.

Black. Americano, he says. Large.

Mother's little helper, Danny says.

Mr Abensur smiles at me when I come over. He's ayeways smilin. And when I says what I want and point to Julian, he looks delighted. He fits a thing like an ice-cream scoop onto the coffee grinder and pulls a lever three times. He undoes it and twists it onto his shiny machine. The smell of coffee wafts up again. Then he takes this like bowl and puts it under the nozzle, presses the red button and the coffee starts to trickle out. When it stops he takes the bowl and holds it under the hot water bit, presses a button. It hisses and steams and the bowl's full of black black coffee.

I take it over, the guy says. No handles. Hot.

I follow him to the table and he sets the bowl of coffee carefully in front of Julian.

Grazie, signor, Julian says. *È molto gentile.*

The guy's eyebrows go up at the Italian. *Prego*, he says.

I think he would've stayed and spoke more, but Julian pulls the cuffs of his shirt down over his hands, cups them round the bowl and lifts it up to his face. He takes a slurp and then keeps the bowl up at his chin, props his elbows on the table and looks out the window. Mr Abensur turns to go.

Grazie, signor, I says, and he flashes a smile at me as he walks away. *Prego, signorina.*

Oooh! Danny holds one finger up to his cheek and makes his mouth into a poncy oh. We all speaka da lingo now, do we? I don't know why he's bein a prick. Julian pays no attention. He keeps his eyes on the street and takes a sip of his coffee now and again.

I'm fed up with this. I want to get out and do something. I says, Is anybody goin out before the demo starts? I would like to see the shops an that.

Shops! Danny says. Shops! You're in Florence for two days and you want to see the shops? Away tay fuck.

Well, I don't know what else to go and see. And I'm no seein nothin sittin here listenin to your crap, am I? I'm goin back upstairs to get the guidebook.

L'Accademia's near here, Julian says. Would you like to go there? He looks at me with they blue eyes again.

What's L'Accademia?

Ah . . . it's where *David* is.

David?

Yeah, Michelangelo's *David*? You know?

Aye, alright, I says.

Well, Laetitia and me's goin to the Duomo, Danny says. He gets up and pushes his chair in. See you back here at two.

Julian watches him goin, then he turns to me. Clare . . . he says. He's lookin down at his coffee. I think he's goin to say somethin about last night and I can feel my heart thumpin. But he just gets up and says, Let's go.

The outside of the building doesny look like an art gallery; there's just a door straight onto the street round the corner fae the B&B. Julian pushes it open. I'm right behind him and catch a whiff of his dreads. I wonder how he washes them. I wonder if he's washed off the snot. There's a woman in a glass kiosk inside the door. Julian hands over some euros and gets two tickets; stuffs them in the pocket of his combat jacket.

The gallery's got a big high ceilin and there's like statues all round the walls. One a them's got one arm behind him, twisted up his back and the other one coverin his face. His feet are still buried and his prick's been knocked off. He looks like he's pure stuck in the stone.

Another one is sorta sittin *in* the stone and he's holdin this big block where his head should be. And then there's one wae a beard and bands round his legs. The muscles on his chest look deadead real. His arm's up over his head like the other one.

Quattro Prigioni, Julian says. No prizes for guessing what that means. He's lookin at the guidebook, then he looks up at me.

I don't know what it means, I says, but they look kinda trapped to me. They look like they're tryin to pull theirsels out the stone. It's excitin . . . and . . . dead sad.

Spot on, Julian says. They're slaves or prisoners. That one's '*Lo schiavo barbuto*', the bearded slave. That's '*Lo schiavo giovane*', the young slave; and that's . . . that poor sod's Atlas with the whole world on top of him.

You should've been a teacher, I says to him. He sounds like a teacher sometimes. Makes me feel like a wean. And what's this one? I says. I point to one that looks like he's lyin in a bed, except he's standin up, stretchin.

That's '*Lo schiavo che si ridesta*', the Awakening Slave.

35

If he lay back down, the stone would fold over him again and cover him up.

And there he is . . . 'the ugliest masterpiece of Western sculpture' . . . according to the guidebook. Julian points at the huge statue at the end a the gallery. The *David*. I look up at it. And then I look back at the slaves. It's like . . . that's it . . . if you manage to get out the stone . . . you . . . you can . . . he's so amazin . . . I don't care what the guidebook says. You've saw him so many times before on like postcards and different things, you wouldny think it would be a surprise. But it is. He's so big. And still. He's got that frown on his forehead and his eyes are lookin into the distance, as if he can see for miles . . . Through the walls of the gallery. Over the city. Right across the fields and the mountains . . . I feel my eyes pricklin.

. . . Clare. Clare? You still with us?

What?

I was saying, look at the size of his hands . . . compared to his dick, Julian says.

What? Oh . . . yeah. He's . . . amazin.

That's not what I said.

What? Julian's startin to annoy me. I wish he would leave me alone.

Come on, space cadet, what planet you on? Julian comes right round in front of me, takes both my hands and stares at me. Why, I do believe you're crying. And for that great adolescent lump of marble too. But he puts his hands up to my cheeks and thumbs away the tears. Then he slides them down to my mouth and I can taste the salt on them.

Clare. He pulls my head towards him and kisses me on the forehead. His dreads all fall forward and cover both our faces. Like hidin under a tree when you were wee. Come on, he says, dead soft. Let's take a closer look.

Julian takes my hand and we walk towards him. *David*. He

36

grows bigger the nearer we get. The floor is dark polished wood. Light from the high windows is lyin in squinty squares on it, crisscrossed with the shadows of the wooden frames. There's hardly anybody else there. Just a guy and a woman walkin about arm in arm. He's got silver hair – no grey, silver – and a long sort a mac. He looks dead classy. She's got blonde hair and a mac too and her hand's in a leather glove peepin through at the crook of his elbow. They look like they're going thegether, even though they must be pretty ancient. Older than my ma and da. We walk past them. The man covers the woman's hand with his and looks into her face, smilin.

Do you reckon we make as handsome a couple as they do? Julian takes my hand under his arm like the guy and pats it and looks right at me and smiles. I get that feelin again low down, sharp and sweet, and my knees go wobbly. But I keep walkin.

He's dead big, the *David*. When we're right in front of him he towers over us. Well, what do you think of our boy close up? Julian says. You know Michelangelo started it when he was about my age, twenty-six, and finished it by the time he was thirty. He pulls the guidebook out his pocket. 'Michelangelo always saw carving as a form of extraction, believing that his task was "merely to release the figure from its stone prison".' Hence the *prigioni*.

Somethin about it makes me want . . . to no talk. Just look.

D'you see what I mean about his hands, though? Julian says. And his prick. Should've kept his fig leaf on. Look – he points to a screen in the corner – there's the interactive computer programme. Let's have a go.

No, you're alright. I'll stay here. He looks at me funny. I want to see the real thing, I says. He goes off to the computer hissel. I just stand there in front of the *David*. And look.

*

37

By the time we start walkin out the gallery there's a lot more folk in. Some a them have badges on and like berets and hats and T-shirts of Che Guevara and must be goin to the demo too. One guy is campin it up for his pal and doin a pose like the *David* wae his hip out and his other knee bent a wee bit. And he hangs his scarf over his shoulder like David's sling.

Let's get out of here, Julian says. If you've seen enough?

Yeah, there's too many people now, you can't see anythin properly.

Julian looks at me and laughs. His dreads look all happy again and dancin. Quite the culture vulture, aren't you?

No I'm no. It's just . . . I've never saw anything like that afore. I feel silly and my face is goin red again. I'm comin back here someday, I says.

We can hardly get by people on the pavement now, it's got so busy. And noisy. And it's no safe to step onto the street, cause the cars and scooters are roarin by that fast. Julian looks around at me.

What a very definite girl you are. At first I think he's takin the piss. But he's lookin at me dead serious. I believe you will. Come back one day, I mean. And it's been my great privilege to accompany you on your maiden voyage.

He stops on the pavement, turns round and takes my hand. But today, come back to the hotel, he says. With me.

It sounds like an order but I know it's really a question, cause his eyebrows are up and his eyes look a bit scared. Dead blue. But scared.

Aye alright, I says. And he smiles and starts walkin faster.

Julian's room's different fae ours. Only one bed. But it's big, a double bed. The duvet's sorta pinky orangey. Colour of a sunset. The walls are yellow. And there's photos of the Ponte Vecchio on them. No Our Lady.

This time, Julian's took his jacket off as soon as we come in and he flings it in the corner. He goes back to the door and turns the key. That's us locked in. He smiles at me, then he opens the other door and goes into the toilet.

I sit on the bed but I keep my coat on. When Julian comes out, the zip of his jeans is still down and I can see his pants. He's got a hard-on already.

Clare. He comes and stands in front of me and pulls me up by the hood of my coat. My head comes to just under his chin and his wee beard tickles my forehead. He pushes me back and takes my face in his hands.

I lick my lips. He takes my hand and puts it to his mouth. Then he bends down and kisses me on the lips . . . kissin and kissin me. His mouth is soft and wet. He puts his tongue between my teeth and touches my tongue. It tastes salty.

Then he steps back. Clare, he says. And he starts to take my coat off. When he's got my arms pinned to my sides with the fur of the hood soft on my bare back, he kisses me again.

We're gonny miss the demo. He's holdin my face and his fingers are up the back of my head. He laughs.

No, we'll make it. Don't worry, I'll get you there. And he pulls me to him and starts kissin me again, all over my face. My coat slips down my arms onto the floor. He pushes me back towards the bed so I have to sit down. Then he puts his knees on too, one either side of me and lies down on top of me so I have to lie back. I push my boots off with my toe on the heel and they clatter to the floor. Julian puts his arm round the back of my waist and hoists me further up so's my head's on the pillow and I'm lyin diagonal across the bed. His dreads are hangin over his face and his white pants are bulgin out the V of his zip. He takes my hand and puts it on his thing. It still feels dead weird to be doin this. I squeeze my hand in over the top of the elastic that says cK cK cK and burrow through

the hair till I hold it in my hand. But he's different this time
. . . impatient. He jumps off the bed and hauls off his boots
and socks and jeans. Then his pants. His . . . cock . . . springs
back up out them when he pulls them down. He gets on the
bed again and starts unzippin me and pullin hard at the
waistband. I push up my hips to help him and he peels my
jeans right off, inside out and flings them across the room.

Julian, wait

It's OK. Just relax. He takes hold of my knickers and rips
them down. The lace scratches me. I can hear it tearin.

Wait . . . Julian . . .

But he's on top of me now and his dreads are coverin my
face and I can't get my hands up to push him off. He prises
my legs open and next thing . . . he shoves into me . . . and
I scream . . .

Julian, stop . . . you're hurtin me.

But it's like he can't hear me.

Julian . . .

He keeps bangin it into me and bangin and bangin.

Please, Julian . . .

And then he lets out a groan and he shudders and falls
heavy on top of me. He's breathin fast into my ear and it feels
all wet.

Oh fuck, he says. It sounds thick and muffled through my
hair and his. Oh fuck.

I don't say nothin. Just lie there. I can hardly breathe the
way he's got me pinned down. I have to just lie there.

The one picture of the Ponte Vecchio is all the traders and
tourists. I have to blink to see it right. In the bottom left-hand
corner there's the edge of this stall with models of the *David*.
They look funny. I blink again, harder. They're too long.
Skinny. The wrong white. Maybe it's the photo. The other
picture is of the bridge fae a distance, with the bits stickin out

like the backs of sheds and the red roofs of the houses. The brown river runnin underneath. Different fae Glasgow.

Totally different.

Julian's breathin quieter now, so I shift under him. He pushes himsel up on his hands with his arms straight. He's still in me. I can't see his face for his dreads but I get the feelin he's smilin. I pull mysel up the bed on my elbows and I can feel his prick wee and soft slidin out of me.

Clare?

I don't answer.

He rolls off me onto his elbow and looks at me. Are you crying? Clare?

I roll over the other way and pull myself off the bed.

Where are you going?

I pick my jeans and my knickers off the floor and go into the bathroom. It's white too, same as ours. I lock the door. My face is pale in the mirror and my hair is stickin to the side of my head where Julian's slavered on me. I set my clothes on the bidet and fill the basin with hot water.

Julian's at the door. Listenin.

Clare? Clare, please talk to me. What's the matter?

I pick up my torn knickers and dip them in the water and squeeze them.

Are you alright? Clare!

Then I wash myself down there. I'm still sore. When I look at my knickers, they're all blood and slime. I rinse them again. The water turns pink.

Talk to me, Clare. Are you there?

I wash mysel and rinse and wash and rinse and wash and rinse. Then I pull the plug out. All the pink water swirls away.

Clare! He bangs once on the door. C'mon. What you doing? You're scaring me.

I take one of the white towels off the chrome rail and dry

between my legs and where the water's ran down them. I hang the towel back up. There's only a faint pink smear. I hope Mr Abensur doesny see it.

He thumps again. Harder. Clare!

I lift my jeans, put my arm down the legs and turn them the right way out. Then I step into them, pull them on and do them up. I make sure the zip doesny catch any a the hairs in my pubes.

Clare, you're being childish. Open the door.

I pick my knickers out the basin, squeeze the water out, drop them in the pedal pin beside the sink. No. I press the pedal again with my bare foot and fish them out. It might be Mr Abensur who empties the bins. Or his wife. I squeeze them a bit more into the sink. Then I stuff them in the pocket of my jeans.

Clare, I'm going to break the door down . . . if you don't talk to me . . . tell me what's the matter.

I slide back the chrome bolt and open the door. Julian steps backwards. It looks like the whole room behind him is full of sun. But it's only the yellow walls and the orange duvet.

Clare. Julian takes my hands and looks at my face. His eyes look worried. Clare, did I hurt you? I'm so sorry. Tell me, Clare. It's just I thought . . .

I'm alright, I says. I walk past him and pick up my boots. Then I go to sit on the bed to put them on. There's a stain right in the middle of the duvet. Like a big red poppy.

Oh God! I start to cry again. Look what we've did . . .

Julian sits on the bed beside me and puts his arm round my shoulder. Clare, it's alright. I'm sorry . . . I didn't realize you were . . . I didn't know you hadn't . . . you'd never . . . you know . . . done it before.

I told you . . . I told you . . . I told you . . .

Shhh, Clare, shhh. It's alright. I'm sorry. It's alright.

42

Somebody hammers on the door. Really loud.

Julian, you there?

It's Danny!

Time to go, man. Demo's due to start.

I stop breathin.

Is Clare wae you?

Julian puts a finger to his mouth and squeezes my shoulder with his other hand.

Julian?

They should be back by this time, Danny says to somebody. Twisted cunt, that yin.

A woman's voice answers. Laetitia it must be, but I don't hear what she says. Danny gives the door one last thump. Then they go away.

Julian comes round the front of me and kneels on the floor. Forget about Danny, he says. He pulls his hand inside the sleeve of his shirt and uses it to wipe my face.

Don't cry, Clare. Please. I'm really sorry. That was insensitive of me.

Is that what you call it? I think to myself. I'm cold. I cross my arms over my chest. Julian takes my arms and pulls them apart. Slow.

Don't, I says.

Clare . . . don't be like that. Please. He puts his hands under my oxters, stands up and pulls me up at the same time. I notice he's got his jeans on again. He presses me to him and puts his arms round me and sorta rocks me. And sways me. Then he like starts to slow dance me round the floor. Singin.

No woman, no cry . . .

He kisses the top of my head.

No woman, no cry . . .

He combs my hair with his fingers and sings about Trenchtown and havin good friends and losin them and dryin my tears. His voice is soft. It doesny sound posh when he sings. He even looks a bit like Bob Marley, only white. He kisses my eyes.

. . . *Everything's gonna be alright* . . .

He sings over my head into the bright room.

. . . *Everything's gonna be alright, now* . . .

Clare, he says. The front of his jeans is hard again.

He dances me slow across to the bed, flings the duvet back and pulls me down onto the rumpled sheet. Then he reaches for the cover, tents it over our heads and kisses my mouth in the warm dark.

This time I know it'll be OK.

When I wake up, Julian's arm is heavy across me and his face is at the top of my head, blowin my hair when he breathes out. It's nearly dark in the room. The sky at the window is a deep kinda mauvey blue. I lift my feet up under the duvet to let some air in. The cold makes me feel the wet between my legs. I get embarrassed even in the dark thinkin about Julian's face there, me holdin on to his dreads with both hands. When he's came back up, he says, Am I forgiven then? And his face is all shiny with slavers and like . . . my juice. He makes me laugh; he reminds me of my aunt Patsy's big daft dog just out the sea at Helensburgh wae a stick. He says, Here, taste yourself . . . He kisses me and puts his tongue right in. And I think maybe I *can* taste me, mixed in with the tobacco and his own salty taste. And when he's came into me again, it's totally different. It's so warm under the cover and he's movin slow and his tongue's in my mouth . . . I don't remember now who's fell asleep first.

I pull my hand out fae under the duvet and look at my watch: four o'clock.

Julian. I lift his arm off me and sit up. He says somethin in

44

his sleep I canny make out. Julian. I shake his shoulder. He turns slow onto his back. His hair's all over the pillow. Then he opens his eyes. I can see the whites of them sorta gleamin in the half-light in the room. He looks a bit creepy. I swing my legs out fae under the duvet and run with my bare feet on the cold marbly floor to the light switch beside the door. The light's as bright as sunshine and the yellow room is there again. Julian squints in the sudden glare but his eyes are back to normal. He's watchin me. I put my arm across my boobs and my other hand over my pubes and go back to the bed.

He laughs, You can't hide from me now; I know you inside out. His eyes are blue and I get that funny feelin again.

Pass me my jacket, will you? Julian says, and points. It's crumpled in the corner where he's flung it. I feel him watchin me when I go over to get it. I try to imagine what he's seein but I can't. He's lookin at me fae an angle I've never even saw mysel. Nobody has. Except when I was a wean. I hold the cold jacket in front of me when I go back to the bed. It smells of Julian. The metal buttons make wee burny-cold spots down my belly. I hold it out to Julian and he takes it from me and pulls me down beside him at the same time.

Are we gonny go to the demo? Close up, his eyes have got wee violety flecks and a few gold ones, and the really really blue bits are round the edges.

Do you want to? He's took his tobacco out his pocket and he's smoothin out a Rizla.

My da'll kill me if don't.

He laughs and takes a big pinch of tobacco out the pouch and sprinkles it slow and even along the paper. Some wee brown strands fall onto the duvet and he picks them up and rubs them off his fingers into the green packet.

Sure, we'll go. I promised I'd get you there, didn't I? His hands are the only bit of him that's no dead white; they've got some sun on the backs and gold hairs, and the fingers are stained with nicotine.

Aye, but . . . when? It'll be all over if we don't go now.

He starts to roll the fag, foldin the thin paper over careful, then workin it between his fingers till it's closed over the tobacco.

Soon . . . when I've had a smoke. He lifts the cigarette to his mouth and licks the edge of the Rizla, sticks it down. He fishes out a clear turquoise lighter and flicks the flame under the roll-up, narrows his eyes and takes a long draw. He clocks me watchin him.

Would you like a drag? He holds out the roll-up like it's one a they spliffs.

No, you're alright. I don't smoke.

What a good little girl you are. He takes his fag back and takes a deep draw. Why's he sayin that? After what we've just been doin? Nobody in our house smokes – no even Danny. My da's dead against it. Says he watched my granda cough hissel to death at the age of fifty-two.

The stain on the duvet is dried now. It's turned more a sorta browny-pink. The colour of Laetitia's lipstick nearly.

What we gonny do about that? I says.

Nothing.

Nothin?

Not a thing.

But—

Clare, this is a hotel; there are people to do the washing. That's what we pay for. He sounds annoyed.

OK . . . Are you mad at me?

Of course not.

It's just . . . you sound mad.

He sighs out a big cloud of smoke. Well, I'm not. Come on. He nips the end of his roll-up and tosses it in the bin. Then he jumps out the bed. His prick's smooth and kinda long and a bit red. But no hard. No wee and wrinkled either. I wonder if it's on the way up or down. He goes into the bathroom and I hear him peein. When he comes out, it looks smaller again. I've no saw it lookin the same way twice.

Right, let's go, he says. And he starts pickin up his clothes off the floor.

It's funny how you can be dead close to somebody, then it's like you don't even know them.

It's no completely dark when we come out the B&B, but it's gettin there. There's still a few light silvery streaks in the sky.

How will we know where to go? I says. Julian's holdin my hand and his fingers are cold. He's got the collar of his combat jacket up.

We'll find it. Trust me. He starts walkin in the same direction as l'Accademia. It feels like a week at least fae we came along here before. The big door of the gallery's shut now and the windows are black. Julian is walkin faster and I'm kinda half runnin to keep up. He doesny look at the place. Funny to think of the *David* in there, gazin into the distance in the dark, his body all white and still. And the slaves strugglin, strugglin out the stone for ever.

We start goin across a big square wae a church at one side and a statue in the middle. It's dead quiet for a Saturday. Maybe everybody's went to the demo. Then we go through some more narrow cobbled streets. Some of the shops have big planks of wood bolted across their windows. They're all closed.

Are the shops always shut like this on a Saturday? Even though he's holdin my hand, Julian seems awful far away.

What?

The shops?

Not sure. Think perhaps it's the *manifestazione*.

The what?

That's what the Italians call the demonstration. *La mani-festazione*. Manifestation. See. He points to a notice on the dark red door of a *ristorante*: *Chiuso per la manifestazione*. Closed for the demonstration. Bastards.

Why?

Don't want the riffraff of Europe coming into their nice clean restaurant.

Maybe they've went to the demo theirsels and that's how they've closed it. I think this might make Julian laugh, but he says nothin and just starts walkin faster again.

We cross another wee square, this time wae trees round it. Some of the leaves have fell onto the street and they swish under our feet. They're different fae the ones in Glasgow. More like old paper. No soakin wet or dry and crumbly like in the park at home. I wish Julian would say somethin.

What kind a trees are they?

Dunno. He's lookin straight ahead and doesny even glance at them.

Only the leaves are different fae in Glasgow.

I don't know, Clare. A tree is a tree is a tree. D'you want to make the demo or not?

I don't say nothin. The next street we come to has leaflets and streamers and things in among the leaves.

Well, here's where they started from, going by the evidence at our feet. He bends down and picks up a yellow leaflet with black writin. It seems to be all in Italian.

So, I guess we just follow the paper trail. He looks at me for the first time for ages and I remember when I first seen him standin in George Square and wondered who he was.

Alright? he says. I nod my head and he starts off walkin fast again.

It's like there really is a paper trail. First it's just leaflets and the odd placard wae a broken stick. But then we come to a bit where the road's wider and there's signs to different towns – Pisa, Bologna, Roma – and we're out of the centre of Florence. There's no old houses here; just modern flats. Concrete boxes for the masses, my da would say. And all over the road there's hunners a wee bits of paper scattered, all different colours. A few of the flats have posters and banners hangin out the windows. I can see right into some a them where the light's on. There's this one . . . a young guy with a bare chest is dancin round the room hissel. He sorta boogies over to the window and looks out. Then a dark-haired girl comes up behind him and puts her arms round his waist and her cheek against his shoulder. The hairs on the back of my neck stand up. I look at Julian and I'm gonny say somethin, but his eyes are far away.

A couple a guys and a lassie are walkin towards us. It looks like they could a been on the march by the style of them. Jeans and T-shirts, green jackets and coloured scarfs. The lassie has on a red and yellow stripy jumper and a floppy rainbow hat.

Buon giorno, Julian says. *La manifestazione?* They look at each other, then start to talk dead slow in Italian and point the way they've came.

Ah, American? Julian says. Hi.

They smile and say, Hi, like it's a big relief. Yeah, just keep right on along this road, then it's on your left? You can't miss it. It's e*nor*mous. Bigger'n any we've seen in the States.

The girl with the hat holds her arms out wide and opens her eyes like she's surprised.

Yeah, one of the guys says, we sure would like to stay for the party, but we're booked into Venice tonight, so we gotta go get the train.

Venice is beautiful . . . a one-off . . . you'll love it, Julian says. He's smilin straight at the lassie. Maybe it's just me he doesny want to talk to.

Your dreadlocks are real cool, she says. I would just *love* to have locks, but my mom would go crazy.

I'm sure your hair is much too pretty as it is, Julian says. Enjoy your trip. *Ciao.*

Yeah, *ciao*, they all say. And Julian puts his arm round my shoulder and starts walkin again. I look back and the lassie's between the two guys, lookin over her shoulder at Julian. I'm glad his arm's round me.

So, just along here and to the left . . . appropriately enough, Julian says.

They were nice, I says.

What, those guys? A bunch of Yanks playing politics while they do the Grand Tour of Europe. I move in closer to his side and press my face into the cold, smooth cloth of his combat jacket.

Hear that? Julian says.

What? I pull my head away from his side. There's a noise like a concert with like music and drums and people shoutin. Is that it? I says.

That's it. The reason you came all the way to Florence from bonny Scotland. He says it in this kid-on Scottish accent, the way American actors do in films. Florrr-ence. Scoat-land.

Oh, reh-ally? I says. And at least he looks at me. Even if he doesny crack a light. We walk along the road, shufflin through all the wee bits a paper in the direction of the music and shoutin.

The next street we turn into, there it's there. The noise! It pure hits me. And the amount of people. Thousands. The whole road's filled fae side to side right up against the buildins. There's a van wae a loudspeaker blarin out songs and there's guys dancin around it. It's movin dead slow. The folk in front are holdin up their banners and shoutin and chantin. An old guy is leanin out his window, givin water to some of the marchers and there's folk at loads a windows up above throwin the wee bits of paper. They float down silver in the lights from the houses, but when they fall they're just bits of newspaper and stuff.

Christ, what a bottleneck! Julian says, and takes my hand. Let's see if we can get a bit further along the column. I hate being at the end of a march; the interesting stuff's at the front. The vanguard.

He starts walkin and pullin me past the end of the road wae the demo, into the next street. It's like he's decided to be nice to me again. Or maybe he's just excited to be here at last. I have to nearly run to keep up. In the distance I can see the marchers walkin past the far end of the road with red banners and yellow placards. It must a looked amazin in the daylight at the start.

When we reach the end of the road and come into the side of the demo, it's the noise that hits me again. Mental. There's more space but, and Julian pulls me into the middle of the row in front of a guy with a placard he must a drew hissel wae BUSH, BLAIR E BERLUSCONI: TERRORISTI! in big red letters. I canny make out a word of what they're shoutin. A lassie dressed in green wae a face tae match and wild curly hair is walkin backwards in front of another lassie, paintin a green CND sign on her face. When she clocks me watchin, she holds up the crayon and lifts her eyebrows. She's even got green eyes! I look at Julian and shake my head. He's pullin hissel up, cranin to see over the folk in front. The lassie shrugs her shoulders and pulls her mouth down at the corners. Then she smiles at me and moves on to the next person. She's got a dead nice smile.

Julian tugs at my hand, Come on, he shouts, see if we can

find the Glasgow contingent. He pulls me out the line round the back of the green lassie, paintin a sunflower on a young guy's face. On her rucksack she's got badges and a wee placard stickin out the top that says: DIE GRÜNEN.

We get onto the pavement, but it's quite narrow and hard to get by folk at first. I hold on tight to Julian's hand. He's goin, *Scusi, scusi*, and squeezin past folk. Just as well everybody's in a good mood; they're all singin and chantin and shoutin and hardly notice us. Eventually we get goin a bit faster. Most of the time you can just see folks' backs and the backs of their banners. I would like to look at them but I'm scared to turn too often in case I lose Julian. He's tall but, so at least his dreads would be flyin over the heads of maist of the crowd.

At the end of this road, we turn into another one that slopes down a wee bit. The march goes right to the bottom and away on by. I don't see how we're ever goin to find Danny and them. I've never saw so many folk – no even at Celtic Park, when my da used to take me and I had to hold on tight to his hand and all I could see was legs and the bottoms of anoraks till he picked me up. And then all his pals would speak to me and smile and sometimes kiss me with their beery mouths. I've still got the scarf one of them gave us. I never told my da I didny like goin.

We pass a line of guys with red T-shirts and black berets. I look back at them. One of them was at l'Accademia this morning posin like the *David*. I smile at him but he looks right through me. When I was wee I used to think it was terrible there was so many people in the world you would never know.

There's a big section next that looks like trade unions. They've got dead professional-lookin banners and official printed placards. At first I think it's all in Spanish, but it isny.

Must be Portuguese. Or maybe Catalan. No the kind I've

learnt anyway. They're about my da's age, a lot of them, and they look a wee bit like him too. The style a them. They're a lot quieter. One a them winks at me and I give him a smile in the passin. Julian's no slowed down one bit. He's on a mission. My hand's sore where he's grippin it tight, but I'm glad he is. If he let go and disappeared I don't know what I would do. I would like to stop sometimes and see what it's like at one bit of the demo, but in a way, it's quite excitin leggin it down the side, past all the different kinds a folk and the colours and the noise and all the different songs.

In front of the trade unionists there's a funny wee group. I look over my shoulder at them. Julian, I says, here's some English banners. He doesny hear me at first. Julian, wait, I shout louder. He turns and slows down a bit. Look, there's some banners in English here. Julian looks. His face is hard and set.

Don't tell me you want to stay with this lot, Clare.

Shh, I says. They must have heard him. But I think they're a good laugh. FAIRIES AGAINST THE WAR, the banner says in spidery writin, with pictures of fairies and elves all over it. The lassie nearest me is wearin white tights and big rainbow Docs with the laces undone; and a pink and white net tutu with a big green jumper on top. She's carryin a tray with like, fairy cakes wae pink and white icing. And she's got on a paper tiara with letters made out of purple sequins that says, Tinkerbell. Hangin fae her tray there's a notice: MAKE CAKES, NOT BOMBS. She smiles at me and holds out the tray.

Would you like a cake?

Thanks, I say, and I take a pink one. Her tray's held on round her neck with a ribbon and she's got fingerless red gloves on. Did you make them?

Yeah, she says, me and Milly. She points her tray at the lassie walkin beside her. Hi, Milly says. She's wee and fat and she's dressed in a floaty yellow and green nylon skirt wae a

combat jacket on top and a big badge that says: FLOWER
FAIRIES FIGHT FASCISM.

We made them at my mother's in London and brought
them on the bus in a fridge box. Pretty cool, hey? This is the
last of them. Would your friend like one? Milly's cakes are
green and yellow; she holds out her tray to Julian, but he just
looks at her. I can see Milly's face goin pink even though it's
quite dark now.

I'll have one, I says. Thanks. I've got to go. I'm lookin for
my brother.

Well, good luck in this mob, Milly says.

Thanks. And thanks for the cakes. I walk closer to Julian.
I've got baith the cakes sittin in my right hand in their crinkly
paper cases and we're walkin too fast for me to eat them.
There's more folk throwin the confetti stuff fae their windows,
clappin and cheerin the march.

Julian, stop a minute. What am I gonny do wae the cakes?

Would you really like me to tell you? he says. He's smilin,
but. Come on, there's a mere five hundred thousand demon-
strators to get past yet. I'm glad he's in a good mood again. I
let go his hand for a minute and stick the two buns thegether
by the pink and yellow icing, then stuff them in my pocket. I
have a quick keek back at Milly and Tinkerbell, but they're
singing a song and ringin wee bells alang wae it. I lick my
fingers and grab Julian's hand. He turns and looks at me.

D'you really think we're gonny find Danny and Laetitia?

Stranger things have happened. But I'd say the odds are a
bit on the long side. He laughs. You've got pink icing on your
face, incidentally. I lick my fingers again and rub at my cheek.
You ought to watch what you eat, you know; never can be
sure what might be lurking in an anarchist's cake.

It's a fairy cake, I says. It's the colour of the icing gives you
the clue. But I don't think he's heard me. He's away like

the clappers again down the side of the demo, weavin past lampposts and marchers takin a break and a wee woman with a dog goin even slower than the demo.

We must be gettin near the front of the march by this time; I feel as if I've walked miles. We're in a more open bit again, a wider road. There's a guy on top of some sorta kiosk – *un tabaccaio*, it's called – holdin his banner above his head like a football scarf, swayin it fae side to side and singin. I should've taen a camera, but I didny think. There's more room here, so I'm walkin beside Julian. He's still no really talkin to me – like he's no that bothered if I'm there or no. He's goin slower but, and we're walkin with a group that's got drums and maracas things and they're dancin round to the rhythm. If Julian wasny here I would join in; I don't think he's in the mood.

There's a big grassy bank wae a railing along and a lot of folk are sittin down there.

That must be the river, Julian says.

It's completely dark now and I canny see any river. What, the Arno? I says. The one the Ponte Vecchio's on?

It's the only river that runs through Florence. Want to take a break? We've seen what there is of the action. Not much more to see.

Yeah, alright. We leave the dancin drummers and cross to the grassy bit. Some folk have spread their coats out and are sittin drinkin out a bottles a wine. Right enough, it doesny feel as cold, but I don't fancy sittin there; it's covered in dowts and I can see at least one lump a dog shite.

It's Danny that clocks me first. I hear his voice comin out the darkness.

Clare! Clare! Where the fuck have you been?

I look round and he's standin up fae among the folk drinkin. He's got a bottle in his hand and he looks mad.

Danny. We've been lookin for you.

Where's Julian?

He's here. I turn round and for a minute I canny see him. But he's kneelin down talkin to somebody. Over there, see?

I've been worried about you all day. Somebody else stands up and moves into the light fae the streetlamp. Laetitia.

Hi, Laetitia.

She doesny smile back. Her face is dead serious. Hello, Clare. We've been sitting here trying to figure out how exactly we would go about finding a missing girl in a city hosting an extra – what? – eight hundred thousand plus for the Social Forum.

Well, I'm here now, I says. I look round, but Julian's still hunkered down talkin. Danny's dead mad, but he doesny come near me. He takes a long slug of wine. I don't know what else to say.

Is that how many people's on the demo? Eight hundred thousand? That's amazin. I bet my da would a loved it.

Loved what?

I turn round and Julian's behind me. His dreads look orange under the streetlights. Hi, guys, he says. Now this *is* amazing. I just said to Clare that the chances of us actually finding you in this crowd were pretty thin. But here you are. Should've bought a lottery ticket today, eh? He makes a kinda oh-well-never-mind face and shrugs his shoulders.

Where've you been? Danny says. His face goes dead dark when he's mad, wae his black eyebrows pulled thegether and his black hair. Why were you no back at the B&B at two o'clock like we said?

What's this, the third degree? Julian says. He's startin to sound a bit narked.

We were worried, Laetitia says. Clare's only sixteen. Danny's supposed to be looking after her. He promised his father.

Well, isn't that sweet? Danny and Laetitia *in loco parentis*.

As you can see, Clare is absolutely fine. She's been with me.

We went to see the *David*, I says.

Yeah, Clare's first naked man, wasn't he, Clare?

And the prisoners breakin out the stone theirsels.

What the fuck you talkin about? Danny says. I've got a feelin he's gonny be in a bad mood for the rest of the night.

Michelangelo's *Prisoners*. They look like they're tryin to escape fae the stone.

Danny takes another slug from the bottle. Some of the people round about are gettin up, shakin out their coats and startin to leave.

Look, let's go somewhere more comfortable, Laetitia says. She still hasny smiled. She pulls her fingers back through her hair. A bunch of the guys are heading to town to Dino's on Via Cavour. They've booked tables. She bends down for her jacket. OK?

A bunch of the boys were whooping it up in the Malamute Saloon. . . Julian says, and punches the air.

Naybody laughs. I'm glad Laetitia's here. Wae Danny in that mood, you don't know what might happen. I start to breathe normal again. I'm no lookin forward to the walk into town, but.

I wouldny've even noticed the place. It's on a dark bit of the street. From the outside it looks like an ordinary house or a close maybe. Laetitia pushes open the door and goes in first. There's another door inside with the top half glass.

Here we are – Dino's. Cheap and cheerful, she says. Authentic Italian. She holds out her arms and turns to the rest of us.

I take a look round. It's a bit of a dive, if you ask me. Kinda like a cave, with an arched entrance and a curved ceiling. The walls are dark wood up to shoulder height and then it's a sorta yellowy plaster above, covered in dunts and dirty marks. The tablecloths are white paper and this time there's no candles on them. Only on the walls in kinda metal brackets. It's hard to make out the faces sittin round the tables at the back.

Great, Julian says. Fasta, fasta, bring on the pasta!

Where'd you like to sit? Laetitia says to Danny. He's no said hardly a word on the way back.

He shrugs his shoulders, I'm no bothered. Anywhere. This'll dae. And he sits down and plonks his half-empty bottle on the nearest table. Laetitia pulls out the seat beside him and hangs her jacket on the back.

Right, I'm off to the loo first, she says. Want to come and help me find it, Clare?

She sorta looks right at me. So I goes, Yeah, OK. I put my hands in the pockets of my coat and I follow her out. That's when I realize the fairy cakes are still there. I pull them out. Laetitia holds open the door of the Ladies for me.

What on earth is that?

Fairy cakes. I got them off a couple a lassies on the demo. Would you like one? They're a bit squashed. I'm only really sayin it for somethin to say, so I'm surprised when Laetitia says, Sure, go on then, I'll have one. I pull them apart. Most of the yellow icing has stuck to the pink. I hold out that one to Laetitia and go to eat the one with no icing mysel.

She leans her bum against a basin, picks a crumb of icing off the cake and puts it on her tongue. What were you playing at, Clare?

What d'you mean? I've got maist of my cake in my mouth now and it's stickin to the roof. I feel like gaggin.

Oh, I think you know what I mean.

Honest, I don't. My voice sounds thick with the cake.

She turns and stares at me. Her dark eyes are lookin right into mine. I can see mysel in the mirror above the basin; my face is dead white.

58

I think I'm gonny be sick, I says. I push open the door of one of the cubicles and lock it behind me. The lavvy's stinkin. I bend over it and stick two fingers in my mouth to scrape the claggy cake off the roof. I throw the stuff in the pan and shake my hand. Then I'm retchin and retchin but there's nothin much to come up, just clear liquid and a few crumbs of cake. I chuck the crumbled bun case in on top and pull the flush.

Clare, are you alright? She sounds anxious. I put down the seat and sit on it.

Yeah, I'm OK. I just need a minute.

Are you sure? Why don't you come and sit in the restaurant?

In a minute.

Look, you've got me worried now. Please come out. I wish she would leave me alone and go back in with the rest of them.

Clare, I'm sorry if I've upset you. It's just you gave us such a scare.

OK, OK. I'm comin. I get up slow and open the door. She's standin waitin for me. I'll just give my face a wash. She moves to the side so I can get to the basin. I don't look at her. I run the cold water and splash my face and drink some from my hand. It tastes different fae Glasgow water. I dry my face on the towel, then my hands.

I'll be fine now. Let's go back through.

Right. Great. She sounds kinda cool with me, but she follows me out the Ladies, back to the table.

Julian looks up, I don't know what you girls find to talk about for so long in the loo.

Clare's been sick.

He looks at me.

I think it was the cake she ate.

I warned you about that. Julian sounds as if he's pretendin to be annoyed. Never trust an anarchist as far as you can throw their poxy cakes.

Oh, for Christsake, Laetitia says. Do you have to make a political point out of every fucking thing, Julian? It was a cake. End of story.

Correct me if I'm wrong, but I thought it was you feminists who tried to sell the idea that the personal is political? He seems to be enjoyin hissel. His eyebrows are arched, lookin at Laetitia, and he's got a daft smile on his face. Certainly the *fairies* who made them seem to think baking buns is a political act? *Bake cakes, not bombs!* Wasn't that their slogan, Clare?

Laetitia pays no attention and sits down beside Danny. He's got his elbows on the table and a stubby glass of red wine in his hands and he's starin into it. I don't know where to sit. The place is fillin up now and it looks like everybody comin through the door is fae the demo.

Julian pats the chair beside him, Come on, Clare, sit down. Tell us what it was about the cake made you sick. The politics or the baking? I sit beside him but I don't say anythin. Laetitia's opposite me and she's reachin for an ashtray fae along the table. She takes out her lighter, clicks a flame to the roll-up in her mouth and draws on it deep. Her face is lit up for a minute and you realize how dark it is in here. The candles on the walls make big shadows that flicker across the arched ceiling when folk go past.

Leave it, Julian, she says, and the smoke comes out her mouth with every word. You've had your fun. Let Clare be.

OK, Mummy, I promise to be good. He's talkin in a wee boy voice. Like Christopher Robin or somebody. Danny draws him a black look but doesny say nothin. I'm wonderin if I could find my own way back to Mr Abensur's fae here.

The waiter's takin orders at the next table, so I pick up the menu fae between the salt and pepper. This time I'm makin sure I get a pizza.

You alright to eat? Laetitia says. She looks concerned and she even smiles at me.

Yeah, I'm fine now. I'll have a pizza wae ham, tomato, onion and mozzarella. I pass the menu to Laetitia.

Pizza. What a good idea. I'll have a pepperoni one. And I'm going to have a side salad too. *Insalata mista, per favore.* And a glass of red wine . . . or three. I'm starving. The waiter comes over and Laetitia gives him our order. What about you guys? she says to Danny and Julian.

They both reach for the menu at the same time but Danny lets Julian take it and says to Laetitia dead low, I'll have the same as you.

Oh, well, Julian says, I see I'm in a minority again. He looks up at the waiter, Can I have today's special? And wine, of course. *Una bottiglia di vino rosso, per favore.*

Il piatto del giorno? E un litro di vino rosso? Sì, signore. Bene. The waiter writes it down in his notebook at the same time as he's walkin away.

You don't even know what it is, Julian. Could be something ghastly. Laetitia blows her smoke straight up. And expensive.

Hey, what's with this parental thing you've developed in the course of the day? Don't let it become a habit, will you? You'll turn into your mother before you know where you are.

Leave my mother out of this. Laetitia looks angry. Maybe she doesny get on wae her mother. Pour us a glass of that wine, will you, Danny? He pushes the bottle he's been drinkin on the demo across the paper tablecloth towards her. There's a pink ring where it's been standin. She waits for a second or two and looks at him. Then she picks it up and pours it hersel into one a the chubby glasses.

Clare, would you like some?

I wouldny mind. Thanks. I hold a glass up to her and she

61

pours. For a wee minute it catches the light fae the candles and looks like a ruby. Cheers, I says.

Cheers, yourself. I'm glad you're safe and sound, Clare.

None for me? Julian says.

Help yourself. Laetitia pushes the bottle across to him.

More wine for the son of Poseidon, he says. He pours hissel a glass and takes a good slug. So, Danny boy, how was it for you?

Danny just looks at him.

The demo. The demo, dear boy. Julian leans across the table. Did you think I meant country matters?

Fuck off!

Julian, cut it out, Laetitia says.

Yeah, yeah . . . tears before bedtime. *Send for nanny, dahling.* Julian pulls his dreads up into a kinda bun on top of his head and sucks in his cheeks. What a spoilsport you are. He sits back, shakes out his hair and sips his drink. Then he starts up again, We met these Americans, didn't we, Clare, doing the Grand Tour of Europe?

Aye, one a them wanted dreads like Julian. A lassie. I think she fancied him.

Oh, shucks . . . *moi?* He points to hissel wae his head on one side. Who is gonna *fancy* liddle ol' me?

Cut it *out*, Jules, Laetitia says.

Shore thing, Lou. Just say the word. He kids on he's zippin his lips thegether. Only the company's a tad on the quiet side tonight, don't you think?

I look round the restaurant. Right enough, it is quiet; maybe everybody's a bit knackered. And hungry. A boy comes past fae the toilet and a guy at the next table clatters his chair back and stands up. He flings out his arms and shouts, I am Spartacus. I get a fright, it's so loud. More guys get up – I am Spartacus . . . I am Spartacus . . . I am Spartacus . . . all round the restaurant. Then I see the boy's got it on his T-shirt: I AM SPARTACUS.

Laetitia rolls her eyes, Quiet, did you say?

What's that mean? I says to her.

Just a boys' joke. Pay no attention.

The waiter comes runnin. *Signori, signori.* Please sit down. No trouble, please.

Danny's perked up a bit. He gets to his feet, C'mon, guys. Nay trouble, ih? Ambassadors fur Glesca an aw that. You can see his face better in the light of the candles and he's no got the knitted brows any more.

Somebody shouts, Away and wank, Kilkenny; we wereny doin nothin.

Danny starts to move across to the guy, but Laetitia's put her hand on his arm. Leave it, Danny. Leave it.

He shakes her hand off, but he sits down. Fuck the lot a them, he says.

Who is Spartacus anyway? I says. But naybody's payin attention. I look at Julian. He's starin at Laetitia and Laetitia's lookin everywhere else except at him.

I'm away to the toilet, I says, and I pick up my bag. Laetitia's gazin at the end of her roll-up and she doesny look up. I shove my chair back and get up to go. The place is hoachin now and I have to squeeze past chairs and tables to get to the Ladies. I look back at our table before I push the door open. The three of them are all still sittin there no talkin. Some night this is turnin out to be.

There's two lassies already in. They're standin smokin and flickin their ash into the basins.

No, one a them's sayin, no I couldny find him. He was with us when we set off. Last time I seen him he was tryin out his Italian on this *raven-haired signorina*, as he called her. Bastard! They turn their heads to me and smile, Here's another redhead. Hi, there. Us redheads and brunettes must stick together.

Aye, right, I says.

And naebody better tell us we're *ginger* or *mousy*.

I look at them again. The brown-haired one's got red eyes, like she's been cryin. No, I says. I push open the door of a cubicle. It's no as smelly in here as the one I was sick in.

Too young to understand, one of them whispers.

Fuck off, I think to mysel. I lock the door, pull down my jeans and sit on the pan. It's wooden and it feels kinda warm. Like somebody's just got off it. That's when I notice it. On the crotch of my jeans. Blood. I can't still be bleedin. That's no supposed to happen. It's no what Mrs Redfern says, anyway, in the sex education class we got. And then it dawns on me. It's my period's started. I should've knew it was comin cause of the coldsore. I nearly always get a coldsore afore my period. In the winter anyhow. I should a remembered. I tear off plenty of bog roll and wipe mysel. It's definitely my period. I look through my bag. I've no got any pads. The pink tiles on the sides of the cubicle have black cracks runnin through them and there's graffiti on the back of the door. A few *fucks*, but mainly Italian. I canny read it. Even if I did have a pad, I've got nothin to keep it on wae. Then I remember my knickers. I pull them out my jeans pockets. They're crumpled in a wee ball and a bit damp but they'll have to do.

The lassies outside the door are still talkin, only they're runnin the water, so I can't hear what they're sayin.

Hey, scuse me, I says. You feel dead stupid tryin to talk to somebody you don't know when you're sittin on the pan. Scuse me, I say it louder. Do any a yous have a sanitary pad? Please?

Sorry I didn't catch that. What did you say? The water stops.

A sanitary towel. Any a yous got one you could gie me? My period's just started. I've no got any.

Oh God, you poor thing. Know the feeling. Here will this do? No pads, sorry. And a tampon appears over the top of the door. I can see the light shinin on the Cellophane between the lassie's red nails.

Cheers, I say. Thanks. I stand up wae my jeans round my ankles and reach up for it. Blood runs down the inside of my thighs. That's great, thanks.

In fact here, have the packet; mine's just finished. And a wee blue and pink box slides under the door. That'll do you till you can buy some. What *is* the Italian for tampons? Don't know, the other one says. Then she says a bit louder, You'll likely be able to pick them up in a supermarket, anyway. You'll no need to ask for them.

Thanks, you've saved my life.

Don't mention it. Been there. Got the bloody T-shirt. And they laugh. That's us away now, love. Back into the fray. Enjoy your night.

Bye, I shout. And their voices disappear into the noise fae the restaurant.

I bend down fae the pan and pick up the box. There's six in it. That was dead nice of the lassie. I look at the one I'm holdin. I've never used a tampon before. I know it's an old wife's tale – even my ma says that – but there was aye a rumour at school you shouldny use them when you're a virgin. I didny fancy it anyway. Stickin something up you. I like the pads wae wings. So do a lot a the lassies at school. Different now, but. I peel the Cellophane off and drop it in the pan between my legs. The tampon's dead wee and it slips in easy. I look at my pubes and the blue string hangin down. That's that, then.

I stick the box in my bag, throw my knickers in on top of

the blood and paper and fasten up my jeans. Then I pull the flush. The whole lot sucks away and the lavvy glugs and gurgles like it does when you put too much down. But I don't care.

The three of them's already eatin when I get back to the table.

Oh, there you are, Clare, Laetitia says. We started without you. Hope you don't mind?

No, I says. I look at my place. My pizza's no there. It's some sorta pasta with like brown stewy stuff on top. Wae bones stickin out. I look at Julian. He's cuttin right through the middle of a pizza wae ham and tomato.

That's mine, I says. I didny order this . . . stuff. They all burst out laughin. Even Danny.

You should see your face, Clare.

Oh, the horror, the horror, Julian says, and swaps the plates round. His blue eyes are laughin at me. You mean to tell me you don't like *pappardelle alla lepre*? A Florentine speciality.

Aye, very funny, I says. And I probably would a laughed too, if I wasny nearly greetin. I sit down. I can feel my face burnin.

Och, don't be like that, Clare, it was just a wee joke, Danny says.

Well, at least everybody's laughin for a change, I says.

Mind Granny sayin how she would never eat rabbit? Danny says. Dirty-lookin dogs, she said, runnin about the countryside eatin rats. No mind?

Is that what that is? Rabbit?

When you were brought up in a tenement in the Gorbals, the countryside was as foreign as . . . here . . . Florence. And he waves his arm at the restaurant.

What you fucking talking about? Julian says. Half of Glasgow is seated here at these tables. He turns to me. Actually, it's hare. *Pappardelle* – that's the pasta. He lifts up a bit of wide pale pasta with the point of his knife. *Alla lepre* – that's the hare; wild hare in fact. And he picks a bone wi reddish meat on out the brown sauce and sucks at it. A dribble of gravy runs down his chin. *Il piatto del giorno*, he says, and wipes his mouth with the back of his hand.

Right, I says. Hare. I take another look at it. It's even more disgustin than the seashells.

First catch your hare, Laetitia says. She's cut her whole pizza up into wee squares and she eats one at a time. Daddy used to shoot one occasionally. And he would skin it himself. My mother wouldn't touch it till it looked like meat and not a furry animal with floppy ears. But, I'm with you, Clare. She smiles at me like she's tryin to make me feel better. Never could eat it. Not even Mrs Beeton's recipe for jugged hare.

Mrs Beeton? She your cook then? Did yous have a cook? Danny says.

Laetitia and Julian burst out laughin at the same time. And they're lookin right into each other's eyes. No, no, Laetitia says, she was a Victorian cookery writer.

Oh well, pardon me, Danny says, for no bein up on my Victorian cookery writers. He shoves a big chunk of pizza in his mouth and swills it down with a slug of wine.

I'm glad I never says nothing; I thought she might be Laetitia's Home Eekies teacher. I pick a bit of ham off my pizza and chew it. It's lovely ham.

Anyway, I says, my granny didny really say that about rabbits. That was just my da's joke. Cause she was my ma's ma.

Family apocrypha. I love it, Julian says. He's got a wee pile a bones at the side of his plate now. I try no to think what bit of the hare they come fae. The smell of it clashes wae the pizza. Sorta like Bisto but spicier. And a kinda meaty smell I've never smelt afore.

67

Aye, she did say it. Danny speaks with a mouth full of pizza. He jabs his fork in the air. I was there. It was afore you were born. I mind my da laughin on the way hame on the bus. Eatin rats!

Mind you, I wouldn't put it past the Scottish rabbits, Julian says. He's pokin through the stuff on his plate, lookin for more of the meat. It looks all bones to me. Rabbitus Scotticus, he says, with a wee rag of meat on his fork. Eats rats and talks shite.

I see Danny lookin at him, but he doesny say nothin.

Did your gran really live in the Gorbals? Laetitia says to me. Wasn't it a bit – well – rough for an old lady?

No, she went intay sheltered housin in Castlemilk a few years afore she died, I says.

You shouldny believe all you hear about Glasgow, Danny says. He's ate all his pizza except the crust, just like he does at hame. Nothin wrang wae Glasgow. It's—

Well, hello, Julian, you old dog. I thought that was you lurking beneath the dreadlocks.

I look round and there's this guy standin behind us with a red plastic bucket. It's got a leaflet stuck on it but I canny read it.

Hector! Julian says. Didn't know you were coming to Florence?

Hector? I think. Where do they get they names?

Julian gets up and claps the guy on the shoulders with his two hands. Danny, Clare, this is my old friend Hector from university.

The guy's face twists as if it's sore to smile. He's got wan a they faces. Like somebody sat on it when it was still warm, my ma would say.

Laetitia stands up and offers him her hand across the table. Hi, Hector. Nice to see you again.

It's been a long time, he says. At first I've thought he was English like Julian and Laetitia, but when you listen closer you can hear he's really Scottish.

Danny, he says. Pleased to meet you. And Clare? The name's not really Hector, by the way. It's Douglas. Acquired the moniker amid the college cloisters.

So, what you selling, Hector? Julian says, and he points at the bucket.

Hector . . . Douglas holds it up and shoogles it. There's a pile of coins in the bottom that rattle and jingle. Collecting for the Carlo Giuliani Fighting Fund. Care to lob in a bob or two? One of the fringe meetings was devoted to him. His mother's mounted quite a campaign. Very impressive.

You don't mean to tell me you've been attending the actual Social Forum itself? Since when did you get so involved? And where's the Harris tweed? Julian pulls at the sleeve of Hector's jacket. It's denim and he's got the collar turned up. Like he's tryin to be cool but he canny.

Long story, old boy. I'll save it for another day. So . . . ? Anyone? He holds up the bucket again.

Laetitia and me fish for our purses in our bags under the table. I watch to see what Laetitia takes out. I think it's two euros. She puts her hand in the bucket and drops the coins in. I've only got a ten-euro note and some cents. I pull out the note.

Have you got change? I says.

Chrissake, Clare. Danny snatches the note out my hand and flings it in the bucket. That'll do for the baith of us. I'll square up wae you later.

Very generous, Hector says, and he looks at Julian.

You know me, Hector, financially embarrassed as usual. He shrugs his shoulders.

The soul of a true Englishman, Hector says.

Perennial student, Julian says.

Oh yes . . . how *is* the PhD coming along? What's it on again?

Julian waves his hand, like he doesny want to talk about it.

The Role of Sex in the Novels of D. H. Lawrence and Henry Miller, Laetitia says. A.k.a. *Wanking for Boys*.

Sit down, Hector, Julian says. It's ages since I've seen you.

No, can't stay. Got a target to reach for the fund. Good to see you, Laetitia. A pleasure to meet you, Clare. Danny. He twists his face again. See you anon, you old skinflint. He touches Julian on the shoulder and moves to the next table with his bucket.

I look round the table. Everybody's watching Hector.

Who the fuck is he? Danny says.

You could at least have put a couple of coins in his damn bucket, Julian. He is *your* friend, after all.

You know I never give money to charity . . . the feelgood, conscience-salving activity of the moneyed classes.

It's a fighting fund, Danny says.

What's it for? I says.

Carlo Giuliani. Guy that was killed by the Italian polis in Genoa at the G8 summit in 2001. Twenty-three years old. Bastards opened fire on the crowd and he was killed. His maw goes round now tryin to raise awareness of what it's like under Berlusconi's fascist regime. Crush opposition with the full force of the state . . .

I aye switch off when Danny starts to talk like that. But *why* was he killed? I says.

Don't be so naïve, Clare, Danny says.

Come to think of it, it was a pretty tame demo today, Laetitia says. Hardly any *carabinieri* to speak of.

Aye, they're shit scared, wae the eyes of the whole of Europe on them. Don't want a repeat of Genoa.

I bet it's a woman. Everybody looks at Julian. Hector, he says. The new threads. Old Hector dipping his wick at last.

Oh, for Christsake! Laetitia says. If it's not politics, it's sex. What is it with you, Julian?

I'm lookin at Julian to see what he's gonny say. His eyes kinda flicker and for a nanosecond he looks dead hurt. Then he turns to Laetitia and says, What else is there? Hmm? What else?

Laetitia takes the wee skinny end of her roll-up out the ashtray, puts it in her mouth and flicks a flame to it. It's that close to her lips, you'd a thought she would burn hersel. She takes one big draw at it, then squashes it hard back in the ashtray and grinds it in with the ash that's already there. She clocks me lookin at her. It's too dark to see properly, but I think she might be greetin a wee bit. I think I see a tear kinda shinin in the corner of her eye.

She smiles at me. You don't miss much, do you, Clare? She lifts her hand to my face and – dead gentle – rubs a smear of ash ontay the middle of my forehead.

What's that for? I says.

Ash Wednesday.

It's in February.

So it is.

And this is Saturday.

Yeah?

Aye.

Danny's pissed off again. He gets up. Hey, Laetitia, want to come and meet they guys I was tellin you about? They're over there. His face is in the light now and he points across the restaurant.

What, now?

Aye, how no?

The place's got gradually noisier while we've been eatin.

71

Folk are talkin and laughin and it feels much mair relaxed. Well – at some a the other tables anyhow.

Later, perhaps, Laetitia says. I'd like another glass of wine.

Danny sits down again, but you can see he's no pleased.

I wish that wee French guy was here the night, I says, so's we could have another singsong. The three a them look at me and laugh.

Oh, to be young, Laetitia says.

Aye, right, I think. Whatever. I stand up and I just catch their faces turnin up to me surprised afore I start to sing:

> Ol' pirates, yes, they rob I,
> Sold I to the merchant ships . . .

The place has went quiet and everybody's starin. I keep singin. I don't even really hear it; the words just sing theirsels. All I see is the faces lookin at me, gold in the candlelight and sort a floatin in the dark. And they're listenin to me. They're listenin to me.

> Emancipate yourselves from mental slavery . . .

Somebody whistles.

> Won't you help to sing
> These songs of freedom?

Some guys have started singin alang wi me now. By the time I'm finished, it sounds like the hail restaurant's singin.

> Cause all I ever have –
> Redemption songs . . .

Then a lot a them's on their feet clappin and whistlin and cheerin. Gaun yersel, darlin, a woman shouts.

Somebody else's turn now, I says. And I sit down. I've got a big riddy. The three a them's still starin at me. I keep my eyes on my glass first, then I take a wee peek up at Julian. I don't know what he's thinkin. His face doesny give nothin away. Danny's mouth's hangin open.

That was lovely, Clare, Laetitia says. What a beautiful voice you have.

Hello there. A lassie's came over to our table. It's her fae the Ladies, the one with red hair. She smiles right at me.

That was crackin, she says. I've never heard 'Redemption Song' delivered like a Catholic hymn afore. Where did you learn to sing like that?

I shrug my shoulders. School, I suppose.

Well, there's hope for the education system yet.

Hey, that you, Bernie, Danny says. How's tricks?

Danny Kilkenny. I didny notice you there. Is this talented young woman a friend of yours?

That aint no Young Woman; that's ma Baby Sister, Clare.

Pleased to meet you again, Clare.

This is Laetitia. And Julian.

The lassie gives them baith a nod and turns to me again.

Listen, if you ever fancy singin wae some like-minded women, come and join our choir. She hands me a wee card wae *Circe* on it and a name, Bernadette McCarvil. It's got my mobile number and my e-mail address. We could do with some new young blood – especially wae a voice like yours. Fantastic.

Thanks, I say. And I put the card in the back pocket of my jeans.

A lassie's started singin over the other side a the restaurant. Bernadette turns round to look.

That's my table, she says. My pal, Shona. Better get back; she'll need handers for the chorus. Really great to meet you, Clare. Hope I'll see you again. By the way, have your pals no telt you, you've got a black mark up here – she puts her finger up between her eyes – on your forehead. *Ciao*, Danny . . . guys, she says. And she weaves away through the crowded tables.

Nice to meet you too, Julian says, even though she canny hear him by now. So . . . Clare, this is the light you've been hiding under that bushel of red hair? He's leanin on one elbow across the table, his dreads all spread out, squintin round at me. His voice sounds mockin but his eyes look serious. They catch a wee gleam of light fae the candles and I get that feelin shootin through me again, sharp and soft at the same time. He dips his fingers in his glass and rubs at the mark Laetitia's made on my head. A drop of wine runs down the side of my nose.

Let's go and meet these friends of yours then, Danny, Laetitia says. She's lookin in her glass and her hair's hangin down, so I canny see her face.

What, now? Danny says.

Yeah, Laetitia says, why not? She stands up and her face is sad in the light just for a second till she turns and walks away. Danny shoots to his feet. He looks dead chuffed when he goes after her.

Julian doesny even glance up when they go; he keeps his eyes on me. Then he picks up a napkin and wipes the wine and ash off my face.

There, he says, that's better. He picks up the carafe and pours some more wine in my glass. And in his. Then he lifts it up to me. A toast, he says. To the sweetest songbird with red hair in all of Florence. He clinks my glass. And the smiliest.

I didny realize I was smilin so much; it must be the wine.

I'm still lookin into his blue eyes and I don't notice Hector till he's right beside us.

Thought I'd take you up on that offer to join you, old man, he says. He puts two wee glasses on the table with this like clearish liquid in them. And he pulls up the chair opposite Julian. Grappa? I brought only two, I'm afraid, he says, lookin at me.

Would you like one, Clare? Julian says.

I'm no bothered, I says. I've got wine. I stare out into the restaurant, so's I don't have to look at Hector's fizzog.

Julian picks up the grappa glass and holds it up to me. All the better to toast you with. Did you hear Clare sing? he says to Hector.

Oh, was that you? he says. Very nice. I've always liked that Dylan song.

Julian and me look at each other and smile. Clare and I prefer the other Bob, he says.

Eh?

So . . . did you reach your target?

Oh, exceeded it, old man. Way over. I'll be taking the loot to the Giuliani fundraisers later. Very gratifying.

Good for you.

No thanks to you, of course.

Never let it be said . . . Julian says. He stands up and reaches into his pocket, takes out a ten-euro note and hands it to Hector.

Fabulous, Hector says. Even better. I knew you couldn't resist a just cause in the end. Or is it the influence of this delightful young lady? He looks at me and corkscrews his mouth into some kinda smile, but his eyes are borin right intay me. He gives me the creeps a wee bit. I can't see him and Julian really bein friends.

Is she not a bit young even for you, Julian? Looks like jailbait if I'm not mistaken.

I'm sixteen, I says, and I must a sounded angry, because he holds up his hands, palms out.

Terribly sorry. Didn't mean to offend.

You never did know when to shut the fuck up, Hector, did you? Anyway, what's with the new gear? Where's that suit you said would last a lifetime? Then Julian turns to me. Hector turned up at Cambridge wearing this bright green tweed suit, 1994. You would think three decades had simply never happened.

I like it when Julian talks to me like this.

That's how he acquired the nickname. A girl in our year – what was her name again . . . ?

Don't remember.

Miranda . . . that's right. Miranda used to say a little rhyme. He clasps his hands together in front of him, wags his head fae side to side and recites.

> Hector Protector was dressed all in green;
> Hector Protector was sent to the queen.
> The queen did not like him,
> No more did the king,
> So Hector Protector was sent back again.

And our Hector was born. Julian waves his hand as if he's introducin him to me.

Yes, well, you're not that hot on knowing when to shut up yourself, old man. Been trying to shake that off for years. But it seems, and he looks right at me with his wee eyes. Once the butt of a joke, always the butt. And I feel kinda sorry for him then. It canny have been much fun at university wi a face like that.

My real friends call me Dougie.

Pleased to meet you, Dougie, I says, and I hold out my

hand to him. I didny like my nickname when I was wee either. I came home fae school in Primary Two all excited one day, cause we had a French lesson and sang a song: '*Au Clair de la lune*', I thought it was about me. For years after, Danny – that's my brother – called me Della Loony.

Hector . . . Dougie laughs then and for the first time his face looks sorta natural. Maybe we should start a survivors' club, he says. Nicknamed Anonymous. Initials, NA . . . Not Applicable. Acronym, Na—

You've lost me now, I says.

That's his problem, Julian says. Loses people all the time.

Uncalled for, old man, Dougie says, and he starts to get up.

Sorry, Hec— Dougie. Sit down, man. I didn't mean anything. Sit down. Tell me what you've been doing lately. It must be – what? – nearly two years since I last saw you. Julian's got his hand on Dougie's arm and he sits down again.

Yes . . . at least two years. What have I been doing? Oh, this and that, Dougie says. Mainly trying to extricate myself from the clutches of the family. What about you? Glasgow Uni actually let you do this PhD? Found somebody louche enough to supervise you? He twists his mouth.

Yeah, no problem, Julian says. My thesis is that recent writing by men is uxorious – you know . . . domestic, emasculated. I'll be looking at the religiosity in Lawrentian sexuality and examining American picaresque – Miller, Kerouac – those guys.

Trocchi? Dougie says.

Yeah, he might merit a footnote. Julian grins. Welsh, certainly. He picks up his glass and lifts it to Dougie. Still waving the saltire, then?

I don't know what they're talkin about. My mind starts to wander. Funny how things work out. Two days ago, I would never a guessed what I'd be doin. I look across the restaurant.

Everybody's getting a bit pissed; they're talkin louder and laughin. I can't see Danny and Laetitia. A guy with a green T-shirt stands and holds up his cigarette to one of the stubby yellow candles on the wall. It doesny light. He reaches up again, pulls it back, looks at the blackened end a his fag. Then he lifts the candle right out the metal bracket, holds it up to his cigarette and takes a long draw. He doesny put the candle back, but; he sets it on the nearest table and carries on talkin to his pals. I can see it happenin just before it does. First a napkin flares. The yellow flames light up the surprise on folks' faces. Then the tablecloth catches at one end and fire whooshes to the other end in a second. I snatch up the wine carafe and run over. Somebody shouts. People are jumpin up. I pour wine on the flames, but there's no much left in the bottle.

The waiter comes runnin over wi a fire extinguisher – *Scusi! Scusi!* – and skooshes the foam all over. The fire goes out right away. What a mess but. The waiter doesny say nothin. Just looks at everybody, shakes his head and walks away, carryin the extinguisher in one hand. The guys on the other side a the table have got white speckles of foam on their claes, some on their faces. They look shocked. Somebody says something and a few people laugh. Then they're all laughin and I laugh too. I realize I'm pure shakin.

Clare?

I turn round and Julian's there. He holds out his hand to me and I go up and fling my arms round him and burst into tears. He hugs me tight and strokes my hair.

Well, what will you be up to next? You little fire-raiser.

It wasny me!

He laughs. I know, I know. Shh . . . He takes me by the arm and leads me over to our table. Dougie's no there. I'm glad. I'm goin to sit down but Julian keeps me standin. He picks up his wine glass and I think he's gonny give me a drink.

Instead he takes a slug hissel, pulls my head to him and kisses me. He opens my mouth wae his tongue and the wine pours in and down my throat. It feels warm and rough. When he takes his mouth away, there's wine on his lips and on mine. I kiss him again.

Come on, he says, let's get out of here. I look round the restaurant. Everybody's startin to get up and go. Two waiters are clearin away the mess on the table and one a them's comin wae a bucket and mop. Party's over. We get our coats and head for the counter.

It turns out Danny's paid for the meal. So Julian just gies the waiter a tip and says, *La pappardelle alla lepre – molto deliziosa. Grazie.* And the waiter smiles and kinda nods. *Grazie, signore. Signorina. Buona notte.*

It's only when we get back into the B&B I realize my hair smells of the fire. I lift a hank of it to my nose and sniff; it's got that horrible burnt paper smell mixed in with the usual cigarette smoke. And underneath, faint and far away, still a wee bit of the rose soap.

What you doing? Julian comes up behind me and takes my rucksack and my coat off at the same time with the sleeves still through the straps.

I'm gonny wash my hair.

What, now?

Aye, how no?

Because I have other plans for you.

The warm, sharp feeling pure shoots through the whole a my insides. I turn and put my arms round Julian. And then I remember.

Oh, I can't! I've got my period.

Julian laughs. Do you really sink, my dear, zhat I vill be put off by a little menstrual blood?

I look at the bed. It's got clean covers on. Pale yellow wae an embroidered bit at the top. Nice.

But it's . . . it's dirty, I says.

Filthy through and through. He kisses the top of my head. Mmm, smoky, he says. I tell you what, if you're so desperate to be squeaky clean, why not use the bidet. I'll watch.

To wash my hair?

He laughs again. This hair. And he touches me down there on the front of my jeans.

I don't know how it works.

Come here, I'll show you. He takes my hand and pulls me towards the bathroom.

No, wait. I'll have to . . . sort mysel first. I pick up my bag and go quickly intay the bathroom and lock the door.

It's definitely no as good as a pad. The tampon's leaked and there's mair blood on the crotch a my jeans. I reach my hand between my legs intay the pan, feel about for the string and pull it out. It looks like a dead mouse. Or like a bit of my insides. Give you the boak. I drop it in and wipe mysel as best I can wae toilet paper, flush it all away. I fish another of Bernie's tampons out the box in my bag, peel off the Cellophane and stick it in. A shower would be so good. Julian's shower's bigger than the one in our room. White tiles and a wee bottle a shampoo on the shelf. It wouldny take long.

I strip off my claes as fast as I can, slide back the door a the shower, turn the knob. The cold water that comes shootin out makes me gasp and I jump out the way. I listen a minute. No sound fae the room. I hold my hand under the rushin water till it starts to feel warm. I'm just in when I hear Julian at the door.

Clare? Not this again. Let me in. C'mon.

Wait a minute. I leave the shower on, slide back the perspex partition, grab a towel fae the rail and open the bathroom door.

He looks surprised. And annoyed. I thought I told you—

It was too temptin. I want to wash my hair.

You bad girl. Good girl, rather. Goody badshoes. He comes right up to me and takes the towel off me. He smells of the fire too. Some of his dreads swing forward like burnt rope. I step back and into the shower. I let it run over me right away. Over my hair and my face and down my back. Some of the water's sprayin out the door of the cubicle ontay the floor of the bathroom. It doesny reach where Julian's standin and he keeps back. Like he wants to stay dry. That suits me. I take the plastic bottle fae the shelf and screw off the cap. It smells lemony. Fresh. I squeeze a good dollop of the yellow shampoo ontay my hand and rub it on my hair. It must be good stuff, cause it lathers up right away. I close my eyes and soap my hair all over. It gies me the creeps a bit, Julian just standin there watchin me. I dig my fingers in hard to get right down to the roots so's I can get rid of the burnt smell of the restaurant.

When I open my eyes again, efter I've rinsed my hair, Julian's no there. The bathroom's full a steam and the towel is lyin on the floor soakin up the water fae the shower. So's my claes. I turn off the water and step out. When my eyes get used to the steam I can see Julian through the open door, lyin on the bed wae one hand behind his head, smokin. I reach for the other bath towel off the rail. It's damp too with the steam. But it's dry enough. I wrap it round my head and rub my hair. The steam's startin to drift away now and I notice Julian isny lyin gazin intay space like I thought. He's watchin me. His jeans are bulgin again at the crotch. I hold the towel in front of me and go to close the door.

Oh no you don't, he says, and sits up on the bed. You must finish washing. Like a good girl. You must wash down here. He rubs his hand round his crotch as he walks towards me. In the bathroom he leans past me, bends down to the bidet and turns on the tap. He lets it run for a bit, keepin his hand under the water. Then he stands up and looks me in the eye.

Now I want you to sit astride this bidet and soap that sweet rosebush of yours.

What d'you mean? I says. But I know fine what he means.

Just what I said. He looks at me for a long time. I feel my face turnin red, but I'm no gonny look away afore he does.

OK? he says. I nod and he walks away back into the room and lies on the bed again. I put my leg over the bidet, over the rushing water, and sit down like he telt me. It's cold on my bum and drops a water's runnin down my back fae my hair.

Oh, for fucksake, he says. And he jumps up and comes into the bathroom again. Here, wait. He reaches into the bidet and eases the tampon out fae atween my legs. We don't want this getting in the way. He stands up and swings it into the lavvy by the blue string. Drops of water spark up and catch the light. I feel blood tricklin into the white porcelain bowl underneath, runnin away down the plughole with the water. Julian turns back into the bedroom and flings hissel onto the bed.

Right, he says. You can start now.

I'm like, Lights, camera, action. But I say it under my breath so he canny hear. I look about for some soap. There's a dish set in the tiles beside the bidet and a wee bar of soap in wax paper same as in my room. I pick it up and unwrap it, drop the paper on the floor and look at the bar. It's yellow like the shampoo. Like the walls of the room. I sniff it. It's lemon too. Julian's watchin me. I keep my eyes on him and reach the soap down into the water to wet it. It slips out my hand and I have to feel about to catch it. I make a lather with my two hands, reach round and start to wash mysel down there.

Soap up that flaming bush, he says. He's rubbin the front of his jeans. I stick the bar of soap in the water again, then rub it on the front of my pubes until they're all covered in bubbles.

Like this? I says.

He doesny say nothin. Just groans.

I must admit I'm getting the melty feeling dead strong too. I keep buildin up the lather and rubbin and Julian keeps on watchin and groanin.

I wonder how long he wants me to do this. Cause I must be clean by this time. And then it happens again. The heat shoots up fae my crotch right up through me to my head and waves come over my whole body. I stop movin my hand and lean forward and groan too. I look down and big splashes of blood are droppin among the white suds and flowin away down the hole. I watch it all disappearin and wait till the waves get fainter. I put my hand under the flow and scoop warm water onto my pubes until all the soap's away. Then I turn off the tap. It's dead quiet suddenly. I get up. My knees are tremblin and blood's tricklin down the inside a my thighs.

Oh God, I says. I lean back against the wall. The white tiles are cold and the shock of them wakes me up. I pick up the towel and stick it between my legs. Then I look at Julian. He's still lyin on the bed, but he's starin at the ceilin now. I walk over to him and sit on the bed.

You weren't supposed to come, he says.

But I've washed as much as I can. How long did you want me to stay there for?

No. You weren't supposed to *come*.

Oh . . . right . . . I'm sorry.

He doesny say nothin.

I didny mean to.

He still doesny say nothin.

I couldny help it.

He just lies there.

*

83

I don't know what time it is when I wake up and hear the tappin. Feels like hours later. I listen for a minute. Julian's half on top of me, breathin slow and steady, still sleepin. It took me ages to get him in a good mood again after the carry-on wae the bidet. Even then he wouldny do it unless I called him Henry. Henry! And he called me Germaine.

Like Germaine Greer? I says.

Decidedly not, he says. But he did laugh. Seems she was a character in a book, this Germaine. *Topic of Cancer* or something.

The tappin comes again. A wee bit louder. I waken up more.

Julian, I says. I think somebody's at the door.

Hhhrmm?

The door. Somebody's there. Oh my God, maybe it's Mr Abensur, I whisper.

Wha . . . ?

Somebody's at the door.

Julian takes his arm off me and sits bolt upright. Who is it? he says.

There's this muffled female voice: It's me.

Laetitia, I whisper.

Can I come in?

Wait a minute, Julian says. And he starts to get up.

No, I says. I grab his arm. Don't let her in. She'll see me here.

He shakes me off, switches on the light above the bed and goes towards the yellow door. Just a minute, he says. His dreads are spread out over his bare shoulders. He's got no claes on; his back and his bum are sorta flushed pink wae the warm. And he's away to open the door.

I scrabble to fling the sheets off me, jump out the bed, run intay the bathroom and pull the bolt. I hear him turnin the key, openin the door of the room and speakin to Laetitia.

Come in, he says. What's the matter?

She's cryin. Laetitia's cryin. I hear her sniffin and sobbin. I listen at the door, but they're talkin dead quiet; I canny make them out.

Great.

The bidet's nearest the door, so I sit on the edge of it and wait.

I still canny hear nothin. I notice my bag's in the corner wae my boots. My claes are lyin on the floor damp, so I pick them up dead quiet and hang them on the radiator. No that it'll make any difference, cause the radiator's off. I'm gettin cold too.

Then I have the idea to take another shower. It'll warm me up. I slide the shower door open. She'll hear it, Laetitia, but I'm no stayin in here all night. Even if it's what Julian wants. That will be right. I reach into the cubicle and turn the shower to high. The water shoots out cold again, but I close the door quick and wait for it to heat. It doesny take long. As soon as the perspex steams up, I slide the door back a wee bit and step in.

I don't want to wet my hair again but, so I wiggle the shower head down the pole and let the water run ontay my boobs and my belly. I find another wee bar of lemon soap and unwrap it. I don't need much of a wash, but I do it anyway. For something to do. I wonder if they're talkin about me.

Wae the water runnin, it takes a minute afore I hear the bangin. I turn off the shower.

Clare? Julian's sayin. Clare, it's alright, you can come out. Clare, can you hear me?

Aye. I'm just comin. I step out ontay the cold tiles. There's only a wee hand towel left on the rail. One big one's soakin and the other yin's in the bed. I hope it did stop the blood

85

gettin on the sheets. I dry mysel as best I can wae the hand towel. I'm glad I didny wet my hair again. It's damp now and the ends are wet, but at least it's no drippin. I get another tampon out the box in my bag, crouch on the bidet and stick it in. Still three left. I'm gettin the hang of them now. Maybe I'll keep usin them when I get home. I take my jeans off the radiator and pull them on. They feel horrible. Cold and damp. All crumpled. My bra's no too bad cause it's nylon. My T-shirt's worse than my jeans. I can feel mysel startin to shiver.

Clare, what's keeping you? C'mon.

I don't say anythin. I don't want to go out there. Maybe she's away. I canny ask but, in case she's no. I pull on my sweatshirt wae the hood and zip it up. It doesny even make me feel any warmer. I fish my socks out my boots and sit on the bidet to pull them on. At least they're dry. I slide my feet intay the boots and do them up.

Clare, for Christsake!

Comin. I go over and take a look in the steamed-up mirror. My eyes are big and my face is dead pink. I try out a smile but it doesny look real. Comin. I open the door slow and look in the room.

I'm expectin them to be sittin on the bed, so first I don't see them. Then something moves in the middle of the room. Julian's standin wae his arms round Laetitia. He's got his jeans on, but nothin else. He takes his arms fae round her, holds her shoulder, looks at her face.

OK? he says. You ready?

Laetitia nods. You can see she's been cryin, cause her mascara's all ran.

Hi, I says.

Julian turns to me but he keeps one arm round Laetitia's shoulder.

Hi, Laetitia says. She doesny smile.

Clare . . . Julian says. And stops. He looks at me. Like he doesny know what to say.

What?

Laetitia's got on a red jumper. It's no holey like her black one. She's got baith her hands in the back pockets of her jeans. She still looks dead pretty even though she's been greetin.

What? I says again.

Her eyes don't seem to be as black in this light. More a sorta dark reddy brown. Maybe it's cause of her jersey. Or cause she's been cryin. I look at Julian again.

Clare, look . . . I . . .

Let's sit down, Laetitia says. She pulls her hands out her pockets, looks round the room, goes to the corner, picks up the gold wicker chair and sets it down in front of me. She's movin dead quick and jerky.

Please, sit, she says to me. She's half bendin over and she's got her hands on the back of the chair. This feels dead weird, but I sit down anyway. Laetitia's hand brushes against my back when she moves away. She comes round in front of me and sits on the end of the bed. She clasps her hands round one knee. Julian sits beside her.

I look at them baith. They don't say nothin. Julian's got his head down.

Good shower? Laetitia says.

Alright, I suppose. I shrug my shoulders.

What happened to your hair?

It's just a wee bit damp.

No, at the back.

I reach my hand round to feel it. Oh, that. Julian was showin me how to start makin dreads. She looks at Julian, but he doesny lift his head.

I see, she says. Well, I think you'd better comb it out, hadn't you, before you get home. Your father wouldn't like it.

I feel my face goin red, but I don't say nothin.

So . . . Laetitia says.

Clare, Julian says suddenly, I think you should go back to your own room. He's lifted his head at last, but he's still no lookin at me. No in the eye, anyhow. I keep lookin at him. His face is white and his mouth is a hard line. Then I look at Laetitia. She *is* lookin me right in the eye. I still don't say nothin. I canny think of anythin to say. Her eyes are burnin right intay me.

I don't get up till I feel the tears startin to prick. I look round for my coat. It's lyin in the corner on top of Julian's jacket. I pick it up, then go in the bathroom for my bag. I keep my head down, so's my hair falls over my face. So's they canny see me and I canny see them. I step over their feet on my way past to the door. My bag and my coat are bundled up in front of me. I open the door, squeeze out, shut it behind me.

It's dark.

I feel for the time switch on the wall and the light comes on. You get about four minutes afore it goes off again. The corridor looks different fae when I came in. Cold. The dark red carpet leads past three other rooms on this floor. I hurry along it. All the doors are closed.

When I get back to my room, I remember I don't have the key. I look at the closed door. I'll have to knock. If Danny's there, he'll wake up and let me in. I hope he's no there. No, I hope he is. If he isny, I'll have to get the key from Reception. I'll have to wake everybody up. Mr and Mrs Abensur. They'll no be pleased. I'm tired. I set my coat and my bag on the floor. There's no carpet on this corridor. Only the same hard marbly stuff like in the room. The wee white and black and grey flecks. They swim together all blurry when I look at them. I press my ear to the door. Nothing. Not a dicky bird.

If Danny's in there, he must be sound asleep. He's no gonny be too chuffed either. The number on the door is 32, two brass numbers screwed on. The more I look at them, the more they melt thegether into a goldy blob. I wonder what happened. Wae Danny and Laetitia. I wonder what Julian and her are doin. The handle's brass too with the keyhole underneath. The light goes out.

I feel my hand along the wall to the end of the corridor and press the switch again. Then I come back to the door and look at the handle. I press it down a wee bit. It doesny make a noise. I press it right down. The door opens. It's been open all the time. I push it in slow. I can see by the light fae the corridor Danny's no there. The two beds are neatly made. I hold the door open and reach across the lobby for my coat and bag. I'm feart the door'll bang shut and I really will be locked out. Even though I know that's daft. I slide my stuff across the floor, in through the door and go in efter it mysel.

I switch on the light. I've forgot how white it is. I keep a hold of the door. It's on one a they springs; it closes slow for a wee while, then it pure bangs shut. I hold it till it gets to the place where the spring jerks, then pull it back a wee bit and let it in slow. It closes without makin a noise. Except the click of the spring, when it's reached the bit.

The picture of Our Lady's still lookin down fae the wall. I look at my bed. My red T-shirt's folded dead neat and laid on the top. Like my ma's been in. I sit down beside it and let the tears come.

I remember the dream dead clear when I waken up. I'm in l'Accademia. It's night-time. It's dark. There must be a moon but, cause there's silver squares lyin on the floor fae the windows. Enough light to see by. I look round. I canny see the *Prisoners*. The Slaves. There're no in the bit they were before. I canny see them anywhere. I look back to where they were supposed to be. This time I notice six big blocks a stone standin on pedestals. I start to panic. Where are they? *Il Prigioni*? Then I remember the *David*. I turn and look down to the end a the gallery. He's no there either. No even a block a stone. Just a pedestal. I cross the silver squares and walk up to where he should be. I keep thinkin he must be there, he must be. I get nearer and nearer. I think maybe I'm in the wrong place. The wrong gallery. And then I notice the computer thing's on and there's a close-up of his head wae his eyes starin intay the distance. And then one of his foot where the guy broke his toe wae a hammer one time. I think, Well he must be here then and I'm just no seein him. I look at the pedestal again. That's when I notice it. The wee white statuette. The size of an Oscar when the actors go up on stage to get it. A wee statuette of *David*.

I wake up and the pillow's wet. My hair too. And my arms and legs are stiff, like efter PE when Miss Roger makes us vault the horse. That was a horrible dream. I think about the *David*, big and still, along the road in l'Accademia. I think about Julian and my throat feels tight. It must be early yet, cause there's no much light in the room, even though I've left the shutters open. But it is morning, cause I can hear the water pipes gurglin in some other part of the B&B. Somebody takin a shower likely.

I peer at my watch in the dark, but I canny see the hands and I don't want to switch on the light. No yet. There's still no sign of Danny. His bed's no been slept in. I can see it there, white and smooth, in the dim light. It feels like a hundred years fae I was in it wae Julian. The tears start prickin again, so I think about other things. If I'll have a shower. Breakfast. Goin back on the bus the day. School on Tuesday. Maybe I'll skip Tuesday as well as Monday. The whole week even. Just go intay town instead. Hang about the shops. Hang about. Maybe I'll . . .

There's naybody in the breakfast room when I come in. No even Mr Abensur. The big silver coffee machine isny even on. There's a cloth draped over the top of it. Like a blanket. Like wae my granny's budgie, so's he would sleep. Joey. So's he wouldny keep my granny wakened all night wae his cheepin. I look at my watch again. It's ten past seven. Breakfast's supposed to be between seven and nine thirty. Or maybe it's different on Sunday. Maybe it's later. I don't want to go back to my room, so I go to the table at the window and sit down. It's gettin light now, but it's still quiet outside. When a car goes by suddenly, it sounds dead loud, rumblin over the cobbles. That echoey way when the streets are quiet. There's a wee bit a sun already, slantin over the tops a the buildins across the street. The colour of honey. Maybe it'll be sunny the day again.

I don't know how long I've been sittin there, when Mr Abensur comes in. He doesny see me at first. He goes straight to the coffee machine, takes the cloth off it and folds it. He's singin a wee tune to hissel. Then he switches it on. You can hear a faint hum. He goes out again and comes back carryin a tray of brioches and croissants. He's away to put it on the table beside the machine when he sees me.

Buon giorno, signorina, he says, like he's surprised. He sets down the tray and comes across to me.

I think, oh no, I'll no be able to understand him. I'll no know what to say.

But he goes, You bed OK? You sleep OK?

Yes, yes, I says, *sì, signore, grazie*. And he smiles at me.

Bene, bene. Molto bene.

I keep my hair kinda over my face.

Tuo fratello? You brother?

He's no up yet. Still in bed.

He looks at me kinda serious for a minute. Then he says, *Cappuccino e brioches.* Like it's the answer tay the questions he canny ask me. Like it's just what the doctor ordered. I can feel mysel nearly greetin again.

Grazie, signore, I says. Thank you.

He goes across to the machine, clatters some cups, presses some buttons and it starts hissin and steamin. The smell of the coffee wafts over. I like the noise it makes. And the smell. He comes back wae a cup and saucer.

Un cappucho, he says. I've no heard it called that afore. The cup's full to the brim wae foam and there's chocolate sprinkled on the top.

Brioches coming. I heat first. He gies me a big smile.

Grazie, signore. I try and smile back but my mouth feels twisted. Like that guy Dougie's. Mr Abensur doesny seem to notice. He doesny crack a light anyhow. He just goes away and comes back a couple a minutes later wae a basket full a brioches. Does he think I'll eat all this? My coffee's still sittin there; I've no started it yet. I take a spoon a the chocolatey foam. The sun's moved further down the buildins now, but this side a the street's still dark. I don't know if I'll be able to drink much of the coffee; they make it dead strong here in Florence. Bitter.

Buon giorno, signora, signore, Mr Abensur's sayin. I look over at the door. There's an older couple I've no saw afore comin in. The woman's got her handbag wae her and a fawn cardigan over her shoulders. The man pulls out her chair for her. Then he sits opposite. They don't say a word to one another. Just sit waitin.

I take one of the brioches out the basket and put it on my plate. It feels warm. I'm no really in the mood for it but I eat it anyway. The jam gets all over my fingers. I'm wipin it off wae the napkin when I hear Laetitia's voice.

Hi, she says, dead bright. Mind if we join you?

My head goes hot and I'm feart to look up. I can see Julian's legs out the corner a my eye. Beside Laetitia's.

Clare? she says.

When I do look up, I just stare. At first I think it canny be him. His eyes look dead big and his face is even whiter than usual.

How . . . why . . . ? I says. What happened?

Behold the penitent, Laetitia says. I know. It's a little extreme. A little OTT. She's smilin at him. His head's no completely shaved, but near enough.

Julian has something to say to you, Clare. Is it alright if we sit down? She's got on the red jersey again and her black hair swings forward all glossy.

I don't say nothin. I can't take my eyes off Julian. They sit down. He's no even looked at me yet. His head's covered wae a pale velvety fuzz and his scalp's showin through. In a couple a bits you can see wee marks. Wee red scratches. Like he's cut hissel shavin. His beard's no there either. He's shaved that off too. He leans forward wae his elbows on the table. He still canny look me in the eye. At the back a his neck there's some longer wispy bits of hair. Curly and soft. Like a baby's.

He looks at me then. Say something, Clare.

I liked your dreads, I says.

I'm sorry, he says.

What for?

Everything. Clare, I wanted to say—

Jesus Christ!

I've no noticed Danny comin in. He's standin beside the table wae his mouth hangin open.

Fucksake, man! What's wae the Henrik Larsson? He starts to laugh. Fuck me . . .

He doesny know. Danny doesny know.

Jesus, Jules . . . He shakes his head and laughs again. Did you know he was gonny dae this, Laetitia?

Excuse me, I says. I stand up so quick, my chair falls over. I've got tay go. I set the chair up and head for the door.

Go where? Danny shouts after me. You've no finished your breakfast.

I'm no hungry, I says.

Clare . . .

Mr Abensur gies me another smile when I pass him at the coffee machine.

Ciao, I says. *Grazie.* Thank you for everything. And I hurry out intay the lobby.

I start to go up the stair. It's got the same red carpet that's on Julian's corridor. I'm gonny go right up tay my room, but I change my mind. Instead I go through the door on the first floor and along the corridor to Julian's room. One of the other doors is open and there's a pile a sheets and towels outside. I tiptoe past. I can see Mrs Abensur makin the bed. I try Julian's door, but it's locked. I stand lookin at it for a minute. Then I decide. I chap the door where Mrs Abensur's workin. She straightens up fae the bed and looks at me. Her face is red and shiny.

Please, I says, could you open this door for me? I point towards Julian's room and mime turnin a key.

She says somethin fast in Italian I canny make out at all.

I left somethin in there, I says. My friend's downstairs havin his breakfast. He says I can go in and get it.

She must understand more English than she speaks, cause she says somethin else in Italian, but she comes out the room, lifts up a key fae a chain round her waist and opens Julian's door.

Grazie, signora, I says. *È molto gentile*. I remember that's what Julian says to Mr Abensur yesterday at breakfast. She gies me a smile, so it must be the right thing. She lets the big jangly keyring drop back on the chain and watches me goin in the room. I smile at her again and close the door.

God! The bed's a pure mess; the covers are in a big jumble, fallin off, and the towel I put on top a the sheet is on the floor. At least there's no much blood on it. I look for the wastepaper bin; it's half under the covers. There's nothin in it except a few roll-up dowts and a couple of tissues.

They must a done it in the bathroom, I think. Then I notice the chair. The gold wicker chair is beside the table at the window and the bin fae the bathroom's sittin next to it. It's no right closed. I go over and open it; my face flashes at me, scrunched up, in the bashed metal lid. I was right. They're there. Julian's dreads stuffed in the bin. On top of one a the hand towels wae smears a blood on it. No mine this time. Fae the cuts on Julian's head probably.

I pick up one a the dreads. They must be all tangled thegether but, cause the whole lot comes out. And the towel. That's when I notice something else in the bin. A dooby. A used one. I drop the towel and the hair back in, untangle one dreadlock and stuff it in the pocket of my jeans. I need to get out.

When I open the door, Mrs Abensur is just liftin up the pile a sheets and towels. I squeeze past her.

Grazie, signora, I says. And I gie her a big smile, like I'm meant to be there. Would you lock my friend's door again, please?

She gies me a look, but she bundles the dirty washin under one arm and goes over and locks the door.

Grazie, I say again. And I get out fast. I wouldny like to be there when she sees the state a that room.

*

My room feels dead calm efter Julian's. I smoothe up my bed even though it'll be stripped for washing in a couple a hours. I take the dreadlock out my pocket and sit down. It's no as fair as his hair looked on his head. Maybe it's one fae underneath. Your hair's usually darker underneath. It feels funny now. More sorta stiff. More dead. Like a bit of frayed rope. I can see where it's been hacked through near his head. I wonder if it was scissors they used or a razor. Or a knife. It canny a been very sharp anyhow, whatever it was, cause the hair's all different lengths at this end. It's the only bit that's like real hair. When I look at it close I can see a few of the hairs have been pulled out by the roots; there's a bit of white skin and then the root wae a wee black oily glob out the – what d'ye call it – follicle. I peel one off wae my nails and rub the oil between my fingers. I do that wae all of them. Then I notice the bits of thread tied round at different points. Julian telt me about them when he showed me how to make dreads.

First you twist a wee bunch a hair thegether; then you backcomb it right up to the roots. And you keep twistin and backcombin and twistin till it stays matted. But that's no the finish of it. It starts to unravel, so you tie wee invisible threads round it. And then you have to rub beeswax on it to keep it all thegether. That's the kinda sweet smell I always get – got – off Julian's hair. I hold the dread under my nose. Smoke. It still smells smoky fae the fire last night. Beeswax. I can feel it too, a wee bit greasy. Julian says my hair's too clean to get the dreads started right. Too shiny and slippy. You dae have to be a bit clatty, like I says. I feel the back a my head. It's took me half an hour this morning to brush out the bit he started for me. Even without the beeswax. Cause my hair's curly, Julian says, it should make it easier. You don't wash it wae shampoo. If they get a bit smoky, you just have a bath wae patchouli oil. That's the other sweet smell I get, but faint. Contrary to popular belief, Julian says, dreadlocks are high maintenance. I hold the stiff, matted bit of the dread and touch my cheek with the cut ends. Soft. Like a makeup brush. Like normal hair. How come he uses a condom wae her and no wae me . . . ?

I wonder what Mrs Abensur'll do wae the rest a Julian's dreads. She'll likely just put them out wae the rubbish. I wish I'd taen more. Maybe she'll stick them in the washin machine. Alang wae the towels. But how would you get the beeswax out? Maybe you could do what my ma does wae candlewax. Iron it wae brown paper on top, so the wax melts intay the paper. It's a good job I've got my period the now, or I might've got pregnant. Funny how I didny even think. My ma would a killed me. The times she's telt me, Use a condom. Never mind the Pope; if it comes to it, use a condom. And I'm like, I know that, Ma. You don't need to tell me. I know. But I never. In the end, I never. I wish I'd have took one more of the dreads. Just one. Then I could keep this one the way it is. And I could undo the other one. I would like to see what his hair's like if you combed out the dread. What it's really like underneath. I think it would be fair and soft and a bit wavy.

Clare.

The door opens and Danny comes in. I stick the dread under my red T-shirt on the bed.

Oh, you're there, he says. He knows now. You can see it in his face. He's got his dark look again. I wonder how they telt him.

Aye, I was just gonny pack, I says. How you doin?

He looks at me then. Like he's never saw me before. His brows are knitted and his green eyes are the colour of his combat jacket.

Aye, alright, he says. How about you?

Alright.

Aye, pair of fucking upper-class wankers, when it comes down to it. He says it low, but he sounds dead angry.

What've they says to you?

Never you mind. Just remember, don't let the bastards grind you down.

No.

C'mon. Better get our skates on. Bus leaves at eleven.

Do you love her? Laetitia?

He gies me a look. But he says nothin.

I roll up my T-shirt wae the dreadlock inside it and push it to the bottom of my rucksack.

It makes no difference, anyhow, he says. She's gettin off in London.

Wae Julian?

No, he says and he looks at me kinda sharp. He's comin back to Glasgow. Forget it but, Clare. Birds of a feather, know what I'm sayin?

Aye, right.

I stuff my book and my CD player and the rest a my clothes in my rucksack.

The train station's hoachin. We have to go through it to get to where our bus is leavin from. There's folk fae the demo all over, waitin for trains. It looks like some a them's slept here. There's a group sittin on the ground. One guy's in a long coat wae a red and yellow scarf, even though it's warm the day. He's rollin a joint right out in the open, like he doesny gie a fuck. Another guy's playin a guitar and a lassie's hittin a wee drum thing and singin. I wish I was goin on the train. I wish Farkhanda was here and we were goin on the train thegether.

The two buses fae Glasgow are parked near the station. I don't see any sign of Julian and Laetitia. Danny slings his

rucksack on the pavement. He's lookin around too, but tryin
no to look as if he is. I feel sorry for him. I put my rucksack
down next to his and stand beside him. I wonder what bus
they'll go on.

Folk are startin to gather. I recognize Bernadette and her
pal standin smokin. She gies me a wave and I wave back. I
know more a the faces now, fae the restaurant. I see the guy
who started the fire speakin to a few a his pals and laughin.
One a them's the guy wae the Spartacus T-shirt. He's still
wearin it the day. It must be boggin.

I feel Danny goin tense beside me. Then he starts talkin in
a loud voice.

Aye, so just leave your bags here and the driver'll stow
them in the side a the bus.

I look round and Julian and Laetitia are walkin towards the
buses. It's funny, even though he's cut off his dreads, I still see
him wae them. Before I see him, if you know what I mean.
I still get a shock at how he looks now.

Hi, guys, Laetitia says, dead cheery.

Danny makes a point a no lookin at her. He bends down
and unbuckles his rucksack, pushes his hand down the sides
as if he's lost something, then buckles it again and stands up
facin the other way.

Laetitia and Julian kinda exchange glances and she shrugs
her shoulders. She doesny seem that happy right enough. No
as happy as she's tryin to sound. And Julian still isny lookin
me in the eye. That suits me. Means I can get a good look at
him. Try and take in what he's done to hissel. What *they* done.
It's funny how bare naked he seems. His face, I mean. And
he's no comfortable, you can see that. Like he needs his dreads
to hide behind and suddenly they're no there. So he doesny
really know where to put hissel. Where to put his face. It
makes him look a lot younger. More kinda scared. Like he's

no really as sure of hissel as he tries to make out. I think it's his eyes. They dae look huge now when there's no hair gettin in the road. I try to remember the exact colour of them when I seen them close up in his bed. Blue. Goldy flecks like wee strands a his tobacco. And I have to turn away, cause I start to get wet and I feel the tears prickin at the same time.

That's when I notice Laetitia watchin me fae under her dark hair. She's standin a few feet away and she comes over to me and puts her arm through mine.

Glad to be going home, Clare?

No really. I keep my face half turned away.

I am, she says. Back to real life.

I say nothin.

It's warm today, isn't it?

If she thinks I'm gonny talk about the weather . . .

It was fantasy, you know, Clare. You and Julian. He's all wrong for you.

I look at her then. Right in her fuckin ballet dancer face. Right in her big chocolate eyes.

Oh, aye? I says. How would *you* know that?

I bend down and pick up my rucksack. Leave her arm hangin there. I can feel the surprise comin off her even wae my back turned. I walk past Danny to the door of the bus. It's still shut and the driver's sittin wae a newspaper spread over the steerin wheel. Must be an old one. Unless he reads Italian. It's the nice driver, but. The one wae the twinkly eyes. No the wee fat grumpy one wae the greasy hair. I chap the door and he looks up. I smile and he pulls the lever that hisses the door open.

Any chance I could get on and get my seat? I'm cream crackered.

Aye, on you go, pal. It's still twenty minutes afore we leave, mind.

That's OK. I hold my rucksack in front of me and climb on. That you? The door hisses shut behind me.

Thanks, Charlie. You've saved my life. Sometimes I hear myself soundin just like my ma.

No bother, hen. He goes back to his paper.

I walk up the aisle to the seat next the long back one. If they're comin on this bus, I'm no wantin them behind me. And they wouldny sit in the back seat. They'll want a seat to theirsels. I take my CD player out my bag, alang wae the book that I've no read a word of since we got here. Then I reach down into the bottom and burrow my fingers intay the middle of my T-shirt. I pull out the dread and stuff it quick in the pocket of my hooded top under my coat, take my coat off, roll it up and put it on the rack. Then my rucksack. And I sit down.

Out the window, everybody's still millin about. Laetitia's got her back to the bus and she's talkin to Julian. His face is pale and it looks like it's floatin over her dark head. Like the moon. No the full moon – a quarter moon, maybe. One wae a bit hollowed out it, like the hollows under his cheekbones. He clocks me watchin him and I look away. I put my earphones on, close my eyes and kid on I'm listenin to a CD.

It's dead hard when you really want to see what's goin on, but I keep my eyes shut till everybody's on the bus. I keep them shut till they're sittin down and the engine's started. Naybody sits next to me. When I open them, I see Julian and Laetitia are sittin thegether a few seats down fae me on the opposite side. Laetitia's in the window seat. Her head's on Julian's shoulder. No sign a Danny. He must a went on the other bus.

Now all I have to do is work out what I need to think about. I count off on my fingers.

One: how far is London fae Florence? I was sleepin half the

time on the way here, so I don't remember. Somebody'll know.

Two: what night is Danny's meetin? Assumin Julian will still be goin to it. Thursday night, I think. Aye, Thursday.

Three: how am I gonny get out of goin to school the rest of the week? Farkhanda'll nip my ear till she pulls the whole story out a me.

Four: I need to think what to tell my da about the demo. That'll be OK. There's plenty there. The Greens and the Spanish TUC. The banners – USA E ISRAELE I VERI TERROR-ISTI. And the fairies. He'll have a good laugh at them. Same as Julian. And I'll tell him about the wee French guy and the singin. He'll like that. Mr Abensur and his coffee machine. Da'll tell me what bit of Africa he probably comes fae, plus the reasons why. And the *David*, of course. I'll tell him about *David* and *Il Prigioni*.

Five: Ma's a different ballgame. She'll take one look at me and know right away. I'll have to keep out her road as best I can, till things settle down. Till I know what I'm doin.

I look out the window. We're already on the outskirts of Florence. I don't recognize any a the streets. Must be a different route fae the demo. When the road opens out, we pass a long line a they tall thin trees. They've got no leaves on them except at the very top. The sun's catchin them, turnin them gold. Like artists' brushes wae dods a gold paint on the tips, pointin to the sky.

Julian's head's leanin on the seat in the direction of the aisle. Laetitia's head's still on his shoulder. I can just see her black hair between the seats and a slash of her red jumper. I want to touch his head. See what his new hair's like.

I feel in my pocket for the dreadlock and close my hand around it. It's warm now wae bein next my body. I rub my thumb back and fore in a wee hollow bit. A wee felty hollow.

Now and again I can feel an individual hair, but mostly it's a thick matted bunch. A piece of rope to hold on to.

I look out the window again. I wonder if there'll still be leaves on some a the trees by the time we get back to Glasgow.

I hope so.

PART TWO

Florence – London – Glasgow

November 2002

Laetitia lay in the half-dark and strained to pick out the furniture in the room. If she could make out their outlines, she was real after all. This was real. All of it. The bulk of a chair draped in clothes detached itself from the lighter dark around it, the nature of the garments indecipherable, their colours smudged. But they were there. They were there. And there was the door to the bathroom, the oblongs of the windows, the slats of the blinds just visible, the quiet pool of the mirror on the wall. Her panic subsided and she shifted her head on the pillow to look round at Danny. Asleep, he looked sweet, with long dark lashes brushing his pale skin, all aggression quieted. A pang of – what? compassion, guilt, regret? – made her almost change her mind. But she lifted his arm slowly off her chest. He grunted in his sleep and turned onto his back.

When he was still again, breathing evenly, with just the suggestion of a snore, she pulled back the cover and slid over the side of the bed. Knees on the cold, hard floor, she tucked the duvet close into Danny's side, so that he wouldn't miss her warmth. She moved slowly backwards, hardly breathing. One thing she couldn't cope with now was having to talk to Danny, tell him what she was doing. Explain herself. She stood now, joints creaking, and tiptoed over to the chair. In the semi-dark, she identified her clothes, almost leached of colour, and disengaged them from Danny's. His belt buckle chinked against a metal button and she stood, cold as a statue, her own flesh gleaming like marble, till she was sure she hadn't woken him. She could feel the wool of her jumper against her chest, irritating her stiffened nipples, the cold denim of her jeans, the lace of her bra and knickers. She bundled them closer and bent down for her boots at the side of the chair. Then she tiptoed past Danny to the bathroom.

The tiles in here were even colder. She pulled the door almost to, couldn't risk the noise of shutting it, daren't put on the light. Her crotch still ached from having been entered. Abraded. Even her orgasm had felt disingenuous. Her body dutifully responded to Danny's surprisingly dexterous touch, but when she came, she felt her mind resist. It wasn't right. And her orgasm fizzled out like a disappointing firework. Why couldn't she just take her pleasure with him? Like men do when it's offered. He was good-looking, had a good body, sturdier, more muscular than Julian's. And he was eager to please.

You'll get none of your wham-bam-thank-you-ma'ams fae Danny Kilkenny, he'd said. I like a lassie to remember a night with me.

In spite of the arrogance of his statement, he was a good lover. Technically at any rate. Knew the right buttons to press. Moved with her. Intuitive. Except he didn't intuit the growing sensation that she didn't want to be there; that started from a thought, then moved down along her body till she felt all her muscles tense. And the thought was? She couldn't really remember. It was more an apprehension. She apprehended something. But what? It felt utterly momentous at the time. Something not to be ignored, or the whole of one's life could be blown off course. It was this that had made her cry as she came. Made the tears come now. She set her bundle of clothes on the lid of the toilet, extricated her bra and knickers and put them on. She had to get out of here. Danny had been concerned when she cried.

Are you OK? Did I hurt you or something?

When she couldn't say what the matter was, he got up, went to the bathroom, came back with a wad of toilet paper, knelt astride her and dabbed her eyes, his balls and cock resting like floats on her stomach. *The peculiar texture of the detumescent cock.* That's what she thought. As if it were the title of a paper she might write. And still she wept. Danny was tender, attentive, his brow creased, stroking her hair off her face, catching the tears as they ran towards her ears.

You'll soak my good pillow, so you will, he said, tutting like a housewife.

She knew she'd have to rally herself or he'd be forced to try and joke her out of it. And she was in no mood for jokes.

I'm fine. Really, she said. Just an overflow of emotion.

Danny took this, as she knew he would, as an expression of her feeling for him and grew even more tender. Eventually she persuaded him that she was alright and he got in next to the wall and curled his body round hers, his wiry pubic hair irritating her buttocks, his arm heavy across her chest. He fell asleep quickly like a child, and his breath, slow and even across the top of her head, finally eased her into a ragged sleep. When, some time later, she jerked awake, panic flooded her.

She pulled her jeans on slowly, so that Danny wouldn't hear the dry rasp of denim on flesh; eased the zip up tooth by tooth. The noise seemed impossibly loud in the dark bathroom. She picked up her black jumper and caught a whiff of the mixture of smells rising from it: smoke, the garlic and oil of Italian cooking and, more enmeshed in the wool, her sweat, overlaid with deodorant and perfume curdling in the fibres. She tossed it on the floor. She'd have to get a clean one from her rucksack. With her boots in her hand, she inched open the door. It didn't squeak; she pushed it enough to slip through.

The room seemed lighter after the windowless bathroom. Danny had turned to face the wall but she could see by the slow rise and fall of his back that he was still asleep. She crept over to the corner, set down her boots, fed her hand into her rucksack and felt about for her other jumper. It eluded her at first till her fingers snagged on its soft wool beneath her journal and tugged it free. Her journal, her lifeline, the thread she clung on to to lead her back to herself; she'd barely written a word in it since she arrived in Florence. It would have to wait. She pushed it to the bottom of the bag. Quickly, eyes still on Danny, she pulled her jumper on over her head and arms simultaneously and smoothed it down her body. Her new jumper. Cashmere and immediately warm and soft against her skin. Like being taken care of. She picked up her boots and stepped carefully across the room, her heartbeat noisy in her ears.

Outside Julian's door, she waited for a minute. Two. Three. What lay on the other side of it seemed as remote as a foreign country. Room 17. The brass numbers concentrated the light from the corridor, as if they had just been polished. Swollen with crying, her face peered back at her, further distorted in each shiny digit. She pulled the cuffs of her jersey over her hands and rubbed her eyes. She was shivering in spite of it, in spite of its colour. Red. Imagine her mother buying her a red jumper. After all the political arguments; after the shock on her mother's face when she admitted that, actually she stood somewhat to the left of Tony Blair. Her mother had blanched. Visibly. Laetitia watched her face drain of colour and her feeble brain tick over to hook into a lexicon of phrases like 'nanny state', 'undeserving poor', 'evil terrorist'. God, she made Laetitia want to put her hands round her throat and shake her till her teeth fell out like a broken string of pearls.

She shook her own head. Julian. What to say to Julian? Even when she pressed her ear to the dark wood of the door, she could hear nothing.

Let him be alone. Let him come to the door with sleep in his eyes, his dreads tangled and take me to his warm bed. Please.

Her hand, still mittened in the red sleeve, reached up to knock, hesitated, dropped to her side. She put her face to the door and whispered.

Julian.

Julian.

The brass numbers clouded.

Julian.

She could feel the tears burning her eyes again, trickling warm down her face. This was hopeless. The closed door. It seemed inconceivable that she could get to the other side of it. Without something cataclysmic happening. Her tendency towards melodrama. Histrionics. *Her*trionics, as Julian called it.

She raised her hand again, pulled back her cuff and rapped twice with one knuckle.

Again.

She heard him then, his voice blurred by sleep, Who is it?

It's me.

Finally there was movement. A scrambling sound, a bang. The door opened before her raised hand and Julian stood there, naked and sleepy, eyes half shut.

Laetitia? What's wrong?

She laid her hand flat on his chest. It was warm, slick with sweat. Can I come in?

Yeah. Of course. He caught her wrist and pulled her behind him into the room. She closed the door.

What's the matter? Has something happened?

No. Yes. I mean no, nothing's happened. It's just . . . hold me, Julian. Please. I think I'm coming apart.

He opened his arms wide, a gesture of total acceptance. Or so it seemed to her. And his face was soft. She stepped towards him and sobbed. His dreadlocks swung forward and covered her face. Her cheek rested on his damp chest. Sweat. Beeswax. Golden Virginia. The smell of him pricked at her senses. She felt her shoulders relax.

We need to talk. I . . . it's crazy what we're doing. It's . . . She could hear her voice rise again, hysteria seeping through.

Julian put his fingers to her lips. Shh, he said. Wait. Clare's here.

Where? Laetitia jerked away from him and looked round the room. Where?

In the bathroom. Look, I'll . . . get rid of her. He was whispering now, his voice soft, tugging at the edges of her panic, smoothing it down like a linen sheet, cool on a bed.

And then she realized what he'd said. Clare? Clare? Julian, she's sixteen. She's a child. You didn't . . . you haven't been? Oh my God! Julian!

It's not like that, he said. It wasn't like that.

So, what *is* it like? Her panic was turning to anger, her face felt hot now, her eyes gritty.

It was only . . . it was . . . it's you I want, Laetitia. You know that. Fucksake, man, I've been telling you for long enough. Come here. He pulled her towards him again and she stayed stiff in his arms at first, then drew back.

Get rid of her? You can't just discard her like . . . like a used condom or something. She's a child. What's that going to do to her?

She'll be fine. She's more mature than she looks. It's just something that happened. A product of circumstance. It just happened. It doesn't mean anything. It's nothing. Honestly, babe, it's nothing.

Laetitia studied his face. It was earnest, his eyes wide. Innocent. Nearly. She laid her head again on his smooth chest, unexpectedly smooth for a man with all that hair on his head. And on his face. Clare wasn't her concern. Julian pulled her so tightly to him that the muscles in his arms trembled and the breath went out of her.

They could have stayed that way all night, but there was Clare. In the bathroom. Clare to be dealt with. Simultaneously they stepped back from each other. Julian exhaled a great sigh. His breath smelt. Of tobacco, of garlic, of the metal smell of his sleep. She breathed in deeply.

Right, he said. Clare. Wait here. I'll sort it out, babe. I promise.

She tightened her grip on his hands till their arms were stretched straight between them before her fingers would disengage. Like the principal dancers in a *pas de deux* about to pirouette and jeté away from each other to opposite sides of the stage. She folded her arms across her chest, cold suddenly, and watched Julian back towards the bathroom, his eyes never leaving her face.

At the last moment he turned, rapped sharply on the door. Vaguely the sound of water running became audible to her. She was having a shower. At a time like this. The girl was having a shower.

Clare, Julian said.

A frisson of pleasure went through her at the thought of the expulsion to come. Defenestration. The word popped into her head. The Defenestration of Florence. A *Star Trek* phaser set on *Beam you up, Scottie; little Scots girl, disappear*. I am a truly horrible person, she thought. This is a sixteen-year-old.

Not much more than a child. An image sprang to mind of herself at sixteen, her gaucheness in adult company, her hands huge, hanging at her side. She shook her head and the muscles on her face tightened.

Clare. Julian knocked again, more sharply this time. Clare, it's alright, you can come out.

The girl wasn't responding. Laetitia felt a spurt of anger. Julian's ear was to the door and his dreads stood out chaotically, pointing in every direction. She smoothed down her own hair and swatted the tears drying on her face. A cursory glance at her hands found they were stained with mascara now, and shaking. She stuck them in the back pockets of her jeans, rocked on the balls of her feet till she found a precarious equilibrium.

Clare, what's keeping you? C'mon. Julian was becoming irritated. His voice had that harsh quality that unsettled her. Now she wanted it to work on Clare.

Clare, for Christsake! Julian said.

Finally the door began slowly opening. This girl was milking the situation for all it was worth. Laetitia stood stiffly on the spot. Julian came to her, put his arms round her. Then he stepped back, let his hands weigh heavily on her shoulders, brought his face level with hers.

OK, he said. You ready?

The girl came into the room.

She looked at the bed. Then her eyes darted round, her enormous eyes. They found Julian, stayed on his face. This girl is determined not to see me, Laetitia thought, either from fear or sheer will. Her dark red hair was tousled, falling onto the shoulders of her white hooded top. She looked lost. She looked . . . She looked . . .

Hi, she said.

She looked like the white girl. Scared and lost. Whistler's White Girl. *Symphony in White Number One.*

This was not going to be easy. But it's my shoulder Julian's arm is round, she thought. *My* shoulder. He could sense her tension, squeezed her arm. Without looking at him, she knew their old attunement was there.

Clare . . . he said.

What?

But Julian said nothing. His fingers squirmed, digging into the flesh of her upper arm. Where were the certainty and irritation of a moment ago?

What? Clare said again. A note of defiance was creeping into her voice. But her pink face had gone as white as her jumper. She stood uncertainly, her left hand plucking at the leg of her jeans.

Clare, look, I . . .

Julian was going to blow this. His voice was growing feebler by the minute. Feeble, feeble, feeble. And he was looking at his wretched feet.

Let's all sit down, shall we? she said. She looked about the room. There was the chair. Gold wicker. No doubt hand-sprayed by the redoubtable Mrs Abensur. She lifted it. Her muscles were so tense, it shot up, lighter than it ought to have been. An image of wings on its feet came into her head. Enid Blyton's flying chair. She set it down facing the end of the bed and looked at Clare.

Please sit, she said. The girl looked back at her, as if she might bolt. A woodland sprite ready to dart behind a tree. A nymph.

Nymphette.

She kept her hands on the chair till the girl came and sat, her hair brushing the backs of them. Damp, artfully tangled, the dew of the forest still on it. A thickness falling down the middle, a single plait, half concealed by curls. No, not a plait. A dreadlock. She looked at Julian. She could kill him. At this precise moment, she could kill him.

She sat on the end of the bed. Her hands were shaking so badly she had to clasp them round her knee to still them. There was a strange lightness seeping into her body. As if she might levitate. As if she needed something to hold her down. A guy rope. Stones in her pockets. She thought she caught a whiff of chloroform. But where on earth could that be coming from?

Julian sat beside her. His weight on the bed reclaimed her. Even though he appeared to have lost it. Totally. He was going to be useless in this. Worse than useless. He was keeping his eyes on the carpet. She looked at Clare.

Good shower? Her voice sounded clipped like her mother's. Strangulated.

The girl shrugged. She was slouched down in the chair, trying and failing to look unconcerned.

Alright, I suppose, she said.

What happened to your hair?

Clare looked up at her, uncomprehending, her eyes darting from Julian back to her. No help for you there, Clare, Laetitia thought. You're on your own. She drew strength from the knowledge.

It's just a wee bit damp. Clare's voice was growing quieter.

No, at the back. She pitched her voice to match Clare's, but the honey was laced with acid. She knew it and couldn't help it. This child was quaking in front of her and here she was peeling off strips of her pale skin.

Oh, that? Clare said, with her infuriating glottal stop. Julian was showing me how to make dreads.

Perhaps now he'd come in. Offer an explanation. Take

some responsibility. But his eyes were still down. He looked ghastly too. Laetitia wondered if she was as pale as the other two. If they were a threesome in pallor. Ghosts at their own feast.

I see. Well, I think you'd better comb it out, hadn't you, before you get home. Your father wouldn't like it.

Clare looked at her hands in her lap. She just sat there.

So . . .

Clare, I think you should go back to your own room. At last Julian had raised his head and spoken. He was even managing almost to look at Clare. Almost. Clare's head was still bent, but she was looking up at Julian through the hair that half concealed her face. Even behind the tangle of curls, Laetitia could see her blush. She felt something close to empathy for her. Close, but not enough to offer any kindness. She wanted her out. Now.

Clare made a move finally. It was painful to watch. She walked about the room, face screened by the red hair, picking up her belongings; stepped carefully over their legs, hers and Julian's, thigh to thigh now on the bed; opened the door and was gone.

I'm home. Laetitia set her rucksack down on the polished wood floor of the hall.

Mummy, I'm home. She breathed in the smell of the place: wood polish, that exclusive room freshener that started off trying to convince you everything was lemon fresh, but soon came out in its true odours – cloying sweetness, with a suspicion of cat's piss seeping through underneath. And fresh paint. What had her mother been decorating now? The depression that invariably accompanied her return started to drift like mist around her.

She turned to close the door. The broken stained-glass

panel above the handle had been replaced. A good match. Near perfect, except that the new red was a little more vivid, the turquoise a touch too green. Otherwise the nymph still stood among reeds on the bank, her brown curls permanently held off her face by a tiny pink hand, her toe dipped forever into the glassy pool. Laetitia's favourite piece of the jigsawed glass; the way the pink foot turned green in the water and, between the two colours, no black leaded line. Consummate artistry, her mother liked to tell guests. She'd never reveal to them that the house was a comedown. After Wellwood House, a severe disappointment. So much more convenient, she'd say, for all one's needs. She made Laetitia wince, she was so transparent; her need for approval utterly naked.

Hello. Are you there, Mother? It's me, Laetitia.

Laetitia heard a sound from above and her mother's black-slippered foot appeared at the top of the stairs.

Is that you, darling? You're back early.

I'm back exactly when I said I'd be, Mother. The rest of her came into view on the stairs.

Well, no need to be touchy, dear. You know how I lose track of time.

Under the hall light, she could see that her mother's hair was a shade or two lighter than it had been when Laetitia had left for the start of term. And it was styled to swing glossily at every move of her head. She'd clearly succumbed at last to the advice of her friends: *Dark hair at our time of life, darling, ages one so.*

I like your hair. It's different.

She flicked it in an exaggerated Miss Piggy gesture from both sides of her face and held her head at a coy angle. Do you think so? I'm so glad, sweetie. I'm not used to it yet. But look at you! She held her arms out to Laetitia and drew her

118

into a bony embrace. Laetitia submitted stiffly till her mother stepped back, keeping a tense grip on her shoulders.

You look lovely, bunny rabbit, my own lettuce leaf. She managed that trick she had of looking deeply into Laetitia's eyes without seeing anything. And she had used up her entire repertoire of endearments in the first two minutes; any moment now, the needling would start.

You're wearing your red cashmere. I'm so glad. Did it keep you warm? It ought to have at the price I paid for it. Shockingly expensive, deValois, but *the* best quality anywhere in the country. Now, come and have a drink.

She took her hand and pulled her towards the drawing room. Something was wrong; Laetitia could feel it. Her mother was even more relentlessly superficial than usual. That brittle sweetness, like the caramelized sugar on a crème brûlée. The image that always followed instantly, a spoon cracking through the crust to the soft mess underneath. Her father breaking the ice on the pond, hefting the pick over his shoulder, crashing through on the first downswing, the explosion of rooks from bare branches, the splash of icy water, the orange flash of the old carp, startling against the white.

Laetitia pulled her hand out of her mother's. No, I'd like to dump my stuff in my room first.

Dump, darling? Her mother turned to look at her, the lines at her mouth etched clear, one side of her face brushed by an upflicked strand of glossy hair. One doesn't dump. Bin men dump. Demolition men dump. I dare say other sorts of tradesmen . . .

Yes, alright, Mother, *I get the photy*, as they say in Glasgow. Laetitia was pleased with her glottal stop, but she'd have to work on ironing out the diphthong. Not that her mother was alert to such fine distinctions: she pursed her mouth and said nothing.

I'll come down and join you for drinks in a minute. Laetitia went to pick up her rucksack from beside the hall table, turned and made for the stairs.

I've moved you.

Her mother stood clasping her hands in front of her, pearlized nail varnish offering reflections of the hall light in subtle gleams. Her chin was up and her mouth was a hard line.

What do you mean, you've moved me? Where to? Laetitia stood in front of her mother and, for the first time she could remember, saw that she looked her age. She was tired, strained, her skin taut across her cheekbones. What's been happening, Mummy? Are you alright?

Oh, perfectly, darling. Her mother's voice warmed at her use of 'Mummy'; no doubt to her it evoked an earlier, simpler time when she had been loved by her daughter. She took a step towards Laetitia and clasped her free hand.

I'm sure you'll like your new room. It's compact and cosy with plenty of space for . . . well, everything you need. After all, dear, you don't stay here permanently any more, and—

Where have you put me?

In that little room at the back.

The *box*room?

Well, I only called it that, but actually it's quite large. It's—

And what have you done with *my* room?

I've had another bathroom put in. A proper one.

A *bath*room!

Yes. I needed . . .

Does Daddy know about this? Have you told him?

Her mother moved away from her and walked towards the drawing room. At the door she turned, held on to the frame. Her face was white and her fingers trembled against the wood.

This is *my* house, not your father's, though you seem to

find it extremely difficult to grasp this simple fact. *My* house. And may I remind you that it was your father who precipitated the break-up of this family with his serial infidelities, and *his* decision that we sell Wellwood and that I move with you into this dreary Victorian terrace, while *he* lives it up somewhere in the sun with . . . with . . .

Clearly she couldn't bring herself to say the name without spitting. Feathers and blood. Nails. Her voice had risen in a crescendo, and Laetitia realized she had walked straight into the trap. Once her mother got into her WRONGED WOMAN stride, there was no gainsaying her. All conversations were structured by this ineluctable fact: she had been wronged in *the* one major area of life, so take care lest you wrong her again by challenging her in any way. Having suffered such a devastating blow, she deserved only to be cosseted and indulged for the rest of her time on the planet. Her tragedy was that there was no one – no one! – in her life with the sensitivity and perspicacity to recognize this and oblige. Certainly not her uncaring viper of a daughter.

First rule of the game: ignore her. Walk away. Laetitia used to fight her father's corner. That induced fainting fits and hysteria . . . well, as good as. Then she tried another tack: sympathy. It was worse, if anything. Drew out that many splendoured thing, her mother's self-pity.

She listened for a moment to her mother's movements in the next room, heard her take a bottle and a glass from the drinks cabinet, chink over to the sofa, sit down heavily, clatter the bottle and glass onto the coffee table. By the fatness of the glug of liquid, she could tell it came from a decanter, that her mother's current poison of choice was whisky. Great! When she'd left a month before it had been Pinot Grigio. So refreshing, darling; cleanses the palate. Things must have gone downhill since then. Whisky meant danger. Whisky meant keep out of her way. Give her a body swerve, as the Glaswegians have it. Steer clear.

Laetitia swung her rucksack onto her shoulder and started up the stairs. She could feel a prickly, itchy heat across the top of her back now as if the soft cashmere had transmogrified into a hair shirt. An allergic reaction. Julian was right about her mother, she *was* toxic. A waste of space. Toxic waste. Best *dumped* away from human habitation. By the appropriate *tradesman*. She allowed the memory to soothe her of Julian's last kiss when she'd got off the bus in London. Sweet and salt. Deep enough to lose herself in. Only the irritant of the ever-vigilant Clare to mar it, watching them through the window of the bus.

She stopped at the top of the stairs and looked at the doors that curved round the sides of the landing. They'd been newly painted. A fresh coat of what her mother called *a hint of spice*, a sort of pallid ginger, if such a thing were possible, with all the warmth and colour sucked out of it. Laetitia put a finger to the first door and ran it down the paintwork, hoping she'd leave an ugly streak. She was in the mood for scribbling on walls with felt-tip pens, easing her fingernails under wallpaper and stripping it away, shred by shred. But the paint was dry. Only the smell of it persisted under the room freshener.

The door of her old room was next to Mother's *boudoir*. For a moment she stood outside, allowed herself, like the hapless victim of a home makeover programme, to visualize it as it had been when she'd left. Only just over a month ago. Her rucksack slid off her aching arm onto the carpet. She opened the door slowly, fumbled for the light. But the switch had been moved outside, of course. A stainless-steel effort, out of keeping with the rest of the fittings on the landing. She pressed it and stepped into the room. Instantly it revealed itself as something straight from the pages of one of Mother's

Sumptuous Homes and Splendiferous Gardens-type magazines: modern, minimal, the acme of good taste. Clearly a designer had been at work; this was no sudden whim. Rows of subtle spotlights were embedded in the ceiling and there were half-concealed lights behind panels facing the mirror, the better to illuminate Mother in the kindest possible way. From somewhere came the sensation of a low hum overlaying the silence, as if the whole room was a precision-made machine, ready to reveal shiny lubricated pistons, working to some mysterious end, should she happen to press the right button. Or the wrong one. The washbasin was clear glass; the shower like the inside of a spaceship, stainless steel and glass; the toilet and bidet were pristine white; the walls a muted shade somewhere between pale dove grey and mauve.

Laetitia felt her throat tighten; all trace of her had been erased from the room she had occupied since the age of eleven, since Daddy had left and Wellwood was sold. The panelled door that had connected her room to her mother's was gone, replaced by a modern flat-planed effort. For years, after the nightmares stopped, the old pitch pine door had been concealed on her side by a bookcase, and on her mother's by a wardrobe. Now the new sleek version stood slightly ajar, offering a glimpse of her mother's bedroom, completely redecorated too by the looks of things. Ah, the master bedroom with en suite. Of course.

Laetitia moved slowly across the bathroom floor, feeling scruffy, her trainers squeaking on the dark grey tiles. She looked in the mirror. Her red jumper seemed to have expanded, to have indistinct edges, which bled into the metallic tones around her. Her brown eyes, her dark hair even, were splashes of colour. Though she could hardly imagine much splashing in here. Not even of water.

Lizzie Borden. Didn't she stand naked in a small basin to

wash away the blood of her butchered parents? Set aside the bloody axe and step into the clean water? Didn't she rinse off every drop without spilling any over the side, without leaving the minutest spatter on her body as forensic evidence? Did that happen? Or had she just made it up? *Lizzie Borden took an axe, gave her mother forty whacks . . .*

There was no bath. There would be no long sudsy soaks, water slopping onto the floor as you adjusted your position for reading. She slid open the glass shower door and looked inside. So clean and modern it was clinical. You couldn't wash away your sins in here; a place like this admitted no sin. No colour, no mess, no sin. The door glided shut again at the merest touch.

What do you think, darling? Do you like it?

How long had her mother been standing at the door watching her?

No. I don't.

But it's so *contemporary*, don't you agree? I thought you'd love it. She stepped into the room, crystal glass held in front of her, whisky glowing like a lamp, scattering pieces of amber light around the mirrored surfaces, little flecks of it dancing on her face. The smell of alcohol challenged the asepsis. It was René Bouchard who did it, you know. The designer? Famous for his cutting-edge ideas?

Never heard of him.

Oh, darling, you must have. He did the Phillipses' bathroom too. Her mother glanced around for somewhere to set her glass, thought better of it, took another sip instead. I think he's done a much finer job here.

This was *my* room.

But, darling, have you seen your *new* room yet? Her mother made her way to the door. She must have taken her slippers off downstairs because she tiptoed barefoot now on the ribbed tiles. It was slate, wasn't it; it would be cold on her feet. Her beige cardigan was over her shoulders and Laetitia thought her retreating back looked hunched. Defeated. In spite of her new light hair, its gloss and upswing. She was downbeat.

I know where it is, Mother. I don't need a guided tour. Her mother cast her a hurt, quivering glance from the doorway, took a slug of whisky and walked to the stairs. Laetitia followed her out and watched from the landing as she shifted her glass into her left hand, so that she could hold on to the banister on the way down. She felt for each stair carefully, as if it were dark, as if she were already drunk.

Fuck, fuck, fuck! Laetitia picked up her rucksack and walked round the curve of the corridor to the boxroom. A strong smell of fresh paint escaped from the cracks round the door. Julian, I wish you were here with me. She breathed in deeply, thought she caught a whiff of his tobacco. The power of the mind. Maybe if she concentrated hard enough she could conjure him up, all of him. They could go into her new room together. A new beginning. She pulled air into her lungs again and opened the door.

Before she switched the light on, she stood, trying to make out the changes in the almost dark, barely touched in this corner by the dim bulb on the landing; she wanted to absorb the room in stages. All the old Wellwood furniture Mother had stored here, piled to the ceiling, had gone: the Chinese dresser and the other pieces of chinoiserie; the Japanese screen with the gold peacocks à la Whistler; the rolled-up Afghan rugs; the paintings. The gewgaws and fripperies, the rest of the expensive tat. What on earth had Mother done with it all?

When the light snapped on she found herself gaping at a modern furniture showroom. *A compact and well-appointed study bedroom* – the estate agent speak instantly parsed itself in her mind. Funny how it had infiltrated the language. Her old single Wellwood bed had been replaced by a futon. Of course. A double one, in cream-coloured cotton, with red and yellow and blue scatter cushions. She picked up a yellow one and hugged it to her. In front of the window, on a brand-new glass-topped desk, was a laptop computer, a standard lamp in stainless steel above it in an elegant arc. The wardrobe looked like birch. As opposed to pine or oak or beech. She opened the door to find her clothes hung neatly, put her hand in between a cotton shirt and a long skirt and moved them along the rail garment by garment. All there. It seemed her mother hadn't taken this opportunity to do a fashion makeover. A Color-Me-Beautiful transformation. They were definitely all there, the ones she hadn't brought down to Cambridge. All there and all black. Most of them. No colour. Or hardly any. Brown. Slate grey. The yellow cushion glowed like something standing in for sunshine against her clothes. She tossed it back onto the futon. The walls were yellow too, a pale, fresh yellow. One was taken up entirely by glass shelves. Her books were there. All those she'd left behind. In alphabetical order by author by the looks of things. The ragged spine of her Blake stood out – *Songs of Innocence and of Experience*; she took it down, flicked through it.

> O Rose thou art sick.
> The invisible worm,
> That flies in the night
> In the howling storm:
>
> Has found out thy bed
> Of crimson joy:
> And his dark secret love
> Does thy life destroy.

Her finger traced the arching thorns on Blake's etching, circled the fat round rose that looked more like a peony, avoided the worm, followed the little figure emerging with its arms outstretched, *the spirit of joy extruded*. Extruded. She remembered that day, sitting on a low wall in the quad, reading the poem, the start she gave when Julian came upon her. And the whole wide universe Blake had opened up shrank instantly to eight black lines on a page. Her backside chilled on the cold stone, her fingers frozen. No matter how often she'd read it since, she could never get it back. That hugeness.

Her stereo was there too; her CDs. Some of her boxes of notes from Cambridge. The toy rabbit Julian gave her in second year, dark brown and furry, nibbling forever on a green silk lettuce leaf, with paler stitching for the veins.

Oh God. She'd have to go down and talk to Mother.

The chair was on castors; moulded wood with slits on the back. She sat down and rolled herself in to the desk. The glass top felt cool to touch. She'd have preferred wood probably. Warmer. But the glass did look good, it had to be said. She bent down and breathed on the pale turquoise surface, misting it over. With her finger she wrote:

LETTUCE
LAETITIA

The mist cleared before she'd finished her name and all the letters dispersed. Nothing there but a few smudges. She pulled her sleeve down over her hand and rubbed at the marks till the glass was transparent again. The edge of it was smooth, curved, opaque like sea glass; she rolled herself closer till her waist was against it. The laptop was one of those titanium affairs. Beautiful. She ran her hand over it. Mother must have spent a packet on this lot. An absolute fortune. The button on the front of the computer released the spring sweetly. She opened the lid. No, better not. She shut it again. Mother would be waiting for her downstairs, drinking herself stupid, nursing her grievances. Love-rat husband. Ungrateful daughter. Wellwood, Wellwood. She stood up, took a deep breath, plucked the rabbit from the shelf and looked into its brown button eyes.

Well, Julian, what d'you think? Shall we stay? Hmm? What's your opinion? Nothing to say for yourself? What, nothing at all! Lettuce worked its soporific magic, has it? Mr McGregor will catch you, if you're not careful. She waggled it till its ears flopped from side to side. If you're not very, very careful. She set the toy down on top of the laptop. Look after this for me, will you. I won't be long.

When Laetitia went in, her mother was sitting with her feet tucked under her on the sofa, whisky glass in one hand. Smoking!

Since when did you start smoking, Mother?

Since I was nineteen actually, darling. If you want to know. Her mother was staring at her with something close to defiance, chin up, looking her straight in the eye. If it's any of your business. She leant forward and flicked a column of ash into a cup on the table in front of her. A china cup! It looked like one of her wedding china sets, the one from Nanny Rosenthal. A strand of her mother's hair dipped in her whisky glass as she pulled herself upright. She took it out and sucked it. It hung like a rat's tail when she let it go, a darker shade of dark gold than the rest, and she tilted her head back to look at Laetitia, waiting for her to say something. Daring her.

Laetitia sat in the armchair nearest the door and leaned forward. My room is lovely, Mother. Thank you. It's not what I was expecting.

Her mother looked at her, took a swig of whisky. Drew on her cigarette. Said nothing.

How did you manage to get all that done in such a short time? The bathroom too. It must have taken a humungous amount of organization. Must have cost you a fortune.

Her mother shifted her buttocks on the sofa, remained silent. Her eyes were down, staring into her glass.

At last she looked up and faced Laetitia. I do try, you know.

I know, Mother, I know. I'm sorry. It was such a shock to come home and discover my room had been translated into a bathroom.

Do you really like your new room?

Laetitia studied her mother's face. The little pads under her eyes were pink and puffy. She'd been crying. Yes, Mummy, I really do like it. Thank you. And I love the laptop.

She blew out through her nose. That was your father's idea.

Daddy? I thought you said he wasn't involved.

How could I have afforded to do all that on my own? On my income? Her voice was raised now and her neck was flushed and mottled. How could I possibly—

OK, Mother, OK. Look, I *really, really* like it. I love the colour. And the desk. The bookshelves. And thank you for arranging all my books and my clothes.

Oh, I didn't do that, dear; the removal firm did.

You got a removal firm in to move my things from *my* room to one a few yards along the landing?

Well, the designer wouldn't do it. We *were* on a tight schedule, you know.

God, Mother . . .

Laetitia could see her teeter on the edge of taking umbrage again. Instead she set her glass on the table, stubbed her cigarette out in the cup, turned to Laetitia and attempted a smile.

I am so glad you like the room, darling. I'm hugely relieved. What about the trunk? Do you like it too? That *was* my idea.

What trunk?

Laetitia's trunk.

What?

Laetitia. Your namesake, Laetitia. Your father's great-great-aunt on his mother's side.

What are you talking about, Mother?

Your father *must* have told you about *her*. Surely. The great free thinker in the family? The great Free Radical? Her mother was waving her hands out from the centre of her chest, as if presenting the woman on stage. The Great-*great* GREAT Aunt Laetitia!

No, he hasn't. Laetitia didn't want to get into what was clearly another fertile region of marital discord.

And I didn't see a trunk. It crossed her mind that her mother might have lost the plot completely; been tipped over the edge by whisky and a surfeit of interior decorating.

Go and take another look. It's beside the futon. There's a lamp on it. It's just the right height for a bedside table when the futon's down. Oh, and you'll find your bedding in the cupboard opposite your room.

Right.

Her mother was reaching for the whisky bottle again, as Laetitia went out.

It was in the corner next to the futon as her mother had said, smaller than the picture conjured up for Laetitia by the word 'trunk'. She'd imagined some great curved-top chest with metal bands running across it and big studs and a huge hasp at the front with an ancient padlock. Like a pirate's treasure chest, sitting at the bottom of the ocean, encrusted with barnacles. But this was small. Laetitia took the lamp off and set it on the floor. It had a flat top. And it seemed to be made of leather, not wood. More of a suitcase really, with thicker leather corners riveted on. Had she seen it before? A vague memory teased at the back of her mind. She kneeled and lifted it out of the corner onto the futon. It was heavy for its size. Full of bricks maybe. Not a body anyway; it was too small for a body. Laetitia had a quick flash of a severed head – Great-great whatever Aunt Laetitia's head – locked away in her trunk for a hundred years, green and mouldering with staring eyes. A grisly discovery. *A twenty-five-year-old West London woman yesterday made a grisly discovery in her newly decorated bedroom. Her mother, under heavy sedation, said: 'We had no idea Aunt Laetitia was in the trunk. We thought she was in the family vault.' A forensic anthropologist will today examine the remains to rule out foul play.* She used the old trick her father had taught her to banish horrible visions and nightmares: make a funny story of it. Implicate Mother. The dead hare, blood seeping from the fur on its side.

Laetitia shifted the cushions out of the way and put her hands on top of the trunk. In the light now, she could see the letters L. G. almost rubbed off. Laetitia. Laetitia what? What did the G stand for? She'd have to ask Daddy. She ran her hands over it. It felt almost warm to touch. Not like something hauled up from the crypt. The attic! That's where she'd seen it. The attic at Wellwood, in the far corner; the pile of boxes and suitcases and things near the grimy skylight. Strange she'd never thought to look in it then. But then her aim had always been to rummage quickly in the dressing-up box, choose her costume and get the hell back down the steps, before they got her. Whoever *they* were. The *they* that lurked in the attic and the barn and all the other dim spidery places round the house. And actually, once her father had overruled her mother and brought the dressing-up box down to the nursery, she never ventured up there again. Not that she could remember.

There were two catches on the front of the trunk, brass apparently. A keyhole under each, also brass. No key as far as she could see. She touched the catch on the left, felt about for a way to release it. There was no give. The one on the right looked identical. She traced the edges of it, eased her finger-nail underneath, pressed the brass circle that surrounded the key-hole. Nothing. Had her mother kept the key? A way to force Laetitia to ask for it? *Oh, I'm terribly sorry, darling. How silly of me. Here it is in the ice bucket.* She wouldn't put it past her. Her knees were getting sore on the wooden floor. She pushed the trunk over on the seat of the futon and sat next to it. Then she saw them. Fixed to the side with masking tape, two small keys on a brass key ring with some kind of round fob the size of a fifty-pence piece.

Sorry, Mother.

The tape came off easily, left a faint scuff on the leather surface. She scratched at it with her nail to remove any sticky residue, rubbed her fingers together till the little pellets of gum dropped off. Two keys. She looked at them lying in her palm. And some sort of medallion. With writing round the edge. Pretty well rubbed smooth, but perhaps decipherable. Later. One key was dulled brass with dark pockmarks, the top formed like a three-leafed plant. Trifolium. Trifoliate. A clover leaf. Or a shamrock? The ring went through a hole in the middle leaf. She turned it over and examined the other; it was made of some kind of grey metal, had a plain flat round head with a rim like a coin, and a soldered loop at the top for the key ring. Two different keys. One for the left lock and one for the right? She laid them side by side on her palm. No, the tiny shafts and the ends looked the same, cut for identical locks. Forged. How were keys made in the late great Laetitia's day?

Filed by hand, most likely. By the blacksmith. Or the locksmith. Some kind of smith anyway. Laetitia, Laetitia. So, that was where her name had come from. Not plucked after all from *Tatler*'s list of the most popular girls' names in 1977. Hardly *popular*, darling. *Distinguished*. What only the *best* families were calling their female sprogs. Two other Laetitias in her year at school; one in the year above. The four Letties. Or the four Titties, depending on whose gang you were in. None of them liked the name. Though it was better than some. Lalage, the babbling brook. Drusilla, for God's sake! Portia. Better than all the Dianas and Fionas. The night Laetitia Latimer was expelled, Mary Underwood singing: *Last night there were four Titties; tonight there'll be but three . . .* Jokes about three-cupped bras.

She got up, set the keys on the glass desk, looked at her CD player. It was jammed into the second shelf, the one set high enough to accommodate her art books. The turquoise LED numbers pulsed into life when she switched on the power. She ran a nail along the edges of her CDs. God, alphabetical order here too. By composer for the classical stuff; by band or artist for the pop. She pulled out Bach's Cello Suites and stuck it on. The sombre bowing swelled into the room, lapped at the edges of the furniture, sloshed about in the corners. Fit accompaniment, Laetitia. She picked up the keys, went back to the trunk and knelt in front of it.

The fancy one, the clover leaf, was the one she tried first. She fitted the key into the left-hand lock. There was some movement, but rusty, a scraping sound; it didn't give. Not even when she wiggled it minutely, ear to the trunk like a safe breaker. Plangent notes rained down on her. She took out the key, looked at it, fitted it in the other lock. The same. It moved, but only slightly, a scratchy noise. Turning harder could break it. The mechanism might be freed by some WD40, if there was any in the house. Or olive oil, *faute de mieux*. But this would mean getting tied up with Mother again. The Gordian knot.

She sat back on her heels and let the cello work her over like a Swedish massage. Her hair-shirt irritation was gone but the back of her neck had grown stiff. She rolled her head in time to the *Allemande*. Reached round and palpated her neck when the *Courante* took off; played the top of her spine like a piano. Did some stretches to the slow *Sarabande*, sat back down on her heels. Breathed.

The other key. The plain one. Dangling at the moment from the right-hand lock. She removed the clover key, inserted the plain round one. The mechanism gave in one smooth click and the catch flew open. Was this some fairy-tale test of character? Deep curtsies from Bach's music, and the quick, light steps ran rings round her. She put the key in the other lock; its catch gave way too, with a mousetrap spring. You dancer! As Danny Kilkenny was wont to say. Jiggety jig! The plain one does it. The hard-working, plain girl, dressed in grey, kind to her father and the crone at the door. The fancy girl, haughty and vain, a bodkin in her poor father's heart. Laetitia pulled out the key, hooked her forefinger through the ring, held it up and examined the two keys hanging together. They looked identical at the business end. No discernible difference. She let them drop with a noisy jingle onto the desk beside the laptop. A mystery.

OK. The lid ought to open now. So what was stopping her? Her hands were resting on the leather top on either side of the letters. L. G. L. She traced it with her finger. G. The letters were old-fashioned as well as faded, a defunct typeface. Like nineteenth-century newspapers. Like *The Times* reporting on the Boer War, or some such distant event, when the metal letters came from a compositor's tray and were set in rows to make up the words for printing. L. G. Laetitia. Laetitia what? Garbo, Gulbenkian, Gardenia? Gilgamesh, Gilfeather, Ghirlandaio? Gabriel, Golightly, Gaddafi? Geranium, Geronimo, Guerlain? Maybe just plain George? Laetitia George. Gordon, Godard, Grant. Gramsci . . . That would certainly consign her to black sheep status in the family. Laetitia Gramsci. No, not Gramsci. It lacked euphony. Letisha Gramshee. Sounded slurred. As if a drunk were saying it. Her mother after a session with the decanter. Aunt Laetitia would certainly have a more harmonious name. Bound to. She moved her hands down to the released catches; pinged them twice; pulled them down till they almost clicked home again. Almost.

Her thumbs could just about squeeze in under the edge of the lid. Slowly she eased it up. It was heavy. Heavier than it ought to be if it were only leather. The inside of the lid felt soft. Velvet? She peered in through the crack. It was dark in there. But there was nothing shaped like a severed head or mutilated limbs, as far as she could see. No bones. She breathed in deeply. A smell of old leather and older paper hit her. No rotting flesh. She opened the lid fully till it leant against the back of the futon.

Oh.

There was hardly anything there at all. A few papers. So how come it felt so heavy? She put her hand in and riffled through the things at the bottom. Just some old papers, fragile and yellowing. A small piece stuck to her nail with static electricity. She peered at it, sat up on the futon beside the trunk. Nothing. There was nothing on it. Fly away, Peter. She waved her hand and the fragment fluttered down behind the bed. There was a small book with a leather cover, smooth to touch. She took it out and set it on the seat beside her. Some envelopes. She picked one up and felt inside. A letter in this one. In them all, by the looks of things. Some quite fat.

Oh, well.

The leather book was intriguing, at least. She took it onto her lap and sat back in the seat. No L. G. on the cover of this. Plain brown leather. Soft. Calfskin, perhaps. Kid. The cover extended beyond the pages and formed a kind of protective lip for the deckle-edged sheets. Tiny stitches ran round it, so close in colour as to be barely visible. She opened the book. The spine creaked slightly and a dry papery smell pricked her nose. Crimson. Oh. The endpapers were deep, deep crimson. Unmarked. They looked new. Vivid. She turned to the first cream-coloured page. It was rather fine, despite the deckling. Not tissue-fine like old bibles, but clearly good-quality paper. It was blank. She turned to the next page. There were a few lines of writing here, a small, neat hand, ink faded to sepia, some words barely legible. It said . . . it said . . .

'Sweet joy befall thee!'

To my darling, darling,
only love, my joy,
my Titia, from your
very own Harry.

Florence, April 1915

Laetitia felt the hairs rise on the back of her neck. Aunt Laetitia had a lover. Or a husband. They knew Blake. And they were in Florence! Or at least Harry was, when he dedicated the book. Nineteen fifteen. During the First World War. Nineteen fifteen? But wouldn't travel in Europe have been restricted then? A soldier. He must have been a soldier. In Italy, though? Maybe he was a foreign correspondent for a newspaper. War correspondent for the *Daily Telegraph*. A diplomat, possibly.

Or a poet. A wandering minstrel, granted poetic licence to roam freely.

She eased her thumb under the next sheet and turned it. The handwriting was different here, a full page of it, bigger, bolder, looping across from the stitching near the spine right to the outer edge. Aunt Laetitia!

> My first entry in the book H.
> has sewn for me. It is a beauti-
> ful thing – the paper, the kidskin
> cover, the blood-red endpapers;
> presented to me a few moments
> ago, wrapped in green satin, tied
> with a lilac bow, while we sat in
> the shade on the edge of the sunny
> Piazza della Signoria, where now I
> write, as Harry reads . . .

Hand sewn?

> A dun-coloured pigeon has landed
> on the replica of Michelangelo's
> David – the fate of all outdoor stat-
> uary – though the sculpture is no less
> magnificent for that . . .

Aunt Laetitia's journal! This was too spooky. Written in Florence with her lover Harry at her side, at the time of the First World War. Her own neglected journal was still in her rucksack; she'd written nothing in it since they'd got on the bus home. The bag was on the floor on the other side of the desk. She unzipped the front pocket and took out the book.

Black, cloth-covered, A5 size, in contrast to her aunt's delicately handmade notebook. The last page she'd written in was marked by one of Danny's leaflets, folded in half, a photo montage of Bush with Tony Blair as a ventriloquist's dummy on his knee, hand up his back. Crude, but effective. Bush's lips were slightly open, teeth closed, in what could easily be a *gottle of geer* expression; Blair was grinning inanely. Danny had drawn in a speech balloon in the white space above Blair's head: *If you do as Dubya asks, you'll get a good one up the ass!* She set it aside and picked up her notebook. There were only a few lines on the page it had marked, written before they left to get the bus:

Sunday, 10 November 2002
    Glad to be going back. Too much tension here. Getting used to J. without his dreads. Don't know if *he* is. Hope we can get onto the bus the Ks aren't on . . .

Bit of a contrast to Aunt Laetitia's musings! She put her journal on the desk, picked up her aunt's book and leafed through the rest of it. There were perhaps a hundred pages and some had been torn out; near the stitching in certain places were ragged edges with traces of ink, the beginnings of letters, trailing their coats, the little tails that lead you in. How annoying! Aunt Laetitia had secrets, things she had written and didn't want read.

She closed the book. This was something to savour, to take her time with. She'd get to know this Laetitia gradually. If she were able to with the evident censorship. The book felt warm in her hands now. Julian would adore it. He'd be dying to see it when she told him about it. Why had her father never mentioned anything about Aunt Laetitia? Something to ask when he next phoned. She set the notebook on the desk side by side with her own journal and turned to the trunk.

OK. Why are you so heavy? The lid and the bottom were lined with what looked like suede: soft, unpolished hide, a shade lighter than the tanned leather on the outside. She looked more closely at the inside. In one corner of the lid, a few of the stitches had come away, leaving a small gap. She pushed her finger into it. Cold. Something cold and hard. She shifted the trunk round so that the light shone directly onto the inner lid. Her finger eased open the hole again and she tapped with her nail at the surface underneath. Metal. Lead? A lead-lined trunk. Bit strange. But possible, definitely possible. Surely she hadn't carted it to Italy with her; it weighed a ton! Hardly practical for travelling. Another mystery.

The handful of letters and papers at the bottom of the trunk didn't look that inviting; she shuffled them to one side and closed the lid, clicked the catches into the slots, reached behind her for the keys and used the roundhead to lock it again. It didn't feel as heavy when she lifted it back into the corner, restored the lamp and the trunk's function as a bedside table. Perhaps Aunt Laetitia's memoirs were a weight off its mind. She slipped the keys into the pocket of her jeans and went to find her bedding.

It must have been a good ten hours she'd been asleep by the time the smell of coffee reached her, and the little scratchy noises her mother made in the kitchen downstairs resolved themselves into something vaguely recognizable. She didn't know where she was at first; opened her eyes expecting the layout of her room in the *pensione*, Italian voices outside in the street. A trick of the daylight, strained through the yellow blind, gave the illusion of sunshine, but she could hear the thrum of heavy rain. At the back of the desk a shimmering silver oblong, the reflection of a strip of window, strung with raindrops, was visible at the bottom of the blind. *Glass beads flung on glass.* Who said that? She closed her eyes again. The oblong stayed, pale green now, moving behind her eyelids.

Light rippled over her face; the room was warm. Beside her Julian stirred, his dreadlocks spilling onto her arm, ropey, comforting. He groaned in his sleep, turned and, in one smooth movement was on top of her and inside her, moving in her. His breath was warm on her cheek and he groaned again when he came and kept moving in her until she came and she

woke

the waves of her orgasm receding

fuck me fuck me fuck me

woke in a strange room to the sound of rain on the window, November outside, masquerading as summer, London pretending to be Florence.

Not Florence. Somewhere else. Where? It had the feel of another time. A different place. Funny she should dream of Julian with his dreads and not his new velvet scalp. Which she preferred really. A flash of his head between her legs, her hands stroking the short fuzz prickling her inner thighs, sand-gold against her dark pubic hair, her fingers convulsing and nothing to hold on to, her nails digging into his scalp, drawing blood, as his tongue brought her to orgasm. But it wasn't then. When was it? The mood of the dream belonged to a moment suspended, a time outside time. When she had no desire to be anywhere else in the world with anyone else. Ever. That was it. And you think the moment will last but it doesn't. Someone has to get up to pee. Or a dog barks outside.

Or a phone goes off in somebody's pocket, in the heap of clothes on the floor. It doesn't last. You revisit it occasionally. Unexpectedly. Like in this dream. As if it's still there, a little pocket of time you can dip into. If you're lucky. If you happen to be wearing the proper coat.

Her mother was at the kitchen table with the *Telegraph*, her glasses low on the bridge of her nose, coffee mug in both hands, the smell of Colombian dark roast like the possibility of warmth between them.

Morning, Mother.

She brought her head up slowly from the paper and regarded Laetitia over the top of her glasses. Did you sleep well? Is the futon comfortable? She said the word with an exaggerated French accent, her mouth pursed for the first syllable, releasing the second, the almost —*ong*, so that the effect was more comic Japanese.

Yes. *Très confortable.*

Her mother smiled. *Bon*, she said, *très bien*. She set her glasses on the paper and got up. *Voulez-vous du café, ma chérie?*

Oui. S'il vous plaît. There was no sign of a hangover. Nothing that looked like the splitting headache she deserved. She could obviously hold her drink. Only her eyes were a little red-rimmed. Laetitia sat down and squinted at the paper. One lens of the glasses magnified the middle of a paragraph; it bulged towards her.

... bogus asylum claims ...
... swamping the town of ...

Fucking typical! Her mother set an espresso cup beside her, white china with a silver rim, half an inch of thick black liquid in the bottom.

141

There you are, bunny. She sat down, put her glasses on again. Laetitia waited, but she didn't deliver her usual line: *This coffee is like tar, darling; it can't be good for one.* Unsaid, it buzzed like a fly between them. Her mother waved her hand, swatting it away. A truce then. They would steer clear of politics, religion, addiction. Don't mention the whisky. Don't mention the war.

The demo was fantastic, since you ask, she said. Seven hundred thousand at least. Some reports said around a million. She took a sip of the espresso and eyed her mother over the cup. The atmosphere was terrific. So many like-minded people together. Fabulous.

Her mother lifted hurt eyes, underlined by frameless glasses, held Laetitia's own eyes past the point of discomfort, bit her top lip and got up, gathering the pages of the paper.

I'll leave you to your espresso, darling. And she went out of the kitchen, closed the door with deliberate gentleness behind her.

Fuck!

Laetitia looked at the window. Rain was streaming down it. Grey, grey, grey. The wet black branches of the plum tree at the end of the garden swayed and scattered droplets across the sodden lawn. No Daddy, no Julian. Just grey and the prospect of greyer. She swilled the treacly liquid round in the bottom of the cup, upended it against her lip, let the thick drops slide onto her tongue and down her throat. It *was* like tar. She set the cup on its saucer and decided.

The big, square suspended clock was easy to locate. She looked for him underneath it, as she came down the platform and, sure enough, there he was, the hood of his parka pulled forward over his head against the Glasgow cold. Instantly recognizable, even so. Julian. Even sans dreads. He saw her and came quickly towards her, pushing through the stream of passengers that poured off the London train.

Tish! God, you're laden. Give me that. He had one hand on her shoulder and reached for the case with the other, a frown of concern on his face.

No, this is the laptop my father gave me; I'll carry it. You take this, if you like.

She set the black case on its edge between her feet, while she shrugged her rucksack off. Her hands were shaking. Julian grabbed her by the shoulders, her elbows pinned to her sides by the straps of the bag, drew her to him and kissed her on the mouth. She could smell him. His tobacco breath, his sweat rising from underneath the parka. She could smell him. He grabbed his hood off his face, pressed his lips hard against hers and pushed his salty tongue between her teeth. He held her there in the middle of the concourse, with people going round them, giving them a wide berth, looking at them sideways.

When he pulled away, their breath merged in one cloud, her rucksack slid off her arms and dropped to the tiles behind her. His face was white and the pale fuzz on his head had regrown a little in the two weeks since she'd seen him. She reached out to touch it, the soft bristle of it, and ran her hand down his face. He hadn't shaved either; there was the makings of a beard straggling through. Four days' growth.

Your hands are cold. He unzipped his parka to his waist, took her hands in his and put first one, then the other inside, crushed them to his ribs under his arms. She could feel the heat of his thin body through wool, the rickety beat of his heart. When she looked at his face again, his eyes were fixed on her, darker than usual, a funny colour in the artificial light. He knew her. That's what it was. That was what she—

Scuse me, pal. Could you spare some change?

The old man was standing right beside them before she noticed him. There were only a few other people scattered about in the station and the crowd off the train had disappeared. He held out an empty cardboard coffee cup; there was still a faint coffee smell off it. Grey synthetic stuffing poked from a hole above the pocket of his black anorak. He was staring at Julian. She wondered what Julian would do and she tried to move her hands from his armpits. He squeezed them tighter, ignored the old man and his cup.

Scuse me, pal, any spare change? He thrust the cup closer to Julian. She could smell some kind of cheap, sweet alcohol. And worse. She tried not to breathe in.

Fuck off, mate, Julian said. Go and rummage in a bin.

With all due respect, sir, there nay bins. That's the point. He turned big watery eyes on Laetitia. Beggin your pardon, hen. No since Nine Eleven. She thought at first he said, *nine a love in.*

He switched his attention back to Julian. Bombs, see. Could be members a the al-Qaeda network anywhere. Even here in the dear green place, dear old Glesga toon. He waved his cup in big arcs. There was a drip of clear mucus on the end of his nose, ready to fall next time he turned his head.

Give him something, Julian. Just give him something.

The old man bowed towards her, kept his rheumy eyes on her face, smiled a little smile. His chin was silver with rough stubble; the drip on his nose quivered. He straightened and turned back to Julian.

And all they would have to do, sir, is pap a few dods a Semtex, tied tay an alarm clock, intay the aforementioned bins and, Bob's your uncle. Central Station blown tay bits. Hunners a casualties.

He moved the cup over the top of her arm and held it an

inch away from Julian's chest. Almost still, but for a slight tremor.

So, there nay bins.

Julian tightened his armpit grip on her hands and they stood like that for what felt like ages, till he smiled and released her. Her fingers tingled.

Here you are, mate. He brought out a pile of coins from deep in the left-hand pocket of his parka, selected a couple and dropped them into the cardboard cup. Did you audition for this role then? he said. Archetypal Glasgow Drunk?

The old man's attention was on Julian's hand, as he returned the remaining coins to his pocket. When he raised his head, the drip was gone, and his eyes looked tired.

No, son. I was born tay it.

They were subdued on the funny little underground train, on the way to Julian's flat. Laetitia still had the papery feel of the old man's farewell handshake on her, saw the look he gave them when he turned to go. She moved her laptop closer to her side on the swirly orange livery of the seat, reached for Julian's hand under the end of his sleeve. It was warm and moist. She laced her fingers through his and he turned to look at her.

Don't worry, babe. It's the Glasgow style. Even the drunks are into politics and philosophy. The whole Rab C. Nesbitt nine yards. *A twenty-four-hour cabaret*, as one of their local writers put it.

On the seat across from them, a young guy was glaring at Julian. He looked about twenty. His hair was cropped with a blond tuft at the front. Like Tintin, she thought. He was holding on to the metal pole and sitting on the edge of his seat.

Julian patted her arm and faced forward again, met the stare of the boy.

What you sayin about Glasgow, ya posh cunt? You don't like it, go back where you came fae. *Glaahs-gey!* It's fuckin Glasgow, man. Glaz-goh! He leant further forward in his seat, jabbed his finger level with Julian's face to punctuate each syllable.

She felt her heart beat faster. Julian tightened his grip of her hand. Around them, passengers were getting up and the train squealed to a stop. Nobody looked at the young guy. Or at them. He pulled himself to his feet by the pole, and made for the door as it slid open.

Fuckin English cunt, he said to the back of an Asian woman getting off in front of him. She pulled a thin green scarf over her head and moved aside to let him out before her.

Laetitia watched him walk towards the exit. The sign on the platform read 'Cowcaddens'. As he passed, he turned to the train and gave them the finger.

Julian looked at her. His face was white and tense. Wee *Glaz-goh* hard man, he said. I rest my case.

Where do we get off? she asked.

Kelvinbridge.

There was a list of stations on the arched wall by the platform. She craned to scan it. Only two more stops.

Don't worry, pal. We're no all like that.

A guy about their age was perched on one buttock on the seat beyond Julian, facing them, a rolled-up newspaper in the pocket of his jacket, one foot resting on the other knee. An empty drinks can, orange and blue, rolled with the motion of the train from beside his other foot and clattered against the seat opposite. He smiled at her.

I know, man, Julian said. Some of my best friends . . .

In saying that, you *were* a bit condescending. Rab C.'s well passé, pal. Know what I'm sayin? Doesny do to patronize the good people of Glasgow.

Oh, here we go, Julian said. He was frowning. She had never noticed before how deep the furrow was between his eyes. Perhaps it was more pronounced with his shorn head. It made him look older.

No, I'm just sayin . . . Piece a free advice, my friend. Simple as that. He took his paper from his pocket, shook it out and started to read.

Julian tensed beside her, ready to engage with the guy. This didn't happen on the London Underground; people rarely made eye contact, wouldn't dream of speaking to other passengers. She squeezed his fingers, pressed herself closer to his side. Those who did were studiously ignored, blocked out by newspapers, averted gazes, assumed to be trouble or mentally ill. She looked out the window. The train was pulling away from St George's Cross platform.

Is the next stop ours? she said.

Julian nodded.

I'll be glad when this journey's over, she whispered into his shoulder. I've had enough of trains for one day.

She didn't realize what Julian was doing at first when he swung her rucksack off his back and fumbled in his pocket in front of a door between a continental grocer and a bookmaker's. It had peeling brown varnish and there were two worn stone steps up to it. She stood on her toes and peered over his shoulder at the square window in the wood. A spider web of cracks ran to the edges from a small round hole just off centre. Beneath this random pattern, she could see that the inside of the glass was marked off with wire into little squares like graph paper. To toughen it, she supposed.

Is this where you live?

Yeah. He turned to her, smiling, and held up a silver Yale key. Welcome to the Palace of Grunge.

What happened to the glass?

Fascist bullet.

No, really, what happened?

Julian jiggled the key in the lock and rattled the door. Fucking useless key, he said, as it gave and the door opened inwards with a strange whine.

Et voilà. He cast her a grin over his shoulder. *Entrez, madame.*

She lifted her laptop case, held it in front of her chest and followed Julian into a dark passageway. It stank of old rubbish.

Landlord still hasn't fixed the close light. Bastard.

What's a close light?

This, my dear, is the close. Julian flourished his free arm into the rank air of the passage. Name for the common entry into tenement buildings. Not the most salubrious specimen, admittedly, this one. Perhaps the landlord is being merciful. No. On second thoughts, revert to original assessment, he's a tight-fisted bastard.

But what *really* happened to the door?

They reached the foot of a wide staircase. Her eyes adjusted to the dim orange glow that made it through the cracked glass from the sodium streetlight outside. And there was some light coming through a window on the landing above, three panes of clear glass and on the others the remains of some kind of painted Victorian scene. She could make out a bird on a branch.

No, a fascist bullet, really. Or so Danny says.

Danny! Danny Kilkenny?

The one and only.

Have you seen much of him?

Certainly. And so will you. He's crashing here for a few days till he can find somewhere else. Fell out with old man Stalin; left because his mother was upset.

Stalin? You mean his father?

Of course.

She was watching where she put her feet on the dark stairs, hugging her laptop to her. On the landing, she stopped. The stink of rubbish was worse here. Close up she could see the painted bird was perched among brown leaves and held a berry in its beak.

But, Julian, why did you let him stay when you knew I was coming?

I didn't. It was Jed.

Jed?

Jed, my flatmate. He and Danny are friends from way back.

Julian stopped and turned to her, hitched her rucksack further onto his back. It was Jed who got Danny into the group. He reached for her hand. Don't worry, Tish. Danny's cool with it. With us.

He looked like a little boy, eyes wide, wonky smile, except for the orange light that hollowed out the planes of his face, and the frown line that might now be permanent.

You've spoken to him?

No-o-o . . . not exactly. Look, he's fine. *All shall be well, and all shall be well* . . . He lifted her hand to his mouth and kissed it. His lips were moist and nuzzled for a moment in her palm, like a pet. Or a childhood secret. He raised his eyes to her . . . *and all manner of thing shall be well.*

Clare's not here too, is she?

No, darling. Clare is still in parental custody. When she's not at St Veronica's – *Holy Mary, Mother of God, pray for us now and at the hour of our death* – learning how to be a good little Catholic girl.

Julian! You screwed her, remember. But she couldn't help smiling in the dark.

There was no one there when they entered the flat. No Jed.

149

No Danny. She breathed again. She had time to take it in, get her bearings before she had to deal with that.

Oh, my God!

You should have been an estate agent, she said to Julian. This was not how she imagined it from his e-mails, waxing lyrical about high ceilings, wedding cake cornicing, the big bay window. When he switched on the shadeless light, it was the sheer scale of the mess that staggered her. Clothes, books, CDs, newspapers, pizza boxes, plates, mugs, glasses, ashtrays, takeaway cartons covered the floor. A sea of detritus. Julian waded in, kicking rubbish aside, clearing a path to the window, inviting her to follow in his wake.

The window, *the beautiful bay window*, was curtainless at one side; sagging over the other was what looked like an old banner, drained of colour by the orange sodium lights outside.

This is even worse than your room in Cambridge. If that's possible. She pressed her laptop closer to her and took a few steps into the room. Her foot caught a polystyrene cup and it wedged on like a toecap. She kicked the air three times before it flew off.

It's not my room; it's the living room, he said. Danny's going to be sleeping here for the mo.

Where? she said. She could see no surface that resembled a bed. It was like a building worked over by a hurricane, transformed by a bomb; no recognizable feature remained.

Sofa bed. There. He pointed to a mound in the middle of the room, where she spotted a filthy bundled duvet underneath a top layer of clothes and papers.

Fucking hell, Julian.

Now don't go all bourgeois and little-womanish on me, he said. Housework and the revolution are incompatible.

Bullshit, she said. Bee Fucking Ess.

He laughed. Attagirl. You're right. Jed and I and Malcolm,

the ex-tenant – Malcolm X, we call him – used to argue so much about who should do what, we gave up on it. Julian set her rucksack on top of a pile of clothes. She fixed its coordinates in her head in case it disappeared amongst the rubble

Malcolm nearly killed Jed one night for not washing the dishes when it was his turn. Hit him over the head with the kettle which, luckily, had not yet been boiled. Left a scar above his left eye, though. Drenched us all when the lid flew off. After that, we held a summit and agreed we'd each just do housework when we felt like it. He reached out to Laetitia. Here, let me take your coat.

She shook her head. In a minute.

And of course – *quelle surprise!* – no one ever felt like it. Malcolm couldn't hack it. Moved out not long after. Bit of an old woman, our Malcolm.

Julian, I don't think I can do this. I'll never get any work done here. She could feel the pricking in her nose, the loosening of mucus, the start of tears. She blinked, sniffed, stopped herself.

Babe! It's not as bad as all that. He held her shoulders and fixed her eyes with his, blue again now in the bald light, the tiny gold hairs on his head like so many live filaments. Hey, Tish, it's only *things*; they don't matter. And my room's much better. *Our* room. Come on, I'll show you.

She wouldn't release one arm from its grip on her laptop to take his outstretched hand. But she followed him as he picked his way back across the room to the door. The hall was too dark to see much, and for that she was grateful. She stayed close to him as he crossed it to open one of the other doors.

In the dark, in the dark. She lay there on her side, trying to make out the noises in the flat. Julian was curled into her back, asleep. His breath fanned her hair; it rose and settled, rose and settled, feathering her cheek. They were on the top floor, so what sounded like footsteps above must be something else. She'd woken up briefly when she heard voices and banging, then slept again. Till now. Now she was awake for the night, for however much of it was left. She couldn't extricate her watch arm from where Julian had it pinned to her thigh. It was too dark anyway to make it out.

He'd been right about his room. It was do-able. Before she arrived, he'd clearly made an effort. The bed was graced with an entirely new set of bedding bought earlier in the day. New thick duvet, new fat pillows, new cover, sheet and pillowslips in white cotton. A bridal bed. The rest of the room was straining to be minimal: a desk with his computer on it; a bulging blue canvas wardrobe, zipped up; one chaotic book-case, stuffed and overflowing with papers, books, plastic wallets of notes; two straight-backed wooden chairs, painted blue, one on either side of the bed. What couldn't be contained had probably been tipped into the living room.

A sly move, to show her the other room first. Anything would have to be an improvement. She smiled in the dark, remembering. The kiss at the foot of the bed, tender, slightly tremulous. As if it was their first time. *Do as you would be done by*, she thought, the white bed gleaming beside them, even when she closed her eyes. It was possible to shut out the rubbish piled next door. *Sail off on a river of crystal light* . . . Children's rhymes were saying themselves in her head . . . *into a sea of blue*. Fragments alighting like butterflies. Where did they spring from? She didn't say them aloud. *Where are you going and what do you wish, the old moon asked the three?* . . . Julian would be forced to scoff, tell her it was mawkish crap. *We have come to fish for the herring fish* . . . Or treat her like a child . . . *that live in this beautiful sea.* Prozac. Could this be a side effect? A portal into all the sentimental literature she'd read as a child? It's only supposed to kick in after three weeks, the doctor said. She didn't care. When he finally came into her under the white cover with its folds from the packaging still crisp, it was as if she had come home.

Home, she said it into his neck, her breath coming back to her, hot on her cheek. I feel as if I'm home.

Home and wet, he said, muffled. Very. Very. Wet. He thrust with each word and he groaned when he came. Stayed inside her. Stayed.

Nets of silver and gold have we . . .

She didn't even care that she hadn't come. They fell asleep entwined.

It was Danny's voice that woke her first, a door banging, another male voice. Jed. Sometime in sleep, she and Julian had disentangled. They lay back to back now, each facing a blue chair covered in clothes. A strange symmetry. Though it was too dark to see the chairs, to do anything other than infer their colour and shape from her earlier observation. Were they really there? She turned and moulded herself to Julian's back, squashing her breasts either side of his bony spine, flattening her cheek on his shoulder blade.

Fucksake man, she heard Danny say, before she fell asleep again.

So now she was awake for the remainder of the night. With her free arm, she reached over the edge of the bed. Yes, her laptop was there in its leather case. She eased open the flap at the front. The rip of Velcro was loud but it didn't wake Julian. She waited; his breathing was steady. Her hand fumbled in the front pocket, wrist encircled by a cool bangle of air outside the duvet, till she found Aunt Laetitia's journal, the kid cover soft and flexible beside the rigid covers of her own. She still hadn't shown it to Julian. Why not? The right moment hadn't yet presented itself. What with . . . But that wasn't it, because she hadn't even told him about it. Hadn't mentioned it to Daddy, when he phoned to ask how she liked her laptop. She'd intended to; felt the words tingle in her mouth, but somehow couldn't release them. Why? The conversation had rushed on, entered familiar territory, cosy, collusive, savouring Mother's latest misdemeanours, laughing at her *deeply shallow* nature. Perhaps it was guilt; the niggling awareness that it was to her mother she owed the gift of the journal, her mother's idea she should have Aunt Laetitia's trunk. Whatever the reason, the moment was lost. Her father rang off and the journal lay quiet in her bag, untalked about. A secret. Like the tiny dead crab she found on holiday once, that she wouldn't throw away, though her mother told her to; kept it in her pocket till they got back to Wellwood, transferred it to a sweet tin, hid it at the bottom of her wardrobe. The whiff of something rotten, fish, seaweed, when she opened the tin again a week later. But still she wouldn't throw it away; it was so pretty with its little white articulated legs, its bleached, brittle body. She covered it with scented petals from the rose garden, to keep it warm, to mask the smell. White rose petals. Only white would do. And she took it from its hiding place two or three times, replaced the browning petals while the roses lasted that summer. Then she forgot about it. Never saw it again.

Now the notebook. She eased her thumb under the flaps of leather, found the edges of the paper, fanned them. Or maybe it was Aunt Laetitia's secret she was keeping, the one contained in the missing pages. So tantalizing. Sketchy accounts of their visits, Laetitia and Harry's, to various tourist spots in Florence and round about. A travelogue. Il Duomo: *such lightness for a building so immense; it lifts one's spirits. Brunelleschi's magnificent dome.* Ponte Vecchio: *the good people of Firenze, the bustle, the smells; all life is here.* A spin to Fiesole in a motor car owned by *a brash young American.* Nothing much more yet. One or two mentions of the war, speculating about Italy's intentions: would she come in on the side of the Allies; would Harry and she be forced to cut short their stay? True, there were plenty of pages still to read, but the overall impression so far was of information withheld, secrets kept.

Julian shifted slightly behind her, gave a great sigh. She let go the journal and pulled her hand back under the duvet, settled it lightly on Julian's arm. He flinched in his sleep, turned over, leaving her to warm her hand between her own thighs.

When she opened her eyes, Julian was gone from the bed. She had drifted off again after all. His voice was coming from somewhere in the flat. His early morning, not-quite-awake voice, an aristocratic drawl, she teased him, when they first met. Ought to be accompanied by the whine of peacocks.

Hark who's talking, he said.

We didn't have peacocks at Wellwood. We weren't that grand.

Oh, yeah! You are the only person I know, darling, who had an honest-to-God, bona fide, old-fashioned nanny. As opposed to a Danish au pair. Or a woman from the village, who *did* for one.

Nanny Rosenthal was my father's. She'd been with the family for years. She wasn't really mine.

Lordy, lordy, one just can't get the staff these days, he'd said, and caught her by the wrist when she swung at him, hoisted her onto his desk and shagged her again.

She shook off the memory and looked about the room. A thin, grubby light was straggling through a bashed venetian blind beside the desk. She leant over and prised two dusty slats apart. Through the gap, she could see some kind of back area

155

with washing lines and a bin shelter, a child's scooter on its side in a puddle. Beyond that, bare trees. The River Kelvin, perhaps. Julian said it was near.

You're awake. He had a roll-up in one hand, a small cardboard coffee cup with a plastic lid in the other, and stood at the end of the bed.

Madame's espresso, he said, bowed, straightened, drew on his cigarette and scattered a few flakes of ash on the white cover.

Oh. She sat up, brushed off the ash and reached for the coffee. You've been out already?

Yeah. Great little café on the corner. There are croissants too. In the kitchen. If you . . .

What? He was looking at her with a strange smile on his lips.

Nothing. You just look . . . You look just . . . right there. As if it's exactly where you ought to be.

She smiled back at him, pulled the edge of the duvet over her breasts.

He straightened, waved his arms. And it is. It's exactly where you ought to be. Here in the Palace of Grunge with Captain Fuckwit. He bowed. At your service.

Charming. Who were you talking to out there?

Jed. He's off out. Doing a leaflet drop with some of the guys. He offered her a draw on his cigarette, but she shook her head. Might do some flyposting too. Sunday morning's a good time for it. Streets are quiet. Fuzz are all shagged out trying to keep the lid on a Glasgow Saturday night.

And Danny?

He went out earlier. Kipped on the floor in Jed's room. Couldn't stand the mess in the guest room.

Not surprised. She was glad he wasn't there. Another brief reprieve. Good coffee, she said, and raised her cup to Julian.

My pleasure, ma'am. Shall I roll you a cigarette too? He was smoothing a cigarette paper, the smoke from the roll-up between his lips making him screw up his eyes.

You're not the greatest of adverts for it! She laughed at his cowboy-contorted features. No, thank you. I haven't felt much like smoking since I got back from Florence. Thought I might as well seize the opportunity and stop altogether.

What? What the fuck d'you mean you haven't *felt* like smoking? How can you just go off it? Normal people take years. Forty sessions of hypnosis, a library of self-help books, multiple relapses, before they finally quit. What kind of a smoker are you, anyway?

Clearly not a *normal* one.

You can say that again. A dilettante, I'd call you, my dear. An amateur. No commitment.

He rolled the cigarette paper into a tiny ball between his fingers and pinged it at her. Take that, traitor!

It bounced off her cheek, disappeared under the edge of the duvet. She felt it trickle down her warm belly.

You realize from now on you're going to have to ask the question abhorred by all hopeless addicts, she said. With her free hand, she explored under the quilt, till she found the little ball. *Mind if I smoke?* She threw the paper towards him, but it fell short and disappeared in the folds of the cover. And I shall say, *Yes I do mind. It is a filthy habit, injurious to one's health, so kindly do not light up in my presence.* It shall be my mission to bully you into joining me on the path of righteous abstemiousness.

No! No! He turned and launched himself backwards onto the bed, his boots leaving great smears of mud at the bottom of the cover.

Julian! You are *such* a Pig Pen.

But you adore me. He reached over and grappled her into

a bear hug, scudded the cardboard cup from her hand. Droplets of coffee scattered onto the white cotton.

Oops! Well and truly christened, he said, and slipped his hand under the cover onto her breast.

She watched the neat arc of spots glisten for a moment, before turning matt black. Later they would dry to dark brown.

You have the soul of a chimney sweep, she said, leaving black footprints on a white carpet.

I'll climb up your chimney any day, honey, he said, and caught her nipple between dry lips.

Danny came back about midday. She heard him in the hall.

Man, that is some day. It's chuckin it down. Cats and dogs, as the wee wumman says.

There was a rustle of supermarket bags, the sound of a coat being shaken. She slipped Aunt Laetitia's diary under the pillow. Who was he talking to? Julian had dozed off again on top of the quilt and she hadn't heard Jed come in. Must be Danny's way of announcing his arrival. Letting them know he was back in case . . . In case what? In case he caught them *in flagrante*; in case she was wandering about with no clothes on? It was quite sweet really. Danny without the tough-guy veneer, the Glasgow machismo. Time to say hello and get it over with. She stood up from the bed and smoothed down her jeans, tugged her brown sweater over her navel.

Julian, Danny's back. Come with me and help break the ice. His chest rose and fell; a faint snore purred from his open mouth.

Julian. The memory flashed into her mind of Danny's face when they'd approached the bus in Florence. The hurt look, quickly extinguished, disguised in a bit of stage business with his rucksack.

Julian. She pinched his bare big toe between her finger and thumb and squeezed. His foot jerked back on the cover, he folded his arms, turned slightly and went on sleeping. The smear of mud was dry now. And the coffee stains. She'd have to find out the arrangements for laundry.

For a moment before opening it, she listened at the door. Some sort of activity was going on; banging, shuffling, knocking. And, skewering the other sounds, a whistled tune. Not one she recognized. She breathed in, stilled her hand on the doorknob, turned it and went into the hall.

The only light came from a fanlight at the top of the outer door and from the wide open door of the living room, where the noises were coming from. She crossed to it quickly before she changed her mind.

Danny didn't see her at first. She watched his dark head bob up and down in front of the big bay window, his face in shadow, as he scooped up armfuls of rubbish and dumped them into one of five black bin bags, arranged in a semi-circle, following the curve of the window. The banner was gone, she noticed. Each time he bent, the tune he whistled was distorted for a moment, before rising sweet and piercing again, as he straightened. The muscles on his arms flexed and unflexed smoothly while he worked, and his white T-shirt was already grimy. *Ah don't want you to be no slave . . .* The words sang themselves in her head, an ironic counterpoint to his mournful Irish air. All she needed was a can of beer to pass him.

Can I help?

He stopped mid scoop, with his arms full of rubbish, his mouth still puckered, and exhaled a low note that could have been part of the tune. Or could have been an expression of appreciation. She felt her ears burn.

He glanced away. Oh, hi, Laetitia. Then in one smooth move, he tipped the load he held into the nearest bag. Aye, sure you can. All assistance gratefully received. What d'you make a they mingin bastards but?

It was going to be OK, she thought.

That Jed one. His granny will be birlin in her grave. He wasny reared to live in a pigsty like this.

She had to hand it to him. Apart from that one faltered note, one would never know there had been anything between them. She waded into the room.

Where shall I start?

That's the game. Get the sleeves rolled up, and then you can choose. This here is the Wastepaper Disposal Section. He turned a pointed finger and a cocked thumb on three of the bags.

Or perchance your aptitudes might lie here in the Crockery Retrieval Department. She followed his gesture; in a small clear space on the floor was a pile of miscellaneous dirty dishes.

On the other hand, mair job satisfaction might be derived from the merry clink of bottles tossed into this particular black plastic receptacle here.

My goodness, spoilt for choice, she said, and he grinned at her.

And, at the risk of causing you to salivate in eager anticipation, further down the line there will be Sweeping and Dusting and Washing of floors.

There's a *floor*!

I can assure you, comrade, there is. And it is our job to excavate it from under myriad strata of archaeological deposits.

Right, let's go to it! With a steady hand and a ready heart. She did a little marching step on the top layer of rubbish, over to where the bags were lined up.

Danny laughed. I think the term you're looking for is *Haud me back*!

And whistle while we work. I do think we ought to whistle. She liked it when he laughed. It transformed his Celtic scowl into something much more open and appealing.

What was the tune you were whistling before? It was terribly evocative.

Now, that is a little oul Irish air me mother sang to me. Tis called 'She moved through the fair' . . .

How lovely.

That it is.

And she made her way homeward with one star awake,
As the swan in the evening moves over the lake.

He held open his arms as he sang, and warbled the grace notes with an exaggerated tremolo. It still gave her a moment of shivery pleasure.

Wow, Danny! Are *all* you Kilkennys such marvellous singers?

She could swear that he blushed. The Glasgow hard man! He bent at once to pick up more papers. Aye, tis a darlin song to be sure, to be sure. But I canny stand around here chattin all day. There's work to be done. He gave her a shy smile before stuffing more rubbish into a bag.

Right you are, sir. She saluted him and started to scrape assorted papers into a bundle. On one sheet she caught sight of Julian's small, neat handwriting, the source of endless ribbing from all his friends, such a contrast with every other aspect of him. Notes for his PhD, it must be.

She sat on the bidet soaping herself and talked to me pleasantly about this and that . . . As she stood up to dry herself . . . suddenly she dropped the towel and, advancing toward me leisurely, she commenced rubbing her pussy affectionately, stroking it with her two hands, caressing it, patting it, patting it. There was something about her eloquence at that moment and the way she thrust that rose-bush under my nose which remains unforgettable . . .

Miller, *Tropic of Cancer*, pp. 49–50

Christ, Julian, she thought.

. . . And while it's all very nice to know that a woman has a mind, literature coming from the cold corpse of a whore is the last thing to be served in bed. Germaine had the right idea: she was ignorant and lusty, she put her heart and soul into her work. She was a whore all the way through – and that was her virtue!

T. of Canc. p. 54

What crap! What self-serving tosh! She glanced over at Danny, but he had resumed his earlier rhythm; bending, scooping, rising, dumping. His face was closed in a frown of concentration.

. . . And it seemed she was like the sea, nothing but dark waves rising and heaving, heaving with a great swell, so that slowly her whole darkness was in motion, and she was ocean rolling its dark, dumb mass. Oh, and far down inside her the deeps parted and rolled asunder, in long, far-travelling billows, and ever, at the quick of her, the depths parted and rolled asunder, from the centre of soft plunging, as the plunger went deeper and deeper, touching lower . . .

She felt the spasm of a giggle, took a sideways peek at Danny, bent in rapt attention over his task, and gulped back the bubble of mirth.

. . . till suddenly, in a soft shuddering convulsion, the quick of all her plasm was touched, she knew herself touched, the consummation was upon her, and she was gone. She was gone, she was not, and she was born: a woman.

Lawrence, *Lady Chatterley's Lover*, p. 181

Plasm! She must remember that. There was one last quote.

'. . . She sort of kept her will ready against me, always, always: her ghastly female will: her freedom! A woman's ghastly freedom that ends in the most beastly bullying! Oh, she always kept her freedom against me, like vitriol in my face.'

L.C.L. p. 292

Vitriol! Wait till he got hers. She cast about the room for somewhere to lay the sheet, begin a pile of items to be kept. There was nowhere except in the window, where Danny had cleared a space. To one side she spotted a high-backed kitchen chair, picked her way over to it, swept the clothes and papers off and set Julian's notes on the seat. When she looked up, she realized Danny was watching this operation with undisguised amusement. His dark eyebrows were raised and his green eyes seemed like the one true colour in the room.

Well, Ms Laetitia, I reckon that puts you in charge of the Search and Rescue Department. I hope you won't mind if us cruder souls in Bundle and Crush just stick to our remit.

Hah! You know what, Danny, you're right. A quick heat flushed up her neck. She picked up the page of notes, crushed it into a tight ball and threw it into one of the open bags.

That's the stuff. Otherwise we'll be here tay the Christmas efter next.

Once she got into a rhythm, she quite enjoyed working alongside him. They hardly spoke. Outside, the sky was grey, though it had stopped raining; and the big bay window, uncurtained, let in a watery light through its grimy panes. She could see that it was a room of elegant proportions, the ceiling higher than those in her mother's house, the decorative plasterwork more ornate. In one corner a watermark reached halfway down the wall. Above it, the frieze of fruit bowls and looping garlands of flowers was missing and had been crudely replastered flat. It must have been done some time ago, though, because this new plaster was almost as grey with dirt as the original cornice.

Danny had started whistling again. Softly this time, to himself almost, like whispering. It was hard to make out the tune above the noises of the rubbish being gathered and dumped. She bent again to concentrate on her own patch. It worked best when she shut her mind off from the specific nature of the objects to be disposed of. The takeaway cartons were the worst by far, with congealed curry from an unimaginable number of days or weeks ago. Perhaps even months. Yuck! A mug with a bloom of green penicillin on the scummy coffee to join the pile of crockery. Bottles and bottles. Newspapers, heaps of leaflets for an anti-war vigil from a few weeks back, paper, paper, paper.

All five bags were filled pretty quickly and Danny tied them up, carted them into the hall, peeled another batch off the fat black roll, and propped them open with carefully placed heavier items: bottles, a chipped mug, a smashed alarm clock. It was good to watch him; he was so organized, precise, efficient, his movements graceful. Yes, she thought, he is graceful.

Through the window she could see the buildings opposite: dull, miserable tenements, not improved by the weather. There was more traffic now, a constant roar, punctuated regularly by the frenetic peeping of a pedestrian crossing she hadn't noticed before. Though the rain had stopped, she could hear the sizzling noise car tyres made in surface water on the road below.

What would you say to a tea-break, comrade? Danny was tying up another bag.

Huh? It took her a moment to come back to herself, to register his words. When she looked up at him, she was struck again by how long and dark his lashes were. How green his eyes. Conjured up a forest pool; reeds and bulrushes, the reflections of trees. Oh, yes, a cup of tea would be lovely. She peered over one of the bags at the now impressive pile of plates and cups. Shall we be required to render the Dish Washing Unit operational first?

Danny grinned and cast a glance over his shoulder as if talking to someone behind him. Hey, she catches on fast, this yin. You'll rise through the ranks in jig time, so you will. Assistant manageress before you know it.

Only Assistant?

Hey, any complaints, comrade, approach your shop steward.

Right, I shall. She wasn't entirely sure she knew what a shop steward was, but she wasn't going to let on to Danny. It sounded like some suitably workerist term. She picked up a last bundle of papers, straightened quickly to throw them in the bag and stumbled forward.

Oh! A wave of nausea came over her and her vision blurred. She reached out for something – anything – solid to steady her.

Hey, you alright? Danny said.

Yes, I'm fine . . . But she felt herself topple sideways and she grabbed his outstretched arm.

Woah, there, Laetitia! I wouldny take a dive onto that floor the now. No yet. His voice was coming from a distance. She felt his arm go round her waist, as he helped her over to the chair by the window.

There. That better?

The seat was solid beneath her. She watched a flock of pigeons land blurred on the roof of the building across. When she narrowed her eyes, they came clear. One alighted on a chimney pot and stood as if addressing the other birds assembled on the tiles below. She turned her head to Danny. His face was close to hers, regarding her with a mixture of concern and amusement, his eyebrows shooting up and down between a frown and a question.

You have beetling brows, she said. Yeah, I'm fine now. Thanks.

What was that all about?

Don't know. Probably lack of food. Haven't eaten anything since . . .

That cheapskate bastard no take you out for a slap-up meal last night? A nice big biryani?

I think a sandwich on the train was the last thing I ate. No, we came straight here from the station. She laid her head down on her knees. I'll be fine. Just give me a minute. Her words came out constrained and lost themselves at her feet among the remaining bits of detritus.

Well, we'll need to see if the management will consider givin you a position in the office, comrade. His hand felt heavy on her shoulder. Your constitution's obviously a wee bit delicate for the mair physical aspects of the job.

Ho, ho, she said. Piss off! She raised her head to find him smiling down at her. Sometimes I simply forget to eat.

Forget? You *simply forget*?

She slapped his thigh. Danny could make her words sound so prissy and silly.

Well, nay wonder the country's going to rack and ruin, if you ask me.

Nobody asked you, sir, she said. She quoted the nursery song as she stood up. And if I don't get that cup of tea pretty damn quick, I'll be looking for this steward chap.

Danny laughed; his face lit up with delight. Right you are,

pal. Up the workers! This way, comrade, follow me. And he punched the air as he made his way to the door.

Somebody had obviously been busy in the kitchen too. The surfaces were cleared and the rank stench of rubbish was gone.

Did you do all this as well?

I certainly did. Up at Krakatoa, while the rest of yous were still in your scratchers, givin it a row a zeds. Look at this, by the way. He picked up a big frying pan and stuck it under her nose.

Yuck, suet, she said, and recoiled.

Aye, look at it but.

She brought her head closer again. There were two neat rows of tiny claw prints scratched into the surface of the congealed fat.

Oh my God, mice!

You're damn tootin, he said. Our rodent brothers have been havin a rare tear in here, I'm tellin you. I kept this to shame they two clatty bastards.

She felt the nausea surge in her throat again and swallowed it down.

Right, he said, set the pan decisively aside and flicked on the switch of a pristine-looking kettle. Unaware as I was that the entire stock of a china shop was buried under the rubble through there, I took the precaution of pur-*chasing* some new crockery. He picked out two fresh mugs from a group of six. One had strawberries printed on it, the other cherries.

They're pretty, she said.

And a kettle. There was nay kettle.

You think of everything, Danny. I'm so glad you're here.

He turned away and busied himself with taking a packet out of the cupboard, opening it and putting a teabag in each mug, before looking at her again.

Nearly there, he said. I'm ready for this, you no?

Sure am, she said.

And here, look, somebody's supplied the croissants. He held a paper bag out to her. I'll warm them up under the grill.

Actually, can I have one as it is? Keep the hounds of hunger at bay. She pulled out one of the greasy pastries and felt a rush of saliva as she raised it to her mouth. It would be alright. It was going to be alright.

Aargh!

Danny looked at her.

Julian, she said. Simultaneously they made for the hall.

Oh my God! Julian said. It's the Invasion of the Mrs Mops. He was standing at the door of the sitting room, his two forefingers held in a cross in front of him. Lord have mercy on our souls.

Aye, very funny, Danny said.

Trust Julian, she thought. She put her hands on her hips and tried for a scolding tone. And just *who* was going to clear this heap of junk if we hadn't?

No one, darling, no one, of course. But I don't care. All young women should be locked in a tower and never allowed to set eyes on a mop or a duster. In case they are overcome by the urge to clean. Lest they turn into – oh, the horror! – *housewives*, charladies, cleaners. One never wants to shag a cleaner. Nurses, certainly. Maids, as long as they're wearing short black skirts with little white frilly aprons and brandishing a stick with feathers on the end. But cleaners! Come awn! Gimme a break! He opened his arms and rolled his eyes. And when *men* are lured by the temptations of housewifery's black arts, well . . . He looked at Danny, held his hand out and dropped his wrist.

She could see Danny's hands tense at his sides and she shut her eyes. No.

When she opened them, Danny was looking at her. He was

white round the mouth and his jaw was working. But he flexed his fingers.

Know what, Julian? You're a fuckin wanker. But I'm no gonny let you annoy me. No the day. No *any* day. But especially no the day. See, it's my birthday. Twenty-five. The quarter-century. And nay cunt's gonny rain on my parade.

He stepped away from them and moved through the hall.

She looked at Julian.

What? He made his eyes wide and pulled his shoulders up to his ears. It was only a joke. Some people have no sense of humour.

Cut it out, Julian. She lowered her voice almost to a whisper. You know damn well what you're doing.

She turned and left him; followed Danny into the kitchen.

Happy birthday, Danny. He was leaning against the sink with his arms crossed and the cherry cup in his hand, propped on the crook of his elbow. You should have said. She stepped up to him and put her arms round his shoulders in an awkward hug. Happy birthday. The heat of his body radiated out through his damp T-shirt, along with the smell of his sweat and something more acrid, a whiff of anger.

Aye, thanks, he said. He stayed where he was, arms still crossed, and gave her a close-lipped smile.

Sorry, mate. Julian was behind her. He put his hands on her hips, rested his chin on her head, pressed each finger in turn into the flesh beneath her jeans. I'm sorry. Happy birthday. You know me, I'm such a prick.

Danny stared forward for what seemed like ages. When he turned to face them, he kept his eyes on her. Aye, I know, he said.

Julian stepped out from behind her and held out his hand.

Danny took his time, but eventually he uncrossed his arms, set his tea down and shook Julian's hand. There was a red ring on the white skin of his inner arm, where the mug had rested.

Oh. She wanted to put her lips there in the centre of that circle and kiss the tender flesh.

Right, Julian said, and clapped his hands. This calls for a celebration! He whirled round like a dancer, displacing the air, as if a freak wind had whipped into the kitchen. She could swear she felt it.

What do you say to an all-day breakfast?

She laughed.

And Danny laughed. I don't know, give us a clue, what *do* you say to an all-day breakfast?

My dear boy, what did they *teach* you in that Glasgow comprehensive? You say, Oh glistening egg, oozing with golden yolk, let me prick your curved belly with my fork. He stopped, looked at the ceiling, drummed his fingers on his chin. Or should that be, fork your curved belly with my prick? No matter . . .

Aye, we get the photy. Danny looked at her sideways.

And those juices that run from the stretched brown skin of your fat little sausages; and your bacon, its pink, succulent flesh; and that sweet, oleaginous – oh, call it not fat! – quintessence of the child pig's yet pure food . . .

Danny looked at her. You've got to hand it tay the cunt, he's never lost for words.

No. True. She smiled at him. Even when they're not his.

You mean, he didny just make that up?

Of course I did! Of course I did! Julian waved his arms about. It's intertextuality, darlings. Interfuckingtextuality.

Well, you can explain that ower the glistening egg. This lassie needs something to eat. And I'm payin. My ma gave us a bung for the birthday.

*

It wasn't what she expected from a Glasgow pub somehow. Julian directed them to a table in the middle and went to the bar to order. She looked around her. There were a couple of old oak dining tables with fat, heavy legs, mixed in with more normal-looking small round pub tables. Staff ran up and down a shaky spiral staircase, decked with fairy lights, carrying orders of food and drink to customers on a mezzanine level above. The atmosphere was busy and relaxed at the same time.

Danny sat down opposite her. The chairs had straw seats and strange little wooden shelves at the back. What for?

What are these for, Danny? She leant over and touched the shelf on his chair back. He kept his eyes focused on hers a second or two longer than was necessary, a reminder she'd have to be careful.

What, they things? he said, turning to look at what she'd touched. That's for your hymn book and your Bible.

Really?

Yeah, really. They no have that down in England? Whenever a church closes, some pub aye acquires the furniture. Fae reclamation yards and that. There's a bar in town uses a baptismal font for ice. Wet the baby's head here, they says; a *spirit*-ual experience with genuine holy ice. Mine's a Scotch on the Rock of Ages, please.

Oh, yeah, she said. And I bet the bar staff dress like vicars.

Danny smiled. She was beginning to get the picture; he liked it when she sparred with him.

Aye, OK, he said. They don't gie special rates to christening parties, but they dae use a font for the ice. Moreover, he said, leaning across the big square table and moving the salt cellar in a circle, there quite a few churches in the city have became bars. What does that tell you about the spiritual health of the good citizens of Glasgow?

Nothing I wouldn't have expected, she said. A godless, drunken crew to a man.

Oh ih, you cut me to the very quick, Ms Laetitia. Me a good Catholic tay. I bet you wouldny believe I was an altar boy.

You're right. In this I am a total unbeliever.

Well, I can assure you I was. He put his hands together, turned his eyes to the ceiling and intoned.

Erimus, erimus, erimus. Catch it.
Erabum, erabum, erabum. Scratch it.

It took her a moment to cotton on to the cod Latin; Danny sang it with all the bright-edged clarity of a Gregorian chant.

Julian came back carrying three pints. He took small steps and kept his eyes on the frothy heads. Drinks all round, he said, and set them on the table. Breakfasts ordered.

Great. I canny wait to talk tay mine.

He sat down at a third side of the big square table, between Danny and her, but stood again abruptly and fished in the back pocket of his jeans.

Oops. Forgot about this. He held Great-aunt Laetitia's diary out to her.

That's mine! She heard her voice rise to a childish whine, and snatched the book from Julian. It was slightly curved now where he'd sat on it, the kid cover wrinkled. She smoothed the soft leather with her palm. You've ruined it, Julian. It belonged to my great-great-great-aunt.

Sorry, babe. I forgot I'd put it there. Found it under your pillow. It's not permanently damaged, is it?

She didn't say anything.

What is it? Danny asked. He was leaning towards her again, his eyes catching flecks of light from the window.

She smoothed and smoothed the bent cover and tried not

to cry. It's a journal that belonged to my great-great-aunt Laetitia. She kept her eyes on it, hoping attention alone would straighten the creases.

How many greats? Julian said. I thought it was three you mentioned last time.

I don't know. And I don't *give* a shit.

Sorry! He scraped his chair round to her side of the table and put his arm across her shoulder. She shrugged it off. Their knees were touching now and Danny was watching them.

My father gave it me. She was an ancestor of his. I'd only just begun to read it. And now . . . A big tear was rolling down her face and there was no stopping it.

Tish, I'm so sorry. Truly, I am. I'm such a klutz, I know.

Understanding was the last thing she needed. Julian's fuzzy cheek was against hers now and Danny's eyebrows were pulled down in sympathy. She sniffed and blinked. Sorry, Danny. Your birthday . . .

Don't apologize. It must mean a lot to you.

Yes, I didn't realize how much till now. The laugh that came out was half a sob, but it did the trick.

Julian drew back, put a strand of her hair behind her ear.

All this attention from two dishy guys could turn a girl's head.

They both smiled at her. Fondly. She squirmed on the straw seat, swallowed, fought to steady her breathing.

Why don't you tell us about it? Danny said. His voice was low. What's in it?

Well, I haven't had time to . . .

I read a page about a WSPU march for women's suffrage, Julian said.

What?

The Women's Social and Political Union, was that not it? Votes for women?

Where?

She doesn't mention the route, I don't think.

No, where in the diary?

I don't know. I just opened it at random and there they were, marching bustle to bustle, banners aloft. She and Harriet.

Who?

Listen, gie the lassie a chance to read it hersel, Danny said.

Of course, of course, Julian said. Sorry. This seems to be my day for abject apology.

The guy who had been behind the bar earlier emerged through a door and laid three huge plates on their table. She was glad of the diversion. Her eyes focused on the yellow seeds of a fried tomato among the potato scones, egg and veggie sausages, as he set down cutlery and three starched white damask napkins.

That's the business, Danny said, and flourished his napkin. How does that go again, Jules? *Oh, glistening egg . . . blabbity blah . . . let me . . .* He paused, looked at her. Ach, fuck it! His broad hands lay open beside his plate. He picked up his fork and knife and addressed the food. I am just gonny wire right intay yous. Any objections? Nane raised. Good. He speared a fat pork sausage, bit it in half and held his fork up to Julian. Pardon me talkin with my mouth full, but sometimes plain speech is the best.

She ignored Julian's anxious face turned to hers and smiled at Danny. But the mood was broken.

Julian moved his chair back round to his original place at the table. You may be right at that, man, he said. You may very well be right.

She slipped Aunt Laetitia's journal into her bag and spread her napkin on her knee.

*

On the landing, outside the door of the flat, she stood at Julian's back as he hunted for his key in various pockets. He was swaying slightly on his heels after the beer he'd drunk.

Sounds like Jed's back, Danny said. Glad we got a carryout. Or maybe it's no Jed at all; maybe it's our rodent friends.

I haven't met Jed yet.

He's a good guy, Jed. You'll like him. Danny was holding a cardboard twelve-pack of bottled beer in front of him. C'mon, for Christsake, Jules, I'm dyin for a pish.

I have it about my person somewhere, Julian said, and patted all his pockets again.

Fuck this for a game of sojers, Danny said. He stepped forward and rapped on the glass. It rattled in its frame. A pattern, engraved and frosted, of a bird among leaves was just visible beneath a layer of dirt, an echo of the stained glass on the window of the first landing. Amazing it had survived this long, she thought. An image of her mother with her crystal glass of whisky came into her mind. Sitting alone on the sofa, her bony feet pulled up beside her.

Jed, Danny shouted. Gonny let us in?

Ah, found it, Julian said, and put the key in the lock at the same moment as Jed's shadowy outline appeared on the other side of the glass.

Julian stumbled forward as Jed pulled open the door. Fuck, he said, and Jed stepped aside, leaving Julian to make a comical entrance, arms flailing, struggling to remain upright. Danny and Jed laughed and pointed. She wasn't sure she was up to this; it all seemed to need so much energy. Her body ached and another crying jag threatened like a bad weather front over the horizon.

Danny put the beer down on an old sideboard that stood, surrounded by fat black bin bags, in the square hall, and made straight for the bathroom.

Hi, Jed said. You must be Laetitia. He held out his hand. She shook it and said, Hi, Jed, pleased to meet you. For some reason she hadn't expected him to be Asian. He was taller than Danny, nearly as tall as Julian, and had a serious face. Or perhaps it was his glasses, heavy black frames round eyes that were equally black in the dim light of the hall. There was a scar over his left eye, pink against his dark skin.

He turned and made for the living room, stopped at the door and looked back at her. I imagine we have you to thank for this, eh, Laetitia? A woman's touch and all that? His accent was Glaswegian, but not as strong as Danny's, and with an extra element that was recognizably Asian, though she'd be hard pressed to put her finger on it.

No, actually. I was only the assistant. It was Danny who organized it. She wondered where Julian was and assumed he must have gone into their room.

Organized what? Danny said. He came out of the bathroom, shaking drips of water off his hands.

Well, in that case, Jed turned to Danny, what the fuck have you done with my uni notes? Maths and chemistry, two big folders?

It didn't take long to shift the remaining junk into a pile to one side of the room and find enough seats to sit on. She could see that Danny was itching to get at it again, finish the task. He kept glancing over at the heap, playing his beer bottle as if it had the stops of a clarinet. She tried to catch his eye, give him an encouraging smile, but he didn't appear to notice her.

There was a poster of Che Guevara on the wall now, a red one with the black iconic image. Jed must have put it up when they were out. And on the wall opposite the window, to the left of the door, was a huge poster with NO WAR! in bold black letters, and one of the DON'T ATTACK IRAQ ones on the other side.

She tuned back into the conversation. Julian was discussing the demo with Jed.

Fucking amazing, man, nearly a million marching. Should've been there.

Aye, well, I told you the problems I had getting into France in the summer. Fuckin four hours detained at *le douanier*'s pleasure before they let me through. Whole a Europe's fuckin paranoid about us dark-skinned brothers. If you're no a Suspected Terrorist, you're a Bogus Asylum Seeker, the new Bogeyman. Best you can hope for is economic migrant status and gettin snapped up by some capitalist bastard to do the jobs nay other cunt wants. Sweepin streets and shovellin shit. That no right, Danny?

What? Danny looked up. His eyes took a moment to focus, his brain to engage. He flicked his gaze from Jed to Julian to her.

Earth to Danny, come in please. Jed cupped his hands round his mouth and said the words small, as if from a long way off. A ventriloquist's trick. She watched Danny gather himself and sit forward, elbows resting on his knees, bottle held in front. His eyebrows lifted and let in the light.

Yo, brothers, he said. And sister. He tipped his bottle towards her, tilted it to his mouth and drank deep.

Aye, he said, it was a pretty white affair athegether. No much sign a the Gastarbeeters.

Biters, Julian said. Gastar-*biters*. *Arbeit Macht Frei* . . .

What?

. . . as they said in Auschwitz.

She tried to flash a warning to Julian, but he was oblivious. For a change, Danny didn't seem interested in rising to the bait.

Whatever, he said. Anyway, we gonny discuss it at the next meetin?

Yeah, it's on the agenda for Thursday. Though I expect most of the meeting will be taken up with planning the asylum seekers' protest in front of the Upturned Boat.

Upturned boat? She had a sudden image of a huddle of desperate people adrift on the ocean in a small boat.

One of our more affectionate names for the Scottish Parliament, Julian said.

Bunch a jumped-up councillors, Danny said.

Parcel a rogues, Jed said. By the way, I collected the leaflets. He eased himself forward in his seat and pulled a crumpled piece of paper from his back pocket, smoothed it on his knee and held it up.

GUANTANAMO
BELMARSH
DUNGAVEL

She couldn't see the small print immediately underneath, but the last line said, END SCOTLAND'S SHAME.

Cool, man, Julian said. And do we know if the Scottish Socialists are on board yet?

Aye, of course, Danny said. They'll probably be makin their ain protests.

She hadn't expected to find the politics quite so foreign here. The issues were the same, but the language was different, names and references unknown to her. She was at sea herself, she thought. *In a beautiful pea-green boat.*

What happened to the glass in the front door? She looked at each of them in turn. I've been meaning to ask.

Fascist bullet, Danny and Jed said in perfect unison. They laughed, half rose from their seats and high-fived.

Julian shrugged towards her. Told you.

Always the dream started the same: the drop of blood glistening on the fur, a red jewel; then the trickle of it, the steady drip onto the table. And, as she watched, eyes level with the carcass, the hole opened to a gash and the blood pulsed from it in dark red gouts.

She struggled awake and reached for Julian, who muttered, turned away, slept on. But it was a comfort to her that he knew the dream, had held her in a bony clinch the first time she woke with it in his bed; sent it up with a pseudo-Freudian analysis. Penis envy. Hysteria. Oedipus complex. Made her laugh at herself. Since then, she'd lain awake whenever it recurred and applied other theoretical frameworks to it. Feminist: male violence, a need to dominate, the *Wille zur Macht*; Socialist: rich man's sport, poor man's food; Religious: sacrificial animal, the rabbit of God; Animal Rights – well, that was too obvious.

But whatever she did, there was no avoiding it; the dream was always followed by the waking memory. The dead hare lying in a shaft of dusty sun on the old wooden trestle in the barn. Her mother's voice rising hysterically, saying, No, she would not – would *not* – skin and cook it. Laetitia couldn't place herself physically in the scene. Not at this moment. But she must have been there, because the memory of the drama unfolding was so clear. She had to have been there. Without effort, she could summon up the dimness of the barn, the dust pricking her nose, the musty smell tinged with the scent of apples, stored above on the wooden boards laid across the rafters. In the corner was the mountain of potatoes her father let her climb; she loved trying to pick her way to the top without starting a landslide. Avalanche! she'd shout, when they rolled away from under her, and her father would come running with mock alarm, tailed by Biddy, the golden retriever, her personal Mountain Rescue team.

But that was BH, before the hare. It was a place of enchantment then, her father's domain, with its liberal culture; a bolt hole from the tense watchfulness of her mother's regime, the strict rules, her constant infringement of them, however hard she tried.

Julian turned again to her, threw his arm across her shoulder, but she shrugged it off and lay on her back. There was no sound coming from the flat. Except that above she could hear the noise that was like footsteps. The mad woman in the attic. Somewhere nearby, music was playing, too faint to be recognizable, stripped down to a drumbeat and the occasional squealing riff of an electric guitar.

Two hares. Her father brought home two hares that day. Look, he said to her, bagged two beauties. And as always, he held open his canvas gamekeeper's bag to show her, so that as a child, she thought to bag game meant to put it in a bag. That particular canvas bag, with the brown leather straps and corners, the leather flap that fastened to a metal button. Through her childhood, he bagged rabbits, pheasants, pigeons, grouse, salmon. And hares. What have you bagged today, Daddy? she'd ask him, and pull at the canvas, Biddy's wet nose nudging her palm, till he bent down to show her. She'd stroke the soft grey breasts of wood pigeons, bury her fingers in the fur of rabbits, loosen the silver scales of salmon with sharp little nails.

The boards in the hall creaked. Danny or Jed going to the bathroom. Whoever it was left the door open. She listened to the stream that gushed into the toilet bowl, the fart that punctuated the last squeezed-out drips, the blind fumbling back to whichever bed.

Aunt Laetitia's diary was back in the pocket of her laptop

case, propped against the legs of the blue chair at her side of the bed. She leant out over the side and patted the case in the dark; she wouldn't lose sight of the diary again. When she lay back, her hand went automatically to the two keys on the chain round her neck. They were warm from lying next her skin, nestled between her breasts; she would guard them like a chatelaine from here on. Her fingers smelt of metal now.

The day he brought the hares home, she worked at the stiff strap till her small fingers prised the metal button back through the slit in the leather. Well done, old girl, he said to her. Newly six, it gave her a thrill that he should call her 'old'. He lifted the canvas flap, and there they were. She stroked the soft fur on the belly of the one on top, wriggled her fingers deeper to the one underneath, in case it should feel left out.

Her mother appeared in the doorway, casting a dark shadow on the yellow sun, spread like butter on the floor of the barn. From that moment, she could see only the two of them leaning towards each other, and one hare limp and bleeding on the table. She herself was gone from the scene except as a pair of eyes, two ears. Her parents shouted into the space between them, words she couldn't understand, couldn't now remember, as she watched their faces change. Her mother was white; little flecks of spittle flew from her mouth, sparked for a moment in the beam of light, and disappeared. Her father grew red, the tendons on his neck raised, a wormy vein pulsing at his temple. She had never seen either of them like that before.

And I will not – I will *never* – sully my hands on your *kill*. It was the word 'kill' that nailed it for her. In the end it was the word. Until then, she had no idea it was what her father did. She knew he took the gun, barrel hung at the crook of his elbow; she knew he shot the animals, the birds; she kind of knew they were dead when she fondled them in the bag. But it was her mother who pulled all the strands together, fixed them in her mind with the glinting needle of that word. It was her mother who ensured that the crack of gunfire in the woods, from that day on, would summon up her father, red-faced; the running, frantic animal stilled for good.

Jed was up, she discovered, when she could lie in bed no longer; it was Jed who was moving about in the kitchen, boiling the kettle, clattering dishes.

Hi, there.

His eyes were startled when he turned to her. Without his glasses his ears were more noticeable somehow; they had long lobes that curved out at the bottom like the god Shiva's, or those on statues of the Buddha. He seemed to take a moment to remember who she was. She wished she'd put on her jeans as well as her old black cardigan, pulled down to the knee on one side by the weight of her aunt's diary in the pocket.

Oh, Laetitia. You gave me a fright there. There's never usually anybody else up when I'm getting ready for my work.

What is it you do?

Och, I'm workin in a call centre the now. Till a real job comes along.

What will the real job be?

He poured boiling water into one of Danny's new mugs, held the kettle up and raised his eyebrows in a question. The pink scar above his eye contracted, half disappeared in the folds of his forehead.

Yes, please. Tea, strong, no milk. Unless you do espresso?

Sorry, no can do. Café on the corner does a good one, though. He glanced at her bare legs. Maybe later, eh?

She felt her face go red. Tea's fine, thanks.

He filled another mug, handed it to her. Aye, a *real* job would be scientific research. I'm a biochemist.

Don't you find the call centre terribly boring?

Too right. Stressful as well. So far I've managed to avoid gettin the old heave-ho. Unlike Danny boy.

Oh, yes. I remember. He said.

Aye, Danny tried to organize the workforce to complain to the management about working conditions.

Didn't you agree with him?

There's nay point, he shrugged. I put my energies into the larger struggle. He opened his arms wide and some tea slopped out of his mug onto the cuff of his white shirt. Shit, he said. Clean on the day. He set down the mug and rubbed ineffectually at the tan-coloured stain. Shit. No, when I get bored, I wait till the supervisor's out of range and I have myself some fun with the customers. I kid on I'm phonin fae Mumbai. *Vhy you are treating me this vay? I have sick mother, vaiting for hospital; she is needing very badly heart operation. Vhy you are putting phone down on me?* His expression was a tragic mask. Pure Bollywood.

She laughed.

That gets tay some a they middle-class bastards. The wankers that object to cold-calling. One even offered to send me money for the operation. Ease their liberal conscience. I would a took it too, if I could a come up with an address in Mumbai she could've sent it to.

Aren't your calls monitored?

Oh, aye. That's what gives the game its edge. That wee extra *frisson*. His eyebrows came together and his face assumed another mask, fear this time. It's a kinda Russian roulette. One in five calls they listen in to.

He glanced at his watch, rubbed again at his cuff. Well, gotta love you and leave you. He unhooked a black suede jacket she hadn't noticed from the back of the kitchen door, pulled it on and turned to her before he went out.

And you never know. This could be my lucky day. A hand snaked magician-like into his jacket pocket, flourished his glasses, set them on his face with an authoritative finger. *Come and see me in my office. At once, Mr Singh, if you will.* He slapped the worktop on his way out. *P45, ya cunt ye!*

And he was gone. Would she ever come to terms with the way they used *cunt*, these boys? The flat door banged shut and she listened to the diminishing clatter of Jed's footsteps echo up the stairwell. Her eyes flicked round the kitchen. It was pretty small. A row of fake marble worktops, a cooker, fridge and sink. Not much room for anything else. At least it was clean now after Danny's exertions, and didn't smell too bad. Other than sneaking into Jed's room, while he was at work, this was the only place in the flat she would be able to spend time alone. Apart from the bathroom, that is. Which did have the advantage of a lock.

The high wooden stool at the end of the worktop looked as if it had been liberated from a pub at some time; it was darkly varnished with machine-turned legs, its edges scarred deep with notches and nicks to make it look old. Distressed. Know how you feel, she thought, and patted it. She tugged her cardigan down over the back of her thighs, perched on the seat, and pulled the diary out of her pocket. It was still a bit curved but not as badly as before. Nothing a few days under a heavy dictionary wouldn't cure.

The cover was warm and supple and the crimson endpapers exposed themselves shockingly as soon as she opened it. Rather than look for the page Julian had chanced upon, she was determined to read the entries chronologically, piece together some kind of narrative of Aunt Laetitia's stay in Italy. Although, if she did march for women's suffrage, it must have been before her Italian trip, before the First World War. All that stopped then, didn't it? And women got the vote at the end of the war. So that entry must have been recalling an earlier period in her life. She turned over Harry's dedication, scanned the beginning of Laetitia's script. And the next sheet and the next. A long disjointed meditation in those first few pages of the newly stitched notebook on the art and architecture of Firenze. Artists like Michelangelo, Donatello, Raphael, Titian, Tintoretto; words such as *eloquence, grandeur, exquisite, awe-inspiring*; no more than appreciative jottings that might be written up at a later date in some other form.

Three sides of this, then, near the spine, the ragged edge of a page torn out. Two pages. She parted them with her nails to make sure. Yes, two. Followed by another few intact pages in similar vein, waxing lyrical about the art and sculpture. Then the trip to Fiesole with a young man called Myron; luncheon on a long shady terrace, looking down on a hillside thick with trees just coming into leaf, *a rather good Prosecco, as fresh on the palate as many a more expensive Champagne.*

And towards the bottom of the page, this: *I do wish Harry would shake off her new-found truculence. It makes it so much more awkward in company to carry off our deception . . .*

She jumped off the stool, walked to the sink. Back again. Her. Her.

. . . which she accepts as necessary, tiresome though it un-doubtedly is.

She. *She* accepts. And that was it. Two sentences then back to: *On the drive down into Florence, the Tuscan countryside was aglow with a light so golden and a sky of such luminous, cerulean blue, that the whole scene might have come directly from a painting of the Italian Renaissance! Our new friend, Myron, was oblivious, but I was gratified to see that Harry seemed somewhat mollified by its beauty.*

Our deception. What deception? Harry was a woman. Dressed as a man? Masquerading as Laetitia's husband, lover? Why? A picture formed in her mind of Laetitia in a wide-brimmed hat held on with a silk scarf, beside Harry, short hair slicked back, fake pencil moustache, in an open-topped automobile, hurtling down the winding roads towards Florence in the spring sun.

Coffee. She needed coffee. There were two soft depressions on facing pages of the diary where her thumbs had gripped it tight. Under one, the letters were newly smudged. Damn! A smear of brown ink on her skin revealed the whorls of her thumbprint.

What's the problem? Danny was at the door, a bag of rubbish in each hand, his dark hair standing on end.

Oh! I didn't hear you get up. She slipped the diary into her cardigan pocket and kept her thumb between the pages she'd just read. As though the passage might disappear, as though it were written in ink that might vanish on exposure to the air.

Quiet as a mouse, that's me. Talking of which, have you seen any a they wee sleekit, cowrin, timrous bastards? He glanced around the kitchen.

What?

Mice. Meeces. What do yous call them in England?

Very funny. No, I haven't. Perhaps they've gone.

Well, paps they have. Let's hope so.

I'm not particularly bothered by them. I rather like mice.

I'm no tickly bothered either. I just prefer it if they don't go to the dancin in my fryin pan.

Are you taking the piss?

Would I do such a thing? He winked, gave one of his winning smiles and made for the door of the flat with the full bin bags bumping and clanking against his legs.

Danny?

Aye? He stopped at the open door, his voice amplified in the echo chamber of the stairwell.

Do you know where this café is that Julian and Jed talk about?

No really. Never been in it. On the corner, they says. Canny be hard to find but, just follow your nose. The words came back to her loud and stagey, then his footsteps, the same percussive diminuendo as Jed's earlier, with an additional swishing noise as a bin bag brushed the wall on the descent. Sounded like the heroine of a black-and-white movie, she thought, sweeping down the staircase in a long silk gown, petticoats rustling. She'd have to remember to tell him that. Why wasn't Julian awake yet?

Silvio's was as good as advertised. Well, the coffee was. The café was small with only about eight tables covered in bright cloths. She could see them through the glass of the door. Yellow, orange, apricot; antidotes to a dingy November day. A bell jingled to advertise her entrance, and the smell of fresh coffee picked her up and set her down at a sunny pavement café in Italy. Once she was inside, the mood was more sombre, despite nasturtiums, so vibrant they had to be artificial, dangled from the ceiling in rustic baskets. Could hardly be real at this time of year, of course. Chrysanthemums it would have to be, *such serviceable flowers*. There were only two customers apart from her: a girl about her own age, at a single table in the corner, frowning, her face lit up blue by a laptop screen; the other, a guy reading a newspaper, taking up two tables to spread it out. The table near the counter seemed the best option, furthest away from the other two, beside a glass cabinet of the day's scones and pastries, homely on yellow gingham.

She was onto her second espresso when he came in. A

silhouette in the grey light of the door, face in shadow, his shaved skull and tall wiry form, the slight stoop, unmistakable. He scanned the interior for her, seemed to miss her until she lifted her hand towards him. When he'd spotted her, he went to the counter, did her a little cup-holding, drinking mime with eyebrows raised, as he fished in his back pocket for money. She shook her head. Truth was she was feeling nauseous again after only one and a half shots of coffee. Perhaps she'd have to give it up as well as tobacco, though she couldn't imagine functioning without the caffeine kick. Her Prozac. She'd forgotten to take it this morning. And yesterday, come to that. She fumbled quickly in her rucksack, pressed a capsule out of its foil in the dark interior of the bag and swallowed it with a mouthful of coffee, just before Julian reached the table.

What's that? he said.

Paracetamol. Got a bit of a headache.

No doubt caused by that strong coffee you drink. He switched on his paterfamilias voice, deep, authoritative.

You sound like my mother.

Oh, heaven forfend! He put his mug of coffee on the table and made the sign of the cross, as he clattered his chair back to sit down. The man with the newspaper raised his eyes and scowled at them; Julian always attracted the wrong sort of attention. He ignored the guy and looked at her a little oddly.

You alright, Tish?

Fine. Why?

You seem a bit . . . I dunno . . . out of sorts.

Do I? No, a little tired I suppose. You know, I've just discovered something amazing. She made an effort to brighten her voice, convey more enthusiasm than she felt. Harry is a woman.

Julian's face was blank. Harry Who is a woman?

Aunt Laetitia's Harry. In her diary. Look. Here. She fished in her bag for the journal. I thought he was a he. A male lover, a man friend. Or a husband. But it turns out Harry is a woman.

Your great-great whatever aunt had a lesbian relationship with a woman called Harry? In 1915? During World War One? How cool is that!

Oh, I don't know if they were lovers. But they were travelling together and one entry refers to their *deception*. She had marked the page with a postcard of the Palazzo della Signoria, bought in Florence for her father but never sent. It seemed appropriate for Aunt Laetitia's narrative. She turned to the page, fretted once more over the smudge, smoothing it with her fingers as if that might restore it. Here. See?

Julian twisted his head round and read out loud. *I do wish Harry would shake off her new-found truculence. It makes it so much more awkward in company to carry off our deception, which she accepts as necessary, tiresome though it undoubtedly is.*

He lifted his eyes to her. So Harry and Harriet are one and the same? She and old Titty march together for the vote, then fuck off to swan about Italy, while our boys are dying in rat-infested trenches. Very fine.

She felt her stomach clench in denial. Julian, need I point out that you're farting about producing the odd bon mot on Henry Miller, while millions starve. What's the difference?

Only teasing.

Well, don't.

Sorry. No more. I promise. He made his eyes look serious, but she could see the corners of his mouth twitch.

Julian!

Sorry. This is important to you, isn't it?

Yes. Yes it is.

Why?

I don't know. She's my father's aunt, I've only just dis-covered her existence and . . . and she's got *my* name. I don't know. It sounded lame. Pathetic. Even to her own ears. But Julian appeared to take it on board this time. He reached across the table for her hand, lifted each finger in turn and bent down to kiss them.

How nice to see two young people in love.

They both turned. A man she hadn't noticed come in was sitting at the next table. Bald on top, with a trim hedge of silver like imperial Caesar, his head was tilted back and he peered through thick glasses, beaming at them. Or she as-sumed he peered. The way the light fell on the lenses, his eyes were completely obliterated, giving him the air of a madman.

It always cheers me, he said, to see young people doing what comes naturally. Orotund was the word that sprang to mind. His voice was orotund, the words carefully enunciated, Scottish but not Glaswegian. No glottal stops. It gave him a peculiarly authoritative tone, like the presenter of a current affairs programme. A contrast to his lunatic gleam.

Fanks, mate. For some reason, Julian decided to affect a cockney accent.

You're not from round here. I can tell by the way you speak.

Can you really, me old fruit? He was going for a music-hall version of an East End barrow boy. She dug her nails into the palm of his hand.

No, you sound rather as if you hail from south of the border.

Down Mexico way?

Pardon?

Nev mind. You're right, mate. We come from good old England. God save the Queen.

Indeed. He lifted his cup. To Her Majesty. May she reign over us many more years.

Er Majesty! Julian raised his cup too. A game old bird, wotever anybody says. May she fall off er orse and flatten er corgis.

The man stopped smiling and levelled his gaze at Julian. She could see his eyes now. He looked less mad and more alarming.

I hope you appreciate, young man, what it is to live in a country where it is possible to say such things and not be taken out and shot.

Of course. I'm ever so umbly grateful. Julian fumbled at the front of his head. I would tug me forelock if I ad any air, but they shaved me ead when I spent time in the Scrubs at Er Majesty's pleasure.

Oh well, I can see why that would make you bitter. But of course it's not the Queen's fault. A fine young chap like you must realize that.

She watched the play of a familiar dilemma pass across Julian's face. *Shall I raise the stakes, wind the silly old buzzard up even more? Or am I already bored?* She held her breath. At one time it had thrilled her, this flair, this bravura, his ability to eviscerate slowly the more asinine views of an unwitting adversary. But lately she hadn't the stomach for it. Perhaps he read this in her expression, because he turned to the old man and said, No. No hard feelings. He stood up and held out his hand. A pleasure to make your acquaintance.

The man smiled, delighted, raised his eyes to be blanked out again by the light, took the outstretched hand in both of his. Likewise, young man, likewise. If he thought it was odd that the cockney had switched to Received Pronunciation, he showed no sign of it.

Without a word, Julian lifted her coat from the back of her chair, draped it over her shoulders, head cocked on one side, a silly smile on his face, and pulled her to her feet.

Come, darling, we must go.

She thrust the diary into her bag and followed him out. A backward glance through the glass of the jangling door, caught the old man craning in his seat, beaming after them.

Danny had been hard at work. All the bin bags were gone from the hall and some semblance of order imposed. His whistle from the living room was underlaid by a peculiar squeaking noise.

Hi, there, she said. He was at the window, his back to her, rubbing the window pane in circles with what looked like scrunched-up newspaper. It squeaked and squealed over the glass.

Hi, he said, without turning round. Just finishin the windies. His voice was distorted by the vigorous windmilling of his arm.

I thought you'd found your nest of mice. All this squeaking.

That made him turn and smile at her. Nah, they're away their holidays; I seen them wae their wee suitcases earlier, headin off tay clattier climes. His hands were black with newsprint.

So they'll be back?

No if I can help it. What d'you think? He threw the ball of newspaper in the air and batted it at the window. Just then the sun came out and filled the room with light.

Crikey! How did you do that? That's the first time I've seen the sun in Glasgow.

Danny shrugged modestly. Just one of my many talents. Explain it we cannot, believe it we must.

She glanced round the room. It actually looked habitable. You've even done the Sweeping and Dusting and Washing of floors!

He grinned.

Six rhomboids of sunlight lay on the wall opposite the

fireplace, illuminating half of a NOT IN MY NAME! poster, and a black-and-white Bob Marley in full swing, dreadlocks flailing.

There's a fireplace! An ornate carved wooden mantel surrounded a cast-iron Victorian grate. On either side, a vertical row of tiles depicted a bird among leaves, a red berry in its beak. It's that bird from the, from the, from the . . .

Aye, fae the landin windie.

She realized he was laughing at her, standing there with her finger pointed and her mouth hanging open. And the door, she said.

What door?

The front door of the flat.

Is that right? I havny clocked that yet. Did Julian get you, by the way?

Yes. He's gone to the university now to explain to his supervisor why he hasn't produced any words for his PhD for the past three months.

Man, I don't know how yous can be bothered. Four years at university, then another five or six studyin some deid writer.

Three years at university.

What?

In England we do three. *Then* five or six studying a dead writer.

Aye well, whatever. What's it got to do with the price of mince? How's it gonny add to the sum of human happiness?

Good question. Have you never thought of going to university?

Nah. Didny stick in at school. Too busy runnin about the scheme wae my pals, gettin into scrapes. Nay Highers, two poxy Standard Grades. My da went mental the day the results came out, did his Big Red Clydesider. Danny straightened his back, jabbed a finger into the sunny room and shouted: *Apart fae revolution, it's education that's gonny liberate the masses! There's nay room for a stumer in the struggle.* He turned and smiled at her. So that was me.

You don't really get on with your father, do you?

How did you guess?

With me it's my mother. She looked at the sun slanting into the room and remembered her mother at Wellwood, sitting by the window in the morning room, writing letters, her dark hair tied back, sunlight streaming over her pale hands on the table, making them seem translucent. She found herself blinking in the brightness and turned back to Danny.

Anyway, you've done a *brilliant* job in here.

He looked at her sceptically. Aye, right.

No, truly, it's . . . Somehow she sensed too much praise would wound him. You've made it . . . almost habitable.

He laughed. Aye, home fae home. Bit of a comedown for you but. You no live in a mansion at one time?

Not quite! Wellwood wasn't *that* big. Anyway, I moved when I was eleven. Unlike my mother, who still lives there in her mind fourteen years after the event. Da— My father calls it Wormwood now.

You still miss it?

This felt like dangerous ground. I miss my father. He left and they sold Wellwood and my mother and I came to live in London. She tried to give it an *end-of-story* inflection in the hope Danny wouldn't pursue it. He didn't.

Instead he walked to the window and scraped at a dried-on splash of something with his thumbnail, rubbed the spot with his sleeve. I still miss the house I grew up in, he said. When Clare was eight months old, we moved out of the high flats to a bigger house, a four apartment in a tenement. I was nine. All my happiest memories are fae our first house.

What's a four apartment?

It's what they call a council flat wae three bedrooms and a livin room. He looked at her a little longer than was comfortable, switched his gaze abruptly and said, But here we are, comrade, standin about and me wi a hot date at the Job Centre. Canny wait. He pounced on the fallen ball of newspaper, kicked it through the doorway into the hall. Oh, ho! Postage stamp! Ya dancer!

It was a relief when Danny went out and she had the place to herself. Quiet. The coming and going of traffic and the odd shout from the street below were like natural phenomena, the sea beneath the hotel balcony on childhood holidays. She had a choice of where to go now. She could sit at Julian's desk at the window overlooking the drying green, the – what did Danny call it? – back court. Or she could stay here in the living room, pull a chair up to the bright bay window and watch life go by below. The seating in the room fell into two categories: saggy armchair in brown cord with scuffed arms and threadbare cushion – times two. Or straight-backed dining chair, its wood scratched, the seat in green velvet with the nap worn off – times three. Where was the fourth, she wondered. And there was the sofa bed, scarlet, aglow in the sunlight, a newer piece of furniture, with Danny's sleeping bag draped across the back. She dragged one of the upright chairs to the side of the window and took both diaries out of her bag, the black hardcover notebook she'd bought in Cambridge and Aunt Laetitia's hand-sewn work of art. It was hers she ought to be writing, but it was her great-aunt's life that intrigued her now. Her own seemed in abeyance, too indistinct to get a handle on. She set her journal on the floor beside the chair and picked up her great-great-aunt's.

The postcard had worked its way loose or else she'd forgotten to insert it again before Julian had hustled her from the café, but the book opened anyway at the page where Aunt L. revealed her irritation with Harry. Deception, deception. What could that be? Harry in drag? Was that really feasible? What else was possible?

A flock of pigeons flew onto the roof above the window, scattering light from their wings into the room. Down in the street, buses crawled towards the junction, the pedestrian crossing beep-beeped and a yellow car did a U-turn, heading back towards the city centre. It was quite like some parts of London really, this little bit of Glasgow. At street level, anyway, the shops: the Asian grocers; the African Caribbean fruit seller with his aubergines, mangoes and sweet potatoes spilling out onto the pavement; the café; the Italian restaurants; a little like Beechfield Road, a few streets away from Mother. But this road was broader. And through the newly translucent window she could see two church spires, one of them slender, elegant, touched gold by the low November sun.

She turned back to the diary in her lap. The depressions made earlier by her thumbs were still there and the edge of the right-hand page seemed to have fused to the one after; she had to ease them apart with the nail of her little finger. On the next page, Laetitia's large looping hand looked slightly different; it had a headlong quality, as if written with excitement at great speed.

15th of April 1915
Today in la Galleria degli Uffizi
we saw a painting of Judith
beheading Holofernes. As soon
as my eyes lit upon it, I knew:

a woman has painted this! And so
it proved. The painter's name was
Artemisia Gentileschi. Her subjects,
Judith and her maidservant,
working together to part
Holofernes from his head,

She turned the page.

while his life's blood gushed and
bespattered their dresses, were so
muscular and alive to each other,
it was clear no man could have
conceived the vision. Why was the
existence of this marvellous artist
hitherto unknown to me? Harry was
dreadfully sour, refused to share my
delight, uttered only five words
together: The maid-servant's name
is Abra. I do wonder . . .

The next page was torn out. Its ragged edge revealed only
parts of letters, tails, a dot, something that looked like the
beginning of a 'b', or could have been an 'h'. Damn! Damn,
bugger and damn! *I do wonder* – what? What was she trying to
hide? Assuming it *was* Laetitia who tore out the pages. Perhaps
it was Harry. Or someone in the family. She reached inside
her jumper for the two keys, pulled them absently on their
chain from side to side.

An account of a search for more paintings by Artemisia
Gentileschi for the next two pages. Then the one Julian must
have seen.

In a painting by a little-known artist
I saw today in the Pitti Palace, the
robes of a bystander at some spectacle
were the very shades of purple and green
we once wore so proudly. It is not yet two
years, though it seems like decades
since we marched, Harriet and I, with the
WSPU, on our pilgrimage to Hyde Park,
resplendent in satin sashes, bearing the
beautiful banner H. had sewn for us, the
voices of women raised freely around us,
singing and laughing and calling for
justice. Oh, how I wish we could reclaim
the innocent fervour we shared throughout
those heady days!

She remembered something: the fob. The medallion attached to the key ring. It ought still to be there. She raked in her bag, unzipped her purse. There it was, the size of a fifty-pence piece, its enamelling largely rubbed off, little scuffed fragments only remaining of white and green and purple towards the edge. And around the perimeter, the inscription: WOMEN'S SOCIAL AND POLITICAL UNION 1903. So, Laetitia and Harry, a.k.a. Harriet, a.k.a. H. were members of the WSPU and worked together for the cause of women's suffrage. What could have happened? Sometime during their trip to Florence, their friendship soured. But why?

There were footsteps on the stair, someone at the door. The letterbox clattered and she heard the sound of mail falling onto the wooden boards of the hall, the footsteps retreating, the outside door banging shut. While she'd been reading, the sun had gone in again and the room had reverted to dingy. Dingy, but at least no longer grungy. She crossed it and looked at the mail lying inside the front door: three letters in white envelopes, a couple of items of junk mail. She went to pick them up. One piece of junk mail was for Julian, the other for Malcolm Finnerty. Malcolm X, presumably. All three bona fide letters were addressed to Arjun Singh. Jed? How did he get from Arjun to Jed? She laid them on the sideboard inside the front door.

She was restless. Glasgow was still a closed book to her. Julian ought to have been back by now, as he'd promised. The morning was gone. *She* ought to be getting on with Virginia Woolf as she'd said. Her new laptop hadn't been out of its case, and she had written not one single word since she was last in Cambridge, before heading off for Florence and the demo. At the moment, Great-aunt Laetitia interested her more than Virginia Woolf and Gertrude Stein. Laetitia and the shape-shifting Harry, who had now appeared to her in several guises: soldier, poet, war correspondent, husband, moustachi-oed transvestite, lesbian lover, seamstress, ardent suffragette. And a woman who would not participate in her friend's enthusiasm for art. Perhaps the letters still in the trunk in London would offer more clues. Perhaps. She clutched the keys on their chain round her neck. If she hadn't brought them, Mother could have unlocked the trunk and sent the letters on. Except she didn't want her to know that she wasn't in Cambridge.

Not that she'd mind terribly; not if she knew her daughter was with Julian Legrozet, who, even with dreadlocks and *unfortunate political views*, came from the proper background.

Tea. *A nice cup of tea*, as they said in Mother's circles. She went to the kitchen and filled the kettle, took the cherry mug from the drainer. The water was almost boiled when she heard someone knock at the door. Julian. He'd given her his key.

Coming, she shouted. At first she couldn't see anyone

through the glass, but that was because it was someone much shorter than Julian. She turned the Yale latch and opened the door.

Clare!

Is Danny here? He asked us to bring some claes for him. She held up a dark blue holdall. I didn't know you were gonny be here. Danny never told me.

Aren't you supposed to be at school?

And I thought he might like this CD player. I couldny carry his whole stereo. She thrust a portable CD player towards her. Her appearance was rather different from the way it seemed in Florence; she was much more an ordinary schoolgirl today, on an ordinary Monday. Danny's little sister, her red hair tied back in a single plait, lying coiled in the fur-trimmed hood of her white coat.

She realized she was looking through a narrow space between the door and its frame, like an old lady trying to keep out bogus workmen. The thought embarrassed her and she opened the door wide to Clare. Won't you come in?

When's Danny comin back? The girl made no move, but kept her big eyes on Laetitia's face. Defiant.

I don't know, she said. He went out about an hour ago. It was funny, she picked up a definite hard gleam at the core of Clare's demeanour, in the set of her mouth, the tilt of her chin, a little nugget of determination to stand up to this bossy cow. An Elizabeth Bennet moment: *My courage always rises with every attempt to intimidate me.* It was odd, this realization that she could be seen as threatening, given how much of a wuss she'd been lately. I don't imagine he'll be that long, though.

Well . . . maybe I will wait then if . . . She tailed off, the *if it's OK* left unsaid, the defiance hard to sustain.

Yes, it's fine. Come in. She turned towards the living room, leaving Clare to shut the door and follow. You can put Danny's stuff in here; this is where he's sleeping.

Clare set the bag and the CD player on the floor beside the red sofa and looked around. Her eyes rested on the Bob Marley poster, then darted away. Laetitia could see the flush rise pink over her face.

I'm making a cup of tea, she said. Would you like one?

No, you're alright.

Well, I need one. Have a seat. It seemed impossible to avoid a school mistressy tone; the girl invited it.

Clare perched on the edge of the sofa, while she made for the kitchen. Why had she asked her in? She'd been caught off balance. Worse, Julian should be back any time, now. The last thing she wanted was a repeat of the scene in the *pensione*. She reboiled the kettle, poured water over the teabag, carried the mug back through and sat on one of the brown armchairs.

I tried him on his mobile, but it's switched off.

Who? Danny?

Aye. He doesny want to speak to my ma. She's dead worried about him. He left a message on her mobile when he knew she would be at her work and it wouldny be on. He said, Stayin wae Jed. That was all. My ma's up to high doh. Clare turned big worried eyes on her, two spots of pink on her cheeks. This was as animated as she'd been so far. She clearly took her role as family intermediary seriously.

Danny's fine. You can tell your mother. He's already organized Jed and . . . he's made a big difference to this place, I can tell you. It struck her as oddly touching that his mother should be worrying about him. If she was. What happened to drive him out? she asked.

Clare wriggled in her seat. Against the red of the sofa, she was the little white girl again. She spoke hesitantly. Him and my da . . . they had a big fight on Thursday. My da didny hit him or nothin, don't get me wrong, but he was shoutin and bawlin. Callin Danny for everythin. He doesny mean it, my da. No really. It's like . . . He just . . . He's like . . .

It looked to Laetitia as if the girl was ready to cry and she wasn't sure she could cope with that. Reassurance seemed called for. She warmed her hands round her mug. Danny shouldn't be that long, she said. I think he was going job hunting – I'm not sure. Wouldn't you rather take your coat off while you wait?

Whatever hard edge Clare had had at the door, she'd lost it now. She did as she was told, unzipped and shrugged the coat off her shoulders. Underneath, she wore a white blouse and a black skirt, knee-length black socks, sensible shoes. No doubt her school tie was in her pocket. Her plait hung fat and red down her back.

And on Thursday night, Danny ran out and naybody knew where he'd went. He didny come here that night. Or the next. And we didny hear nothin from him.

Doesn't he have other friends?

Aye, we checked wi all the ones we could think of but and he wasny there. My ma was goin mental. She got my aunt Patsy to come up fae Helensburgh and drive her round the streets a Glasgow lookin for him. She even phoned the hospitals, the A&E departments, in case he'd landed up there.

Why was your mother so worried? Danny's pretty capable of looking after himself, I should have thought.

Clare gave her a look she couldn't quite read, but she had a sense it accused her of being obtuse. There was heat in her little Glasgow voice when she spoke again.

You don't know what it's like in the scheme. Two a Danny's pals fae school have topped theirsels this year already. And another yin tried last month. I know my da's worried about that too, even if he kids on he's no.

Topped themselves. There was nothing she could say to that. A circle of light wobbling on the ceiling was the reflection of her tea. She studied the strong black liquid in the mug, looked out the window. The pigeons were on the roof across the road again, perched in grey serried ranks. Perhaps it was they who made the sound of footsteps overhead at night. A glance at Clare told her she was struggling to contain herself. Danny's fine, Clare. Really. He'll be back soon.

Clare stared at her feet, didn't answer.

Of course, it would have to be Julian who came back first. She let him in and tried to signal to him that Clare was there, as he launched straight into a tirade against his *fucking stupid supervisor*. But subtlety wasn't his strong point.

Julian, Clare's here, she said finally, overloud, and jerked a thumb back towards the living room. He looked startled for a moment, a little flustered. But only a moment.

Oh, right, good, he said, pitching his voice to the same volume as her own. Come to see her big brother, has she?

Her mum is worried about Danny, she said, shrugging her shoulders and making a *don't ask me* face to Julian as they reached the door of the living room.

Hi, Clare, he said. He flung himself down in the brown armchair. She'd put her coat back on and had it wrapped close across her middle with folded arms.

Hi, she said. She gave him the merest glance.

Fuck me, this place has been transformed! His voice was forced and jolly, though Clare probably wouldn't notice; he was avoiding looking at her altogether.

Yes. It was Danny, she said. He's worked wonders. I told you, didn't I, Clare, that he was sorting Jed and Julian out?

Oh, I wouldn't say that.

The place was a tip, Julian! A pigsty! Totally uninhabitable.

203

She was jolly too. She felt very English suddenly. This was a game of Punch and Judy for Clare's benefit.

And Clare was watching them now, less self-conscious, frankly interested. You mean Danny's been doin housework? He never does any at hame. Even her voice was pitched to cheery. As if she'd already sussed out the game and was now making her play. My ma calls him Dirty Dan. She smiled, looked from Julian to her.

Julian smiled back. She waited for the smart remark, the subtle putdown, but it didn't come. Not at first. Well, he's a regular Mrs Mop here, isn't he, Tish? he said finally and glanced at her.

If it weren't for Danny, I'd have been out of here, I can tell you. The words were hanging in the air before she realized, but she continued in the same heightened tone. He simply got down to it and transformed the place.

Well, jolly hockey sticks! Julian said, and sat forward in the sagging chair.

Clare was glancing from Julian to her with those great eyes.

Your brother, the magician, he said. The Worker of Wonders. He was looking straight at Clare now as her eyes darted about for some means of escape from the headlight dazzle of his gaze. It struck her that their eyes were similar: big and blue, though Clare's were darker, closer to grey. And she hadn't yet learnt to use them the way Julian did, as weapons in the various skirmishes of life. She ought really to have had Danny's green eyes, though, to go with her red hair.

Well, you've got to admit it, Julian, you and Jed *had* rather let it get out of hand. This was not a role she relished but she felt somehow squeezed into it, scolding the boys for their mess, an ally suddenly of Clare's mother.

She heard the footsteps on the stairs for some time before

registering them, then a key turned in the lock and Danny was in the hall, whistling again.

The man himself, Julian said, and got up from the chair. There was something oddly middle-aged about the move, as if in the presence of Clare, they'd automatically become the older generation.

Danny came straight in, holding some keys, yellow and silver, in the palm of his hand. Got a couple of sets of keys cut, he said and stopped. Clare? Is everything OK? You alright?

Aye, I'm fine. She stood now too, her arms hanging at her sides, though she looked as though she'd like to fling them round her brother. My ma's dead worried but. I brung you some claes like you says. And a CD player. She pointed to the bag and machine on the floor.

Well, here we all are again, Julian said, clapped his hands once and rubbed them together. Isn't this spiffing?

And here . . . Clare reached into the pocket of her coat. Here's your birthday present. It was obviously a CD, though it was wrapped in pale green paper with a squashed rosette of emerald ribbon on the front.

Aye, thanks, Clare. Danny took the gift from her. He seemed ill at ease. Almost bashful. He turned it over a few times in his hand, studied it.

No gonny open it?

Aye, I will. In a minute. Just gies a chance. He looked from the present to the keys in his other hand. Oh, before I forget, here's a set for you, Laetitia. Jed left us his and I got another couple cut. One for you and one for me.

Well, don't you just think of everything? Julian said. The forced jollity had a sharper edge now. She read the signs and they spelt Danger.

Thanks, Danny, she said, and would have slipped them into

the back pocket of her jeans, but she looked at Julian and thought better of it. Aren't you going to open Clare's present? The two of them looked at her blankly. Well, I'll leave you both to it, she said to them. I'm off to our room. She hadn't meant to emphasize the *our* quite so much. Julian didn't follow when she made for the door.

She was halfway across the hall when she remembered Aunt Laetitia's diary and hurried back. It was on the chair by the window. Forgot this, she said, waving it into the room. It was as if she were in some dreadful stage drama, miscast in a role she didn't know how to play. But the attention of everyone was elsewhere. Julian was sticking down the edge of a STOP THE WAR poster, concentrating overmuch, she thought.

Danny had the paper off his present now and held the CD up to look at it. Snow Patrol? he said. Never heard a them.

You will. They're great. I seen them at King Tut's a couple a months ago wae my pal Farkhanda. Clare put a finger on the back of the plastic casing. That's a crackin song. They're an Irish band. I think you'll like them.

Laetitia took a last look at the tableau of characters in their different poses, and slipped out of the room again, unnoticed.

She stayed in the bedroom for the rest of the afternoon. There were various comings and goings. Julian went out without saying goodbye to her. Danny and Clare were in the kitchen at one point, rattling dishes. She tried to get back into her aunt's looping handwriting, but it was hard to concentrate. More art galleries; more descriptions of paintings. There were some children playing out in the drying area, though it was already dark by three o'clock. Two of them, a girl of about eight and a younger boy, got involved in a scuffle over a silver scooter. It glinted in the available light as they pulled its handlebars this way and that. The girl won the contest and the boy went howling towards one of the other back doors. It banged shut behind him and cut him off mid-shriek. At about half-past four she heard the door of the flat again and Jed's voice joined Danny and Clare's. Still no Julian.

To hell with this!

The three of them were in the living room when she came through. Clare was on her feet, zipping up her coat. She'd loosened her plait; her hair spread now over the white hood, a dark red cloud, as if it had been rendered in pastel crayon, smudged at the edges.

Hi, Laetitia, Jed said. Did you get your espresso this mornin? He had his black suede jacket, hooked on one finger, slung over his shoulder; one corner of his white shirt was hanging down the front of his jeans.

Yes, thanks, she said. Two, actually. It's a good little café, that. Great coffee.

Clare's just away, Danny said. He turned to his sister. Mind an tell Ma I'm fine. Everythin's hunky-dory.

The girl gave her brother a smile that was close to adoring and put her arms round his neck. Danny looked embarrassed and unhooked her. Right, Wee Yin, better get hame before my ma clocks you've been doggin the school the day.

You been doggin it? Jed said. Oh, ih! Naughty girl. Watch you don't go the way of your wastrel brother. Slippery slope.

Danny punched him on the arm. Who you callin wastrel? One a they wee animals that slink about the countryside?

That's a *weasel*, ya daft cunt.

Clare was laughing and Danny was grinning. Jed looked at them and a light dawned. Aye, right, he said. Ha, ha. He punched Danny's arm now. A familiar routine, obviously.

And the three of them moved to the door to let Clare out, Danny and Jed still jabbing at one another.

Bye, Clare, she called out. Nice to see you again. There was no reply from Clare; just her feet echoing down the stairs, the slam of the outside door.

The two boys came back in, laughing at a joke she must have missed. Jed tossed his jacket on a chair. Any mail for me? he said.

Oh, yes, she said, I believe there is. That is, if your name is Arjun? There are three letters for Arjun Singh.

That's me alright.

So, why Jed?

Jed – Arjun – shrugged.

He's a Jedi Knight, Danny said. He leapt up on the arm of the chair and started waving a virtual light sabre. *May the force be with you.*

Jed was watching him, but she noticed he wasn't smiling.

Danny jumped down again. It was great. I had a green light sabre and Jed had a blue one.

It was the other way about, Jed said.

What?

I got a green one and you got a blue one, but you says you should have the green one cause you were Irish. So in the end we swapped.

I don't remember that, Danny said. He looked perplexed; his black brows were down. Anyhow, we played Star Wars that much, Arjun changed his name to Jed.

No, you did.

What? What you sayin, man?

You decided I should change my name.

I decided?

Yeah. Look, forget it. Where's my mail, Laetitia?

On the sideboard in the hall, I think. He went off to fetch the letters. Danny still had a frown on his face. She could see his mind ticking back over the past and drawing a blank.

Jed came back in, ripping the envelope off one letter, another already open. He unfolded the sheet inside, gave it a cursory glance and tore at the third. Same old, same old, he said. Three *We regrets*.

What are they? she said.

He spread the letters out like a fan and spoke over them. His black-framed glasses gave him the air of a newsreader. *We regret to inform you that, on this occasion, you have been unsuccessful. The standard of candidates was extremely high. Thank you for your interest in our company. And may we take this opportunity to wish you every success in your future career.* She wondered why he used an English accent to deliver the speech.

Is that they jobs you went for a couple a weeks ago? Danny asked. They biochemical research jobs?

The very same.

Aw, man, I'm sorry. That stinks.

To high heaven! Jed said, pitched his voice like a drama queen, and flung the letters into the air. Danny caught one; the others landed on the floor at their feet. He picked them up too.

Aw, man. How many's that now?

Don't rub it in! I've lost count.

Bastards don't deserve you.

Aye, right. See if you say, *What's for you'll no go by you*, I'll fuckin kill you.

Would I? *Moi?* What I will say is this . . . Danny paused, looked at them both with serious eyes, arched by his great black brows.

What?

. . . *Qué sera, sera.*

And she watched them trade play punches and slaps again till they collapsed laughing, limbs tangled, on the red sofa.

None of them heard Julian come in. He'd spoken before

she realized he was in the doorway behind her. She turned to look at him.

Oh, hi, Julian. Where have you been? He'd clearly got caught in the rain; drops of water were dripping off his chin and his parka was soaked. Underneath his eyes had those bruised circles again. She hadn't noticed them earlier in the day.

Out and about, he said. Here and there.

It was hard to make out his mood. What did you say when you came in? I didn't hear.

I merely remarked on what looked like a bit of homoerotic bonding, that's all. And, I might add, the audience did seem a tad voyeuristic. He was smiling at her, but it felt strained.

Jed rose smoothly from the sofa and minced towards him. Och, you're just jealous. He pecked him on the cheek. You've been readin too much a that D. H. Lawrence. Anyway, I'm starvin. Is there any food in the flat?

Danny and Jed went racketing into the kitchen, leaving her with Julian. Better get out of these wet clothes, he said. He avoided her eyes. As nanny would say.

He locked the bathroom door behind him. There was nothing she could do but go into their room and wait.

Next morning, early, she leaned over the bathroom sink, held the shampoo bottle above her. It blurted an icy dollop onto her head and she shivered. The last few hours had been cold comfort one way or another. Julian, his back to her the whole night, resisted all attempts to cuddle up to him; remained rigid and angular at the edge of the bed, the knobs of his spine jutting, a deterrent to intimacy. She'd spent the night chilled, replaying conversations, oscillating between guilt and anger. Finally driven from the bed by cold, she got up to wash and dress, warm *herself* up. Quickly she massaged the shampoo into a lather, digging her fingers into her scalp, working in small circles. She counted to a hundred, and plunged her head into the water, rinsing off what she could. Again. Shampoo. Lather. Massage. On the surface of the water now, a thousand thousand golden bubbles, lit by the bare bulb overhead. She was counting again as she massaged. To fifty only for the second wash.

That was when she saw the eyes. Every bubble was an open eye staring up at her from the basin. Different sizes, big and small, all with eyes staring.

Oh, she said, and she wobbled backwards. Oh God.

She wondered why she was looking at the bottom of the sink pedestal, at the balls of fluff that had rolled there; why her feet were against the bath. Cold. Jed was talking to her, but she couldn't hear what he was saying. His face looked big; it hung over her and his mouth was moving. He sat her on the edge of the bath and made her put her soapy head on her knees. But some of the shampoo ran into her eyes and stung. She sat up and blinked. He held on to her arm while he reached for her towel. First, he wiped the soap from her face. Then he wrapped the towel round her head and, with one twist, made it into a turban. It stayed in place.

How d'you do that? she said. Her voice sounded slow, blurred.

It's in the genes. Right, if you can stand up, we'll rinse that soap out your eyes.

The eyes!

Yes, your eyes.

No, the eyes in the basin. They were all staring at me!

What? Look, are you OK to sit there? I'll get Julian.

No, don't leave me here. Please don't leave me.

Right, OK. There are no eyes in the basin. Do you hear me? Stand up and I'll show you.

He helped her to her feet and held her so that they both looked into the water in the sink. The bubbles were still there, still yellowed by the bare lightbulb, but there were no eyes.

See, no eyes, Jed said.

But I saw them. I was washing my hair and they were staring at me.

You imagined it. Must have been a reflection or somethin. He was keeping a firm grip on her. The front of her T-shirt was wet and it felt cold against her belly and thighs, pressed to the edge of the sink.

A reflection? She pulled off the towel, dropped it to the floor. Hold on to me, she said. Hold on to me here. And she pulled Jed's hands to her waist. He did as he was told, though she could feel his discomfort. She put her hands on top of her head, stretched her arms to the side. There they were again. The eyes staring. But her head was the iris, the curve of her arms the shape of the eyelid, her jutting elbows the corners. She could see now. It looked like an eye. Her reflection, repeated in a thousand bubbles, stared back at her.

It's me, she said. It was me. Oh, Jed, you're right. Thank God. Thank you. Thank you. She turned and looked at his face properly for the first time. His eyes had the slightly naked look of one used to wearing glasses; he was frowning with concern. It was only now she realized that she was shivering and tears were running down her face.

Don't tell, Julian, she said. I feel such a fool.

He took a lot of convincing, but finally, once she'd rinsed her hair, towel dried it, sneaked into the room, retrieved some warm clothes from her bag and put them on, made them both a cup of tea, perched on the bar stool in the kitchen to drink it – finally, finally, Jed was prepared to leave her and go to his work.

Well, if you can stay up on that stool, I guess you must be OK.

I hope I haven't made you late, she said.

He made a face and a dismissive movement of his hands.

Thank you, Jed.

But he was gone, clattering down the stairs.

The river was fat and brown and slick, moving slowly, with little rapids here and there, past islands of vegetation. Low bare branches of what she supposed must be willows stretched in some places half across the water. A pungent loamy smell rose from the bank. They walked upriver along a narrow path. Somewhere above to their left was a school; she could hear the voices of children raised in play.

It's wonderful to have this on your doorstep, she said.

They'd been walking in silence and her words sounded false, even though she meant them. Last night's tension still hung like a miasma between them, noxious, refusing to disperse; it had taken two long hours of skirting round the edges of it, before she could persuade Julian to go out with her.

Hmm, Julian said. The great consolation of Nature.

Well, doesn't it console you?

What, a murky brown river full of plastic bags and supermarket trolleys? That *flash upon the inward eye, which is the bliss of solitude.*

She laughed. They were on familiar territory again. I don't see any supermarket trolleys.

That, my dear, is only because of the recent rain; the river is swollen now and mercifully covers the urban detritus. In summer, you'll discover all conceivable varieties of supermarketus trolleyus.

Now that he'd pointed it out, she noticed rags of coloured

plastic littering the banks, clinging to the rotting vegetation, and now and then a bag, snagged on a branch, bellying out whenever a breeze caught it. Through it all, the river flowed, ponderous and dark. But it was a bright day, fresh after yesterday's heavy rain, and it dispelled the vision of the eyes in the basin.

I decree the plastic bags shall be bunting and today a festival of . . . of . . .

Of rubbish?

No . . . of renewal. It's good to be out with you like this, Julian. Blow away the cobwebs.

Cobwebs? You have cobwebs? You didn't tell me that. But he took her hand in his and kept it there when joggers or cyclists raced past and they had to flatten themselves against the railing.

They stopped by a weir where there was room to stand, out of the path of walkway traffic. At the bottom of the miniature falls, two footballs and a tennis ball bounced and whirled on the surface, prevented by the churning water from escaping downstream.

I think I may give up the PhD and do some research into Aunt Laetitia instead.

What, throw over Ginny and Gertie for Titty?

Yes. Is that a problem?

Will Daddy still finance you, if you do?

I don't know. Maybe I'll get a job.

A job? What kind of job?

I don't know. A call centre? A bar? A café? Something in publishing? There are plenty of wine and coffee bars in Glasgow. And Scotland *does* have one or two publishing houses. Doesn't it?

Julian said nothing. They watched the water rush over the weir. Towards the middle, a wooden spool for holding cable had come to a halt on the lip. Behind it, twigs and branches collected. An island in the stream.

They had let go of the railing to walk on to the Botanic Gardens, when it came, a sudden darkening of the blue above. A heron. He landed on the wooden spool and folded big grey wings.

Julian looked at her, smiled, said nothing.

The heron stood and watched.

PART THREE

Glasgow – London – Glasgow

February 2003–January 2005

February 2003

They blew up the high flats yesterday. I went wi my da to watch. Ma was at work, but she didny want to see it anyhow. A part of my past, she says. Our past. The family's past. Wild horses woudny drag me up that hill to watch them tearin down they buildins.

I don't remember it but, stayin in the high flats. We moved when I was eight months old. Danny remembers. He loved that place. Says his life changed for the worse when we moved to Kirbister Street. I think he blames me. Pardon me for bein born, I says to him, but he didny laugh. I told him he should come and watch the demolition, but he says, Will my da be there?

They've been preparin the explosives and that for the past couple a months. And they upped the security at night, in case anybody got any ideas. Such as settin fire tay the buildins afore they were ready. Or detonatin the explosives. Maybe even stealin them for – I don't know – *terrorist purposes*, like they're aye sayin on the news.

Anyhow, when we gets to the top a the hill, me an my da, there's already quite a crowd round the barrier. And polis keepin everybody back. Some folk are lookin up and pointin. That's where we lived. Fourteenth floor. See there. That wan wi the broken windie. I look up, but most of the windies are broken, as far as I can see. Right up to the top storey. I wonder who tanned them all in. Probably that's how they've decided to blow up baith blocks at once; stop any more vandalism. There's a right cold wind up here, even though it's no that cold down in Kirbister Street. A boy standin next to us is chitterin. He's only wearin a wee thin jacket and he's got his hands stuffed in the pockets and his shoulders are up round his ears. I think I've saw him at the school, even though he doesny look old enough to be in secondary. His lips are pure blue. Just as well my ma's no here; she'd be takin him hame to our house for his tea and wrappin him up wi woolly scarfs an jumpers.

Somebody's singin. It sounds like a couple a they jakies that hang around the shops. I look back through all the folk. Aye, the pair a them are dancin, arm in arm, both wi a can a lager in the other hand, singin. *Start spreading the news . . .* Some a the boys are standin round clappin, eggin them on. *I'm leaving today . . .* My da looks ower his shoulder.

Walter Fairlie, he says to me. Aye, that's old Walter. Used to work wi me in Thomson's. A great guy, great workmate. Do anythin for you, for anybody. Couldny do it for himsel, but; couldny get hissel off the drink. Damn shame.

I look at them again and canny imagine either a they guys workin wi my da. They're aye at the shops wi their cans durin the day, drunk as skunks, till somebody phones the polis. Don't know where they go then but. I never make eye contact with them. You don't know what they might say to you. *These vagabond shoes . . .*

What one's Walter? I says to my da, but he's no listenin.

I want to be a part of it, New York, New York . . .

There's more and more folk crowdin round the barrier. Somebody presses right up against me and I have to take my hands out my pockets and brace mysel against the railing. It's dead cold and for a wee minute I think my hands are goin to stick to the metal at the top. I'm glad I'm wi my da. He turns round and says, Here, nay shovin, pal; that's my lassie. His breath comes out in a big cloud. It's no dead aggressive, the way he says it, but the guy behind me stops pushin. Naybody messes wi my da, even if he isny that big. He puts his arm across my shoulder and pulls me closer to him.

Tell me again what flat we stayed in, I says.

Seventh floor. He points up. Fourth window along. Used to have red curtains. I mind standin at that windie wi you in my arms lookin out to the hills in the distance. You could see right ower to the Campsies. I seem to remember they had snow on them, so it must've been no that long efter you were born.

Was Danny there?

My da looks up at the window again. Canny remember. Probably. I mind the day we took you hame fae the hospital. You were sleepin. Wrapped up like a parcel in a shawl your granny had knitted. Just your wee red napper pokin out the top. We stepped out the lift and . . .

I know, Da, I started yellin and everybody on the landin came out their doors to see what the racket was. You've telt me that hunners a times.

And Mrs O'Brien said, If that lassie can sing as well as she can greet, she'll be on stage at the Sydney Opera House some day.

Da, I know. *They can probably hear her in Australia the now.*

Well, it's a good story, hen. Somethin about your life to tell your ain weans some day.

Aye right.

Good pair a lungs on you.

I squint up again at the block we lived in. The sky's that funny overcast way, grey but bright at the same time; you canny look at it for very long. Imagine stayin in they flats but. They look horrible. Big loomin towers, all grey wi sorta like darker grey bits where water's run down them. Broken windies. For the past year, there's been hardly anybody livin in them. Except some a the asylum seekers. Poor bastards, my da says, sent up here to live in they conditions. They've survived persecution, wars and torture, and now they've to contend wi British hospitality. Fuckin scandal.

I wish they would get on with it; it's pure Baltic the day. There's guys goin about wi fluorescent jackets and hard hats on, but nothin seems to be happenin. Along the barrier a bit, I see Big May fae Skaill Street. I used to be dead scared of her. When we were wee, she was aye out on her veranda, especially if her Robert was wi us, goin her dinger, givin it, *You weans, get back to your ain bit, comin ower here makin trouble. Robert, get your arse up that stair right now.* But we wereny makin trouble; we were only playin. At the time my ma thought it was maybe cause we were Catholics. Tell her you're a communist, my da says. Tell her religion's the opium a the masses and sectarianism's a mortal sin. She'll do no such thing, my ma says. It's alright for you at your union meetings; the weans and me have tay survive in the scheme. That was years ago. Big May's no as big now, probably cause I'm taller. She's thinner too; doesny look that well.

People's voices are gettin louder; some a them seem to be excited. I suppose no much happens in the scheme. If you're stuck in the house all day, it must be deadead borin. My da's talkin to the guy next to him.

Aye, 'eighty-six we moved out. You could see the way the high flats were goin even then. We needed a bigger house anyhow, when the wean was born.

When's he gonny stop callin me *the wean*! I can't hear what the other guy's sayin, but when he leans forward on the barrier, I can see he's cryin. Tears are rollin down his face and he's no even tryin to hide them. He's got big bushy eyebrows, black wi flecks of grey, and bags under his eyes; he's about my da's age probably. He leans his arms on the top of the fence and hangs his head.

I tug my da's sleeve. He's went all quiet. Da, what's the matter with him? I whisper in close to his shoulder, so the man willny hear me.

Tell you later, darlin, he says, dead low. And then louder. They're away to start now.

And right enough, I've no noticed, but there's a guy wi a hard hat standin back holdin a thing a bit like a walkie-talkie wi a pink cable comin fae it. He presses a button and looks at the furthest away tower. Suddenly there's a crack and a low rumble, and the tower kinda sinks down on itself; grey dust billows out at the sides low down, like it's doin a curtsy and the dust is the skirts spreadin. Then the thunder gets louder and the whole thing collapses in slow motion into a pile a rubble wi the dust risin in a big cloud above it. I don't know what I expected. I think I thought there would be a man kneelin down at a square box wi a plunger, like in they old films, and the whole thing explodin intay the sky and flames shootin up.

Some people cheer. The man next my da turns away fae the barrier and starts to barge his way back through the crowd. He's still got tears streamin down his face. Watch where you're goin, pal! somebody says.

A woman's came into the space he's left. She's tryin to catch the attention of one of the guys in the hard hats, but he's ignorin her.

Son, she's shoutin, Here, son, gonny tell me somethin? Gonny tell me where you take all this rubble when you've finished? Son!

Why is it you need to know that, hen? my da says.

She looks at him as if she's no noticed him afore, as if she's no noticed anybody. Her eyes are kinda wild and her mouth's a hard line, like she's determined. I want a bit of it to keep, she says. A memento. I reared my family in they flats. Four weans. My youngest boy's in the army. Last time he was hame on leave, he says, Ma, I want a brick fae our house when they knock the flats down. Her face goes soft, and her eyes. Know what he done? He broke intay the flats and went to our old house and he chipped away some a the plaster in the livin room; scraped away at it till he was down to the bare concrete. And then he taen a paintbrush and some paint and he wrote his name on it in big red letters: ALAN. He says, Ma, I'm goin back for that concrete block. Find out where they take the rubble.

She turns to the demolition men again and shouts, Here, son, gonny tell me where you take all this when you're done?

Come on, my da says to me, let's go hame.

But they've no did our one yet.

One's enough. He takes my arm and starts to weave back through the crowd. I hang on to him.

Why was that man cryin afore?

He stops and turns round to me. His face is so tired. It was his boy jumped off the high flats last year, he says.

What was it like, Farkhanda says, the high flats coming down?

We're sittin in English, waitin for Mr Forbes. He's ayeways late and when he comes in he shouts and bawls at us for no gettin on with the work. So we've baith got our copies of *Sunset Song* open on our desks, kiddin on we're readin. The boys in the back are carryin on as usual, pingin bits a chewed up paper at the ceilin, makin them stick. The whole ceilin is covered in them, like a bad case of acne.

Och, it was nothin spectacular. I only really seen the one tower properly; my da wanted to go hame. I looked back at the exact same time the second one was collapsin. It just like – sunk down on itsel and the dust came up in a big cloud. Nay massive explosions, nay flames leapin intay the sky. A bit borin.

My dad wouldn't let me come. Stay away from buildings being demolished, he said. It's dangerous. I argued with him, but he wouldn't listen. You don't know who's going to be there, he said. And Shenaz chimed in, You should listen to Dad, Farkhanda; it's no safe for Muslims to be out among crowds like that. I hate her.

No you don't. She's your sister.

Aye, I do hate her. She's never off my back.

I looks at Farkhanda. She sounds dead serious. I don't think she's forgave Shenaz for makin her wear the hijab to school. I was mad at Shenaz too, when Farkhanda telt me. She's got such beautiful hair, dead thick and black and shiny, wi a smell like flowers. We used to take turns brushin each other's sometimes. When I did hers it would be normal to start with; like mine, a wee bit wavy and tangled, hard to get the brush through. Sometimes Farkhanda would yell and tell me no to be so rough. And then it would turn smooth as dark water runnin down her back; and if I kept goin it would crackle and like blue sparks come off it. A couple a times we plaited a bit of her hair and mine thegether, just to see what it looked like, the red and the black.

I nearly burst out greetin the first day she came in with the headscarf on. All her lovely hair under a horrible white scarf. White or black she's allowed, to go with the school uniform, and she has to pin it under her chin. It makes her face round and her eyes look dead sad, starin out fae under that cloth. It was hard enough for her before, some a the boys callin her Paki cow and stuff. Now it's like: *Osama, Osama in excelsis Deo* . . . in assembly. And they run up behind her in the corridor, slap her on the bum and yell, *Jee-haad!* I says to her when she started cryin, Look, never mind they morons; it's just the same as them callin us lezzies when we were brushin one another's hair.

225

Aye, but that was the two of us, she says, and a big round tear ran down her chin and soaked into her headscarf.

I think that was when I decided about the dreads.

Mr Forbes comes in then, stinkin a fags, shoutin, Right, who is going to delight us today with a reading from our favourite book?

He's dead sarcastic, old Four Baws, and he thinks he's bein funny. He goes to his desk and picks up his copy of *Sunset Song*. I'm sick to death of this book. By the time it gets to the exams, I'll know the whole thing off by heart. This is like the second time we've went through it.

Farkhanda, he says, will you do the honours? He often asks Farkhanda, cause he says she speaks better English than some of the rest of us. No scruffy Glasgow; more polite. Ooooooh! the boys all shout. It used to get up my nose sometimes, like you canny speak right if you come fae here. But no now; now she needs all the encouragement she can get, even fae old Forbesy. He's talkin shite anyhow; Farkhanda was born in Glasgow too.

From where we left off yesterday, please, he says.

'. . . Chae Strachan came up to Blawearie one night with a paper in his hand and a blaze on his face, and he cried that he for one was off to enlist, old Sinclair would heed to the Knapp and to Kirsty. And Ewan cried after him, *You're havering, man, you don't mean it!* But Chae cried back *Damn't ay, that I do!* And sure as death he did and went off, by Saturday a letter came to Peesie's Knapp that told he had joined the North Highlanders and been sent to Perth . . .'

I think Farkhanda likes readin out loud; she ayeways gives it loads of expression and puts on the different voices. She even does the teuchter accent better than Mr Forbes.

Then one or two a the boys start up. State a her! they says.

Sir, sir, what's *havering*?

Read that bit again, Farkhanda, *Damn't ay, that I do!*

No, it's a sin for her to say they words. She'd get a public whippin off the Taliban if they heard her.

QUIET! Turn round and be quiet, Thomas Docherty. Listen and learn.

It's no me daein the whippin, sir.

It'll be me doing the whipping in a minute, boy, if you don't be quiet.

You're no allowed, sir, you'll get the jail.

Ayeways the same; they run rings round old Forbesy and we get one paragraph done if we're lucky. I'm glad I read the book afore we started it in fifth year. When my da heard we were gonny dae *Sunset Song*, he went intay the room and came back out with this old hardback, *A Scots Quair*. There, read that, he says, the hail trilogy; greatest Scottish book ever, especially the third part, *Grey Granite*. So I reads it. To please my da as much as anythin. And I dae like it, at least I did afore we started it in school, but it's dead old-fashioned; all that country stuff and farmin. Naybody I know lives like that.

The bit I remember best is out the middle section, *Cloud Howe*, I think. It's more like a poem or somethin.

> Funny and queer that you were with a man!
> You did this and that and you lay in his bed,
> there wasn't a thing of you he might not know,
> or you of him, from the first to the last.

It comes back to me when I think of bein with Julian. Only I canny imagine knowin him that well. Or Julian knowin me. If I say the words in my mind, I'm back in that room in Florence, watchin him sleepin, his dreads spread over the pillow. That feelin pure hits me in the gut, and my head goes hot. I wind one of my own locks round my finger; it makes a wee twizzly noise when I rub it.

I don't realize Mr Forbes is talkin to me till I feel Farkhanda nudgin my arm with her elbow.

Would you care to grace us with your presence, Miss Kilkenny? Hmm? Miss Roberta Marley? Sometime this century? He leans on my desk on his knuckles. His shirt has wet patches at the oxters and his blue tie is hangin in front a my nose. I feel like givin it a good yank, but he's already too close to me. Instead, I look at my book, lyin next to his hand. The fingers are yellow with nicotine and his breath's pourin down on my head like ash.

I says, it's about the conflict in the community and whether or no the men should be enlistin to fight in the First World War. I can half see Farkhanda beside me, crossin her eyes, makin hersel skelly, and I have to bite my lip so he willny see me smilin.

Yes? And? he says.

And Chae's went and joined up, but Ewan thinks he's off his head.

Chae's WENT and joined up, has he? You know better than that, Clare. What have I told you about the Glasgow past participle? You'll never get your Higher English if you persist in using it.

Chae has GONE and joined the army; Ewan thinks he's GONE quite barmy. *Baahmy*, I says, rhymin it with *aahmy*. I get away with bein cheeky, cause he knows fine I can dae the work. I look up at him. He's smilin. He takes his hands off my desk and goes back to his seat. Thank fuck! I look at Farkhanda; her eyebrows are up under the edge a her white hijab and her mouth's twitchin. She looks like a wee woodland creature wi her round black eyes, peepin out fae under the snow.

I canny wait to get home and wash the smell of ash out my hair. Then I remember I canny, cause a the dreads. And even if I could, I canny; Farkhanda and me's goin to the anti-war vigil in George Square straight after school. She never asked her ma and da; she thought, no way were they gonny let her go. But the second time we went, Shenaz was there too. So it was alright. She tells her ma now that Farkhanda's goin wi her, so Farkhanda doesny have to lie any more. I think she's glad. What do you dae? I says. Us Catholics say a few Hail Marys and we're OK. No that I dae that but. Farkhanda ayeways says she doesny like to talk about her religion.

Well, you're no allowed to eat pork, I says, so I suppose you're no meant to tell porkies either.

Aye, very funny, she says. Heard the one about the mean Scotsman and the stupid Irishman?

God, you're so prickly! OK, sorry, I says. I didny mean it. It's just . . . we've been pals since second year and I still haveny a clue what Muslims dae.

Aye, you do. We blow up buildins, chop people's heads off and eat babies.

She can be dead fierce sometimes, Farkhanda; makes me feel it's my fault Muslims get a bad name. All of a sudden, her face goes dark like a storm cloud. No unlike my brother, Danny, come to think of it.

We threaten civilization as you know it, she says.

George Square's no exactly hoachin when we get there, but it's early yet. The faces of the people already here are gettin quite familiar. There's a CND guy and a few Christian *swords into ploughshares*-type older women, wearin purple cords and pink scarfs, and one or two Palestine supporters all hangin about on the red tarmac. There's some guys fae other schools too. Boys even. We couldny persuade the boys in our school to get involved. I suppose the lassies have fell away too but. Maybe people are savin theirsels for the big demo. And the nights are gettin lighter now as well; it was mair fun when a crowd of us came here in the dark and burnt candles. The wax all runnin down ontay the cardboard tray, people's faces lit up.

I look at Farkhanda. She's changed intay a dark red velvet hijab and stuck her white school one in her bag. It suits her far better. It's no pinned under her chin either, just draped over her shoulder. We walk round the edge of the square to see if Shenaz is here.

The statues are all standin about, towerin above us, dark in the eerie light. I don't even know who the half of them are, except the big tall one's Walter Scott. There's a seagull perched on Queen Victoria, another one on Burns. *A man's a man for a' that*, my da would say. *Sceptre and crown Must tumble down, And in the dust be equal made With the poor crooked scythe and spade.* He's aye quotin bits a poems, my da. The seagulls look like ghost birds in this light.

Are there any speakers tonight? Farkhanda says.

I don't know. Don't think so. No sign a Tommy, anyhow.

There's a few more folk gatherin. Scottish Socialists, Stop the War Coalition. I can't see Danny's lot. And I keep lookin but Julian's never came either. Danny doesny talk much about him, and Laetitia's movin wi Julian into a different flat in a few weeks. Bankrolled by their mummies and daddies, Danny says. I think he's just pissed off but, cause Julian's takin Laetitia away fae him. Again.

There's Shenaz, Farkhanda says, and she walks over to a group a Muslim lassies standin thegether all laughin and talkin at once in Urdu. As long as Farkhanda checks in wi her big sister, she's alright. A lassie I've no saw afore, in a black hijab, comes ower and holds ontay her shoulders and talks to her nineteen to the dozen. Next thing I know, Farkhanda's greetin and the lassie's huggin her and wipin her face wi the tail of her scarf. I want to go over, but I don't know what to say. Farkhanda seemed alright a wee minute ago. Maybe a bit quiet on the bus comin down, but that's no unusual.

I stay where I am and wait. There's no really that many more folk came, while we've been walkin round the square. Same old faces. A boy comes up to me and asks if I want to buy his paper. He's haudin them up in front of his chest. No, you're alright, I says. The headline in big black letters is: PLEASE MR BLAIR, DON'T TAKE US THERE. Which is a bit mair polite than some a them! Underneath, there's a picture a dead weans lyin in the dust. The guy wanders over to the next punter. I've got a whole pile of leaflets and stuff about the war, lyin at hame; I never seem to get round to readin them all.

I try to get a look at what's happenin with Farkhanda, without them clockin me. She seems to have calmed down a bit and stopped cryin. I even hear her laughin at somethin one a the lassies says to her. She's got a great laugh, Farkhanda, dead giggly and sorta like musical. Like it could be the notes of a song you've no heard afore, but you would sing it too, if you knew it. Only the next time she laughs, it's that wee bit different, so you can never ever learn it.

The lassie claps Farkhanda on the back and I see her lookin about for me, so I sorta step forward.

Clare, she says, I'm goin to go with Shenaz and her pals to a meetin after the vigil. Will you be OK getting the bus yourself?

Can I no come to the meetin too?

It's in the mosque. It's for Muslim girls. There's dark blotches round her eyes with cryin.

Oh, right, I says. Aye, of course I can get the bus mysel. Are you OK? Why were you cryin?

Aye, I'm fine. It's too hard to explain, Clare. See you in school tomorrow?

Oh. Alright. You goin the now, then?

Yes, they're waitin on me.

I look over at the lassies. They're all talkin among themsels except Shenaz. She's standin watchin. She gives me a wave and I wave back. I feel daft but; she's only five feet away.

Bye, then, Farkhanda says.

Bye.

She walks over to the group and I go to turn away, but she runs back to me and says in a quiet voice, I'll phone you later about the *Sunset Song* essay, OK?

If you like, I says.

She gies one of my dreads a wee tug. I like, she says, and goes back to Shenaz.

It's nearly dark when I turn and cross the square, and most folk are driftin away. The boy with the papers reaches into his pocket and scatters somethin for the pigeons. They all run about his feet like mad, peckin, peckin. It looks as if he's got the same amount a papers as before, held up against his chest.

I don't know why, but I start to run. The pigeons explode into the cold air like a burst of applause and my dreads are flyin, whackin me in the face and thumpin on my back. I keep on runnin till I jump on the bus.

You been runnin? my ma says, when I get in.

My heart's pure thuddin. Aye, I says. Fae the bus stop.

She's sittin cross-legged on the sofa with a pair of my da's big woolly socks on her feet. The TV news is on with the sound turned down. I never understand why she does that. Dubya's on the screen, mouthin like a fish in a tank. My ma looks at me for a minute ower the top of her book, then carries on readin. We've no been gettin on so well, me and my ma, since I got the dreads done; since Danny moved out even, no long after the Florence demo.

There's some spaghetti bolognese in the pot for you, she says, and she turns her page. You can heat it up in the microwave.

I'm no that hungry, Ma, I says. What you readin?

She holds up her book so I can see the title: *Persuasion* by Jane Austen. She ayeways reads right through the complete novels of Jane Austen when she's stressed, my ma, startin wi *Sense and Sensibility*. I think *Persuasion* comes near the end. Her nails are pure bitten right down to the quick, since my da and Danny had that fight. I notice her daein it when she thinks I'm no lookin. If it was me, she would give me a right bollockin. At least she's no started smokin again; my da would go through the roof.

How was the vigil?

Aye, OK. The usual suspects. Farkhanda went to a meetin in the mosque wi her sister and her pals, so I just came away.

How's she gettin on since she started wearin the veil?

It's no a veil, Ma, it's a hijab. She doesny wear a veil.

Well, the hijab, then. How's she gettin on?

What d'you think?

I don't know; that's how I'm askin. Jeezo, Clare, you're a right nippy wee besom sometimes. She lays the book down open on her lap.

Aye well, who do I get that off?

I was only askin a civil question. Is it beyond you to gie me a civil answer these days?

I sit down on the chair across fae her. Our glorious leader, as my da calls him, is fillin the screen now; on his hind legs in parliament at the dispatch box, giein it laldy. Weapons of Mass Destruction, I'll bet you.

I don't know, I says, she has to put up wi a lot more crap off some a the boys. It upsets her sometimes.

What sort of crap?

I don't know, Ma, names and things. The usual.

Has she talked to any of the teachers about it?

No, I don't think so. No, definitely no.

Maybe you should persuade her to tell Mr Perry, offer to go with her to his office.

No way is Farkhanda goin tay Perry! It's bad enough the now, without him jumpin in with baith feet. Her life wouldny be worth livin.

Well, you canny just stand by and watch your friend bein made miserable by a bunch of ignorant boys.

Aye, Ma. Whatever, I says. I jump up before she can see me startin to cry, and run through to my room.

I'll say this for my ma: she knows to leave me alane whenever I go into my room now. It used to drive me mental when she would come in durin the day if I was away at school and tidy things up, make my bed and stuff. But since Florence, she's gave me a bit more space. She let me paint my walls again, even though it wasny that long since they were done afore. I couldny live wi that peachy pink any mair, and the frilly bed mat and the matchin curtains. So she let me choose my own colours and got me a blind and I bought an Indian throw for the bed. It took me a while to get the right paint; I wanted the same colour a yellow as Julian's room in the *pensione*, so the sun would be shinin in it, even when it was dark and rainin outside. But the funny thing is, it's only really the right colour when the sun *is* shinin in the windie. The rest a the time it's kinda dull, especially at night, the colour a brown paper. I'm wrapped up in a brown paper parcel.

The throw's good but; all gold and ginger and like . . . russet, wi embroidery and wee mirrors that catch the glow fae the lamp and scatter it into seeds a light all round the walls.

I thought Farkhanda would love it, but she says, It's alright, I suppose. Very Indian.

And my ma says, You realize, of course, it'll have been made in a sweatshop by twelve-year-olds for a few cents a day.

How was I supposed to know! It wasny on the label.

You know because if the work that's went into it was paid at a decent rate, you wouldny be able to afford it in a million years.

Aye, OK, Ma. I've bought it now, so it's goin on my bed, right?

I'm just tellin you.

Och, leave her alane, my da says, she's a young lassie; she's got plenty a time to get intay all that.

Aye, is that right? If you were even half as understandin of your son, it would be somethin.

I don't know who I'm madder at, my ma or my da. I just picks the cover up off the sofa where I've opened it out, fold it and take it away intay my room. I can hear them still at it when I've shut my door.

Anyhow, I like my throw. I spread it over the duvet and put all the cushions on – the colour a pomegranate, the woman in the shop says – and my bed turns intay a big sofa. When I'm sittin on it, I can see mysel in my granny's dressin table mirror. It's dead old-fashioned, but it was my granny's, so I'm no gonny part wi it, even if it is a bit big for my room. It's got two side bits, wings that move, so's you can see yoursel fae every angle.

Which came in very handy when I done my dreads. I shut mysel in my room one Sunday wi a tub a beeswax, and twisted and waxed and back combed, till I had did the two sides a my hair. The only bit I couldny really do mysel was the back. So I waited till my ma and da went out to dae the shoppin and I phoned Farkhanda and she said she would come ower and help me.

I never telt Farkhanda what happened in Florence – well, wi Julian, anyhow; I telt her about the demo. Sometimes I thought if I didny tell her, it would be hard to stay pals. And sometimes I thought if I did, it would be even harder.

Afore she arrives, I take Julian's dread out the back a my drawer where I keep it wrapped up in a poly bag inside my red T-shirt. One time I thought my ma must've saw it, cause the T-shirt was folded different. I'm nearly sure it was. But, if she did, she never let on, didny say nothin. So, I takes it out and lays it on my dressin table. Funny how it brings everythin back! I hold it beside my new dreads; it looks dead scabby beside mine; frayed and tatty and a bit dirty. Probably cause I slept wi it under my pillow and carried it around for ages in my pocket, so's I could rub it between my fingers under my desk at school. It's a bit of a funny colour too. I used to think it was dark blond, but no now. It's hard to describe the colour really: a kinda no-colour colour.

The basin's ready. I take one last look at the lock the way it is, hold it up to my nose. Even the smell's faded a lot, the beeswax and patchouli. It's mair like – I don't know – old matted hair, just. But I can still see Julian the way he was when he had dreads; afore that cow got tay him wi her scissors.

I put on the rubber gloves, lift the dread and lay it lengthwise in the basin, makin sure it's totally covered; I don't want any a the original colour comin through in case somebody guesses. How long does bleach take? Half an hour should be long enough; another half-hour to get it dried wi my hairdryer. By that time, Farkhanda will be here. First it was gonny be the same colour as mine; then I thought I would never know what one it was if I done that, except for where I fix it at the roots. So I decided on bleach instead.

By the time Farkhanda's came, the whole room's stinkin of it. Piss and chlorine.

Clare, for goodness' sake, what you doin? she says. And she coughs and covers her face wi her hijab. And then she laughs, You're mental, she says. Mad. Wired to a Mars Bar!

I'll open the windie, I says.

Too right. I don't want to be asphyxiated.

Is it that bad? I've no noticed it so much, cause I've been in here all the time.

It's that bad, Clare. She coughs again. Oh God, it's a wonder your mother and father haven't smelt it.

They're out gettin the messages. And they'll likely go for a pub lunch after. Aye, so my da's no here; you can take off your headscarf if you want.

It's a light blue one the day; goes wi her jeans. She unravels it fae her shoulders. It's got weights sewed into the hem to keep it down, to make sure it doesny blow off in the wind. Tiny wee weights. Farkhanda squeezes one out through the stitchin to show me; a wee silver ball bearin.

Weird, I says.

No as weird as they matted bits a rope hangin fae your head, she says.

I think I've offended her. But then she laughs and pulls her scarf right off and throws it on the bed. All her lovely hair comes tumblin down.

Oh, Farkhanda, I says.

What?

I don't know . . . just your hair . . . it's . . .

Are you cryin?

No.

Don't cry, Clare, please; you'll set me off. Come on, let's get started. She puts her hands on my shoulders and looks at me dead serious. Her eyes are back to how they should be, dark, dark brown and shinin, with her thick dark hair round about.

I'm OK. Let me empty that basin first. Your hair smells of honey and ginger; don't want it to end up stinkin a bleach!

When I've came back in, Farkhanda's sittin on the bed, wi Julian's dreadlock in her hands, turnin it round and round, examinin it. It's near pure white now, and the fuzzy bits are like wee strands of light.

She looks up at me. So what's the story with this one? she says, and holds it out to me. Why one white dreadlock among the red?

When I take it out her hand, I'm thinkin, Should I tell her, should I tell her; no, probably no. Then I says, It's Julian's.

Sometimes I don't know what I'm gonny say till it's out my mouth!

Julian's?

Aye, that friend a my brother's I telt you about, that I met at the demo in Florence.

I know who Julian is, Clare; you're never done talkin about him. I mean, what are you doin with one of his dreadlocks?

Well, his girlfriend cut them off after the demo and . . . I got one.

His *girlfriend* gave you one?

No exactly.

No exactly?

I just took it.

She's lookin at me like a wee owl; big round eyes.

And you're goin to do what with it?

Questions, questions! You're as bad as my ma.

I need to know what it is I'm involved in here. She pulls her mouth intay a pout like she disapproves.

Naybody's forcin you to help me.

Theft of a dreadlock's a serious matter, she says.

238

I notice her lips are twitchin at the corners.

In some cultures it would be seen as an act of witchcraft.

Aye right, I says. I could stick pins in it and gie him a sore heid.

And she laughs, thank goodness, like clear water runnin ower stones.

We better get a move on before your parents get back, eh?

Yes. Listen, thanks, Farkhanda. I really appreciate this.

She pulls her eyebrows up and dimples her cheeks. Don't mention it.

Still, I don't think I could tell her about Laetitia's diary.

I sit in front of my granny's mirror, wi Farkhanda standin behind me, and we start. The sun's shinin in and the yellow walls are pure Florence. Julian's dread looks silver in my hand.

So, I just kinda twist a few strands of hair together first? Farkhanda says.

Aye, and then take the comb and backcomb it. Right up to the roots. And seal it all in with some a the wax.

Easy peasy, she says, and I feel the tug of the comb like a burst of pain on my scalp.

Ooh, ya!

Sorry! She looks at me in the mirror and smiles. I've never noticed afore, her mouth goes up more at one side than the other. I gie her a smile back and wonder if she sees me different too. And then I catch sight a my dreads. I mean, *really* look at them. My head goes hot and I pure panic! I pull Julian's dread tight between my hands.

Maybe this is no such a good idea.

What?

The dreads. Do you think they're a good idea?

Too late now! Farkhanda steps back a bit and bends down to look at me in the mirror. She has to haud her ain hair back wi her hand, so it doesny fall all over mine. It makes your hair shorter and thicker, she says. More sticky out.

She's right. My hair does seem a couple of inches shorter. All that backcombin. I feel round the back where Farkhanda's workin on one, twistin and screwin it tight. There's only a wee bit normal hair left. I smoothe it down one last time.

Right, I says. Go for it.

Darker too, Farkhanda says, workin away. Must be the wax makes it darker red.

There's wee points of pain on my scalp where the new dreads are; like when your bunches were too tight when you were wee. I suppose they'll loosen a bit in a day or two.

OK, that's it. So, what do you want done with Julian's dreadlock?

I canny really believe that was only a few weeks ago. And now Farkhanda's goin to meetins in the mosque. Well, *a* meetin. I wonder if she'll still want us to go thegether to the demo on Saturday. Or if she'll stay wi Shenaz and her pals. A bit of the embroidery on my cover's loose. I've been sittin in a dream, pullin at the thread, and one a the wee mirrors has came out. Really it's a bit a silver metal. It looks like a fishscale lyin on my finger. I flick it wi my thumb. It lands back down on the bed and disappears among all the other mirrors.

I'm used to my dreads now. My granny's mirror's used to them. I like them. Julian's one hangs down at the left-hand side. I made Farkhanda *promise* she wouldny tell naybody. I didny know if it would work, but she done a really great job, Farkhanda. She wound some thread round and round at the top of one a my dreads, and I did the same wi Julian's. Then she *sewed* Julian's dread ontay mine, without jaggin me once with the needle. And she snipped some of the loose hairs off Julian's, cause it looked mair frizzy than mine, no to mention a totally different colour!

Some a the other lassies at school asked me how I done it;

how I managed tay bleach one dreadlock without getting dye on any a the rest.

Farkhanda looks at me and we wink at one another. It's witchcraft, she says. Magic.

And that pure pisses the lassies off. They ask if they can touch my hair. Or have a wee piece of it.

That *will* be right! I says. That *will* be shinin bright! Away and make your ain dreads. And I fling my head forward then back, so the dreads go flyin, just to annoy them.

I kneel up on the bed, to get a better view of mysel in the mirror. Dark red wool wi one white strand. Is that birdshit? one a the boys had says. But it shines in the light; sorta sparkles. I wonder what my granny would think of them. Patsy'll like them, I bet, even if my ma doesny.

When I walked Farkhanda to the door that Sunday, I ran right intay my ma and da, didn't I, comin in the door wi the messages. My ma gasps and says, In the name a . . . ! Then she burst intay tears and says, Oh, Clare, your beautiful hair!

It was pure embarrassin, Farkhanda standin there with her hijab back on.

Phone for you, Clare, my ma shouts through fae the lobby. I must've been miles away; I've no even heard it ringin.

Where is it? I says. My ma's still sittin readin. She's took my da's socks off and she's playin wi the toes of her left foot on the sofa, and holdin her book in her other hand. She doesny look up.

Over there.

Where? Then I see the handset, perched on the arm of the chair. Is it Farkhanda? I says.

Uh, huh.

I don't know what my ma'll dae when she runs out a the Jane Austen. I don't think it's did the trick this time.

I pick up the phone; the wee green light is blinkin. Hi,

Farkhanda, I says. I'm gonny take the phone through to my room, OK?

When I'm settled back on my bed on the pomegranate cushions, I say, Hi, how was your meetin?

Alright, she says. We were – – kin at – – – ges – – Qu'ran.

You're breakin up, Farkhanda. Put the phone nearer your mouth.

Is that better?

Aye.

Listen, I don't have much time, Clare, my father's waitin on a phonecall. It's Monday the *Sunset Song* essay's due, isn't it?

Aye, but we've got the demo on Saturday, mind, and we were gonny make placards on Friday night. Are you still up for that? . . .

Hello? Farkhanda?

Yes, I'm still here. I canny manage on Friday night now, Clare. I'm goin to another meetin after Friday prayers.

Oh.

I could come round early on Saturday mornin? Would that suit?

Aye, I suppose so. OK. What time?

Ten o'clock?

Ten! That'll no gie us enough time. The demo starts at eleven. By the time we get the bus—

Alright, alright, keep your dreadlocks on! Nine, then. I'll be round at nine. You got all the stuff we need? Pens, big sheets of paper and that?

Aye, and my da's bringin hame some scrap wood fae his work for handles.

Great. Right, see you in school tomorrow. Bye.

And that's her away. I press the button on the phone and toss it on the bed. I've no even heard how her meetin's went.

My face looks dead pasty in the mirror. Peely wally, my granny would say. And my dreads are bigger.

I suppose I'll need tay make a start on the essay mysel. I lean ower the end a the bed, dig my English folder out my bag and find the sheet.

With close reference to the text of Sunset Song, *explain the various conflicts – political, personal, national, local – at work in the community of Kinraddie and round about, in relation to Britain's involvement in the First World War.*

I take a piece of paper and write at the top: *Sunset Song Essay, S5, Mr Forbes.* The thought of him with his fags and his sweaty oxters puts me right off. It'll be easier in the exams, cause it willny be him markin my paper. I don't know why I feel that; he ayeways says nice things about me.

Well done, Clare. This is very good. No taint in your written work of demotic Glasgow speech, I'm delighted to see!

Demotic. I had to look it up.

I canny be bothered daein this the now. I stick the essay sheet and the piece a paper back in my English folder and stuff it in my bag. Sunday'll be time enough to think about it. I lean forward on the bed, lift up the edge of the throw and squeeze my hand under the mattress to see if Laetitia's diary's still there. It is. Still in the exact same place. That's why I make my bed every mornin afore I go out now. My ma's amazed. The throw's too heavy to sleep under, so I take it off at night. In the mornin, I smoothe up my duvet, spread the throw on top, pile all the cushions back and prop them against the wall. I says to Ma, It's cause I want my room to be mair like a bedsit. But that isny the real reason. It's cause I don't want her comin in, strippin the bed, turnin ower the mattress. Findin the diary.

One last time. I'll look at it one last time. I have to get off the bed to get it out. I kneel down beside it, slip my hand in under the cover, ease it in between the mattress and the base and pull out the bag with the diary in. It's the bag I made in Primary Seven, wi my initials embroidered on. C. K. Green embroidery on a yucky colour a pink. Everybody had to make one; the boys' ones were blue. Miss, what's this for? they says. And they were all pure manky by the time we finished makin them. The teacher had to take them hame and wash them. I never found a use for mine till now. Laetitia's diary fits in perfect, with room at the top to pull the drawstring, made out a the same green embroidery thread as my initials.

I sit back up on the bed again and loosen the string. My heart aye starts beatin faster when I do this. It's black, the diary, hardback, covered in cloth. I didny realize what it was when I first seen it. It was lyin on the floor at the window, beside a chair in Danny's room in the flat in the West End. Well, the livin room, really, but Danny's sleepin in it the now, till he finds somewhere else. I wouldny even a noticed it, but Laetitia came back into the room and picked up a wee brown leather book off the seat.

Jed was there at some point that night, and Danny. Julian was there for a wee while, but he went out no long after Laetitia's went through to the bedroom. That was the first time I'd saw him again after Florence. My heart was pure thumpin, when he walked through the door. I was sure they must be able to hear it, but they didny seem to notice, him and Laetitia. He was taller than I remembered and his hair had grew a bit. Still short but. Take him a few years to grow back his dreads, if he felt like it.

I wasny plannin on takin the book. Julian was away; Laetitia was in her room; Danny and Jed were having a carry-on. And I seen it lyin there. First I thought it was an ordinary book, but when I opened it, it was all handwritin. I thought it might be Julian's, cause I've never saw his writin. As soon as I read the first paragraph but, on the page it opened at, I knew it was Laetitia's.

> Julian has asked me to go with him to a demo in Florence the weekend after next. European Social Forum – anti-war, anti-globalization. Strictly comrades, he says. Strictly compañeros. Don't know if it's a good idea; I've only recently re-established some kind of equilibrium, after the split. Only recently begun any worthwhile work on my thesis. Do I really want to risk opening Pandora's Box again? Why haven't I immediately said NO!?

I've got that bit off by heart now. And some other bits. I had my back to Danny and Jed, but I slung a quick look ower my shoulder. They were laughin and jokin. Naybody was lookin, so I slipped the diary in my bag.

I flick through it to find my favourite bit. The book falls open at the page. God, if ever I dae manage to get this back to Laetitia, she'll know right away what bits I've been readin!

> Julian, Julian! What is it about you that draws me to you? Keeps drawing me back, even after all that's happened? Even after I've decided CATEGORICALLY, that it's no good; our being together invariably ends in tears. Yet, here I am in a pensione in Florence, on the eve of the European Social Forum demo, my heart beating faster at the thought of seeing you in – what? – an hour or so, when your bus gets in. This will be a good test of our resolve to stay apart. My resolve, at any rate. MY resolve.

She writes dead strange – like she's talkin to hersel and Julian at the same time. It's funny to think of her sittin in her room, writin away in this book, just as our bus is comin into Florence, wi me and Danny on it, as well as Julian. I mind how weird I thought he was then, wi his posh voice and his dreads.

I lift my head up to see mysel in the mirror. If I half close my eyes, I can even imagine I *am* Julian now. Him in the mirror, *his* eyes half closed, lookin at me on my bed. I take his dreadlock in my hand. I can ayeways find it dead easy, cause it feels different fae my ain dreads. Different texture. Mair spongy and fuzzy. Ayeways I see it glintin out the corner of my eye. Silvery. Sometimes I think I feel a kinda vibration in it. A wee kinda tremor, as if it's alive. And I get a bit spooked then, rememberin what Farkhanda says about witchcraft.

I turn the page to the next bit I like, skip the first half about Laetitia and Danny, cause I'm embarrassed readin it – God, if Danny knew, he'd kill me! – and get to my favourite bit.

> Danny's young sister, Clare, is a stunning girl. Sixteen with a
> wild cloud of dark red hair surrounding a pale Pre-Raphaelite
> face. A cross between a Burne-Jones and a Waterhouse
> vaguely, with hair by Rossetti . . .

I didny know all they names at first, but I looked them up. *Stunning*. It was that word surprised me.

> . . . The entire effect is somewhat compromised, however,
> by a Glasgow accent thicker than her luxuriant hair. Those
> glottal stops!

That's the part I *don't* like. As if her voice is anythin to write home about. Frightfully, frightfully, dahling!

But here's the best bit.

And now a café, a caffeine injection, and a nicotine boost,
while Danny's off buying postcards, before heading back to
the pensione to meet up with Julian and Clare and go on to
the demo . . .

Julian and Clare. Clare and Julian.

. . . I did wonder at breakfast if there was something going
on between those two. But no, not with a sixteen-year-old.
Not even Julian. And anyway, it's pretty obvious he hasn't
got over me yet; he behaved abominably in the restaurant
last night . . .

Somethin goin on – aye, if you only knew! Snooty bitch! The
first few times I read it, I was like, dead upset, cause a what
happened in the end, Julian goin back to her and that. Then
when I thought about the nice things she'd says about me, I
felt bad. Really guilty. Specially for pinchin her diary. Specially
when she looked that no well the day I went round to the flat
wi Danny's things. Thin and white, mair white than me. Her
hair all straggly. It's hard to stay mad at her when I think of
her like that.

I need to try and get it back to her somehow. The only
other time I was in the flat, I had it in my bag. I was gonny
try and slip it down the side a the sofa, but that's where Danny
sleeps; he opens it out every night. It's a couple a months since
I took it, so he would a noticed. Either that, or he would get
the blame for it; they would blame him for takin it, cause he's
still got a thing for Laetitia. I would feel even worse if that
happened, and Danny would be pure mortified. But I didny
get a chance to leave it anywhere, cause there were folk there
all the time. Danny, Jed, Laetitia. No Julian. I was dyin to see
him too. And when Danny had to go out, I couldny really

stay; it would a looked a bit odd. So . . . I'm gonny have to get intay the flat again sometime. On Saturday, maybe, efter the demo. Danny says they're all goin. We've to meet at the edge a Glasgow Green, beside the war memorial, cause the march is startin there. I canny wait.

Farkhanda says she would be here at nine the day, but it's nearly ten the now, and she's still no came. I've made two placards, cause she'll no have time when she gets here. One says:

WAR ON IRAQ?

NOT ON <u>YOUR</u>

LIFE!

And the other says:

BUSH, BLAIR,

BERLUSCONI

WANTED FOR

TERRORISM!

One's in black and the other's in red. I couldny really think of anythin else to write. My da's got one a the

NOT IN

MY NAME!

posters, and my ma's made her ain too,

NO BLOOD

FOR OIL!

I've stuck my two ontay the batons wi the staple gun. My da sanded the wood, but he says to me and my ma, Better wear gloves in case you get a skelf. My ma gies him a wee peck on the cheek then, and he lassoes her wi his scarf, pulls her tay him and gies her a big kiss on the mouth. That's about the first time I've saw them bein nice to one another since Danny's left!

Do you think Farkhanda's comin, Clare? my ma says. We'll need to get goin soon.

Don't know. She says she was. Could we no wait ten minutes longer?

My ma and da have got their coats on already. I'm no really wantin to wait either; I'm scared in case I miss Danny. He'll be wi Julian. And Jed and Laetitia.

Yous go yoursels. I'll wait a wee while longer, I says.

You sure now? It's gonny be a huge crowd the day, they're sayin.

Aye, Ma. I went to Florence, remember? There was a *million* folk marchin there.

Oooh, awful sorry, she says. A seasoned campaigner already.

My da gies her a wee squeeze round the shoulder and winks at me. Right, hen, we'll see you . . .

And the doorbell goes at this point.

Farkhanda, I says.

My da's nearest the door, so he opens it and I hear Farkhanda's voice.

Hello, Mr Kilkenny, sorry I'm late. Is Clare still here?

She sounds a bit upset.

Aye, hen, come in, come in. I wish my da wouldny do that, call my friends *hen*. It's bad enough when he does it to me. He stands to the side to let her in, and she steps into the lobby.

I'm lookin at her and I don't know what to say.

My ma looks at me, then at Farkhanda. Hello, Farkhanda, she says. How you doin?

She's dressed in black fae head to toe. No just her hijab. She's wearin a sorta long black coat right down to her feet.

I'm sorry I'm late, Clare. I couldn't get away any earlier. There's tears in her eyes, but she blinks them away. I made my own placard in case we didn't have time. She hauds up this big piece a white card. It's got red writin on it. Urdu, I think.

What does it say?

Death to the Infidel.

What?

No really. She smiles for the first time and looks ower at my ma and da. No really. But a brother a one a my sister's pals wrote that on his banner. His mother made him burn it.

Good for her, my ma says, though you can understand why people feel that way.

So what *does* it say on your placard?

Tell you later.

You've no got a handle for yours, hen. Would you like one?

There's nay wood left, Da.

Well, we'll just need to improvise, my ma says. You go and get your coat on and we'll find somethin.

Thanks, Mrs Kilkenny. Farkhanda follows me into my room. I pick up my coat and my bag off the bed. I've already got Laetitia's diary in it. I've no forgot.

Clare?

What?

Will you do something for me?

Depends what it is.

She's standin wi her back to my granny's mirror. Fae the front she looks dead young, wi her big round eyes. But the reflection of her in the mirror is like the back of an old woman.

Out a fairy tale or somethin. The old woman in the forest wi a long black cloak. She reaches intay a pocket in the side a the coat and pulls somethin out.

Will you wear this for me? she says.

It's a braid of her hair. Black and smooth and glossy, about the same thickness as my dreads. And she's wove a ribbon through it, the same dark red as *my* hair near enough, and tied it off with thread at one end and a red bead at the other.

I know I shouldny greet, but I have to swallow and swallow to stop mysel.

We've no got time for that, Clare. Will you wear it or no?

I nod my head. I canny speak.

Thanks, she says. You're a pal. And she gies me a hug. All I can see is this black cloth. Thick black cotton. Her body feels hot underneath.

She pulls away. There's no time to sew it the now. Maybe after. But this should fix it for the day at least. And she takes out this vicious-lookin hairpin.

Holy Mary . . . ! I says. Watch what you do wi that. I don't want my brain skewered.

I look at her standin there, wi the pin in one fist and the braid in the other, her black robes blottin her out, and we both laugh.

She holds out her hand and the braid uncoils on her palm. I pick it up. It's plaited really tight. Black and silky with the red ribbon through it, and it smells of jasmine and lemons.

It's beautiful, Farkhanda. Maybe I should a done my hair like this. Thank you.

She turns round. My room feels dead small all of a sudden, and there's no much space to move between the bed and the dressin table. The two of us look in the mirror.

OK, where do you want it? she says. The other side fae Julian's?

There's a chap at the door and we both jump. That's us away now, my ma shouts, fae the lobby. Your placard's standin here, Farkhanda, outside the door. See yous later. Enjoy the march.

Aye, alright, I shout back. You too.

And we hear the door close behind them.

No, I think I want it at the same side, about here, I says. I hold it up just in front a Julian's. Fix it here.

It takes her about three seconds and there it is. A black plait hangin next to the white among the red. And nay sign a the pin.

That's magic, I says.

She's lookin at me in my granny's mirror, wi her lips pulled in ower her teeth. Then she smiles. A sad kinda smile. Aye, it's no bad, is it?

I put my coat on, my white coat, and we stand for a minute lookin at oursels. Me wi my dreads spread ower my hood; Farkhanda wi her brown eyes in her round face and her long black claes.

The black and white minstrels, Farkhanda says. Come on, let's go.

I pick up my two placards. Maybe somebody at the demo will use the other one. Farkhanda's placard's just outside my door, propped up against the wall. My da's took the handle off the kitchen mop and stapled Farkhanda's card to it. The pole's the same red as the writin.

She holds it up high. Hah, she says, I've got a better handle than you. It stands out great against her black coat.

Aye, so you have. You gonny tell me what your placard says now?

She points to the last squiggle and moves her finger back along the line. It says, Dreadlocks and Hijab Unite Against War in Iraq.

252

Aye, right.

She laughs her beautiful laugh and we step out the door and slam it shut behind us.

This is impossible; we're no gonny find them. I've never saw so many people thegether in the town. No even the Saturday of the cup final at Hampden. There's folk pourin into Glasgow Green fae all directions. No wonder the bus was goin so slow. We couldny work out why at the time. Farkhanda went and had a conversation in Urdu wi the bus driver, but I seen him shruggin his shoulders. He pointed to her placard then, and made some comment and they were baith noddin. But she still willny tell me what it really says.

We were pure inchin along the road at two miles an hour. Eventually we says, the hell wi this, and we jumped off at the lights to get the subway the rest of the way. It was worse! There was this big queue right out the front and along the pavement. Never in my life saw it like that afore. You could tell a lot a the folk in the queue were goin to the demo. Apart fae the fact some a them were carryin placards and one guy had a banner scrolled up around two poles meetin in the middle, other folk had badges and rainbow scarfs and stuff, and there was a kind a quiet buzz about everybody. You knew they wereny goin into town to do their shoppin. I heard one guy behind us in the queue sayin to another that a delegate to the conference – *an actual delegate* – he says, wasny allowed in for wearin an anti-war T–shirt, *because it might upset Mrs Blair*! That canny be true, the other guy says. Surely no. Aye, I wouldny put it past that pusillanimous shower! the first guy says.

What does *pusillanimous* mean? I whisper to Farkhanda.

I'm no exactly sure. Feeble-minded, I think.

Soft in the head?

Somethin like that.

No, it means they've got nay guts, hen, nay backbone, the guy behind says.

We look round at him. He's beamin at us, a guy about my da's age. I smell beer off his breath.

Though feeble-minded's no far off the mark either. What's your placards say?

I turn them round for him to read. Aye, that's the game. And the other guy says, That's the berries. What about yours, pal? he says to Farkhanda. She hauds it up and thinks a minute. I'm waitin to hear what she's gonny say.

Same, she says. Same as hers.

It took us about half an hour even to get ontay the platform, the queue was right up the escalator as well as the stairs. When we finally, *finally* got there, the platform was mobbed too and we couldny get on the first train that came along. It was amazin.

By the time we arrive at the Green, we're knackered and I'm needin a pee. So is Farkhanda. But Farkhanda canny go into a pub, even to use the toilet, and every café we've came to is stowed out the door. We're just startin to think we'll need to go behind a bush, when Farkhanda spots a row a Portaloos. The queue's no too bad and they turn out to be no even all that boggin yet, just the chemical smell. So that's us sorted. A bean's a bean, but a pee's a relief, as my da would say!

When I come out, Farkhanda's waitin for me, a figure in black, starin into the distance, her placard upside down at her feet, her hand on the red pole like it's the handle of a parasol. Come to think of it, we could do wi a parasol the day; it's brilliant sunshine and the sky's dead bright, hurts your eyes to look at it. Cold but. I jump down the steps and put my arm around her shoulder.

OK, where do we start? I says. You sure Shenaz is gonny be here?

Well, they says they would be. Her and Mumtaz and Aisha and Kalsum.

Are they all gonny be dressed in black too?

Yeah? So?

I'm only askin.

No, you're not, Clare. You don't approve of us wearin Muslim dress.

It's no that. Honest. It's just . . .

Just what?

Just . . . it seems like it's tryin to – I don't know – rub you out or somethin; make you disappear.

Well, it is in a way. Do you think it's better having men looking at your bum all the time, ogling your breasts, spiking your drink, so they can follow you and rape you?

She's got dead angry all of a sudden and her face has went dark. And I'm thinkin, How did we get into the middle of this?

Keys, I says, and I stick my thumbs up, like we used to do when we were wee and didny want to fight. Gonny no fall out wi me? No the day.

She's turned her back on me now and I want to put my hand on her shoulder, but – I don't know – I canny. I go round the front and look at her instead, through the one wee window in the black. Her face is closed down, and I don't know what she's thinkin.

Farkhanda, I says, truce. Please.

Her face is still shut.

I pick up her braid at the side of my head. You want this back? I says.

She tuts and gies a big sigh. No, she says. Don't be daft. And she nearly smiles again. The march'll be movin off soon. Let's see if we can find your brother and my sister.

We prop our placards on our shoulders and move towards the sea of people. At least we can see the war memorial stickin up into the sky. What is it you call they things again? An obelisk? Aye, I think it's an obelisk. We have to fight our way through the crowd to get to it. There must be a lot of people usin it as a meetin point, cause we canny get right up to it. Wee weans wi face paint and home-made banners are runnin about. There's even a choir, a bunch of women in three rows, practisin their anti-war songs.

Gonna lay down those guns and bombs,
Down by the riverside . . .

They're singin in harmony too. It sounds really good. Old-fashioned maybe, but good. I wonder if it's the choir that woman Bernadette told me about in Florence. Circe, it was called, I think, wasn't it? I never rung her up when I got hame, like she says. No sign a her in the rows. They're all a lot older than me, anyhow. Some a them's older than my ma even.

I think I see Shenaz, Farkhanda says. She's jumpin up and down to look ower the heads of the folk next to us.

I jump up too. Oh aye, I see her, I says. With they other lassies. I don't dare to say it to Farkhanda, but they're no that hard to spot; a wee huddle a black in a sea of colour. We gonny go and say hello?

Yes, if we can get through. Any sign of Danny?

No, I've no clapped eyes on him yet.

It's Julian I'm really lookin for, I think to mysel. He's taller, should be easy to spot in this crowd, even without his big hair.

Hi, Wee Yin. I get a fright. Danny! Standin right next to me. I look round at him. He's thinner and his hair's longer. It seems like ages since I seen him.

Then I watch it dawnin on him. His face is a picture. Jesus

Christ! he says. When did you do that to your hair? Aw no, Clare . . . no, wait a minute . . . You're no still . . . ?

No! No, I'm no. I can feel my face goin red and Farkhanda's lookin at me funny.

Hi, Danny, she says then.

Oh hi, Farkhanda. How you doin? Alright? You no talk some sense into Clare?

I helped her to do it, she says. She's wearing one of mine too. And she reaches ower and picks up the black plait to show Danny.

I wish she hadny says that. I know she's tryin to stick up for me, but I wish she hadny says it. I move my head back and she lets the braid fall.

Don't tell me you've got dreadlocks under that scarf and all!

No, she says, and she giggles. But maybe I should pretend I have. Make me more mysterious.

I always had a feelin she fancied Danny.

You're already a mystery in your own right, Farkhanda. Don't need dreads for that.

And she's like, smilin at him wi her head on one side. Funny how he can just switch it on, Danny. Charm the pants off the lassies. Does it to my ma and all; twists her round his little finger.

The place is even mair crowded now and we're gettin shoved about the more people jostle into the space. That's when it dawns on me.

It's started, I says. I can hear some drummin at the front.

And right enough, you can feel the movement all goin in the one direction now, away fae the Green.

It'll no be very easy reachin Shenaz, I says to Farkhanda. We look back; it's solid rows a folk as far as you can see.

Impossible, she says.

257

But she's no one bit bothered; she's quite happy walkin between me and Danny. She holds up her placard and I remember mine. My hand's sore wi carryin them; the batons have got sharp edges.

Would you like one a these? I says to Danny. I lift them baith so he can see what they say.

No, you're alright, he says. I can never be bothered with they things. What's your one say, Farkhanda?

She turns and beams at him. It says, If Bush said jump into this hole, would you jump, Mr Blair?

Aye, dead right, Danny says. Good question.

So, now I know, I think to mysel, but I don't say nothin. I flick my dreads out the back a my coat, so they spread right across my hood, and I pull Julian's one ower to the front, so I can half see it hangin there out the corner of my eye. Danny's no even mentioned the rest a the gang – Julian and Jed and Laetitia. I wonder where they are.

Where we marchin to? Farkhanda says.

The Armadillo, Danny says. He's havin to shout now over the noise. Alang at Finnieston, where the Labour Conference is. Blair's done a runner but, fucked off afore he was scheduled to, helicoptered out. Couldny face us.

Cowardy custard, Farkhanda says, and smiles when Danny laughs.

There must be at least fifteen in the line we're in. It'll need to thin down a bit, so we can get along the streets. Then I realize we're at the Saltmarket already, afore I've even clocked we're out of Glasgow Green. It's dead disorientatin being stuck in the middle a this many people.

I catch the tail end a some singin somewhere behind us; it must be the choir. A snatch of an old Scottish song. I'm sure I've heard my da singin it, somethin about wind and clouds . . . *blaws the cloods heelster-gowdie ower the bay.* I mind it now.

> Broken faimlies in lands we've herriet
> Will curse Scotland the Brave nae mair, nae mair . . .

It would be good fun singin alang wi them. Better than chantin.

> . . . Black and white ane til ither merriet,
> Mak the vile barracks o' their maisters bare.

We're kind a near the drummers. They're in front on the back of a lorry wi all sorts of drums, big ones and small ones and medium-sized ones, batterin them and dancin to the rhythm. A kind a Latin beat. *Sambayabamba*, it says on their T-shirts. Wouldny mind a go at that as well. Everythin looks mair fun than just walkin wi a placard! I wish I'd a took a whistle instead, and some maracas. I seen two lassies wi plastic bottles full a lentils, shakin them and dancin round each other, blowin whistles, as they're walkin along.

> Sae, come all ye at hame wi freedom . . .

We're goin uphill slightly now, and the whole sky ahead's filled wi banners; CND, Unions, Church groups, Muslim groups, SSP, SNP, Lib Dems, Greens, SWP, every colour stretchin into the distance. No Labour but; no that I can see. All they banners make me realize we're no near the front at all. I think folk must be joinin in right along the route; same as me and Julian done in Florence. I need him here to drag me up to the front. To the *vanguard*. That was cool.

Polis on horses are goin up and down the sides, their long navy coats spread ower the horses' bums. Somebody in the crowd shouts, Gaun yersel, Shergar! In the row in front, a woman squelches through some horseshit and yelps. Which is just as well, cause that warns me and I manage to keep my feet out it!

There's guys wi megaphones, stewards, wearin fluorescent jackets and armbands, makin sure the rows areny too long and keepin everybody chantin.

> Who let the bombs out?
> Bush, Bush, Blair.
> Who let the bombs out? . . .

Farkhanda's shoutin wi the best a them. I don't know why I'm surprised. The noise all around is deafenin. Whistles. Drums. Pipes. Maracas. It's funny but, you're wi all they people chantin and you still feel a bit embarrassed. I would rather sing. A couple a rows back some students are singin 'Give Peace a Chance'. But our bit's all chantin. Except for Danny. He's walkin along wi his hands in his pockets. I bet he'd like to sing too.

Then somebody comes along the line handin out sheets a paper. She says, We're gonny try and get this section singin; hope you'll join in.

Aye, sure, if I know the tune.

You'll know it, she says, and hands a sheet to Farkhanda.

And then it's started afore I've even read what's on the sheet. I do know the tune; it's 'If You're Happy and You Know It' . . .

> If you cannae find Osama, bomb Iraq.
> If you cannae find Osama, bomb Iraq . . .

So I'm singin and Farkhanda's singin and maist of the folk round about are too.

> . . . Make war not love this season
> If you cannae find a reason, bomb Iraq.

We dae it twice. Danny's no singin but. He's got his mobile out, textin somebody.

This is supposed to be a protest, I says, and you're just textin your pals.

Aye, but one a them's at the demo in Amsterdam and the other yin's at the one in Rome. He shows me the text fae somebody called Ruaridh in Rome.

> Ciao Danny.
> Give it laldy!

How come you know people in Amsterdam and Rome? I says.

He looks at me like I'm daft and puts his mobile away again.

Anyway, this Ruaridh guy says, gie it laldy, so . . .

So . . . ?

So gie it laldy!

> . . . Make war not love this season . . .

And it's great, cause he's the only guy singin in our bit. Farkhanda smiles at me and we sing louder too.

> If you cannae find a reason, bomb Iraq . . .

Next thing somebody behind me's tuggin at my dreads. I turn round ready to gie them a right bollockin, whoever it is. And it's Julian! I get the fright a my life.

Well, look at you, Clare, he says, and he's grinnin fae ear to ear. His hair's a bit longer fae the last time I seen him and it's bleached at the top! My hand goes to his dread afore I can stop it, but I don't think he's noticed anythin. He's gelled his hair up into spikes and round the sides is still his ain colour.

Hi, Clare.

Oh, hi, Jed. I never seen you there.

What?

I says, I didny see you. I shout this time. Jed's different too; he's got his hair tied back in a wee ponytail and he's no wearin his glasses. Maybe he wears contacts now.

Cool dreads, he says, and smiles. He's dead nice, Jed. Aye-ways makes you feel everythin's OK. Except it's no, cause my heart's lowpin and I'm pure tryin my hardest no to look at Julian. He's talkin to Danny now.

Jed, this is my pal, Farkhanda, I says. Farkhanda, Jed, Danny's flatmate.

Hi, Jed, she says, pleased to meet you. Excuse me if I don't shake hands; I need both of them for my placard.

What does it say? Jed says.

You no read Urdu?

No. Punjabi, and no much of that. A wee bit Hindi.

It says: War Breeds Hatred; Hatred Breeds War.

Ain't that the truth!

I'm lookin at her. She didny even bat an eye!

Who's your friend? she says to Jed, and looks at me with her eyebrows up and her mouth puckered.

Oh, sorry, Jed says. Julian, meet Farkhanda; Farkhanda, Julian.

Julian? she says, like she's surprised. Very pleased to meet you. I've heard a lot about you.

I fire her a look, but she's high as a kite; enjoyin hersel; windin me up.

All bad, I hope, Julian says. He's still smokin roll-ups, I see.

Of course, she says. What else?

Julian looks at me then, takes a long drag on his wee thin rollie, and like my insides pure turn to liquid. I think I'm gonny drop my placards.

Any a yous want a placard? I've got one spare.

Julian's hand covers mine like an electric shock. I'll relieve you of this one, if you like. What does it say? He turns it round to read it: BUSH, BLAIR, BERLUSCONI, WANTED FOR TERRORISM. Ace. Last time I saw this message, it was in Italian. And he looks right at me again. Turns the blue headlamps on full beam. Even though I know it's a trick, it still works on me. My legs are pure jelly!

Where's Laetitia? I says. I remember her diary and put my hand ower my bag. That's when I realize it's getting heavy, even though I've no got that much in it, the strap's cuttin into my shoulder.

Julian stops smilin. Frowns. I could kick mysel!

London, he says. Gone to see Mummy. But she's at the big demo down there as we speak. He takes his mobile out, flicks it open and shows me a text.

Ldn packed
At least 0.5 M
Prob more. Lx

Trust me for mentionin her! Great, I says. Is that bigger than here?

He throws back his head and laughs. Yes, I'd say so. Just a tad.

Well, this feels as big as Florence to me, I says.

It's certainly big for Scotland. He looks sideways at me. Great turnout.

I look away fae him out to the sides of the march. I canny believe we're halfway along St Vincent Street already. You never take in where you are when you're goin along wi the crowd. I notice a lassie walkin back down the line. She's got short cropped hair and her placard says:

Julian clocks her too. He gies her the thumbs up, waves his placard and shouts, Right on, sister! Even though she's away by and canny hear him.

I thought you would be wantin to be at the front, I says. In the *van*guard.

He shoots me a look and then he smiles a slow smile. Only at demos on foreign soil, my dear. He bends down and whispers in my ear, And only après sex with a beautiful redhead.

I take a quick look along the line at Farkhanda and Danny and Jed. Don't think they've heard. I hope no. I hope they canny see what a riddy I've got either. I bend my head so the dreads cover my face a bit.

Is Scotland no foreign soil, then? I says. I'm lookin at him through the bars a my dreads.

Oh, the most exotic of all forreign countrries . . .

I hate it when he tries to do a Scottish accent.

. . . but that fulfils only one half of the necessary preconditions.

What's he talkin about? Oh aye, right; I get it. No that I let on.

Preconditions for what? Danny says.

For a nanosecond, Julian looks a bit flustered. Then he says, We were talking about going to the front of the demo. But I do that only in circumstances where it's possible to steal a march, so to speak, on some rival group. This is much too broad a coalition to bother with that.

I breathe again! How does he do that? Come up wi a lot a shite like that off the top a his head?

Danny puts on an American accent. Why do I get the feelin you're blowin smoke up my ass, as they say in the movies?

His eyebrows are up and a smile's hoverin about his mouth waitin to land.

Moi? Julian says.

Aye, *you*, Danny says. He's walkin sorta sideways, so he can see Julian better. I don't *think* he's angry; he sounds like he's bein funny. What rival group have you ever ousted fae the front of a demo? For some reason Danny doesny want to let this go. Maybe he did hear after all.

What's this, the Spanish Inquisition? Julian says.

It's weird the way guys communicate; sometimes you would think it was all in code.

Aye, the rack and the thumbscrews are too good for you, ya cunt.

Great way with words, your brother, Julian says to me. He's got the handle of the placard under his arm and he's concentratin on rollin another fag. Wee strands a tobacco are flitterin fae his fingers and blowin away.

How much further is it? Farkhanda touches my arm. She looks hot, even though it's a cold day.

Canny be much further, I says. We're comin to the end a St Vincent Street by the looks a things. It can only be about, ten, fifteen minutes to the Armadillo now.

That's right, dear. A woman in the row in front turns round to speak to us. Ten, fifteen minutes at the most. D'you know, the end a the march is still no started.

You're kiddin!

No, my husband got stuck in traffic, couldny get parked, so he's away at the end. He's just phoned me; they've no even left the Green yet.

That's when I turn and look back. All you can see for miles through the streets a Glasgow is thousands and thousands a people. The road's pure jammed right across. It gies me a funny feelin in the back a my throat.

Farkhanda's looked back too. They surely can't start a war with all this opposition, she says.

Of course they can, Danny says. They've already decided. They don't gie a fuck how many people march.

I look at Julian. I'm afraid I agree with Danny, he says.

So what's the point a marchin? I says.

Farkhanda's lookin upset now, like she might start greetin.

I think Jed notices. He says, You have to hope it makes a difference; it sure canny if all you do is sit at home and shake your fist at the TV. You have to hope that all these people together means *some*thing; that it sends a message to the Bushes and Blairs of this world.

Like I says, he's a really nice guy, Jed. He's cheered Farkhanda up already.

I agree, she says. You have to have hope. But it's not up to us. *Inshallah*, war will be avoided.

God, I've no heard her sayin that afore! She must a got right into all the religious stuff.

Jed gies her a kinda questionin look. We'll need the whole panoply of gods for this one, I think. The whole jing bang.

Hail Mary, Mother of God, I think to mysel, pray for us now in the hour of our need.

Soon I see the aluminium roof of the Armadillo glintin in the sun and hunners a folk all millin about. The start a the march looks like it's been there for ages already. When we come right up to the open bit round the conference centre, I notice all the polis in their fluorescent yellow jackets.

Fucksake! Danny says. Must be the entire membership a the Strathclyde Police Force here the day.

I think he must be right; I've never saw so many polis althegether in one place.

To protect our glorious leader, no doubt, Julian says.

That's what my da calls him too, I says.

Danny draws me a dirty look.

Wow! Look at that grass, Farkhanda says. Have you ever seen grass that green?

No in February, I says. Must be fake.

That's a good one, Jed says. The greener grass is always fake; the evergreen illusion. He chuckles to hissel. Jed's dead deep sometimes. You don't really know what he's talkin about.

Anyway, here we are. It'll be ages before the speakers start but. At least there's mair space – for a wee while, until the rest of the demo gets here. I turn and take a gander round about me. It gies me a chance to look at Julian without him noticin. He's standin wi his shoulders hunched and another rollie in his hand. He must be cold; he's chitterin slightly. He could a done wi his big parka the day, no that wee thin combat jacket. The corner of his black and white Arab scarf is stickin out the pocket. His hair's the colour a glass in the sun. Like that spun glass.

Farkhanda comes and stands beside me. I can feel the heat comin off her in waves; her face is dead flushed.

Alright? I says.

She gies me a kinda sharp look. Why should I no be?

Just askin.

Hey, Julian, she says, what do you think of Clare's dreadlocks?

Julian turns to us and the look he gies takes us both in at once. Very fetching, he says. His eyes stay on me a bit longer.

How d'you like *his* haircut but? Danny says. No think he's the spittin image of *Oor Wullie*? All he needs is a bucket to sit on. *Oor Wullie, Your Wullie, A'body's Wullie.*

Who is Oor Willie? Some arcane Scottish folk legend?

He doesny look nothin like him, I says. You don't look nothin like him. Julian gies me a quick smile.

I keep my eyes off Danny, and turn away again to watch the marchers comin into the square. Folk are getting fed up

267

holdin up their banners and placards, but you can still read a few. NO BLOOD FOR OIL; BLIAR!; BUSH THE FATHER KILLED MY SISTER, BUSH THE SON IS KILLING ME; IF WAR IS THE ANSWER, WHAT IS THE QUESTION? There's a woman that looks like a granny, white hair, walkin around carryin a wooden tray in front, with a strap to hold it on. The tray's covered in sandwiches. A card on her chest says, MAKE PIECES, NOT WAR. Reminds me of the fairy cakes! She's goin about offerin a piece to anybody that wants one. I wouldny mind one mysel; I'm quite hungry. Jed is pure psychic; I see him goin up to her and choosin a handful a sandwiches. He offers her money, but she laughs, willny take it, shakes her white head.

Farkhanda, he says when he comes back, you can have first choice. Most of them are roast ham, but there's an egg and a cheese one.

I've no really noticed afore, but Jed's quite good-lookin; in fact, without his glasses, you would say he's definitely handsome. You canny hardly see the scar now where that guy Malcolm kettled him. And his ponytail – that makes him look different too.

Thanks, she says, could I have the cheese?

Rest of yous alright with ham? I would prefer the egg.

Don't tell me there's another veggie in our midst! Julian says. Heaven forfend.

I propose a competition, Danny says. He takes a piece off Jed, and stuffs half of it in his mouth right away, chews it fast and swallows it. One pound prize for the best slogan spotted.

So we all start shoutin and pointin at once.

BLAIR! DON'T BE A PUPPET TO A MUPPET!

POVERTY IS A WEAPON OF MASS DESTRUCTION.

Look at that yin. BLAIR STOLE MY HOMEWORK AND STARTED A WAR.

I've seen a good one, Farkhanda says. VOGTS OUT!

In the end we decide no to stay for the speakers. We'd already been hangin about for over an hour and marchers were still comin into the big square. I stood up on a concrete bollard and I seen Shenaz and her pals, so Farkhanda finally went and joined them. It was kinda obvious she would rather a came wi the rest of us, but there was no way. She'd a been in deep shit wi her family if she had. Serious soapy bubble. In a way I was glad when she went, cause it was getting to be a strain. Knowin that Shenaz would be lookin for her; knowin that bein wi me was against the will of Allah or somethin. She telt me one time that some Muslims think all Western lassies are whores and prostitutes. That made me feel horrible. How d'you think I feel? Farkhanda says.

I watch her startin to weave through the crowd towards where I seen Shenaz; her wee black figure tryin no to collide wi marchers millin about and weans runnin. She looks a lot mair unsure of hersel than she done on the march. You can see that the long black coat doesny make her feel invisible at all. No yet, anyway. It makes her stand out mair; people are starin at her, when she goes by. I canny stand it. I run to catch up wi her and start walkin beside her. She turns round, surprised.

Where you going? she says.

Thought I'd come and say hello to Shenaz.

She stops and faces me. No, don't, Clare. Please! she says. And I'm like kinda taken aback at how anxious she sounds.

OK, OK, don't worry. I won't then. I'll just walk alang wi you a wee bit.

You don't have to.

I want to.

Please yourself.

I think she's mad at me cause she doesny really want to go wi them and she knows I know, and that makes her even mair annoyed.

Anyway, I was gonny thank you again for lettin me wear your braid.

That's alright.

It's beautiful.

Don't mention it.

Will you come round themorrow and sew it on properly?

Maybe.

And we could do our *Sunset Song* essays thegether.

I said maybe, Clare. She's stopped again and it's obvious she doesny want me to come any further.

Alright, I says. See you on Monday, if no themorrow. And I leave her there.

The other reason I'm glad she's away is cause a Julian and what might happen later.

I walk back through all the folk and when I'm gettin close to where we were standin, beside the bushes, near the burger van, I'm like, Oh no! There's my ma and da. I half think of hidin till they're away, but they've seen me already.

My ma's talkin to Danny. She's a lot happier than I've saw her for months. She nearly looks young. Danny's turned half away fae my da and my da's talkin to Jed. Julian's standin a wee bit to the side, lookin spare. But when I come right up to them, the exact same moment, I hear my ma saying to Julian, And how's Laetitia?

How does she know about Laetitia!

Oh, she's over the worst of it now, I imagine.

Worst of what? I'm thinkin.

When's the baby due? my ma says.

July, Julian says. Mid to late July.

Baby!

Danny must a saw the look on my face, cause he says, Did I no tell you, Clare? Sorry. Aye, Laetitia's pregnant; nearly four months.

I look at Julian. He's starin down at his feet on the cement path.

I want to sit down but there's nowhere to sit.

I want to take my placard and whack him right across his stupid face.

I want him to put his arms round me and sing Bob Marley songs.

I want to be home in my own room, sittin on my bed, lookin in my granny's mirror.

My da comes forward. You alright, hen? You look a bit pale. Better get you hame.

No, Danny says, she's comin back to the flat wi us. Post-demo party. She'll be fine wi some grub in her belly.

Why's he sayin that? Is he tryin to protect me? Does he no realize? Why's he sayin that?

That what you want, hen? my da says.

I notice my ma eyein me up, tryin to kid on she's no.

Aye, I'm fine, Da, I says. I'm goin to the flat for a wee while. I'll no be late.

He pulls a tenner out his pocket and hands it to me. Make sure you take a taxi hame, he says.

We come up fae Finnieston and walk through the park. The demo's startin to disperse now; a lot a folk are walkin away fae the Armadillo in this direction. Julian's went off somewhere to get more tobacco. That's what he says, anyway. The sun's still shinin and I'm frozen. Jed's talkin to me but I canny concentrate on what he's sayin. Somethin about the birds you can see further up the river.

Aye, he says, there's a heron and cormorants and goosanders. He's countin off on his fingers. Mallards, moorhens. I'm told there's kingfishers too, but I've no seen them yet.

Danny's been quiet walkin along, but he says, Kingfishers? In the middle a Glasgow? You sure you've no been pallin about wi the junkies down there? Gettin a hit aff them? Away wi the birds and the bees?

No, seriously, he says. Kingfishers. Ask anybody who's down there a lot: parkies, guys fishin, dog walkers. They'll all tell you. There's kingfishers nestin along the Kelvin. You ever seen one, Clare?

What?

A kingfisher.

A kingfisher?

Yes.

No.

Would you like to?

What?

See one.

A kingfisher?

Aye.

Suppose so, I says. I get the feelin Jed's tryin to cheer me up, but I canny picture a kingfisher. I canny imagine the colours. No the now.

They're probably all aff their faces down there, Danny says. Jed looks at him. Who?

The guys fishin. The parkies. The fuckin dog walkers.

Your cynicism ill becomes you, Mr Kilkenny.

I'm tired a this conversation. I want to be on my own to think. I walk away fae them a wee bit. Folk fae the demo are all travellin in the same direction through the park. The path we're on comes near the river at this point. I look ower the railin at it; I don't see any birds. Just dirty brown water wi the usual junk. Across on the other bank, there's some a they giant hogweed, the dried-out stalks a them, about six feet high wi the spray of wee jaggy stars at the top. You're no meant to touch it; they telt us at school a couple a years ago. It's poisonous. There's an old pram sittin on an island in the middle of the stream, just sittin in the middle of the river, the water flowin by, draggin long grass like green hair in the current. Wonder how it got there. Wonder where the baby is that used it last.

A baby!

We're just finishin the carry-out when Julian comes in, a roll-up in one hand and a bottle a wine in the other.

Any nosh for me? he says.

You, ya spongin bastard!

In exchange for some excellent weed? He waves a wee poly bag wi some green stuff in. Same colour as his combat jacket.

I keep my head down and my eyes on my chicken korma and dip a piece of naan in the sauce. It's better than the curries you get in the scheme, a lot a flavours I've no tasted afore. I dip and dip the naan till it's soaked up as much sauce as possible, but I canny lift it to my mouth to eat it. I leave it in the gravy and lick my fingers instead. The napkins you get in they places are no any better in the West End; wee thin things that fall to bits as soon as they get wet. I take my packet a hankies out my bag and wipe my hands on one a them instead.

By the time I look up again, Julian's went and got a plate fae the kitchen and he's helpin himsel to saffron rice and lamb tandoori and dhal and they lady's finger things – okra, Jed called them. He sits down on the red sofa, at the other end fae me and starts eatin. Jed hands him a bottle a beer.

Wonderful! he says. Heaven. I could smell this coming up

273

the stairs. Started the juices going before my key was in the lock.

Aye, Ali's is the best, Danny says.

I try to look sideyways at Julian wi my head still down, keepin my dreads out the gravy. The gel in his hair's started to wear off and it's no stickin up as much, but it's still straight and spiky. And bleached. It makes his face look as if it's got mair colour in it and his eyes are darker. He takes a mouthful a curry and holds his bottle up.

Nay offence, Tish, as they say in Glasgow, but it's good to be able to eat a curry without the sound of vomiting as background music.

Jed and Danny both hold their bottles up.

I'll drink to that, Jed says.

Aye, thank fuck she's ower that stage, Danny says. I thought she was gonny disappear althegether, she got so thin.

I'm like, shocked. At Jed especially; he ayeways comes across as dead understanding.

Danny looks at me. You no want the rest a your chicken, Clare?

Aye, I do, I says. I'm havin a break.

Keep your hair on; only askin.

So, what did you think of the demo, Clare? Julian says. How does it compare with Florence?

I glance up at him quick, but his face doesny give nothin away. Maybe it's a straight question. It feels a bit like at school, when a teacher expects you to gie an intelligent answer, but no much comes into your head. I shrug my shoulders.

Don't know. I think I had mair hope at the one in Florence. Like, that maybe it could achieve somethin. I look at Jed when I'm talkin, no Julian.

Jed says, I thought today was hopeful. No matter what happens – and I don't have any illusions that war will be averted; Blair's hitched his wagon to Dubya's horse and they cowboys decided long ago – but, no matter what happens, there's a different mood.

Think so? Danny says. Is that no your romanticism? It'll take mair than a war in distant places, mair than a few hunner thousand dead Iraqis, mair than a few of our boys hame in body bags, to shake the great British public out their apathy.

It's great when guys talk politics; you can sit there quiet and think your ain thoughts and naybody notices you. Same wi my da. No Julian but.

What's your view, Clare? Didn't you start a group at school? He's tryin to get me to look at him. School kids interested in politics; that hasn't happened in a long time?

Naybody's interested normally in what *school kids* think. I say this to Jed.

True, Jed says. He's lookin at me dead sympathetic. But it was great to see you and Farkhanda there, and all the other . . . young people.

I know he's tryin to say the right thing, Jed, but he's makin it worse. I feel about five now. I stand up and hand over my plastic curry tray to Danny.

Here, I says, I'm no wantin any mair.

I pass Jed on the chair and go round the back a Danny sittin on the floor, so's I don't have to step ower Julian's legs to get out the door.

Where you goin, Clare?

For a pee, if that's alright. Or am I meant to ask for permission?

Was it something I said? Jed says.

I sling him a deafie, ignore the lot a them and cross the hall to the bathroom. It's dead different, the flat, since they painted it. Or since Danny painted it; I think it was Danny done maist of it. The hall's dark red now, like bein inside a heart. I switch on the light. Somebody's hung a mirrored globe up beside it, and wee slivers a light appear on the walls, shivering.

The bathroom's a sort a pale blue and there's a mirror above the sink wi a weird kind a mosaic in blue and green, like hunners a eyes watchin you lookin at your reflection.

Mirror, mirror on the wall, I says . . . I don't suppose you know fuck all.

That makes me feel better! I even catch mysel smilin in the middle of the starin eyes. They've put a fancy shower curtain up above the bath now, sky blue, wi a huge print on it of a painting. I pull it straight on the rail to see it properly. The metal rings rattle along it. It's a picture of a bare naked woman comin out a tree grabbin for this guy, who looks like he's tryin to get away, but she's clutchin him round the waist. He's bare too, except for a wee bit of see-through cloth coverin his privates. Only it's bunched up, so's you canny see anything interestin through it. At the bottom it says *Tree of Forgiveness*. It looks like a Burne-Jones. I'm nearly sure it is; the faces are mair or less identical to the ones I seen in the paintings on the internet. *King Cophetua and the Beggar Maid* was one. That beggar maid was nothing like me, I didny think. I couldny work out what Laetitia was talkin about in her diary.

Which reminds me . . . it's still in my bag; I've no had a chance to put it anywhere yet.

I lock the door and put the toilet seat down. There's a smell of antiseptic in the room that makes you think of hospitals. I bet they scrubbed it to get rid of the smell of sick. How come Danny never mentioned to me about Laetitia bein sick? About her bein pregnant? I imagine her sittin on this seat doin a pregnancy test.

I wonder when they all knew. I suppose the last time I really seen Danny properly was at Christmas, when my ma persuaded him to come hame for the day. A truce was called. It was like him and my da were walkin on eggshells round about one another the whole day. I felt sorry for my ma, she'd went to such a lot a trouble, cooked the biggest turkey I've ever saw.

I feel like Tiny Tim, Danny says.

And my da says, Does that make me Bob Cratchit?

Who's he? Danny says. And it was obvious my da thought he was takin the piss. But I don't think he was; he really hadny heard a Bob Cratchit. They hardly said a word to one another after that. I found my ma in the kitchen later, takin big gulps a wine, lookin at the steamed-up window, wi tears pourin down her face.

Christmas, she says. Peace and Goodwill to All Men. And she tipped up her glass and finished her wine in a oner.

But Danny must a telt her about Laetitia at some point. Maybe he was askin her advice. People are aye askin my ma advice about medical things, cause she works in the doctor's, even though she's only a receptionist. Like Mrs Hazel in the top flat. It was my ma discovered it was her daughter, Jenny, flingin the bags a sick out the window onto the back green. All these poly bags a vomit, the handles tied in a bow. The women started to notice them when they were takin their rubbish out, thought at first it was the alkies daein it. But it wasny; my ma found out it was the lassie up the stair. She took her maw up a stack a leaflets about bulimia and spoke to her for hours. Mrs Hazel never knew a thing about it. You would think you would suspect *some*thin, if your daughter was throwin up all the time. But my ma says sometimes the people closest to you are hardest to fathom. She says I should talk to Jenny sometime, ask her in. But I don't really know her; she's a quiet lassie, a couple a years younger than me, and she goes to a different school.

That shouldny matter, my ma says, where's your sense of community?

It was you sent me to St Veronica's.

That's no the point, she says. I'm no talkin about Catholics and Protestants. I'm talkin about a lassie that stays up the same close as you, for heaven's sake.

This happens wi me and my ma all the time now.

Somebody tries the bathroom door and I get a fright.

You alright in there, Clare?

It's Danny. I stand up quick and pull up my pants and jeans. I've no been in *that* long, have I?

Aye, I'm fine, I says. I press the flush and shout over the noise. You wantin in?

No. Just wonderin where you'd got to.

I'll be out in a minute.

I put the plug in the basin and run some hot water. The eyes round the mirror are kinda spooky. Except when you look at them close up; then you can see all the wee bits a tile and glass. It doesny look like a bought mirror; I wonder who made it. It's no the kind a thing Danny would do. And I canny see Julian havin the patience. Must be either Jed or Laetitia. But you would think, if it was one a them, it would be brown; they've baith got brown eyes. The blue's a bright blue, like Julian's, but brighter. The green's an emerald green, like naybody's eyes I've ever saw. And there's a sorta peacocky shimmer on the blue *and* the green. A red tinge too, deep inside.

That's when I realize there's a reflection of me in every single eye; every one's a wee mirror. The red is my dreads flarin. It's like they can really see me. Mesmerizing. I can hardly tear my eyes away fae them, but I force mysel to focus on the normal mirror and I have to laugh. I'm like some kind a startled animal; a creature peepin out its burrow, wi the eyes of all the other creatures a the forest starin out all round. My dreads are tangled, a bit of a mess. I pick them up, a bunch at a time, and separate them. Farkhanda's braid's as black and glossy as ever; the hairpin's no moved since she fixed it.

And Julian's. Julian's is getting fuzzy again. It's like a stick of light wi a kind a haze round it. Julian.

Clare?

A whisper outside the door. It's like he can hear me thinkin!

I'll no be long, I says.

Can I come in?

I'll no be a minute.

I want to see you.

His mouth must be right up against the door, cause I can hear him and he's definitely whisperin.

I look at mysel one more time in the mirror and I pull back the bolt.

He's in before I know where I am and he's bolted the door behind him. He birls round and looks at me. Full on. Like I says, I know it's a trick, but . . . He's standin right under the light and his bleached hair's sparklin. I put up my hand to touch it and he grabs me round the waist and pulls me to him.

Danny, I says. He'll hear us. And Jed.

They're stoned, he says, and he bundles all my dreads round the back and kisses me under my ear. I can smell his ordinary tobacco and the waccy baccy mixed thegether, alang wi the curry. His stubble prickles my neck and I breathe out, push him away.

What about Laetitia?

For a second, his eyes go far away, then he turns them on me again. She's not here, he says. I want *you*, Clare. I *want* you. He nuzzles under my dreads.

And even though I know. Even though I know . . .

Wait, I says. I reach in my back pocket. Use this.

He steps back. His eyes open wide and then he smiles, takes the condom off me. He kisses me hard on the mouth; our teeth crash together; I taste the sour taste of tobacco off his tongue. He pushes me towards the bath and pulls back the shower curtain; the lassie disappears into the tree and the guy goes wae her. He starts undoin his belt and his zip.

Get in the bath, he says. I climb in and he comes after me. He takes me by the shoulders and shoves me against the tiles and unzips my jeans. Pulls them down wi my pants inside, down to the top a my boots.

Now, just stand there.

I do as I'm telt. The tiles are cold against my bum. He pulls the curtain along the rail again and I'm lookin at the back a the painting, over his shoulder; the skin's kind a gold, transparent, wi the light shinin through fae the other side.

And then, he's fumbling wi the condom, rippin the paper off, pullin his ain jeans down at the same time. He's too close to me, so I can't see what he's doin. The smell a my dreads reminds me of him, reminds me of Florence. Then there's a snap and a sharp stink of rubber and he's pressin against me, guidin himsel into me and

Oh!

I put my hands on his bum and feel the way the cheeks hollow out every time he thrusts and he's inside me and my bum presses harder into the cold tiles and this is the third time I've did this and I don't even know if I want to and I do want to and I

Aaahhhh. He groans and jerks and shudders and goes slack against me. His breath is hot on my cheeks and my ear is wet.

And then he's out of me, takin off the condom, pullin up his jeans. He moves the curtain to one side, steps out the bath, turns, wipes his mouth on his sleeve, leans forward and kisses me on the forehead, a wee dry kiss, stands back and looks me up and down, pats my pubes, smiles.

Nice pussy, he says.

And his hand is off me. He tiptoes to the door, listens, unbolts it slowly, slowly, quietly, and steps outside. Closes it behind him. The curtain ripples a bit in the draught he's left. The lassie in the tree tightens her grip on the guy. Then it goes still again. Back to normal.

And I'm standin in the bath wi my jeans at my feet and the condom lyin beside the plughole, oozin spunk, and the wrapper torn in half down at the other side of my boots.

Clare! Clare, gonny come out a there for fucksake! I'm desperate for a slash. Danny's voice sounds slurred.

Comin. Just gies a minute.

I haul up my jeans and cover them with my jumper. At least Danny doesny know the door's no locked. I pick up the condom and wrapper, shift the curtain the tiniest wee bit, so the rings willny rattle, and climb out quiet onto the floor. I search about for a bin, then think, No, unroll some bog paper and wrap it in that.

Come on, Clare, I'm gonny piss mysel.

Comin.

I look at the window; it's dark outside now. I don't see any way to open it.

Clare.

I shove the whole mess in my jeans pocket, pull down my top and open the door.

I thought you'd a grew out a that by now, Danny says. His voice is slow and hazy. Spendin fuckin hours in the bathroom.

I'm away hame now, I says. I'm gonny get my coat.

Right, he says. But he's stoned. He doesny gie a shit.

I'm back in the spangly red hall and the livin room door's shut. I tiptoe across to it and peep in. No sign a Julian. Just Jed, lyin back in the armchair wi a wee squashed end of a joint in his hand, starin softly into the distance. There's a bank a blue smoke driftin across the dark window, ower the top a the carry-out trays and beer bottles. The whole place smells a dope and curry.

Hi, Clare, Jed says, and waves the dowt at me.

Where's Julian?

Gone to crash out he said.

Right, I says, and I pick up my coat and bag. Say cheerio for me, will you? He waves the fag end again.

On second thoughts, don't bother.

He isny bothered. He's away wi the bees.

First bin I come to when I get down the stairs and out the close, I dump the mess fae my pocket. Some of it's leaked out in my jeans and the slime's all over my hand. As soon as I'm sittin in the taxi, I look in my bag for my hankies.

That's when I see it. Laetitia's diary.

March 2003–October 2004

21 MARCH 2003 – GLASGOW

Well, they've done it: despite protests the world over, the Americans have dragged us into war and are bombing hell out of Iraq. The other day, Julian, Danny, Jed and I watched the Commons debate on a pub TV; watched Blair, reeking of Righteousness, stand his moral high ground, use his oratorical skills to persuade Parliament it was the only thing to do. But we were all a little stunned when the first missiles landed on Baghdad, in spite of knowing it was inevitable. Danny and Jed were unusually subdued. A cloud of hopelessness descended on the flat and not even Julian's best comic efforts could dispel it. Jed went out and bought an enormous, widescreen, ex-rental television – a bargain, he said – so we can follow events as they unfold. But after the first evening, I couldn't watch it and left them to their obsessive channel-hopping. Coverage seems to be 24/7: unreal night vision targets flare momentarily as 'smart bombs' pick them off; reporters on hotel balconies wear flak jackets, try not to flinch when shells whizz and bombs crack in the city behind them; 'ordinary' Iraqis, i.e., men in cafés, give guarded responses to questions about Saddam Hussein; and the first footage of limbless, crying children in narrow hospital beds has begun to filter through. Unbearable.

At least it has prompted me to take up my journal again. Not to record the horrors, but to track where I am in it all, what with the baby coming. I finally, *finally* stopped lamenting my lost journal and bought this new notebook the other day, a rather fine one, covered in turquoise silk with green embroidery, a bright little talisman against the darkness, one that won't so easily slip from my grasp. Still can't for the life of me remember what I did with my last one. I know I had it the day Julian and I met that peculiar man in Silvio's café, but none of the staff would admit to having seen it. Perhaps our friend with the blank-eyed stare and the sonorous voice found it. Appalling thought! That a stranger might read it! When I try to recall what was in it, what incriminating details, embarrassing revelations, I come up with very little, even though it covered most of last year and all of the year before. It makes me think I must try to be more conscious of what I commit to these new pages, treat this notebook as something other than a repository of self-reflexive outpourings.

I already regret not recording the start of my pregnancy. And yet, would I have written anything during the months of sickness? Probably not. I have *never* felt so ill, so utterly wretched, so totally in the grip of a process at once part of me and a thousand times more powerful. It was hard not to think I was carrying some alien life form. Yet, now I'm better than I've been for months, especially since I've felt the baby kicking. All the old clichés turn out to be true: I'm 'blooming', the nurse at the clinic told me; Weary, Cheery and Dreary, the three trimesters, have suddenly clicked into place and I'm enjoying a welcome break in Cheery-land. Progesterone sure as hell beats the pants off Prozac as a mood enhancer! Which is just as well, since I couldn't keep the damn capsules down. It's such a *relief* to have stopped vomiting, anything afterwards would be heaven by comparison. But it's more than that, I'm full of energy, joy almost. Against all reason, it has to be said, what with Mother's frank aversion to the news when I told her in

London last month, the disappointment in Daddy's voice pulsating darkly down the phoneline, Julian's wild oscillations about the prospect of fatherhood. And I don't care. I don't care. 'I've boarded the train there's no getting off.' I'm having this baby and that's that. Perhaps the feelgood factor is some dastardly trick one's hormones play, to convince one to see the pregnancy through. It's certainly become more of a reality in the past few weeks; I can believe there *is* a baby now. I ought to have let them tell me the sex when they did the scan, then I could assign a pronoun, make it even more real: *she*'s kicking; *he*'s peaceful today for a change. But I'd rather wait, somehow. Generic BABY is as much of a concept as I can cope with at present. And it's *definitely* as much as Julian can handle. He goes quiet sometimes and I wonder what he's thinking, but he's never once suggested he won't go the distance and stay with me. With US. With me and little Letty, as he calls the baby. For that I am truly grateful.

10 APRIL 2003 – GLASGOW

Baghdad has fallen to the Americans; the statue of Saddam toppled. Comical Ali, so-called, the Iraqi Information Minister, denied it right up to the end. 'If the Americans come to Baghdad, we will hit them with shoes!' he said. Danny told me a whole cult has grown up around him – website, T-shirts, badges, the lot. 'Wait till you see, that cunt'll turn up on the Parkinson show!'

Meanwhile, yet another demo last weekend, though much smaller than the enormous ones in February. Is there any point? Is anyone listening? Somehow, being pregnant makes it more urgent. Imagine bringing a baby into a world where people do such things to one another. And yet, there's my father supporting Blair too. Demonstrations and banner-waving, those are the politics of adolescence, he said to me; you have to grow up eventually and that means making difficult decisions and abiding by the consequences. As if it's Blair or Bush who will have to suffer for what they have unleashed. The most they will endure is political defeat, followed by the publication of their war memoirs and many lucrative years on the after-dinner speech circuit. Well, Blair, at any rate; I doubt if George W. will leave the golf course! I have never felt so cut off from Daddy as I did during that phonecall. He even used the odious euphemism, 'collateral damage', when I spoke of the images of maimed and orphaned Iraqi children. This I might have expected from my mother, but not Daddy. As for my 'difficult decision' to go ahead with the pregnancy and 'live by the consequences'? That was another matter: You're throwing your life away. It's your grandchild, I said, but he was unmoved.

Julian is in London to speak to his parents about the baby; I wonder if he'll have more success. It meant he wasn't at the demo, which I was glad of in the end. Danny was there, Jed, the watchful Clare, complete with dreads(!) and her little Muslim friend, Fariah (I think). Clare was wearing a T-shirt she'd had printed Katharine Hamnett-style with a message of her own:

WHERE ARE THE
WEAPONS OF MASS
DESTRUCTION?
SEARCH ME!

Very effective, I must admit. Wish I'd thought of it. Together, they made quite a statement: Clare, like some fierce but diminutive Celtic warrior princess, white T-shirt, black slogan, flaming, snaky hair; her friend in black from

head to toe, carrying a placard with the same message –
English on one side, Urdu on the other. A jovial policeman
walked alongside us for a bit, told them it was a dangerous
invitation to make to him and his colleagues. Clare shot the
poor guy a look to wither his manhood! And Fariah
unleashed a stream of invective in Urdu. Or at least, that's
how it sounded. They both seemed so young and – what? –
unencumbered, that I had a flash of myself in my current
state, cow-like, ponderous. And, if I feel that now with over
three months to go . . .

Jed was very sweet, told me my new top was the exact
shade of the kingfisher's wing he'd seen last week down by
the Kelvin. Made me realize it's my colour of the moment,
kingfisher, the same as my new diary. I asked him if the bird
was as vivid as its reputation and they all seemed surprised –
assumed I'd have seen flocks of them at Wellwood. I was
immediately uncomfortable. Of course there was a river, but
we'd left for London before I became interested in such
things. It was pure iridescent, man! Jed said, his eyes alight. I
began to tell them about the heron Julian and I saw by the
weir last November, but caught a glimpse of Clare's scowl
and let it drop. She's unvaryingly sullen towards me now,
despite my best efforts to be friendly. Whatever Julian says,
she read more into their Florence adventure than he insists it
warranted. I tried to broach it with Danny after the demo,
but he gave me such a look! I was mortified; I forget
sometimes, that we had our own brief ~~liaison~~ situation.
Mostly it's fine, no tension that I can detect. But this time,
Danny said, Is your head full of wee boxes? Some you keep
locked up, so the things that don't suit can't escape and
damage the official version? I guess I deserved that, though I
was a bit taken aback by his ferocity. It sounded rehearsed
too, as if he'd given it some thought. The good thing about

being pregnant is that one is so completely *taken up*, one's body and mind surrendered to the process, that these things recede quickly into the background. Next day, he brought me a mug of tea and asked, a trifle anxiously, if I was alright. He's so solicitous, Danny, about my condition, protective even. I struggled out of the sagging armchair and gave him a hug, told him I really appreciate his support. That seemed to mollify him and he went off to work quite happy. God, that sounds as if I'm simply exploiting him, but truly, I do depend on his being here, especially with Julian away.

Had a sudden urge – several months overdue! – to dig out my thesis again, while the hormones remain favourable. By this time I ought to be on the outskirts of Drearyville but, fingers crossed, so far I still feel good. I got as far as reading my notes on *To the Lighthouse*, but when I went back to the novel to check out some quotes, I found Lily Briscoe so arid, so thoroughly two-dimensional, that I couldn't imagine how I ever perceived her struggle to paint as heroic! It must, I think, be another trick of the pregnancy; childless women seem so *pointless*. Mrs Ramsay, who struck me before as unbearably smug and interfering, now seems rounded, complete. I didn't even bother to open the Gertrude Stein. The whole thing will have to be done again from start to finish. Frankly, my dears, I don't give a damn!

17 MAY 2003 – LONDON

What was I thinking of, coming here? I'm sitting at the glass-topped desk in 'my' room at Mother's. When I look out the window, I can just see her, chair camouflaged in the purple shade of the plum tree – The blossom this spring was simply stunning, darling. Such a shame you missed it – nursing a cup of coffee, flicking too quickly through the pages of a magazine to be actually reading it. I'm starting to calm down again – deep breaths – but why is it that she can get to me so? Why did I think this time would be any different? I was feeling good when I walked in the front door, absurdly happy to see the stained-glass nymph still dipping her toe in the pool, actually looking forward to spending time with my mother, grandmother of my child-to-be. And what was the first thing she said? God, darling, you're so big! I do hope you are using cream to prevent stretchmarks. And that was the *least* offensive of her remarks. She poured us a coffee then launched into – Celia Legrozet cut me dead at a charity dinner last week. The child *is* definitely Julian Legrozet's, is it, darling? Only, there are rumours that the family doesn't believe so. This last line she delivered to my back as I walked away from her. Hence, my retreat to my room and Mother's to her garden. Julian certainly didn't tell me his parents were harbouring such thoughts. He did say they may be 'a little ambivalent' but that 'they will come round'. Deep breaths. Think of the baby. Last time I sat at this desk, I could roll right in to the edge. Now the baby informs me in no uncertain terms just how close I am allowed to come to hard objects! I feel him kick at least twenty times a day now.

I'm so glad I saw Daddy last night, before coming here. Once I got over how stylishly cool the restaurant was – glass and light minimalism with a Japanesey feel, and me like a stranded whale among the sushi! – I began to relax. He was looking well, Daddy, if a little greyer, and clearly pleased to see me. I was determined to make the most of this meeting, since he's going abroad again. OK – don't mention the war, I thought. And what does Daddy do once the starters are on the table and the waiter has withdrawn? As I guide the chopsticks to my mouth, he says, So, what do your anti-war friends say to Iraq now? Evil dictator out of the way;

temporary UN-backed administration; road to democracy embarked upon. Everything rosy! I mumble a few things about warring factions, Sunni and Shia, American oil interests, dead children, recruitment of new generations of suicide bombers. But there is no way my father is going to listen to any of that. He sits there in his expensive suit and holds forth between mouthfuls, shiny and solid with that assurance of his place in the world, which I have always envied. Everything he says comes with such easy authority, I find it difficult to stand my ground.

I knew I had to change the subject if I was going to rescue the evening. The portions of food were fashionably tiny and I was still starving after two courses. I asked for another dish and Daddy raised his eyebrows, Eating for two, is it? I realized that was his first allusion to my pregnancy. But then suddenly he leant across the table, took my hand and launched into a litany of questions and concerns: Was I alright? Did I really want the baby? Would Julian do the decent thing and support me? What about my PhD? What about my career? Did I need more money? It was my old daddy again. I almost expected Biddy to bound up and lick my hand! From there, we found our way back to the more familiar and comfortable terrain of our days at Wellwood.

It wasn't till we got to the hotel – as plush and sumptuous and dripping with red and gold tassels as the restaurant was trendily bare – and were sitting in enormous armchairs in the residents' lounge, that I asked Daddy about his great-aunt Laetitia. I was too tired and hormone-befuddled to take in the genealogical details; it was the story I wanted. Not much to tell, he said. But Mother said you really admired her. That's what I told *her*, he said, and winked. He must have seen disappointment on my face, because he did his best then: I do know she was involved in the suffragette movement before the First War. What happened to her afterwards? I asked. She became a campaigner for rights of one sort or another, squandered the family fortune on various 'good causes' – he didn't need to wiggle his fingers; his intonation conveyed the inverted commas round the phrase – lived till her nineties and died in penury. And Harry, I asked, what about Harry? Who? my father said. Never heard of him. Her, I said. Harry was a woman. Never heard of her, he said. And that was all I could winkle out of him. We went to our separate rooms then – what luxury after the flat! – and this morning shared breakfast before Daddy headed off to the airport and I came here to Mother's.

Talking of whom, where has she gone? She's left her magazine and cup on the seat under the plum tree. I'd better go and make some kind of peace with her. Tonight, Aunt Laetitia's trunk . . .

18 MAY 2003 – LONDON–GLASGOW TRAIN

Well, Daddy's account of Aunt Laetitia didn't offer any new insight. I have her diary and the letters from Harry I found in the trunk last night spread out in front of me here. As things stand, the two brief letters I've read so far don't reveal much more: the address, 15 Larchfield Road in London; date: 19 Sept. 1915. Then –

Dearest Laetitia (that gave me such a strange feeling!),
    I have at last recovered sufficiently from our European adventure to risk reaching out to you again . . .

They must really have fallen out in the end.

. . . I write to ask if you would be willing to meet with me to try, in some small way, to re-establish our relations on a more friendly footing, away from the baleful influence of the 'arrangement' we lived by in Florence. I had thought that, should you agree, we might choose somewhere public and open, such as Kew Gardens, and see how we go from there.

And it ends –

I await your reply, and remain forever
  Your loving Harry

There's no indication of whether or not the meeting happened, no surviving entry in Laetitia's diary around that time, just a few ragged edges near the spine. Then, in another letter, dated 14 October 1915, two lines and a photograph:

Mr Haldane, the young American we met in Florence, sent me this photograph taken in Fiesole. I thought you might like to have it. H.

The photo is not particularly clear. It shows two women sitting at a table on a terrace in dappled sunshine. The one in the foreground is smiling from under a wide-brimmed hat, squinting a little, her face turned up to the sun; the other, further back, is almost totally obscured by the shadows of leaves. On the back of the photo are the words: 'Laetitia Gardener, Fiesole, April 1915'. The writing is Harry's, same as the letters, same neat hand from the dedication in the notebook. It's fascinating trying to cross-reference the letters with the journal, 'read' the ripped out pages, guess at the mysterious 'arrangement'. Unbearably tantalizing! How odd to erase sections of one's life like that. I should think one would want to hold on to all of it, especially the parts one can't expose to the public gaze. Perhaps she foresaw that someone from the future would rummage about in her personal writings, pore over her private papers, ferret out her secrets. Had she known it to be her namesake, would it have made a difference? Why won't you tell ME, your great-great-niece, Laetitia? Will you mind very much if I find you out? Before we parted, Daddy said he would try and find out some more information about Laetitia.

18 JULY 2003 – GLASGOW

Bright sun again today, not particularly hot, I'm told, but I'm finding it close to unbearable, what with the traffic fumes and the migrainey shimmer above the cars. Silvio's wasn't much better, the hiss of steam from the espresso maker apt soundtrack to my discomfort. So, back in the cool of the flat, before the sun moves round and makes sitting in the window impossible.

Another dream last night, like most nights since I came back from London in May. This time, the action has moved on; it's more like a half-submerged memory. I need to nail it before the baby comes. So here goes . . .

The point disappears soundlessly in the soft fur between the legs. There is a sudden stink: blood, raw meat. A hand works quickly to withdraw the knife, lay it on the bench. In the dusty light a flash of the blade. Pink fluid oozes from the slit in the body, as fingers probe the lips of the wound and pull apart. More pink revealed. I am unprepared for the WHACKWHACK! of the cleaver. My eyes are level with the edge of the bench and I blink and blink. The furry feet set aside look wrong; white knuckles of bone gleam. When I turn to you again, you are pulling the skin like socks off

stumps of limbs, folding the fur back on itself along the
hare's body, rip, ripping it away from the naked flesh. Why
are you taking his jumper off? I ask. The skin reaches the
front of the body, stops at the base of the skull. WHACK!
goes the cleaver again and the head is off. You toss it by an
ear to the side of the bench from where one dead eye
regards me. The neck is ragged, trailing strings of blood,
Two more whacks then silence. I stare at the naked body,
the glistening headless doll . . .

I sat up with a cry and Julian held me. Shh, shh, it's OK,
it's OK. Was it that pesky wabbit again? Shh, it's alright. And
so we added another to my list of theoretical frameworks to
tame the beast: Looney Tunes. Elmer Fudd gets lucky and
bags Bugs Bunny. That's all, folks!

By the time I calmed down, we were fully awake. Julian lit
a roll-up. He'd avoided the discussion till now, but this time
when I asked what we should call the baby, he said, If it's a
girl, she could be Florence after the place of her immaculate
conception. And if it's a boy? I ask. Let's see what Joyce has
to offer, he says. He jumps naked out of bed, takes down
Ulysses from the shelf, opens it at random and reads off a list
of names. I remember some of them: Goodman, Simon,
Blazes Boylan, Horatio Nelson, Theobald Matthew . . .
That's just the first two paragraphs, he says and reads out
another list, ending with: Dedalus, Dignam, Bloom. He
looks up and smiles, See, a rich crop! Never fails. Any among
that lot tickle your fancy?

How about Matthew? I say.

I favour Dedalus myself. What do *you* say? He puts his ear
to my belly and the baby kicks hard. He agrees, Julian says.
Unequivocally!

Danny came in at that point in my musings and turned on
the TV. Dr David Kelly, the Iraq weapons expert, has been

found dead. There are pictures of an area of woods, cordoned off with crime tape, and a stricken Tony Blair disembarks from a plane in Tokyo. Now the shit will really hit the fan, Danny said. Will it? I said. Action and events, things happening, are unimaginable to me now; the world has stopped for me till the baby's born.

27 JULY 2003 – QUEEN MOTHER'S HOSPITAL, GLASGOW

My baby boy was born at 3.00 a.m. He's asleep in the Perspex crib beside my bed. So much black hair – such a red face. So beautiful! Quiet now among the white beds after the clamour of birth. Julian fetched my journal so I could record it. The night nurse is reading in the nurses' station opposite. Earlier, Danny and Jed brought flowers. Danny had a tear in his eye, I know he did, called the baby 'Wee Man'. How you doin, Wee Man? Julian's gone back to the flat for a sleep – white as a ghost after staying with me through labour. He has bruises on his arms where I

9 NOVEMBER 2003 – KELVIN QUADRANT, GLASGOW

A long gap since the last entry – no time, what with Matthew and getting our new place ready. And now I have *two* journals to choose from. Funny my lost one turning up on the day we moved out of the flat. It was behind some books on the shelves in our room. How it got there, I can't imagine. I stopped among the packing cases for half an hour to look through it. It's as if it belongs to someone else, someone in a different age. I blushed to read my preoccupations before Matthew was born. It's so strange to think that's the person I was less than a year ago; even stranger to transport myself to a world without Matthew, in which his cry had never sounded, the cry round which my entire existence now revolves. A chill came over me at that moment, kneeling on the floor in the flat, with the light dying at the window. I was struck by an unbearable longing to hold him close and rock him and feel the weight of his little body in my arms. But I couldn't. He was at Peter and Maeve's. I got hold of myself and the feeling passed, but not without a surge of resentment towards P. and M. Unfair. They have been incredibly kind, looking after him for us. And the best of it is, they never made it seem like an imposition; they so delight in Matthew, that it's rather as if we were the ones doing *them* the favour. ~~Sometimes I wonder if they~~

When I think of my hesitation in taking up their offer! I don't know *what* I expected that first day; some ghastly high rise with broken lifts and graffiti and used needles abandoned on the stairs. But their house is warm and comfortable – a good close, as Maeve said. There's plenty in the scheme not so good, but this stair's not bad. Danny was there to introduce us and he stood back smiling when Maeve took Mattie from me. I found myself swaying in unison with her, as she rocked him, cooing, his little red face peeping out from under his hat, his eyes squeezed shut. Your mammy can't take her eyes off you, she said to him. No she canny. And it was true. I liked her immediately. She has a faded version of Clare's red hair, dyed a kind of strawberry blonde to hide the grey, and Danny's green eyes almost, though more of a blue-green. And when she looks at you, she has a level gaze that could cut through any bullshit. A little unnerving. She's obviously very close to Danny too. I was slightly anxious the atmosphere would change when Peter came in, but I needn't have worried. Danny and he have clearly arrived at some sort of workable truce. He was quiet that first day, Peter, quite formal when we were introduced, more reticent than Maeve, I thought. But since then, it's an absolute joy to watch him with Mattie. He walks about the floor with him and sings him funny little Glasgow songs, as well as Van Morrison and other golden oldies. ~~I sometimes wish~~

Clare is the only source of tension in the house now, the only fly in the ointment. Most of the time she keeps to her room, but occasionally she doesn't escape soon enough when I turn up to drop Matthew off, and it's obvious she's miserable. The whole family is very edgy around her, since she didn't sit her English exam in May and consequently ruined her chances of going to university this year, despite doing rather well in her other subjects. She dug her heels in and left school, with no plans to sit the exam next time round. Now she seems to do nothing but mope around the house all day.

14 DECEMBER 2003 – KELVIN QUADRANT, GLASGOW

Mattie asleep, fitfully; teething I think, his cheek red. Julian gone to buy him some rusks and a 'playstation', as he calls it – a 'command centre' of spinning, clacking, rattling coloured plastic – for his Christmas!

A letter from Daddy today – not coming back before the end of the year after all. Still hasn't seen Matthew.

Saddam Hussein captured, hauled from a hole in the ground in Tikrit, bearded and filthy. Americans cock-a-hoop.

12 APRIL 2004 – SILVIO'S CAFÉ

Haven't been in here for *ages*. Danny taking Mattie for a walk in his buggy in the hope the movement will induce a nap. A chance to catch up with myself before Julian comes. Coffee and a scone, I think. So tired. Mattie up again most of last night. Not even Maeve could get him to sleep last time he was there and she's the champion. Nearly puts *me* to sleep with her rocking and crooning! Met her sister Patsy on Thursday. No mistaking *she's* from the same family – a mass of red curls, pale skin, dark blue eyes. She and Clare were deep in conversation when I arrived – they could easily be sisters – till Maeve introduced me. Clare scuttled off to her room then as usual, leaving the real sisters to argue over who got to hold Mattie first!

US began bombing Falluja on Good Friday. Happy Easter, from the civilized Christian West!

15 JULY 2004 – KELVIN QUADRANT, GLASGOW

Less than two weeks till Matt's first birthday – can't believe it! It's passed in a flash at the same time as feeling like eternity. How does that work? Thank God he's sleeping better now – I'm starting to feel vaguely human again. Dug out Aunt Laetitia's journal once more, determined to get to the bottom of it. Read it cover to cover this time; realized I *had* actually seen it all before, I just didn't feel as though I had. Not surprising, given the removal of half its pages – kept having the sensation I was just missing something. But I was right first time round – mainly art criticism, travelogue stuff, a quest for the paintings of Artemisia Gentileschi. Nothing more about Harry. A mystery. A closed book. Daddy still hasn't found out anything about Laetitia – or at any rate, hasn't sent me it.

Round at the old flat yesterday, all of us glued to Jed's giant TV for the Butler Report. Talk about Teflon Tony! Hutton, now Butler. Couldn't stay till the end – Mattie was crawling around, 'into everything', as Maeve puts it. Danny's done a great job holding back the tide of grunge, but there are still too many hazards in a flat geared towards starting the revolution!

*

Waiting for Danny to bring Mattie down from the flat when he wakes up. He sent me off for coffee and a chance to read my letter from Daddy again properly, without Matt grabbing for it. Typical Daddy – he writes me a letter instead of phoning. He's had to cancel his visit again – or rather, *postpone* it, he says. But he's sent information about Aunt Laetitia – as a softener, no doubt. So let me get it down here.

. . . Laetitia was a leading light in the suffragette movement, an embarrassment to the family, with all her banner-waving and unladylike activities. She narrowly avoided disinheritance by marrying well at the eleventh hour – some silly sod who was besotted with her, Lord James Gregory by name. Marriage only lasted four years – or rather Lord James did; he died suddenly, done in, so the story goes, by his helpless adoration of the beautiful but difficult Laetitia Gardener. (See photo enc.)

The photo is of them on their wedding day in 1921; L. in flapper gear, cloche hat, dark bob, looks straight at the camera, a determined set to her jaw, striking rather than beautiful. Lord James, in some sort of military get-up, has failed to watch the dickybird; his face is a soft blur, though the angle of light reflected in his eyes suggests he's gazing fondly down on his bride.

It seems there was a child, which died in infancy, broke Lord James's heart. As for Laetitia's political activity, you might imagine not much of a record was kept by the family, but I managed to acquire the enclosed booklet – you'll never guess from whom – Nanny Rosenthal! Do you remember her?

Of course I bloody remember her. Though, if I'm honest, I rather thought she was buried somewhere in the grounds of Wellwood – with Biddy, under the horse chestnut!

She lives in sheltered housing now, but is sharp as a tack and appears to have quite an archive of family memorabilia. I thought the booklet might satisfy some of your curiosity. In answer to one question, I can tell you that you weren't named after the late, great Laetitia. Good Lord, no! Your mother got the name from some magazine.

Thanks a million, Daddy!

Give my grandson a big kiss from me (thank you so much for the delightful pic!) and I promise to come and see you both before he starts school!

The booklet is yellowing, musty. Its unadorned cover bears the title: *Magdalen Mothers*, and is subtitled: 'An Account of Work in East London with Prostitutes and Their Children. Authors: Laetitia Gardener and Harriet Martin, 1927'.

Harry!

Started to look at the pamphlet, when Danny popped in with Mattie, both of them in a good mood, grinning at one another. He's taking him down by the Kelvin to see if they can catch a glimpse of 'that fuckin kingfisher'! Matt's going to have a very salty vocabulary for one so young! But it's sweet of Danny to give me a chance to read. Come to think of it, it's a lovely day for the river. L. & H. can wait; I should still be able to catch up with Danny and Matt if I run . . .

November 2004

This'll be Elvis's second Christmas. The first he'll know about but; he was too wee last year. Already this year, when my da picks him up and takes him to the window, he points to the Christmas lights in the house across the road and says, Pity.

Aye, you're right there, son. Pity the scheme's got so little goin for it, the Christmas lights go up at the start a November.

I'm sittin on the sofa behind them, wi my book open on my knee, watchin the pair a them. He's tryin to say *pretty*, Da, I says.

And my da turns round and smiles. Is that so? he says. Well, bless my soul. Is that so, Matthew? Pretty? Eh? Pretty? And he shoogles him up and down and Elvis shrieks and laughs.

That's his right name, Matthew, after Laetitia's father, but I still canny call him that. He'll ayeways be Elvis to me. It's cause a the shock a black hair he was born with; it doesny matter what way Laetitia brushes it, it ayeways ends up in an Elvis quiff.

I was mad at first when my ma offered to look efter him a couple a days a week. I couldny understand it.

We're helpin the lassie out till she gets on her feet, my ma says. And, anyway, look at him; look at they long dark lashes lyin on his cheeks; who could resist him?

Me. I could.

I would get in fae school and there they would be, the three of them, playin happy families. Danny too, sometimes, dependin on his shifts in the pub. My ma sings to Elvis when she's trying to get him to sleep, even though she canny sing to save hersel.

. . . *My brown-eyed boy*, she sings. *Sha la la la lalala* . . .

It's pure excruciatin! And Elvis's wee face sits on her shoulder, quite content, when she walks about the room, his mouth poutin, like he's tryin to say somethin, or he's just gonny burst into song alang wi her.

Farkhanda's as bad. She thinks he's *dead cute*. If my da or Danny's no there, she comes in and takes off her hijab; she's allowed to do that in front of Elvis, cause he's a baby. He loves her long black hair. When she holds him, he gets his fingers all caught in it and it takes ages to disentangle him. He hangs on, the wee bugger, willny let go. I don't let him near my dreads.

At first, when he came, when he was a new baby, I showed her his Elvis mouth. You stroked his cheek when he was lyin sleepin in his pram and his mouth would go up at that side, into a wonky Elvis grin. Skew-whiff. Farkhanda laughed her silvery laugh and tried the other side. Same thing. My ma caught us at it and laughed as well, at the same time she was tellin us off. But it's dead obvious, *they* all think he's like Elvis too.

When he's greetin loud and willny stop, Danny sings, *You ain't nothin but a hound dog, Cryin all the time.* And that quietens him down. One day, I came in and caught my ma and da dancin slow round the livin room, Elvis between them in my ma's arms, sleepin, his head on her shoulder, hair all quiffed, and my da wi his arms round the baith a them, singin 'Love Me Tender'. Pure gie you the boak!

Who's King? Danny says, and picks him up and birls him round. Eh? Who's the King? And Elvis laughs and screeches and skirls.

Nearly as good a pair a lungs on him as you, hen, my da says.

It's Julian collectin him the day, so I'll be disappearin into my room till he's came and went. Maistly it's Laetitia picks him up; Julian sometimes. I try to be out when it's his turn, but it's hard to predict. Now and again even Danny comes ower for him, when he's no workin, and takes him back on the bus to Julian and Laetitia's. His tongue's still hangin out whenever Laetitia's around. Wouldny put it past him to go on the *Trisha Show* and ask for a DNA test. He's on a hidin to nothin but. Birds of a feather, Danny; you said it yoursel. I didny think he would be that interested in the wean, but he pure dotes on him.

Check his wee face, he says once, when Elvis was younger, he's really concentratin, look at him, thinkin great thoughts.

Don't be an eejit, I says, he's deain a jobby. There, see? Smell his great thoughts now?

. . . They said you was high class,
Well, that was just a lie . . .

Danny was pissed off wi me and took him into the bathroom to change his nappy. But I must admit, I was fooled by it too the first time I seen it, though I wasny gonny let on to Danny. I'm readin my book; Elvis is lyin on his bouncy chair, bouncin away, his hair swept back, reachin for the mobile danglin above. Suddenly he stops and goes dead still and his eyes are starin straight ahead, the way you see folk doin when they look like they're gazin into the distance, but really they're thinkin about somethin else entirely. Then comes the stink.

Oh, pooh, Elvis, I says to him, you mingin wee bandit! And I go for my ma in the kitchen.

I'm choppin onions here, Clare? Could you no change him for once?

No way, I says. I don't know how to.

Oh, grow up, Clare, for heaven's sake, my ma says, you're no a wean any mair.

That makes me pure furious and I stomp back through.

Right, you wee minger. I lift him out his bouncer and lay him on his changing mat. His legs are goin nineteen to the dozen and he grabs for my dreads, so I gather them up and stick them down the back a my jumper out the road. He's no bothered; he's blowin bubbles through his Elvisy lips. One a my shorter dreads at the front slips down and he stops brrrrr-in and starts swinging his hand in the air, cross-eyed, openin and closin his wee fat fingers, trying to catch it.

Ah, ah, I says. No, you don't.

His denims are easy enough to get into – his denims! Probably *Armani*, knowin Laetitia – they've got poppers on the inside at the legs. I would hold my nose if I could, but baith hands are needed for this operation.

Pffaww! I try no to breathe in. Elvis doesny bother his shirt; he's lyin there in his stinky nappy, his red socks wavin in the air, smilin at me and gurglin away.

What you laughin at, you wee toerag? What you laughin at? Eh?

I tickle his belly just above his nappy and he laughs mair. He's like a wee manikin wi his teddy-boy hair. A homunculus, that's a good word. A munchkin. I don't see nothin a Julian in him. He's got Laetitia's brown eyes. Wouldny matter what colour of eyes the father's got, Danny says, the brown-eyed gene is dominant. Well, that's no entirely true, Jed says. And he gies a lecture on genetics that goes right ower my head, about how it all depends on the combination a genes on baith sides a the family.

Right, Pongo, I says. I hold my breath, rip off the stickers at the sides a his nappy and open up the surprise package.

Feuch!

First thing he does is stick the heel a his red sock right in the bright yellow shit.

Och, Elvis!

I pull it off dead careful by the toe, then he goes and does the exact same wi the other one! And when his socks are off, he's stickin his bare feet in. I grab his ankles next time he kicks and hold them together. It's all over my hands now too. Elvis gies a husky chuckle.

OK, you wee shite, very funny.

Wi my one hand I pull him up by the feet then manoeuvre the shitty nappy out fae under him wi the other. I take some babywipes and clean my ain hands first, then wipe all round his bum. I make sure that's a shite-free zone, afore I start on his willy. It's like a wee bud peepin out fae his – what d'you call it? – scrotum. I don't really like touchin that. It's all red and wrinkly and it takes me ages to clean the yellow shit out all the creases. There's somethin no right about me handlin Julian's wean's wee pointy prick. Elvis is lovin it but, cooin and burblin, now and again makin a swing for my dread. Like father, like son, I says. I dry him wi his Scooby Doo towel, fae the set my ma got in Poundsaver's, Scooby and Scrappy and Nemo and the characters fae *Toy Story*.

I'm reachin for a clean nappy fae the big bag behind the sofa, when he pees in the air, this sorta high golden arc. He turns and pure hits me wi it right under the chin!

OK, pal, that's you had it, I says. You done that deliberately.

The pee runs down my neck, trickles down the inside a my T-shirt, into my bra. And there's a puddle of it under him on the changing mat, soakin into the back of his denims and his red top.

Fuck, I says.

By the time my ma comes through, I've got all his claes off

and I've cleaned him up. His smooth bare body's sittin on my knee, smellin a wee bit better, and he's still tryin to get a haud a my dreads. My ma laughs at me. What's my boy doin? she says. What's Matthew been doin to Clare? He squeals and flaps his hand at her like a baby seal.

He only got shite all over his socks and my hands, peed down my jook and soaked his claes for good measure. Apart fae that, he's been perfect, I says.

He's only a baby, Clare. Be fair. He canny help it.

Aye, well. I canny help it if it gies me the boak.

And my ma looks at me then, a right long look, as if she's tryin to figure me out.

Well, don't worry, Clare, I won't be askin you to do it again.

And that makes me feel rotten. Bad. Horrible. Thing is, my ma doesny know what's at the back of it for me.

She picks Elvis up off my knee and goes to his bag to find him some clean claes. He gies me a big lopsided grin ower her shoulder and reaches out to me. I canny help smilin at him. No matter what's goin on at the other end, there's never a hair out a place; still the same slicked-back style wi the quiff looped forward, like somebody done it wi gel.

I blow a wee kiss at him behind my ma's back.

> You ain't never caught a rabbit
> And you ain't no friend of mine . . .

I've only just went into my room, when I hear the door and Julian arrivin and my ma goin, Look, Matthew, who is it? Who is it? It's Julian, that's right!

I ayeways get the feelin she's tryin a bit too hard, like she has to be nice to Julian to get her hands on Elvis.

Joo, Elvis says. Joo-joo.

Hello, Matt, Julian says. Have you been a good boy? Have you been a good little boy for Maeve?

He's been perfect, my ma says. Come in, Julian.

I'm thinkin, how nice! Maeve! How terribly, terribly. Awfully, awfully. Frightfully, frightfully. Nice! I look at mysel in my granny's mirror and I've got a face like fizz, but I canny help it.

Hello there, Julian, I hear my da sayin.

Hi, Peter, how's the hand?

I hate the way he's so palsy-walsy wi my folks.

Aye, no bad, my da says. So, so. He's no that sure a Julian either. No really.

He's been off work a week now, my da, wi Dupuytren's contracture, waitin for an operation. His mates were all laughin at him, gettin the same thing as Maggie Thatcher. It's carryin that handbag, Peter, they says. We telt you it would be the ruin of you. And my da's pure mortified he's developed the same condition Thatcher had, even though he tries to make a joke of it.

Could be worse, he says, I could be doolally an aw! It's the Viking blood; only thing I'll ever admit to having in common wi her Baronessity.

Aye, that and a hatchet face, my ma says. *Look for the Baronessity* . . . And he chases her into the kitchen.

Underneath, you can see my da's quite down but, and my ma's worried too. Before this happened he hadny been a day off work in the last seven years, or so he's ayeways tellin Danny. The management said he didny need to be off his work for this either, cause, wi him bein the supervisor, he hardly ever has to operate the machinery these days. But he wouldny budge; a health and safety issue, he says, and the union backed him. Away hame and put your feet up for a while, Peter. You're due it, they says.

Personally, I think it's mair to do wi Elvis; my da loves lookin efter him. Mind you, I seen him workin away, massagin his hand the day, when Elvis was down for his sleep, tryin to get the fingers to straighten out. You can see it's just gettin worse; they're curlin right into his palm.

Have you tried physiotherapy? I hear Julian askin him.

I've got an appointment next week, my da says. Maybe that'll dae the trick.

First I heard of it. I sit up on my knees on the bed to look in the mirror, and pick up Julian's dread. It's clatty again. I've bleached it twice already since the first time; it gets manky cause I'm rubbin it between my fingers so much, I suppose, even when I don't realize it. It's amazin naybody's twigged; no even Julian; even though he knew the dreads were about him. Aye, he knew that alright.

But Farkhanda's kept her word and no telt naybody. Sometimes she says, Is it no time you moved on, Clare, and got rid of the Peroxide Dread? She says it like it's got capital letters, like it's some kind a poxy disease.

What about yours? I say. You want me to get shot of it tay?

Suit yourself, she says. I'm no bothered.

But I don't think that's the truth; I think she likes to see a bit of her hair out in the open; *hidden in full view* was the way she put it. She gets a thrill bein there when people ask me about it. I make sure I don't look at her and say, Oh, I just like variety, so I done a couple a dreads different for a laugh.

Cool, they says. Or, I see. Dependin on the age a whoever's asking me. And Farkhanda smiles at me when we're on our own again. She's eighteen, same as me, Farkhanda, and she's started at university, so you would think she would stop wearin the hijab. But I've got a sneaky suspicion a bit of her wants to wear it. She's used to it now. A bit of her wants to say to the world, I'm a Muslim, any objections? Come over here and give us them.

Aye, well. No really, but that's the feelin I get sometimes. At least she doesny have to wear the dead heavy black claes she wore last year for the big demo and right up to the so-called end of the war. I was worried she was gonny start wearin a chador, a burkha even. But it turns out it wasny her ma and da after all; it was a group Shenaz and her pals set up theirsels, Daughters of Palestine or somethin, to show their solidarity wi the Palestinians.

There must be better ways to give your support than coverin yoursel up, I says.

What? she says. Name them.

And I couldny think a nothin. Except signin the odd petition in the city centre on a Saturday and payin attention when it comes on the news. Mair houses bulldozed; mair weans shot for throwin stones.

Point taken, I says.

I'm dead jealous a Farkhanda bein at uni. I could a been there with her if I hadny blew it, no sittin my Higher English. Why did I no? It's hard to remember now. I was on a real downer after the Glasgow demo and what happened wi Julian. And then the war started anyway and I thought, what's the point? What is the fuckin point? But when my da heard I'd dogged it, he was that disappointed, I thought he was gonny greet, so I sat the rest a them. At least that's somethin, he says.

I tune into what's going on in the livin room again. It sounds like ma's gettin Elvis into his snowsuit, you can hear him squealin – I'm gonny get him a white one wi rhinestones and big flares – and my da's talkin to Julian about the American election.

Nah, my da's sayin, Bush is in. A dead cert. The Iraq factor's worked in his favour.

The polls aren't so certain, Julian says.

Well, we'll see. Only two days to go. You can nearly hear my da's brain tickin over goin, *Who does he think he is, this upper-class twat, comin into my house tellin me about politics?* Only he wouldny say *twat*.

That you all ready, sunshine? That you wrapped up warm for the winter's night? We'll need to get you a Celtic scarf, wee man; bring you up in the true faith. Eh?

Thank you very much again, both of you, Julian says. Tish and I really appreciate it.

Tish and I! *Tish and I . . .*

Not at all, my ma says. He's a pure delight. Aren't you, Matthew? A pure delight. She squeezes her voice thin and high. And she must be ticklin him through his padded suit, cause Elvis obliges wi a *pure delightful* shriek, on the way out the door.

Hey, wee man, I wouldny be surprised if they heard that in Australia, my da says. Great pair a lungs.

I need out a here.

January 2005

My da says, That bus goes through every damn scheme between Glasgow and Helensburgh. Take the train, hen, for Christsake.

And I should've, but I was still mad, so I stood in the cold at the stop on Glassford Street, across fae the Trades Hall, and got on this bus that's windin in and out every wee street behind the St Enoch Centre.

It was my ma's idea.

You'll be able to take Barney for walks down the shore, blow away the cobwebs. It'll dae you a world a good, she says.

Aye, what she really meant was it would do *her* a world a good. I know I'm pure daein her head in these days. Think of all the people, she says, that have died or lost everythin in the tsunami. Think a the weans in Iraq or Darfur. What have you got to complain about? She knows what buttons to press, my ma, makes me feel pure rotten. I'm in the wrong all the time the now.

But I'm lookin forward to seein Barney. He's a big daft slobbery bugger and he ayeways cheers you up. Last time I seen him, he put his paws right up on my shoulders and nearly knocked me flyin. They treat him like a wean, my aunt Patsy and uncle Davey, cause they've nay weans a their ain. Which is fine by me, cause it lets me off the hook.

We're startin to get out fae the tangle a wee streets at last, and the driver's built up a bit mair speed on the straight road beside the Clyde. It's an old bus, rattlin and shakin along, and the seats are threadbare and lumpy. A woman across the passage is tryin to catch my eye, tryin to start a conversation, but you know yon way when you just don't want to talk to anybody; you just want to sit and think your ain thoughts. I keep my head turned away fae her and look out the window. It's a kinda hazy day, no exactly grey, but no sunny either. We're chunterin past derelict sites and warehouses mixed in wi loads a new designer flats bein built. The gentrification a the Clyde, my da calls it.

Anyway, I'm glad of the chance to get away; things have been tense at home, to put it mildly. It would be different if I wasny hangin about the house all day. Jed's right about one thing, if I'd a sat my Higher English when I was meant to, I could've been enjoyin mysel at uni wi Farkhanda the now. As it is, every Tuesday and Thursday I'm pure keyed up, wonderin if it will be Laetitia or Julian collectin the wean. Yesterday it was Laetitia. She makes a point of talkin to me, bein nice, but the nicer she is, the more my face willny behave itsel. It's like I've got Bell's palsy or somethin, same as Mrs Graham across the landin. Twisted and ugly. And to put the tin lid on it, my ma's aye sayin how great Laetitia's lookin.

She's fair came on, that lassie. Positively blooming.

Positively fuckin make you sick!

The thing is too, you can't help lovin Elvis. He makes you. No that I let on. It would be different if he wasny their wean. We have a carry-on when my ma and da's out the room. Him and me's pals on the QT.

There's the Armadillo. No so shiny the day; the overlappin plates of the metal roof look as if they could do wi a polish. It seems like a hundred years fae we marched there. Aye, and look at Iraq now. What was the point? I says that to Jed, when we went to the pictures a couple of weeks ago and he says, Come with me. He dragged me by the hand along the road to an internet café, sat me down in front of a computer and logged onto the Sorry website. Hunners a photos of Americans, holdin up handwritten messages: *Sorry, World! We tried our hardest and Bush still got back in. We'll do better next time. Please don't hate us.* They looked dead normal, ordinary, like us. Makes you realize that's no the usual picture you get of America; Bush, Rumsfeld, Cheney, Rice, rampagin about the world *kickin ass*. Negroponte, for God's sake! The Sorry website cheered you up. Which I think was the whole idea. I've a feelin it was Danny put Jed up to it. A film and then a good talkin to about sittin my Higher English, applyin to uni. Aye well, maybe.

We pass the sailin ship moored on the river, but you canny see it right, only the tops of the masts; there's a big warehouse blockin the view. Wouldn't it be great to sail away on that boat; out the Clyde estuary with the white sails flappin, down past Galloway and the North of England; through the Irish Sea, past Wales then Cornwall; along the west coast a France, round the corner a Spain, intay the Mediterranean; up the boot of Italy to the mouth of the Arno, and straight up the river to Florence! Aye, you wish! I'm gonny go someday but. I'm definitely gonny go back. Me and the *David* have some catchin up to do.

I must tell Patsy about him and *Il Prigioni*. I like Patsy. She's a couple a years younger than my ma and – don't get me wrong – dead similar, but – well, she's no my ma. I can talk to her, for one thing. And for another, she doesny know nothin about me and Julian. My ma and her never spoke for years after they had a big falling-out. Danny thinks it was all to do wi Davey workin at the Faslane naval base. Which makes sense. Davey maintainin the Trident nuclear submarines; my ma and da campaignin against them. I asked my ma how they patched things up. Water under the bridge, was all she would say. Life's too short.

I sit wi my nose to the window when we pass the cranes, but I canny see nay sign a work goin on. Except there's a half-built boat, grey, a ferry, by the looks a things, wi an open stern for the cars. When I sit back, I get a surprise again, catchin a faint glimpse a my reflection in the window. Nay dreads. I rub the short fuzz on my head to check it's true. Aye, it's true. It took me ages to pluck up the courage to cut them off. You get used to them; I couldny imagine bein without them. After I decided, I tried to get a hold a Farkhanda to come and help me, but she was tied up at the uni, workin day and night on the election campaign for the rector. She's been supportin Mordecai Vanunu, the Israeli scientist that blew the whistle on Israel's nuclear programme. She telt me all about him the last time she came to the house, but I canny mind the half of it. I was mesmerized, couldny take my eyes off her; she was so excited about the campaign, sittin on my bed, her hair round her shoulders, face all lit up, eyes big and shiny. She was rattlin through the reasons why the students should support Vanunu, countin the points off on her fingers one by one. She phoned me up pure ecstatic afore Christmas and telt me they'd done it. He was elected. Now all they have to do is get him freed fae house arrest in Israel. Oh, is that all? I says. Uni's been great for Farkhanda.

Anyhow, I had to cut my dreads off mysel. I'd already let them grow out a bit at the roots, so I sat down in front a my granny's mirror and took the scissors to them. I tried to concentrate on the hair and no look at my face; lifted every lock individually and crunched through it wi my ma's big scissors, leaving as much a the new hair as I could. I laid them one at a time on the dressing table, stretched out longways, side by side, till there were too many and I had to stack them on top a one another. They looked like a bundle a ginger sticks.

My da was dead right; the bus *is* goin in and out of all the wee schemes round about Clydebank and Dumbarton. The road we've just came into could be comin up the hill to our house on Kirbister Street. They all look the same, the schemes; all the ones that haveny been *regenerated*.

I saved Farkhanda's braid and Julian's dread till last. Farkhanda should a been there; we would've had a good laugh at the whole operation. Instead, I lost my concentration and caught the full blast in the mirror of what I done to mysel; jaggy tufts a new hair and the four dreads that were left. State a me! Two big tears appeared fae nowhere and ran down my face; I felt dead sorry for mysel. By the time I cut the last ones off, my reflection was a blur and the colours all ran into one another; black and red and peroxide. *The Peroxide Dread*. Maybe it was just as well I couldny see mysel properly; wee bunches of new hair in rows with white scalp crisscrossin my head in between.

I met my ma comin out the bathroom, when I was goin in. She didny say a word, but her face said it all.

What? I says, and locked mysel in afore she could answer.

I made a point a no lookin at myself again till I'd washed my hair and dried it, and the separate wee clumps had merged thegether. Then I snipped away at it till it was all the same length, a soft fuzz like the nap on velvet or somethin. Russet velvet. I couldny bear to go back to my room and face the pile a dreads, so I went through. Danny was in. I seen my ma shoot him a warnin look, but he says it anyway.

Fuck me, if it isny Sinead!

Aye, very funny, I says.

315

Sing us a song now, won't you. A darlin song from the oul country.

Fuck off!

Clare, what is *wrong* with you these days? my ma says. There's no livin with you.

And that pure set me off. I ran into my room, threw mysel on the bed and buried my face in a cushion. I must a howled for three whole hours. They all came to my door at different times, my ma, my da, Danny, but I couldny stop sobbin. I heard my ma sayin, Leave her. Leave her be. Let her have her cry. And that made me worse; I wanted them to leave me and I didny want them to leave me. I didny know what I wanted.

Anyway, that was a week ago. I left the dreads like a bundle a twigs on my granny's dressin table for days. I couldny bear to handle them again. But yesterday mornin, I got up, took one look at them, ran through to the kitchen for a poly bag and stuffed them all in. Then I thought better of it and fished out Farkhanda's plait and Julian's dread, still attached to two of my ain dreads. I untwisted a bit of the hairpin skewerin Farkhanda's braid to my hair – she never did get round to sewin it on – and I bent it round the top of my mirror, so the black and the red hung down thegether. I'm gonny keep it there till Farkhanda's seen them anyway. It looks good. The red ribbon wove through the braid is a bit duller than it was to begin wi, but Farkhanda's hair's just as black and shiny. And mine's like a strand a really thick red wool.

I lit an incense cone and set it on the windowsill. I took Julian's and my dreads, one in each hand, and yanked them apart like a wishbone. The thread holdin them ripped and unravelled right away. It was weird lookin at the two of them separate in my hands. I closed my eyes and rubbed them baith wi my thumbs; they felt the exact same, couldny a telt them apart. I put mine in the polybag with the rest, tied up the handles and stuffed the bag into the kitchen bin. I picked up a roastin tray fae the cupboard on the way out.

Then I sat on my bed wi a box a matches and the tray on my knee. I laid Julian's dread out straight. It was startin to look a bit grubby again since the last time I bleached it. Tarnished. I lit a match and held the flame to the end a the dread. The hair sizzled and crackled and spat. The stink was pure revoltin. The whole operation took at least fifteen minutes and maist a the box a matches. It was worth it. I watched the dread meltin and turnin black and frizzlin away to nothing. Then I opened the window.

So that was that.

Elvis was funny the first time he seen me without my dreads. I come through the door and he charges at my legs as usual, wraps his arms around them. Kay-kay, he shouts, Kay-kay. I pick him up and smoothe back his quiff and he looks at my face wi big brown eyes. Then he keeks round the back a my head, baith sides, to see where my dreads are hidin. He looks at me again and his face pure crumples and I feel a wail getting ready to start. I have to shoogle him up and down and sing to him afore he gets the picture it really is me. Eventually he puts his wee fat hand up to feel my spiky hair, touches my face and laughs, that deep throaty chuckle he does. *Uh-huh-huh.* And that's it. He never mentions it again – if you know what I mean. Weans, they just accept you, don't they, whatever you're like.

I look out the bus window. We're on a mair open stretch a road now, runnin alongside the Gare Loch. There's snow on the hills and you can see towns and cranes, all a sort a hazy blue round the edge of the loch. I'm wonderin if one a them's Helensburgh; we must be gettin near it by this time. I could ask somebody, I suppose. The woman in the seat across is no there now; she must a got off somewhere along the line and I didny even notice.

We come round a bend and the sun breaks through a narrow gap in the blue haze and lights up one a the towns in the distance, turns it gold. Just the one.

Excuse me, I says.

The bald man two seats in front looks round.

Is that Helensburgh?

Aye, he says. That's it now. Looks like the sun's shinin there.

Aye, it does, I says.

Right. OK. I'm no gonny take it as a sign. *Pathetic fallacy* and all that. I'm no daft. It cheers me up anyway but.

So.

So, I'll take Barney for walks on the front. Spend some time wi Patsy. I've no spoke to her for ages. Last time Laetitia was there wi Elvis. The time before was when she came through to Glasgow to help my ma look for Danny. They went off in her car, my ma worried sick, Patsy haudin on tay the steerin wheel for dear life, and Barney sittin up in the back seat, as if he was directin operations. If I hadny been so worried mysel, it would a been funny.

And I'll see what the town has to offer. It's no exactly Florence, but it'll make a change fae sittin in my room. I'll maybe even check out the Peace Camp at Faslane. There's gonny be protests there just before the G8 this summer. Jed says three women got into a wee blow-up dinghy a few years back, steered it out to one a the nuclear submarines, climbed up and done some damage wi wirecutters and glue; jammed winches, wrecked computers, chucked stuff ower the side. The Trident Three. One a them was over sixty! Another time two women *swam* out and boarded a submarine to protest

against weapons of mass destruction. Must a been pure freezin
in that water, but they done it.

OK. Couple a weeks in Helensburgh. And that'll be me.
Then back to Glasgow and
who knows.

Acknowledgements

The Creative Writing course run jointly by Glasgow and Strathclyde Universities gave me the impetus to turn my secret vice into a public one. Thank you to all the staff, especially my tutors, Zoë Wicomb and Janice Galloway, whose writing and teaching always inspired; Willy Maley, whose unfailing optimism nudged me towards publication; Liz Lochhead for her enthusiasm and encouragement; and to the students, particularly my editorial group, Ailsa Crum, Griz Gordon, Ann MacKinnon, Heather Mackay, Clare Morrison and Maureen Myant, for their creative criticism and friendship.

Thank you to my editor, Judy Moir of Penguin, for liking the book after part one and having faith that parts two and three would follow.

The time I spent in Castlemilk is woven into the fabric of my life; the people I worked with gave me so much. I heard echoes of conversations I had there every time I sat down to write. Thank you all. In particular, thank you to Janette Shepherd, whose generosity of spirit has touched so many people.

My friends kept me going when I faltered; Usha Brown, Mary Patrick, Maureen Sanders, Allison Linklater, Anne-Marie McGeoch, Jean Barr, Cynthia Fuller deserve special mention.

Ewa Wojciechowska and the group listened to my first attempts at prose and helped me on my way; Eileen MacAlister too.

Staff in Great Western Road Costa, the Tinderbox and

especially Stravaigin provided a constant flow of cheer, as well as good coffee, food and wine.

Leanne Crisp at Controlled Demolition Ltd was very helpful.

It was in my Orkney family that I developed – among all the other things – a love of words and a fascination with the workings of groups. Thank you to my mother, Irene, to Stuart, Catherine, Maggie, and Iain Miller and, in memory, my father, Sonny, and brother, Alan. Thank you also partners and next generation: Gordon, Helen, Rachel, Lewie, Sonny, Lana, Darren, Alan, Gemma.

Extra thanks to Maggie Miller for taking the photos in front of the peat shed door.

Last and foremost, my Glasgow family, Liam, Norna and Ewan Stewart gave me the love and encouragement that saw me through.

Alison Miller
April 2005